TWO HALVES
DANU'S PI
19 70
ONE TRUTH
I0742051
CONFIDENTIAL

First published by The Rose Verse 2025

This novel is entirely a work of fiction. The names, characters and incidents portrayed in it are the work of the author's imagination. Any resemblance to actual persons, living or dead, events or localities is entirely coincidental.

First Edition

Cover art by Annalise Jensen @annalisejensen
Editing by Annalise Healey @beeandquilledits

ISBN: **979-8-9986729-0-3** (Paperback), **979-8-9986729-1-0** (Hardcover), **979-8-9986729-2-7** (Ebook), **979-8-9986729-3-4** (Audiobook)
Library of Congress Control Number: 2025907736

First Edition: May 2025

To those who see their brokenness and wonder if they're enough.

Remember, even the full moon needs the stars to illuminate the night. Every jagged piece of you carries a hidden light, a spark that can love, heal, and shine in ways yet unseen.

Embrace your fragments. They are not your weakness, but the very force that makes your brilliance unbreakable.

CONTENTS

TRiGGER WaRDiNGS

This book contains scenes that may depict, mention, or discuss:

- Alcohol consumption
- Animal death
- Anxiety
- Attempted murder
- Blood depictions
- Bombing depiction (off-page)
- Consumption of blood (for magic)
- Dead bodies
- Death of parents
- Death of loved ones
- Death by fire
- Disappearance and presumed death of parents
- Grief & loss depiction
- Hallucinations (caused by magic)
- Kidnapping
- Murder
- Medication dispensing error
- Near drowning (off-page)
- Nightmares about traumatic events
- Occult
- Panic attack depictions
- Passive suicidal ideation (caused by magic & limited)
- Physical assault (choking) & knife violence (battle scene)
- PTSD
- Socioeconomic hierarchy (based on magic)
- Stalking
- Violence

PRONUNCIATION GUIDE

Welcome, readers, to Eldermoore! This magical city is inspired by the charm of 1970s Derry, Ireland, but transformed into its own unique fantasy realm. You'll come across many names and phrases with Irish roots throughout the book, along with a few that we've put our own unique twist on. Below, you'll find a pronunciation guide if you need it, but feel free to pronounce the names however you like.

Main Characters

Elodie O'Grady: Eh-loh-dee O'GRAH-dee

Rowan O'Grady: ROH-uhn (rhymes with "loan") O'GRAH-dee

Aiden O'Connor: AY-den O'CON-ner

Declan Finnegan: DEK-lan FIN-eh-gan

Aisling Ryan: ASH-ling RY-an

Maeve O'Connor: MAYV O'CON-ner

Saoirse Murphy: SEER-sha MUR-fee

Lennon O'Donnell: LEN-nun O'DON-ell

Niamh O'Neill: NEEV O'NEEL

Leila Hassan: LAY-lah HAH-sahn

Liam Hassan: LEE-um HAH-sahn

Lorcan O'Rourke: LOR-kun oh-ROHRK

Shade: SHAYD (rhymes with "paid")

Council, Guard, and Doctor

Headmistress Caitriona Flynn: Kah-tree-na FLIN

Ms. Siobhán Maguire: Shi-vawn Muh-GWY-er

Dr. Artí Collins: AR-tee KOH-linz

Mrs. Bridget Flanagan: BRID-jit FLAN-a-gan

Headmaster James Doyle: JAYMZ DOIL (rhymes with "foil")

Darragh Flynn: DAH-rah FLIN

Mr. Eamon Brennon: AY-mun BRENN-un

Dr. Pádraig O'Keefe: PAW-drig oh-KEEF

Students

Rónán Clarke: ROH-nawn (rhymes with "own") CLARK

Patrick Malone: PAT-rik muh-LOHN (rhymes with "stone")

Case: Missing Mittens

Ms. Síle*:* SHEE-la

Irish Stoat*:* STOHT (rhymes with "coat")

Mrs. Byre*:* BURN

Sailors

Finn & Tadgh*:* Fin & Tige (like tiger, but without the "r")

Colm, Piaras, & Mick*:* KOL-um, PEE-ar-us, & MIK

Extras

Ciaran O'Grady*:* KEER-an O'GRAH-dee

Deirdre O'Grady*:* DEER-dra O'GRAH-dee

Heka Priest/Si-Osire*:* Heh-kah/ See-oh-SIRE ("sire" as in a father)

GLOSSARY

Spoiler Alert

Some of the terms below might spill the beans on the plot twists or ending. Proceed with caution—once you know, you know! If you want to keep the surprises intact, feel free to skip this section until the end. But hey, no pressure—just a friendly warning! If you are a bit of a rebel like Rowan or a note-taking fein like Elodie, we have categorized the words for your reading convenience.

1970 Slang & Other Phrases

- ***A proper knees-up-*** Lively or full of energy; A good time.
- ***A load of blarney-*** Nonsense.
- ***A right bighead-*** Arrogant.
- ***Codswallop-*** Nonsense/rubbish.
- ***Cool cat-*** A person who is confident and stylish.
- ***Eejit (EE-jit)-*** Idiot.
- ***Finding my bottle-*** Finding courage.
- ***Gaga-*** Confused and out of touch with reality.
- ***Ginger-*** A term of endearment for a spirited personality or temper.
- ***In her bad books-*** Holding a grudge towards someone.
- ***Magnets for bother-*** Easily attract problems or trouble.
- ***Mdju nctjcr-*** An ancient logographic script; hieroglyphs.
- ***Moulid an-Nabi-*** Egyptians celebrate Prophet Muhammad's birth.
- ***May the stars guide you well this night-*** A blessing of guidance, safety, or good fortune.
- ***Natter-*** A talk.
- ***Ni neart go cur le cheile-*** There is no strength without unity.
- ***One-fingered wave-*** A form of "flipping the bird."
- ***Right ol' slog-*** A difficult or exhausting task.
- ***Rubby-dubby-*** A combination of fish parts used as bait while fishing.
- ***Scales of Ma'at-*** Balance between order and chaos, good and evil, truth and falsehood.
- ***Scáth-*** Shadow.
- ***Trial of Lir (LEER)-*** Based on the myth of Lir's children who endured trials after being transformed into swans.
- ***What's the crack?-*** Similar to 'what's up?' or a way to ask what another person has to say.

Runes

• *Bréagadóir (Bray-guh-DOHR)-* Liar. (Leila)

•*Duine a chasann (DWIN-ya ah KHAS-uhn)-* A person who obstructs. (Liam)

• *Éagóir (AY-gore)-* Betray. (Caitriona)

• *Mallacht (MAL-uhkht)-* To be cursed. (Rowan)

•*Tosach n-echto (TOSS-akh n-EKH-toh)-* Beginning of murder/slaying. (Rónán)

Magic

• *An neamh-draíocht (uhn nyav dree-uhkt)-* The non-magical.

• *Draíocht dhorcha (Dree-ukht ghor-kha)-* Dark magic.

• *Draíocht-* Magic.

• *Draoi-* A druid or person with magic who heals.

• *Féth fíada (Fay fee-uh-dah)-* A magical veil used to hide oneself from human eyesight.

• *Gáe Assail-* The Spear of Lugh in Irish mythology.

• *Heka-* The deification of magic and medicine in ancient Egypt.

• *Mianta na Focail Fírinne-* Words of truth.

• *Púca (POO-ka)-* An ancient Otherworld creature known for mischief and wisdom.

• *Réalt (reel-t, ré rhymes with 'ray-alt')-* Star (aka the magical).

• *Sidhe/Sith/Sí (SHEE)-* Fairy folk or the realm they inhabit.

• *Sluagh (SLOO-ah)-* Hosts of the unforgiven dead.

• *Súil-* Eye (Aiden's magic of sight similar to a third eye).

• *Abhartach-* An Irish Vampire that is part of a Londonderry legend from the 5th century.

Gods

• *Áine-* An Irish goddess of summer, wealth, and sovereignty.

• *Bastet-* A fierce protector of women and children.

• *Cailleach (KAL-yakh)-* Known as a Celtic goddess often depicted as a hag that embodies winter and the destruction and creation of nature.

• *Danu-* Revered as the matriarch of the Tuatha Dé Danann, an ancient race, she is often depicted as a maternal and commanding force, symbolizing nature and its abundant blessings.

• *Duat-* The realm of the Egyptian gods, demons, and supernatural beings.

• *Isis-* Goddess of magic, healing, and protection. She is revered for her maternal love and symbolizes rebirth and resurrection.

- *Lir*- Irish god of the sea.
- *Lugh*- As one of the most important Celtic gods, Lugh represents the sun and light and is known to be an all-seeing deity and great warrior.
- *Ma'at*- The Egyptian goddess of truth, justice, and cosmic order. She is often depicted with an ostrich feather on her head, symbolizing her role in maintaining balance and harmony in the universe.
- *Mórrígan/The Morrígan*- Irish goddess of war.
- *Osiris*- Egyptian god of the afterlife. He is associated with the cycle of life and death.
- *Tír na nÓg (Teer nah noh-g)*- Celtic Otherworld.

Nicknames

- *An Marfóir (Awn MAR-fur)*- The Slayer.
- *Leanaí (lan-ee)*- Children.
- *Mo siréine bheag (Muh shih-RAY-nuh vyahg)*- My little siren.
- *Mo thrioblóir beag (Muh hree-uh-BLOHR byag)*- My little troublemaker.
- *Sionnach glic (SHIN-ukh glick)*- Sly/cunning fox.
- *Ó, a grá (Oh, ah graw)*- Oh, my love.

Locations Within Eldermoore

- *Acadamh na nGnáth (Ah-kah-dav nah nuh-gnaw)*- Academy of the Ordinary.
- *Balie na Muintir (BAH-luh nuh MUN-chir-uh)*- Town of the people.
- *Bóg (bawg)*- A wetland area with waterlogged soil, often found in Ireland.
- *Gleann na Réaltaí (GLAN na RAYL-tee)*- Valley of the Stars.
- *Lough Foyle (LOKH FOYL)*- Inlet of water connected to the Atlantic Ocean.

Locations Outside Eldermoore

- *Blackthorn Glade*- Outside the territory lines of Eldermoore towards the North. It is known as an unruly and unlawful neighbouring town.
- *Cairo (KAI-roh)*- Located far South of Eldermoore. It is the capital of Egypt where the Hassan twins are from.
- *Creevan*- South-west of Eldermoore.
- *Príosún Fear Marbh (PREE-uh-soon far mahr-iv)*- Dead man's prison with maximum security in Creevan.
- *Shadow Glen*- Another territory outside Eldermoore in the East.

WELCOME TO
WETHERBRIDGE ESTATE
FOYLE HALL
THE STOUT & SIP OF ÉIRE
THE SHAMROCK & SCARAB EMPORIUM
Whispering Willow
Spellbound Way
THE O'CONNOR HOUSE
O'CONNOR INVESTIGATIONS
MORGUE
Nocturne's Nook
Kildare Road
Wisp Alley
Fiddler's Lane
Witch's Walk
Arcane
Crescent
DANU'S PI
FLYNN MANOR
Echo's End
Hollow Way
OBSIDEAN VEIL
N
E
S
W

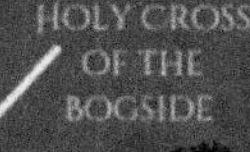

LDERMOORE
HOLY CROSS
OF THE
BOGSIDE
Specter's End
WOOD
EST
AISLING'S
HOUSE
ACADAMH
NA NGNATH
Spellbound Way
Scholar's Grove
Twiblight
Terrace
COVE COURT
Obscura Path
THE ARCANE
SCRIPTORIUM
Lighthouse Ln
RAVENS
DOCK
Seafarer's Walk
THE
RADY
OUSE

LAWS OF THE OBSIDIAN VEIL

1. *At the age of 13, children who exhibit magical abilities will receive an invitation to Tara Hall, where students will be trained in the responsible and ethical use of their powers until the age of 18.*
2. *Children without power will attend Acadamh na nGnáth, where they will receive a conventional education apart from the arcane arts.*
3. *The Obsidian Veil will prevent all of an neamh-draíocht, who cross into Gleann na Réaltaí, from learning or retaining information about Draíocht unless on formal business or with special licenses afforded to them by the Council.*
4. *A Réalt must conceal the nature of their powers from an neamh-draíocht, who are forbidden from learning witchcraft or accessing magical knowledge.*
5. *Access to books and artifacts referring to Draíocht is restricted exclusively to those within Tara Hall and authorized scholars.*
6. *The practice of Draíocht Dhorcha is strictly prohibited across the entirety of Eldermoore.*
7. *Engagements or relationships between individuals from opposing sides of the Obsidian Veil are strictly prohibited to maintain peace and civility among us all.*

Any individual caught breaking these laws will face severe consequences. Detention without trial and punishment proportional to the offense are the standard penalties, ensuring that both of Eldermoore's Districts remain orderly and secure.

Established on the twenty-first day of October in the year of the Réalt one thousand nine hundred twenty-five by the Eldermoore's Founder, Darragh Flynn, and fellow council members, the new policy is set to take effect immediately.

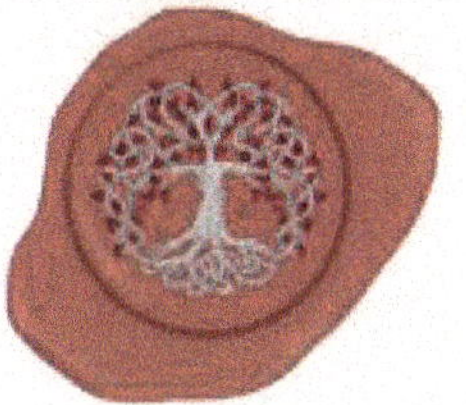

Darragh Flynn

i

PRESENT DAY

The night has a thousand eyes,
And the day but one;
Yet the light of the bright world dies
With the dying sun.

The mind has a thousand eyes,
And the heart but one;
Yet the light of a whole life dies
When love is done.

—Francis William Bourdillon

1

BAD OMEN

ELODIE

I walk in the darkness towards a familiar voice. Its warmth encompasses me as shadows continue to press in, leaving a cold chill against my bare shoulders. The tank top and shorts I wore to bed do nothing to protect my skin from its icy grip. My breath hitches as the voice begins to sing a soft hymn. The note of the woman's voice gets carried on the wind.

> *In twilight's shroud, I stalk the night;*
> *No man nor beast can flee my bite.*
> *It's said in ancient lore of Tír na nÓg*
> *That even fate may rouse from its quiet bóg.*

I continue to search for the woman who has haunted my dreams for the past fortnight. Her bright aura calls to me— the same as her voice. If only I could see her face— could ask her what her song means. "Elodie." A voice tries to pull me from sleep as the woman continues her riddle:

WHEN THE RAVEN SOARS

They see me not, nor hear my call;
On Raven's wings, I swiftly glide.
With Weaver's Knot, they try to stall,
Yet the veil remains undetectable.
And each must take their final stride,

For, in the end, I am inevitable.
What am I?

"Elodie, wake up!" The faint outline of the woman starts to form in my dream.

"One more minute, please!" I plead to the incessant voice prodding my vision. My hands tingle, and the hair on my neck raises with awareness and giddy excitement. This will be the night I finally see her.

"That's it, you forced my hand. We have somewhere to be," the girl states, sounding much like my sister's disgruntled voice. I feel myself pulled out of bed.

And then, the woman is lost once more to the shadowy realm of my dreams.

-Elodie's Journal-
Entry #7: October 1st @ 3:00 AM
"The Dark Prelude"

October 1, 1970 - 3:48 a.m.

Truth is said to be power, and yet the universe tends to deal it to me in halves.

I straighten my legs and rise from my crouched stance, taking in the scene at Tara Hall, where dozens of ravens lie scattered around a lifeless body. Their wings flap incessantly as their sleek, iridescent beaks peck at the ground. The early morning air carries a chill, made colder as I stand next to the wall of shadows that divides our quaint town of Eldermoore. The grey wisps of fog

4

from the Obsidian Veil roll in, and morning dew glistens on the grass, adding to the unsettling sight. As I pull my plaid woollen scarf higher over my reddening nose, I turn to see my twin sister Rowan comforting Headmistress Flynn, whose face has suddenly gone pale, her eyes open wide in alarm.

"This can only mean one thing," she breathes shakily in her heavy Irish accent. "Death has found its way back to Eldermoore."

Despite being well into her later years—her exact age is obscured by magic—she hugs her slender arms as she begins rocking back and forth, whispering to herself incoherently. Rowan's black leather gloves creak softly in Auntie Cait's white-knuckled grasp. Plopping down on the cold steps of the academy behind her, she almost drags Rowan down with her. My sister's eyes meet mine in a plea for help, which I return with silent laughter despite the somber mood. Deciding to take pity on her, I move to Auntie Cait's side to take her statement.

"Can you tell us the name of the boy?"

"Yes, his name is Rónán Clarke. He's a Senior here at Tara Hall— top of his class. The lad would have done great things, I'm sure of it." Her shaky voice hardens as she remarks upon his achievement. "I just don't understand how someone could do something like this." Her voice softens as her light cornflower blue eyes glaze over with unshed tears.

Offering Auntie Cait a few minutes to compose herself, Rowan resumes counting off requests of things we will need on her fingers. "Does the school have any CCTV footage we can review? We will also need his academy records and a complete faculty and student list for the time he attended Tara Hall."

"No, no. Our students here rely solely on their magic and the protection of the spells that I and a few chosen teachers use to ward the grounds. I saw no need to install such codswallop." Her lips pull back in a grimace. Then, as if remembering Rowan and I live on the other side of the Obsidian Veil, in Balie na Muintir, she gently adds, "I hope you're not taking it amiss."

I wave off the remark with an untroubled heart, knowing that after practically raising the both of us herself, she had not meant any slight but was merely voicing her usual disdain for technology. Having lived in Eldermoore much longer than anyone else I know, she had more power than anyone we knew and spent so much time in Gleann na Réaltaí that she often made remarks that could raise eyebrows. However, I like to think that raising us softened her prejudice.

"And I'll have those papers printed out and sent to your office by noon," she adds with an affectionate smile filled with a deep, maternal warmth.

"Can you think of anyone within Gleann na Réaltaí who knew when you'd be arriving at the school and might try to scare you like this?" My hand quickly reaches for my spiral-bound pocket notebook, its compact size making it easy to fit in my trench coat pocket. Flipping it open to a blank page, the metal coils creaking faintly from overuse and the wet Ireland air, I wait for Auntie Cait to reply. Noticing how she has remained silent, I look up to find her absently staring off into the distance with fear again visible on her face.

Before Rowan or I can ask her if she's alright, she snaps her head towards us again. "I haven't the foggiest notion, but I knew I had to call you when I discovered this tragedy. You're the only ones I truly trust."

Hearing the distant ring of the clock tower ding at precisely 5 o'clock at Foyle Hall, she declares, "I'm sorry to do this to you girls, but I must go and prepare for our faculty meeting before the young lads and lassies begin filling in for class. If I can be of any more help, you know where to find me."

As she disappears into the building, my eyes meet with Rowan's, and we exchange another knowing look. "What a right old pickle this is!" she proclaims.

Nodding in agreement, we begin making our way towards the school parking lot, where our shiny blue 1962 Ford Cortina is currently haphazardly parked in a spot marked as reserved. Yikes! I guess I should've let Rowan make me that cup of tea before we left the house after all. From the corner of my eye, I see Rowan's lips twitch in a faint smirk, a small laugh escaping, which she tries to cover with a cough as she finally gets a good look at the tires crossing the white parallel lines. I shove my elbow into her side gently, sending her into another fit of giggles. "Sure, keep it coming, and you'll be driving next time!" I threaten with a slight chuckle.

Upon hearing my half-hearted attempt to intimidate her, she quickly sobers. With a straight face and eyes dancing with mirth, she quips, "Aye, and the moon's made of green cheese! Now, pop the trunk, ya eejit."

With a soft click of the lock, I pull the trunk open and grab the protective gear that all licensed neamh-draíocht investigators must wear while on official investigations. The black body suit's stretchy material gives off a soft, iridescent glow from the dozens of charms woven into the fabric to prevent diseases, bacteria, or dark magic from entering our bodies. I hand Rowan her suit as she pulls her grey woollen blazer off. The soft fabric wrinkles immediately as she rolls it into a ball and chucks it into the trunk. Some things never change, I chuckle. Even when we were kids, Rowan was always rushing about, and much to Auntie Cait's chagrin, she always had clothes thrown across the floor of her room. When we enrolled in the necessary extra classes at Acadamh na nGnáth 5 years ago to become investigators, she was hopeful the school would tame Rowan's chaotic nature. Despite the military-style training, strict protocols, and our instructor's orders to maintain our uniforms, her habitual tidiness ceased abruptly after graduation. It seems the academy's rules for neatness would never wear off on my wayward sister.

Grabbing the yellow police tape after zipping our suits up, we head back to the crime scene. Rowan begins the necessary process of taping off the area as I walk towards the boy's lifeless body, causing the flock of ravens to fly off and settle in a nearby tree. Looking down, I see the boy's face—Rónán's face— now frozen in eternal fear. Trails of crimson escape from all visible extremities, yet I am unable to make out any discernible puncture wounds.

"What do you make of this?" I prompt as Rowan navigates under the perimeter line she just created, and I move to give her a chance to complete her own analysis.

I place my hands on my hips and give the grounds of Tara Hall a swift glance to see if there are any entry and exit points besides the main gate Rowan and I entered through earlier. As I walk towards the right side of the tape border, my rubber boots sink into the wet grass. With each step, I hear a faint squelching sound as small patches of mud splash on my suit. See, it protects us from harm and saves our outfits! It's a jack of all trades, I mentally argue as I think back on Rowan's constant assertion that Eldermoore's laws hinder an neamh-draíocht from learning any protective charms and is just another demonstration of elitism. Catching a glimpse of a wrought iron gate hidden behind the school, I jot it down to tell Rowan back at our office when her voice startles me out of thought.

"Elodie, come get a closer look over here. I can't believe I almost let it slip by; there seems to be some kind of rune along the left side of his neck."

As she shifts Rónán's shirt collar lower with her right hand to help me get a better look, she hands me the camera she holds so I can take shots of the marks for us to research later. Decreasing the lens's magnification, I spot a thorn hidden in his closed fist. The camera shutter fills the silence as I take another rapid series of photos while Rowan measures it and places it into an evidence bag, which she time stamps '6 am'.

"We'll have to check with Leila and Liam at the Emporium to see if they have any artifacts or books that can tell us what these symbols mean," I reply to Rowan's earlier guess as I examine the strange lines one last time, Rowan finishes zipping the body bag so that Dr. O'Keefe, who Auntie Cait called down to the Academy, can transport him to the morgue for further examination.

The school bell rings, startling us out of our routine motions of cleaning the scene. Soon, the chatter of young children and teens can be heard, each one headed towards the front lawn that is now devoid of all evidence. Rowan and I both look up as children from some of the wealthiest and most powerful families in town rush towards the main hall in their navy and white uniforms, oblivious to their classmate's recent death.

"We've got a lot of work to do," Rowan mumbles.

Yes, and if the woman in my dream sings the truth, I fear this may only be the beginning.

2

ONLY THE BEGINNING
ELODIE

Peeling off our suits, now slick with sweat from the humid air, Rowan gives an audible sigh of relief as she pulls her jacket back on.

Is it really that awful to wear your protective suit?" I laugh.

"I'd rather freeze than put that on again."

As if answering Rowan, the skies darken, and the first drops of rain begin to fall, pattering softly against the pavement. I raise my eyebrow as I turn to look at her. *You had to open your gob, didn't you?*

Rowan pointedly ignores my stare as we both quickly get into the car, slamming the doors shut just as the rain begins to pelt against the windshield. Finally breaking the silence, Rowan remarks, "Looks like we just dodged the rain, and a good thing, too, or else we could have lost our only evidence so far."

"Let's head over to the office to get those pictures developed. We can look through our notes and see what we can find out on our own before Auntie

9

Cait sends those files over," I suggest as I shift the car into gear and drive towards Eldermoore Avenue.

With forlorn looks on both our faces, we sit in comfortable silence, clearing our minds on the short ride. *Well, it was a nice ride* until Rowan and I groan in mutual annoyance as we pass by O'Connor Investigations. *What a disaster of a day*, I think, spotting the devil himself, Aiden O'Connor, as he gives a smug wave in our direction before entering his office, which, just our luck, is the building lot right across from ours.

"Ugh, he's a right bighead and a pain in the arse. I'd like to give him a clip around the ear. I don't know how Maeve is related to him," I grumble under my breath.

Unlike Aiden, Maeve's presence in the office is a breath of fresh air. Though we have our differences with her brother, Maeve is driven and passionate. Every day, she arrives with an intense focus, her nose often buried in case files or her eyes scanning through books to unearth crucial details. She's here not to flaunt her abilities, but to prove herself through her work, even if it means keeping her magic in check around us.

After graduating as one of Tara Hall's top students, Maeve had a multitude of prestigious job offers at her fingertips. Yet, she chose to join us instead. Auntie Cait recommended our PI shop as the perfect place for Maeve to showcase her skills, and she's quickly become an invaluable part of our team. Even better, her dedication and work ethic add a thrilling edge to our friendly rivalry with Aiden, making each competition to see who can solve a case first more exciting—especially when Aiden finds himself on the losing side.

Since moving to our current office—purchased legally and with all the proper licenses, despite what some people *cough* Aiden *cough* might argue— he has somehow always been able to get the jump on a new case before us. Normally, I'm much more even-tempered than Rowan, but he seems to get under my skin like no one else. He might be two years older than us with his feet firmly planted in his family's investigative firm, but investigating is our passion too. *Must he ruin everything?!*

Our passion, which slowly became an obsession, began when our parents disappeared. Their case was never closed and their bodies were never found. It wasn't until Rowan and I turned 13 and we failed to exhibit any powers that Auntie Cait demanded we stop looking. *She was just scared the same would happen to us. That without powers, we wouldn't be able to protect ourselves— that, like her old friends, she would lose us too.* With every new achievement or celebration, their absence became a more profound ache. With the house paid off before their disappearance, our sole financial burden lay in paying the rent for our investigation office, Danu's PI. Yet, Aiden continued to reel in clients with deep pockets while he left us trying to pick up the odd jobs he didn't take.

Just last month, Ms. Síle from Cove Court called us in a desperate panic. It had been late one evening when she was returning from a walk along the docks with her dog, Mittens. In hysterics, she claimed to have seen a serpent-like creature jump out of the fog frightening her so much that she dropped the leash, and poor Mittens ran into Grimwood Forest. With no idea how far he went, and no matter how much she called after him, the small Dandie Dinmont Terrier never returned. Rowan and I spent days searching the forest as we sent Maeve to talk to her neighbours.

Upon talking to Mr. Kelly, Mrs. Quinn, and Mrs. Byrne it became quite apparent that Ms. Síle was quite well-known for being "pissed as a newt" and "blind as a bat" when she went without her spectacles, which she later confessed to never wearing the nights she frequented the Stout & Sip. In her intoxicated state, she had mistaken an anchoring rope from a trading boat for the serpent and poor Mr. Mittens was in reality an Irish Stoat known to frequent the docks in search of a meal.

With this new case, though, we might be seeing a bit of sunshine after the rain

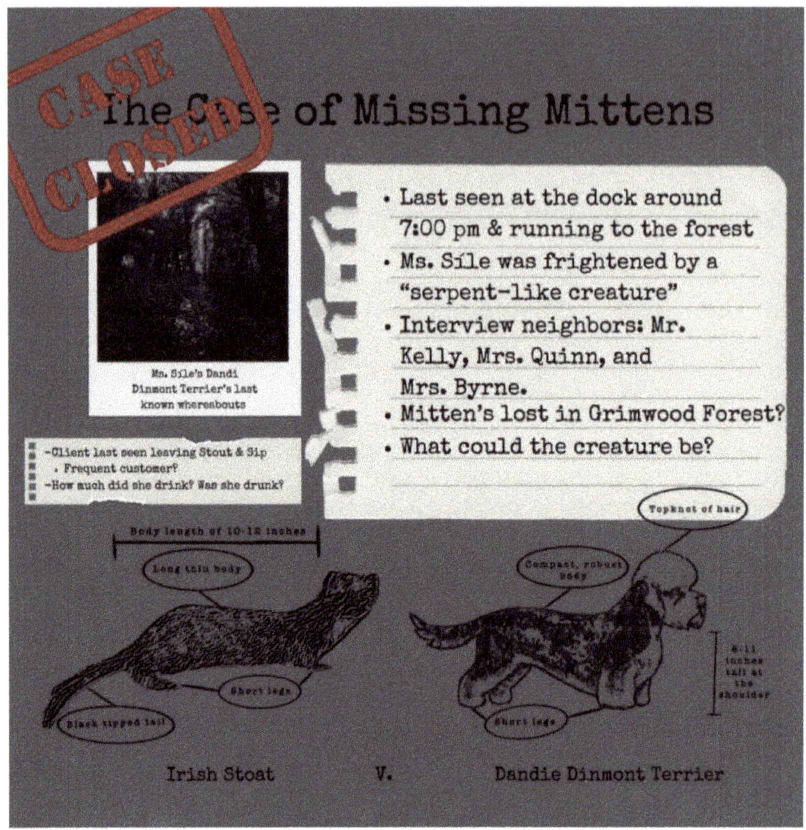

Mr. Mittens- Property of Danu's PI

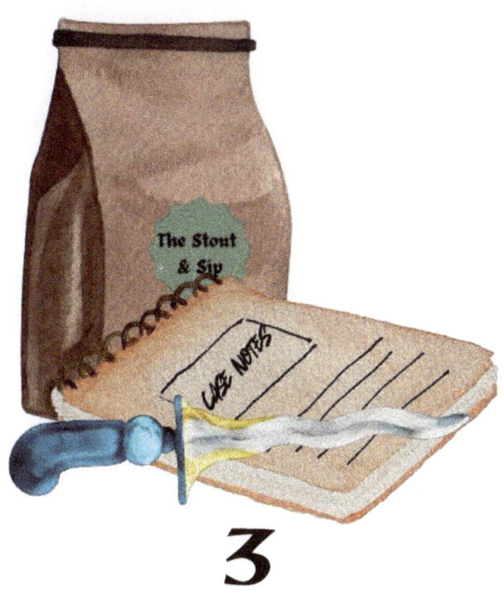

3

GAME ON
AIDEN

I give a soft chuckle as I look in my rearview mirror thinking back to this morning when I watched Elodie O'Grady climb out of her car. Her blue streaked hair blew with the winds of the dying storm, and she flashed me the one-fingered wave like the rebel she and her sister Rowan have always been.

"She'd have you in her bad books for sure," Declan notes, accurately guessing what I'm thinking with his uncanny ability.

I can't help but nod in agreement. As my oldest and most loyal friend, he always helps me solve cases. Acting as my informant and spy, he often lurks in shadows- easily going undetected. Oh, and did I mention he's dead? His ghostly form levitates inches above the passenger seat, just like this mornin' when he peered his head out the closed window to see the O'Grady twins enter their office without a backward glance.

"Do you have any information about this meeting with Caitriona Flynn?" I ask Declan, seeking answers about the mysterious conference the

Headmistress of Tara Hall had called me about only moments ago. Although it was not unusual for high-paying and powerful clients to reach out for my detective services, receiving a call from the woman who had tried to keep me in line during my school years was something I hadn't anticipated. Once again Elodie comes to mind. I can only guess that it has something to do with her and Rowan.

"I heard that Rowan and Elodie were on the school grounds earlier this morning. I visited while students were in class but found nothing amiss. If there was a problem, they did a fine job cleaning up. If I were to wager a guess, Ms. Flynn likely called regarding the two of them," Declan echos my growing suspicion.

"We shall see. I mean, how much trouble could those two get into before dawn?"

Tara Hall - 10 a.m.

I stand corrected. Elodie and Rowan are magnets for bother.

"If you could somehow tag along on their investigation," Ms. Flynn continues, "it would put my mind at ease. I hate to think of them out there unprotected. Besides, I think you could be a real asset with the extent of knowledge you have on draíocht. You were my best student." She gives me a searching look, waiting to see how I'll react.

"You know we are not allowed to share our information with an neamhdraíocht. That's why the Obsidian Veil continues to divide our parts of town, which, might I remind you, your granda enacted," I snap at the woman who appears no older than forty, yet I know to be at least fifty years my senior based on her family's history in this town.

Her eyes squint in anger. "I know, I know, don't be so cheeky. However, the council member and I spoke this morning and we have granted you and the girls special permission under the current circumstances." Calming down, she continues, "As a protective measure, we will need you all to come to Foyle Hall so we can perform a protection spell. It will only allow information you share in the presence of an neamh-draíocht to be heard by Rowan and Elodie or anyone deemed necessary to the investigation. There may be slight differences in how the bond affects you all though. From the past accounts I've read, the spell of the Cailleach can only truly be felt between three." A hair from her tight chignon slips into her face obscuring the left frame of her thin-wired glasses as she finishes detailing the properties of the spell. She pushes the piece behind her ear and uses her index finger to slide her glasses further up her nose as she waits for my reply.

"Do I even have a choice? It seems you've made up my mind for the both of us" I grunt, my lips pulling back in a sneer.

"I'm glad you've finally realized that. My request for this meeting was to inform you of what time you and the O'Gradys need to meet the council. I'll expect you to be at Foyle Hall tonight at 8 o'clock and not a minute later. I'm sure you'll need time to prepare what you will tell Rowan and Elodie. I know you've had some trouble getting along in the past," she quips with a knowing smirk, her eyes twinkling with mischief.

Not too long ago, I had mistaken that same smile for concern. I've been taking cases she has deemed too dangerous for months now. She was able to easily wipe her hands of the mess she made, but my good deeds have left me as the sole target to be barraged in the girls' crossfire.

I look past Ms. Flynn and see Declan holding back a laugh. His quiet presence, which usually settles my thoughts, only causes my blood to boil further as he struggles to rein in his mirth. Storming out, I barely let Declan catch up as the faint gleeful laughter of Ms. Flynn trails behind me. The hinges to the doors to Tara Hall creak as the ornate wood smashes against the building, causing several students in the hall to begin whispering to one another.

Oh, for feck's sake." I fume, picturing how this will end as I start the drive back to my office.

I take the longer route, winding past the Emporium and Stout & Sip, hoping the detour might cool my simmering frustration. Yet, it does little to quell the storm brewing inside me. On my third loop around the block, Declan's influence over electromagnetic currents makes its presence known. A sudden, invisible force jerks my car to a stop, the engine sputtering as if ensnared by an unseen hand.

"What'd you do that for?" I snap, my irritation crackling in my voice as I twist the key in the ignition, hoping the car will roar back to life. The engine reluctantly rumbles, but before I can turn onto Witches' Walk, it stalls again. "Cut it out!"

A woman walking her dog jumps in surprise, quickly bending to scoop up her slow-moving pet. Clutching the dog tightly, she hurries across the street, throwing a cautious glance over her shoulder.

I turn to glare at Declan, who, despite my frustration, is barely containing a grin. His eyes twinkle with mischief as he offers an apologetic shrug.

"Listen, if you're so worried about what they'll say," he begins, his tone shifting to a sage-like quality, "I've seen a thing or two in my time. Girls, for some reason, seem to appreciate surprises. Take a tip from me: sugar seems to soften the blow of bad news. Why don't you swing by Lennon's bakery? Grab some of those cinnamon buns and chocolate squares. His sweets have a way of winning hearts; after all, he managed to charm Saoirse, and that's saying something."

The mention of Stout & Sip's owner and occasional bouncer, cools my temper. If Lennon's pastries could win over her, the most formidable swordswoman and Knight to graduate from Tara Hall, maybe they'd work their magic on Elodie, too. "Alright, you've convinced me," I grumble, giving in with a sigh as I start the car.

As I push open the glass door of the bakery, a rush of warmth greets me, instantly melting away the chill from outside. The rich, inviting scent of freshly baked bread, cinnamon, and chocolate envelops me like a cozy blanket. My stomach growls loudly in response, a stark reminder of the breakfast I had missed earlier due to the lengthy meeting.

The bakery's quiet ambiance and the gentle hum of its soft background music stand in stark contrast to the tense morning I've had. On the ground floor, it also offers a serene escape from the bustling pub that operates above. This early in the morning, the pub's usual clamour is subdued to a distant murmur, allowing Saoirse to prepare for the night ahead.

"Morning, Lennon. I need to grab an order to go. Four cinnamon buns, four chocolate squares, and toss in some of those jam doughnuts Maeve seems to like." My stomach rumbles again, and I add, "And a black coffee, no cream."

Lennon looks up, a smirk playing on his lips. "Aiden O'Connor, coming in for an apology? Who's the lucky lady?" His laugh carries a hint of mischief, recalling the countless times I'd turned down girls at Tara Hall, leaving them in tears.

"What makes you think they're not for me?"

"Yeah, right! You eating sweets? That's almost as funny as that time you got so plastered you—" His sentence is cut short by a swift punch to his arm. He chuckles, rubbing the spot where I hit him. "Alright, alright, keep your secrets. Here's your order. I made sure to grab the freshest ones, just in case there really is a girl involved."

I slap a few bills on the counter and snatch the paper bag and coffee, my irritation simmering but slightly abated by the hope of winning the twins over. As I storm out, his laughter trails behind me. *A reoccurring theme today, it would seem.*

I can only hold off confronting them for so long so I might as well get this over with. Finding my bottle, I spy the girls through their office window. With the peace offering in hand, I grip the door handle and step out, ready to tackle the inevitable conversation. Walking quickly, I force a welcoming smile as I open the door marked "Danu's PI," the soft chime announcing my arrival. *Clever name.* I wouldn't give them the satisfaction of a compliment, though.

"Welco—" Elodie's soft voice cuts off abruptly, and her warm smile quickly fades into a grim line as she realizes I'm not a new client.

"Morning, ladies. I thought I'd drop off some baked goods for you all." Seizing their moment of shock, I place the baked goods on Elodie's desk and take in the space.

The twins' desks are set on opposite sides of the room, each reflecting their distinct working styles. Elodie's desk is meticulously organized, with carefully stacked paperwork neatly arranged in precise piles. The business logo is prominently painted on the white brick of the fireplace behind her, its edges darkened from its use this past winter.

Across the room, Rowan's desk is a chaotic contrast. Papers and tea cups are scattered haphazardly, and she types furiously on the keyboard of her computer. Her screen is filled with lines of code, and her focus is intense as she likely searches for clues on *our* new case.

Alongside the window, two additional desks are arranged: one is piled high with books on Eldermoore's history and is currently occupied by a girl with bright red hair—Aisling Ryan, a local historian and close friend of the girls. The smaller desk, looking fairly new, stands empty near a bookshelf crowded with legal texts and case notes. On the tabletop next to a plant, a small, framed photo shows the girls crammed together in a booth at Stout & Sip—likely the result of my sister's insistence on 'capturing the moment', as Maeve often jokes when she sticks a camera in my face.

The walls are adorned with pinned newspaper clippings, charts, and a large town map, creating a tapestry of local intrigue. Two light brown leather Kengu chairs are paired with a plush green sofa, centered by a small glass table, making for a welcoming spot for visitors—even if it's seldom occupied, I note, the corners of my mouth lifting at the reminder of our one-sided rivalry. In the background, the soft hum of a Riz radio accompanied by my sister's voice can be heard coming from the loft above as she sings along.

As I glance back at Elodie, I worry that my mask of friendliness has indeed slipped, judging by the twins' looks of clear disdain.

"What's the crack," Rowan asks, looking bothered by my entire existence.

"Look, ladies, I've been asked by Ms. Flynn and the Council to assist you both in your current investigation. I haven't been debriefed yet, but I hope we can put our dislike for each other aside long enough to solve this case." Not pausing to see how they react, I reiterate Ms. Flynn's orders, ending with our scheduled meeting at Foyle Hall. Taking a moment to breathe, I stare at Elodie and Rowan as they seem to share a silent, yet angry conversation between themselves. When their glares turn on me, I brace myself for a tough road ahead.

"This is beyond belief. How does she expect us to work together? You are the most impossible person to deal with in all of Eldermoore," Rowan snaps.

"Well, to be honest with you, I wasn't given much choice either. Working with you two is not something I'm looking forwards to. I'd solve this quicker on my own. Unfortunately for all of us, Ms. Flynn calls the shots, and, as I'm sure you know, her word is law around here."

Knowing I am right, and I'm sure hating me all the more for it, Elodie barks back as she shoots to her feet behind her desk, "This is unreal! We may have to work together, but mark my words: you'll be in for a rough time."

Never one to back down from a threat or challenge, all I can say as I walk out the door is, "Game on."

4

'HOMEWORK'
ELODIE

When the bell rang, announcing a visitor, I readied myself to greet them with my warmest smile, certain that even a brief show of friendliness could draw in clients.

That was until Aiden O'Connor walked in; his grin was too bright—too calculated—and he carried a bag of baked goods, as if trying to sweeten whatever he was about to say. His scrutinizing green eyes roved over our office with a thinly veiled sneer, clearly underestimating me as he tried to mask his shifting emotions behind a veneer of charm. And as if he hadn't just bombarded us with his unwelcome news and self-righteous hints of sacrificing his precious time for the safety of Eldermoore, as he left, he dared to mutter "game on." If he thought I was an easy mark, he'd soon find out just how hard I could bite back.

Now, as I watch him through the office window, I focus on calming my racing thoughts with deep breaths. Inhaling and exhaling in slow counts of three,

I gradually unclench my fists and soothe the crescent-shaped indentations left by my nails. Just a few hours ago, Auntie Cait had been in tears, lamenting that she trusted no one but us. *What a load of shite!*

As I squint and move closer to the window, I see Aiden's lips moving, clearly conversing with someone beside him. Then suddenly his arms flail around as if swatting flies, making him look like he's having a full-on meltdown. My eyebrows must be reaching my hairline because Rowan and Aisling quickly abandon their desks and join me at the window. They press their noses against the glass, fogging it up as Rowan's eyes widen in shock and Aisling's mouth drops open in surprise. With a loud snort that clears the fog, Aisling chuckles, her voice thick with an Irish lilt. "That one sure is cracked in the head," she says, voicing what we were all thinking. "Does Ms. Flynn really expect us to work with that gaga?"

"Are you talking about that eejit big brother of mine?" Maeve comes down the steps from the photography room, rolling her dress sleeves back down now that she's finished applying the chemical solution to the photos I took earlier. She strides towards the window beside us with long, purposeful steps, rising onto her toes to peer over our heads. Her blonde curls, mostly unravelled from their braid, cascade onto our shoulders as we watch her brother push open the front door of O'Connor Investigations. "It's unusual for him to drop by the office. Did he kick up a fuss?" she asks, her curiosity piqued.

Shaking my head, I pause mid-sentence. This conversation deserves more than a casual chat. "Oh, you have no idea! There's quite a lot to catch up on, but we'll fill you in over a cuppa. And wouldn't you know it, your charming brother also left us some sweets." My voice takes on a sarcastic tone, though I have to admit, I'd never turn down a good pastry. As we make our way over to the green sofa Rowan and I picked up at the Emporium for a song, each of us munching on our sugary pieces of heaven, the chime above our door rings again. This time, a young lad, likely no older than 15 rushes in. As I see he struggles to hold a tall pile of folders, I point him towards my desk. Placing them down, he cracks his knuckles and stretches his arms across his chest like he's preparing to enter an aerobics class.

"Not even a proper introduction before barging in," I say, placing my cinnamon bun down on the nearest surface. "Though I'll let it slide this time seeing as your arms were full. What is all this?" I can't help the smile that comes to my face at his current state of havoc.

Breathing heavily, the boy answers, "Ah, sorry 'bout that, miss. Name's Patrick Malone. I'm in me third year at Tara Hall, so I am. Headmistress Flynn sent me to drop these files off during study hall. I'm not too sure meself what's in all these papers, but Ms. Flynn called it your homework. I didn't believe her at first; I thought folk like you were done with assignments now that you're working and all." Without missing a beat, he continues, "I was tryin' to get here before the noon bell, but Ms. O'Neill stopped me. She said she'd gotten a call from the Headmistress and would be happy to help—whatever that means." Sweat beads across his forehead as he bends forwards, hands on his knees, taking his first real breath since he arrived. "Well, I gotta run now, but have a grand day!" he calls out, his voice trailing off as he dashes out the door, sprinting back towards the academy.

"Well, he's a real character— and the lot of you thought I was chaotic!" Maeve's laughter spills out, her voice trembling as she wipes at her eyes. Her sea-foam green gaze softened by her tears of amusement.

"I guess it doesn't matter which side of the Veil you're on; school seems to drive everyone bonkers!" Rowan banters back with a lighthearted chuckle.

Leaving them to settle down from their amusement, I move to take a closer look at what 'homework' Auntie Cait sent. Peering at the front of the topmost files I see each one is marked with the name Rónán Clarke. These must be the academy records we asked for. Homework, indeed. *She sure does work fast, I'll give her that!*

"Hey guys, take a look at these. It seems like our Auntie Cait sent us the records for Tara Hall. We should all take a pile if we have any hope of reading them all," I suggest to the others.

"Divide and conquer, eh? At least that's what I always say—much easier than trying to herd cats!" Rowan laughs, recalling her recent encounter with a black cat in the Nocturne's Nook alley behind Stout & Sip.

We all burst into hearty laughter as we remember her chasing the stray up and down Fiddler's Lane last week during the Fall Equinox refusing to let us help her. Rowan's always had a soft spot for feline friends, and her attempts to catch the poor creature were nothing short of entertaining.

"Alright, girls, fun's over. Time to get down to business and show what we can do!" Turning to Maeve I explain, "With all these files, it looks like our long chat will have to wait. For now, to get to the crux of it, your brother is under strict orders from the Council to help us solve this case." Maeve's mouth widens in a silent gasp at my brief explanation before she presses her lips together in discontent. Grabbing a stack of files to look through, we all follow suit, feeling the need to find anything that could help."

+)ﾠ)●((+

I sit back in my chair, my half-eaten cinnamon roll long forgotten and my tea now ice cold. I interlock my fingers and stretch them behind my head as I push backward in my chair, trying to ease the discomfort in my cramped muscles. Moving my hands to cover the back of my neck, I attempt to rub the knots that have formed from reading all morning. From the other side of the room, I hear Rowan sigh for the hundredth time. Knowing she's getting restless, I stand and glance at the girls.

"Rowan and I will take a trip to the morgue to see if Dr. O'Keefe has found anything of interest. You two can keep at those records. Maybe the answers are hidden in plain sight." As I grab my coat, Rowan follows my lead, and Maeve and Aisling nod with renewed focus as they dive back into their work.

"Don't forget I have an appointment at 3 o'clock today that I can't miss." Aisling throws out a quick reminder as Rowan and I head towards the door.

5

A PROPER SEND-OFF
Liam

Raven's Dock - 2:58 p.m.

The sound of the Lough Foyle can be heard alongside the docks as the tide washes over the weather-worn boards with the coming and going of ships. Sailor's boisterous laughter echos contagiously, seemingly much less disconcerting in the day than when walking the docks at night.

I glance at my watch for the hundredth time, enduring what feels like the longest minutes of my life. The rhythmic tick seems to sync with the racing of my thoughts. I shift my weight from one foot to the other, trying to ignore the unease tightening in my chest. Each time I flick my wrist, I pretend to adjust the strap, but my eyes are always drawn back to the hands of the clock, willing them to move faster. *Any second now.*

The click-clack of dress shoes hit the worn boards behind me and I breathe a sigh of relief. *Finally!* I turn with a bright smile, trying to mask my

24

earlier anxiety. "Ah, I was starting to worry you wouldn't make it. I know I've already asked you to come with me, but is there any chance I can convince you to reconsider?"

Instead of the familiar face I'd been expecting, I am met with a shadowy figure looming behind me, their presence sending a chill down my spine. "Oh, I am sorry, I thought you were someone else," I hurry to say.

Stepping into the dim light of the gloomy afternoon, they reveal a smirk that sends a shiver through me. "I'm afraid your expectations were a bit off," the figure drawls, their voice smooth and cold. "But don't worry, I've come to deliver a different sort of farewell."

As they draw closer, I glimpse a dangerous gleam in their eyes, causing me to take a step backward.

The figure's smirk widens, and they chuckle darkly. "I wasn't planning on this encounter just yet, but when opportunity knocks, you don't ignore it. I couldn't let you slip away before I had a chance to… tie up loose ends." Their eyes glint with a dangerous resolve.

"You see, Liam," they continue, their tone almost conversational, "I couldn't let you leave without reminding you of a few things. Consider this your proper send-off, as it were."

Their eyes narrow, and a sinister smile curves their lips. "Oh, and don't worry about your dear one. Once I'm finished with you, she'll be my next concern. You'll both meet again soon enough." The weight of their words sends a shiver down my spine.

With a chilling finality, I watch their hand move to a hidden pocket and pull out a small, dark hagstone. A lifetime of erosion is evident in how the light goes through it directly towards me, pulsing with a power I haven't seen in years. Their final words echo in my ears as a searing pain spreads throughout my body, blurring my vision. As I slip towards the water's edge, the shock of the cold closes over me. My last sensation is the whisper of the current against my skin as my consciousness fades.

6

THIRD TIME'S A CURSE
ELODIE

"Anything new, Doc?" Rowan asks, standing on tiptoe to peer over the shoulder of the elderly man in a white lab coat, his attire marked by the stark, clinical air of the morgue. His silver hair peeks out from beneath a worn cap, and the edges of his coat are slightly frayed, hinting at years of service. As we watch him write on the paper clipped to his brown clipboard, Rowan's curiosity is obvious.

He arches a thick white eyebrow as he steps away from my impatient sister, his shoes emitting a faint squeak on the grey linoleum floor. "Well, I would estimate his time of death at around 1 o'clock this morn'. But this case has me stumped," he says, removing his hat to lift a hand to his balding head, giving it a thoughtful scratch. "I have examined the body thoroughly but could not find any external puncture wounds to account for all the blood," he continues, shaking his head in bewilderment. "I remember reading about this sort of ailment when I was a lad at Tara Hall. Back then, it seemed like nothing more than a myth or a tale passed down through generations. I never thought it could be real."

"Well, what is it?" I press, trying to keep my impatience in check.

Doc places a wrinkled hand on my shoulder, the chill of his touch seeping through the fabric of my knit jumper. He leans in close, his breath brushing my ear as though he's about to unveil a closely guarded secret. His voice, though intended to be a whisper, carries more like a muted growl as he says, "The only thing it could be is draíocht dhorcha." He cups his hand to shield his words from Rowan's view, but the intensity of his tone betrays the effort to keep his revelation discreet.

"Dark magic!" Rowan's gasp draws his attention.

He glares at her, as if offended by her interruption, before turning back to face me.

"Yes. As I was saying, it appears the cause of death was a direct result of a curse," he murmurs, as if saying it aloud might summon the evil eye upon us. "Nasty things, curses. Painful, too. I reckon the boy endured a slow and agonizing death. Only a monster could inflict such cruelty." He shivers, his face contorting as his jacket rustles, and he begins to tremble like a cat in a bath, clearly unsettled by the notion. "You should have Ms. O'Neill down at the library examine these runes on the boy's neck. They might be the key to catching your culprit," he concludes with a decisive nod.

"Thorough job, Doc. Thank you for your help," I say, handing him a small business card with our office's phone and fax numbers. "If you think of anything else, don't hesitate to call us. We'll let you go now, if that's all." When my statement is met with silence, I take it as our cue to leave.

I grab Rowan's elbow to guide her towards the exit, but Dr. O'Keefe suddenly blurts out, "Oh, I almost forgot! I found a crumpled note in the lad's hand. The killer must have left it there before departing." He hurries to his cluttered desk, which is piled high with papers and surgical tools. He retrieves a clear evidence bag containing the note and hobbles back towards us, favouring one leg that seems slightly longer than the other. "I'm afraid you'll need to examine it at your office, lassies. I'm meeting my missus for dinner, and I can't be late again. She's threatened to serve me a cold shoulder if I don't show up on time!"

"Not a problem at all. We'll be on our way," I tell him as Rowan and I head out, ensuring the morgue's door is securely closed behind us. Handing her the evidence bag I add, "Let's get to the office and see what the note reveals."

With excitement bubbling over our first real clue, I place my hand on the back of Rowan's seat. Channelling the precision of a scene from The Quiet Man, I expertly manoeuvre the car out of the parking spot. The gravel crunches under the tires as I execute a flawless K-turn, the move looking as if it's been lifted straight from the telly. Shifting into drive, I smoothly guide us onto Eldermoore Avenue, a sense of triumph welling up inside of me. What started as a dreary day is clearly taking a turn for the better. With a grin, I think to myself, *we'll catch this fellow soon enough.*

+)⟩●⟨(+

"Alright, let's give it a gander," Rowan proposes after making a photocopy to preserve the original in our evidence locker. "Wow, would you get a look at this? We're dealing with a right lunatic here! I mean, seriously, they even went so far as to give themselves a name."

Reading over the note myself, I can't shake the growing dread that the worst was yet to come. "It also seems like Rónán's death might have even excited them, almost like it was a game just to lure him to his death. I wonder if this means Rónán might have known his killer beforehand."

Adding to my observation, Maeve exclaims, "You might be onto something there, Elodie. I think we can also check off that this was premeditated considering he had enough time to write this down. Plus, Aisling and I found nothing in the lad's file so far to hint that he was heading for trouble. One thing I'm wondering is, what's the story with all this seeking revenge business? I mean nothing big like this has happened in Eldermoore for over 20 years."

"Looks like we'll have to sort that out. I think we'll need to speak with Ms. O'Neill sooner than anticipated."

Leaning our hands on Rowan's desk, with our heads bent over the file, the chime of our door startles the three of us. Thinking it's Aisling returning from her appointment, I turn to give her a smart remark about being late. Instead, two men enter. Both are clad in heavy, dark-blue oilskin coats, the fabric stiff and speckled with traces of salt. The high collars of their coats are turned up to cover their rose-coloured ears, offering some shield against the chill that had followed them from the docks.

"Good evening, lassies," the one who entered first begins. "Name's Finn, and this here is Tadgh. Sorry for the interruption, but that nice fellow over there said we should talk to you," he explains, giving a slight nod of his head towards O'Connor Investigations. I force myself not to roll my eyes at the man. "I've got some news about a boy we found in the water by Raven's Dock as we were making port. Our watchkeeper says he saw one of those selkies bring him up from below. A few of me lads took him over to the Doc in town, but I find it hard to believe he'll survive the night, given how he looked."

"Good gracious! Two incidents in one day: it's got to be more than just a coincidence," I exclaim, turning to Rowan.

She nods in agreement, swiftly grabbing her jacket from the chair and slipping it on, followed by her black leather gloves. "Right then, lads, lead the way." Her voice is set with grim determination.

I throw my long coat over my jumper and tug Maeve towards the front door. "Mind locking up tonight? I don't reckon we'll be back before our meeting at Foyle Hall." I pause, then add, "And if you happen to track down Aisling, bring her along to the docks to question witnesses and gather any evidence. Let's hope the scene isn't too muddled by now. Just in case, here are the keys to our car— maybe driving there will give you a better chance of finding something left."

With a final glance and a nod of understanding from Maeve, I hurry to catch up with Rowan and the men who are already halfway down Hallow Way Road and, unfortunately, chatting with Aiden. *Well, isn't this just grand? A proper knees-up, now.*

The shadow of death fell upon him,
Fast and quiet, his light grew dim.
In the dark, I weave deceit;
I lured him to where nightmares meet.
For blood and vengeance, my anger spreads;
No light will enter where my wrath treads.
As darkness deepens and terror grows,
The night unveils what the fog forebodes.
Whisper my name, feel the fear it inspires;
For An Marfóir, in dread, never tires.

Rónán Clarke- Property of Danu's PI

7

a black car's fate

rowan

hat a load of blarney. As we walk, Aiden boasts to the sailors about how he'll likely be able to solve this mystery before the week's end. At least Elodie hasn't caught up to us yet, else she would likely stay true to her word and plant him a big ol' shiner.

"Sorry to cut this charming chat short, lads, but we'd best get a move on. If he's as bad off as you've described, we need to find out what he can tell us before it's too late," I say, stepping to the front of the group and picking up the pace.

With no true doctor in Balie na Muintir, the closest medicine man near the docks is likely Headmaster Doyle, who resides in Cove Court. If that's the case, it will be a good 20-minute walk across town before we reach his 'clinic'. A real bleeding heart that man is: educating children by day and saving lives by night— or at least, trying to. I never understood why the town Council continues to reject the idea of removing the Obsidian Veil. The laws only cause the citizens of Balie na Muintir to suffer the loss of healers. Having a dual education that explained the arcane arts and various types of protective spells so that we ordinary folk could protect ourselves might have made more of us pay attention at the academy. It's a good thing I had Elodie to keep me in check.

As if simply thinking her name conjured her, Elodie approaches the back of our group. "Thanks for waiting for me to catch up. Don't mind me, I'll just be back here trying to catch my breath," she murmurs as she blots tiny beads of perspiration from her brow.

"Out of shape, are you? I thought you said I was the one who'd be in for a rough time. I could offer some breathing tips—just let me know when you're ready for my expert advice." Aiden's snarky comment makes Elodie's face beet red in anger.

Her lips open and close as she searches for a comeback, ending with her stomping in front of him. As I turn to help her, I catch Aiden's eye lingering on her, a flicker of something softer behind his smirk.

Hmm. It looks like I have more than one puzzle to piece together. For now, though, I'd settle for just getting out of this never-ending walk.

I don't bother knocking as I approach the apartment door numbered 13. I twist the door handle, its brass surface dulled and scuffed from countless hands that have turned it. The door creaks open with a groan, revealing a dimly lit interior. The room smells sterile, with an undercurrent of copper that clings to the air.

The sound of the sailors' boots echoing softly can be heard as they back away from the room, their task of bringing us to the boy complete. As they make their exit, they exchange light comments about the lad's condition, their voices hushed but tinged with concern.

Elodie, always eager to dive into the heart of the matter, strides ahead until she reaches Mr. Doyle. Aiden follows a few steps behind, close on her trail.

Mr. Doyle's honey-coloured eyes, previously shadowed with fatigue, brighten momentarily at the sight of us. Yet, as we take in our surroundings, they cloud with sorrow once more. He raises a hand in a weary gesture of welcome. His usual expression, highlighted by the deep richness of his skin now displaying the effects of stress, reveals lines of profound disappointment and concern.

Standing up slowly, he carefully peels off his stained medical apron and gloves. The weariness in his movements speaks volumes about the gravity of the situation.

"I'm afraid the lad doesn't have much longer," he says, his voice heavy with regret. "Without a draoi to wield their magic, all I can do is ease his suffering and be there for him as the curse takes hold."

"Blast it!" I exclaim, my voice trembling with frustration. If what Mr. Doyle says is accurate, this lad will be the second victim of the self-proclaimed Slayer.

I watch as Elodie approaches the bed. Her light blue eyes, which had been clouded with grief at Mr. Doyle's news, widen in shock. Her fingers fly to her mouth, and she turns to me, her expression a mix of disbelief and horror. "It's Liam!"

Stunned, I step closer. Liam lies motionless, the blood-soaked sheets a stark contrast against his tan skin. The dark curls of his hair are matted and dishevelled, partially obscuring his face. Despite the blood and the violence, the angular lines of his jaw and the shape of his features unmistakably mark him as the same man we knew. The tragic reality of the scene sinks in as I glance over the familiar form. His shallow, rattling breaths come in uneven gasps, barely perceptible despite the stillness of the room.

As the four of us look at Liam's face, the thought of his twin sister, Leila, tugs at my heart. The thought of delivering such devastating news makes my stomach churn. Beside me, I catch Elodie's gaze and I can see the same pain mirrored in her eyes. The shared silence between us speaks volumes. The grief for Liam feels personal, as if it were our own. I shudder to think of a world without Elodie by my side, the void that would follow a loss so profound.

Determined to seek justice for Liam and his sister, I crouch beside the bed. Gently placing a hand on his shoulder, I tap him softly, hoping to wake him from his restless slumber. His hazel eyes flutter open, squinting against the soft glow of the candles as if the light itself is a torment.

"Liam, who did this to you? Can you tell us what happened?" I gently inquire, so as to not cause him further suffering.

His voice, weak and trembling, begins with a silent plea, "Osiris...," before he manages to whisper, "It was... a nightmare—Scáth..." His words are edged with a profound sense of dread. His eyes, fill with deep-seated terror, as he seems to look past me. As his breath falters, he grabs my hand adding, "Don't trust a..." His final warning lingers in the air as he drifts away, leaving behind a heavy sense of doom at his unsaid words.

Gently withdrawing my hand from his loosening grip, I feel a piece of parchment slipping from his fingers. Unravelling the crumpled paper, I forgo wearing gloves, feeling some kind of preservation charm beneath my fingertips, and begin to read it aloud.

Another prey fell by my whim,

As ravens caw o'er the water's brim.

You thought to escape from shadows deep,

But in your flight, you sowed what I reap.

For deeds of the past, my heart does yearn.

In this dark game, the wheel will turn.

Eternal and fierce, no force can bind;

A shadowed ally freed me from chains unkind.

My path is far from its final fall;

The night is young, and my shadows still call.

"It looks like we've got more than one player in this game," Aiden observes, his gaze shifting restlessly between the window and the empty space beside Mr. Doyle. He seems to be caught in a repetitive motion, his eyes darting back and forth as if driven by an uncontrollable tick. It reminds me of how Elodie and I used to silently signal each other across a classroom, our covert exchanges hidden amidst the teacher's lecture and our classmates' chatter.

"It would seem that way," Elodie agrees distractedly, glancing at her watch. "If we don't head to the Emporium now, we'll be late for the Council meeting." She turns to Aiden and continues, "Rowan and I will see to Leila and then meet you at Foyle Hall. If you wouldn't mind staying a bit longer to get Mr. Doyle's statement, I'd be grateful." The reluctance in her voice reveals her discomfort in asking him for assistance.

Still distractedly glancing at the window, he doesn't offer a snarky retort. He simply nods and pulls out a spiral notepad from his pocket before approaching Mr. Doyle, who stands beside the bed with tears brimming in his eyes. Without another word, Elodie and I close the door behind us and head out to find Leila.

As we pass the alley next to the Scriptorium, a black cat darts past my feet, jolting me from my thoughts. Its tiny paws tap sharply on the cobblestones as it begins to trail us from a short distance.

"Well, isn't this just the icing on the cake: two deaths in one day and now a black cat shadowing us," I mutter, casting a sharp look at the feline. It stares back with an air of indifference, its purple eyes gleaming with indifference. The white patch on its chest makes it unmistakable—the same cat I tried, *and failed*, to catch last month. It hisses softly, as if remembering our previous encounter. *Seems like the cat still has a bone to pick.*

MAEVE

Raven's Dock - 6:40 p.m.

The salty sea breeze rustles the hem of my dress, pressing the blue fabric against my legs and making it cling uncomfortably. My neatly braided hair, now tousled by the wind, has a wayward blonde curl falling across my eyes. Though

I could easily use my magic to calm the gusts, the wind's persistent playfulness is a deliberate reminder of my gift and an unwelcome nudge of its own power. With so many of the neamh-draíocht eyes around, I resist the urge to use my abilities. Instead, I push the rebellious strand behind my ear with a huff.

As I do, my gaze falls on Aisling, wrapped in her striking red cloak. I'd helped her pick it out from the Emporium just last week, and it stands out vividly against the muted, grey backdrop of the docks.

Her head swivels from side to side as she scans the area, searching for someone.

"Aisling, over here!" I call out, my voice cutting through the din of the bustling quay.

At the sound of my voice, she begins to jog towards me.

"Oh, hi Maeve! What are you doing here? Shouldn't you be at the office?"
Aisling's eyes dart back and forth nervously.

"Some sailors came by while you were out and reported a boy found in the water. Elodie sent me to track you down and gather some witness statements. Looks like she found you first?"

"Yes, that's right. Elodie and Rowan mentioned it. Did they say who the boy was?"

"No, they didn't. The girls went with my brother and the sailors to check on him. Now that we're both here, we need to find someone to interview. There should be plenty of sailors around who can shed some light—after all, they can talk the hind legs off a donkey."

I give Aisling a reassuring smile and grasp her arm as we head towards the group of men stationed by their ships. The sailors are gathered around a makeshift dinner table, enjoying their meal with hearty laughter and loud conversation. However, as we draw closer, the camaraderie fades. They avert their gazes, their joviality dimming as they become noticeably more reticent.

With a bright, determined tone, I announce, "Good day! I'm Maeve O'Connor, and this is my friend Aisling Ryan. We've heard from your mates earlier at Danu's PI about a boy found in the water. If you have a few minutes, I'd appreciate it if we could ask you a few questions."

A young, striking sailor steps forwards from the group, his presence commanding immediate attention. His golden hair, tousled by the sea breeze, catches the sunlight and frames his youthful, chiseled features. Noticing my lingering gaze, he arches an eyebrow and lets a half-smile curl at the corners of his lips. Resting one foot casually on a nearby barrel, his stance is relaxed yet self-assured. The warmth spreading across my cheeks only spurs me on, and I plunge into my questions, determined to make the most of this encounter.

"Hello, sir. Can you tell me if the boy who was found is part of a crew or if he's been seen hanging around the docks recently? Could he have perhaps bumped his head and accidentally fallen into the water?" My questions tumble out in a rush, fuelled by a mix of urgency and the hope of asking the right questions as Rowan and Elodie taught me.

"No need to be callin' me 'sir'," he says, his deep voice carrying a light chuckle. The minty freshness on his breath mingles with the briny sea air as he steps closer. "The name's Lorcan O'Rourke, but you can call me Lorcan. As for the lad, I've seen him around, always with a different bird, if you catch my drift. Come to think of it, I caught him askin' around for a way out of here a few days back. Said he needed safe passage for two, maybe three, as soon as possible."

"This is great news, sir!" I exclaim, deliberately choosing to use his title despite Lorcan's request. I quickly pull out a small notepad to start jotting down his words. "Could you describe the women he was meeting with?" I inquire, my pen darting swiftly across the paper.

Out of the corner of my eye, Aisling begins to fidget. Sensing her unease and eagerness for me to wrap things up, I quicken the pace of the interview. Before closing my notebook, I ensure the notes are complete, knowing Rowan and Elodie will need every detail. The prospect of uncovering more about the boy's situation fills me with a renewed sense of purpose.

ROWAN

The Shamrock & Scarab Emporium - 7:00 p.m.

Stepping into the Emporium, the air carries the earthy scent of aged parchment and worn leather, blended with the faint smokiness of burning herbs. Warm lamplight casts a soft glow on shelves crammed with treasures from distant lands. In one corner, antique furniture, from intricately carved chairs to elegant wooden tables, stands for sale. A dedicated section for more mundane clothing beckons us closer with its eclectic charm, showing Leila's dedication to both the an neamh-draíocht and Réalt. The other side of the store is blocked off by what Leila and Liam once compared to our crime scene tape when we were curious. While we have never been able to cross into that section, Rowan and I have always been mesmerized by the enchanted garments. Each robe and dress is adorned with intricate patterns and runes, promising their wearers both style and subtle power.

"Good evening and welcome. May the stars guide you well this night." Leila's rich voice calls out from the back room. As she steps into view, her eyes light up with recognition. "Oh, hello, girls. If you're here for more furniture, I'm afraid you'll need to wait for my brother to return. I don't have the same muscle for heavy lifting as he does," she adds with a melodic laugh, her Egyptian lilt making the words sing as she reminisces about the time Liam had to help us carry the green sofa down Witches' Walk to our office. He struggled without the use of his magic but determined nonetheless.

Noticing our silence and the absence of our usual camaraderie, Leila's smile fades, replaced by a concerned frown. Her eyes dart from me to Elodie, sensing something amiss. "What's going on?" she asks, her voice wavering as she steps around the front desk and places her hands on her hips, a gesture of both confusion and growing unease.

"Leila, please, sit down," I urge gently, my voice barely above a whisper, as I guide her towards the desk with a tender touch.

She shakes off my hand, her posture rigid and defiant.

"Leila," I begin, my throat tightening with the effort to steady my voice, "there's been… a terrible incident. Your brother was attacked at Raven's Dock earlier today. Headmaster Doyle tried to save him, but he arrived too late."

As my words hit her, her face crumples in shock. My heart aches as I watch her, and I place a hand over my chest, trying to steady the tremor in my voice. "I'm so sorry to bring you this news. It's an unimaginable loss, and I wish there was more we could do. We're here for you. Whatever you need, you are not alone."

A sob escapes her lips, raw and unrestrained. She collapses to the ground, her grief palpable as if it were a living, breathing entity.

I kneel beside her, my heart breaking as I lay a comforting hand on her trembling shoulder. "I wish I had more answers. It happened so suddenly, and we're still piecing together the fragments we have."

Taking a deep breath, I search for the right words. "Leila, there's more to this. There's a dangerous individual on the loose, and your brother's death appears to be connected. We're doing everything in our power to find this person and seek justice for Liam." I hesitate, then gently add, "If you're able, we need to ask you a few questions. We're trying to understand why Liam was at the docks and if there's any detail that might help us unravel this tragedy. There's no rush, though, if you want us to come back later."

"No," she responds, her sobs easing as she gathers herself. With a determined effort, she rises, using the stool beside her for support. Her eyes, though red-rimmed, reflect a newfound resolve. "It's alright. I will do everything in my power to help you find who did this to him. The scales of Ma'at will weigh the truth. Ask your questions."

"Do you know why Liam was down there? Did you have another delivery coming in today?"

Leila's face tightens for a moment, her eyes flickering with something unspoken. She quickly masks it with a calm exterior. "I don't know why he was at the docks. He always kept his plans close to his chest—ever since we first came to Eldermoore. However, he'd been going there more frequently. He was always worried, but these past few weeks he had been acting strange."

Her voice falters slightly as she continues, "He'd come home late, looking over his shoulder. He tried to hide it, but I could see the stress in his eyes. He even started talking about making a big change, though he wouldn't tell me what it was. He always brushed off my concerns with a smile, saying it was nothing to worry about."

"That's really helpful, Leila. We just have one more question: Do you know if Liam has been meeting someone recently, perhaps starting a new relationship?" Elodie suggests hopefully.

Leila's shoulders slump as the weight of her grief overwhelms her again. Her eyes fill with tears, and she struggles to speak through her sobs. "I'm so sorry… I don't know who Liam might have been seeing. All I know is that sometimes he would say he was meeting a friend and would leave on foot, so they must have lived nearby. But then again, Eldermoore isn't that large. It's just… too many possibilities. I wish I could help more, but—."

"It's alright, Leila. You've been through so much. Please, take all the time you need to grieve. If you remember anything else or think of something that might help, we're only a phone call away."

Placing a shawl from the chair over Leila's shoulders, Elodie adds, "We're going to take our leave now, but we'll stop by tomorrow morning to check on you."

Making our way towards the door, I hear Leila's voice tremble from behind us, barely rising above a whisper. "What am I going to do?"

As we step outside, my shoulders begin to shake, and a tear slips down my cheek, unable to be held back any longer.

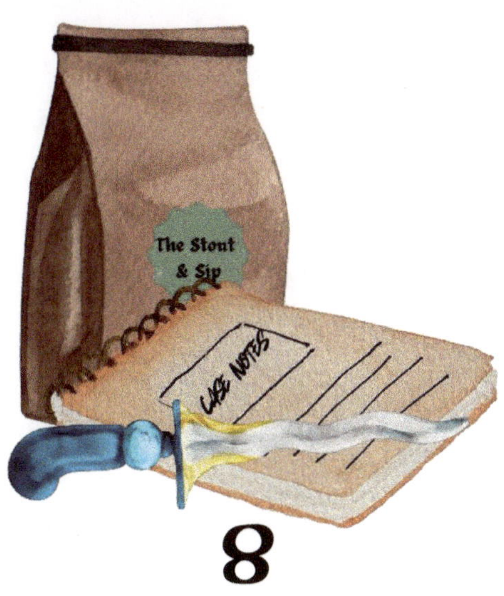

8

TIME TO GET STUCK IN
AIDEN

Apartment 13 - 6:30 p.m.

I watch as Rowan, with brisk and purposeful movements, turns the worn handle of Apartment 13 without so much as a knock. The creak of the door echoes in the narrow hallway. As we approach, my shoulders stiffen, anticipating trouble. The sailors' hurried exit still echoes in my mind, a silent testament to their unease. While maintaining a calm exterior, I prepare to call upon my Súil.

As I concentrate, the hues of the room effortlessly shift, colours deepening with my focus as naturally as drawing my next breath. Shadows stretch and contract, revealing hidden auras and energy fields. My surroundings transform into a kaleidoscope, each colour revealing hidden emotions and potential dangers. With every breath, the apartment sharpens, gradually painting a clearer picture of the threats that might lie ahead. The girls themselves emit a soft brown glow, hinting at their anxiety.

Elodie strides in after Rowan without taking a moment to assess our surroundings. Her anger is sharp and her eyes blaze with irritation at my earlier jest, which is confirmed by the additional red tint of her aura. Close on their heels, I can't help but wonder how the girls have survived this long without running into trouble.

When the door swings open, I know immediately who this newest victim is and my breath catches. Liam Hassan lies on the bed, his body unnaturally still. Though he had graduated from Tara Hall the same year as me, he had always remained quite a recluse. Whenever Lennon and I tried to invite him to the pub after our classes, he was always insistent that he had to return home to care for his sister.

As I draw closer, a shiver races down my spine. The air around Liam feels dense and oppressive, thick with a dark energy that feels unmistakably like a curse. Looking closer, I can see the spectral hints of death clinging to him, shadows that only someone with my sight would notice. My Súil reveal a ghostly aura that has begun to overtake his usual muted indigo aura, a clear sign that his time is running out. Every instinct tells me he won't last much longer, and the grim reality sets in; we need to act fast.

Lost in thought, I barely notice Rowan and Elodie moving closer. Rowan asks Liam a series of calm, measured questions. Her tone, though careful, betrays a hint of the worry she's trying to mask. Beside her, Elodie's face is a canvas of concern and sorrow, her eyes reflecting a deep sadness that echoes the gravity of the situation.

Suddenly, a familiar chill brushes against my senses. Declan materializes beside me, his translucent body barely disturbing the air. His eyes, always sharp, scan Liam's frail figure with a mixture of sorrow and apprehension. "Aiden," he murmurs, his voice tinged with melancholy, "we're out of time." I glance at Liam, my heart sinking as I see a faint, shimmering light rise above Liam's form.

No stranger to death, I prepare to see the bright orb dissipate in its final farewell before leaving the mortal plane. Yet, Liam's spirit slowly becomes a ghostly apparition, disappearing through the closed window on the back wall. *Well, that's new.*

Trying to get Declan's attention—his gaze fixated on Rowan as she slips her hand from Liam's grasp—I clear my throat and give him a pointed look, then subtly nod towards the window.

I must be worse at silent communication than a fish at a dance because he simply gives me a look of confusion as he asks, "Did ya go and kink your neck again?" *Honestly, how is he my spy?*

With a look that could kill if he weren't already dead, I slow my movements, making them more deliberate as I try again to get him to look out the window before the wisp of Liam's form disappears entirely.

"What the devil? I will go see where he's headed!" Declan exclaims as he finally notices, his voice almost indiscernible as he passes through the glass pane. *Well, of course, why didn't I think of that?*

Suddenly, I sense the curse—dark and bloodthirsty—reaching out, trying to find someone new to latch onto. Quickly realizing the girls are without protection uniforms to ward off the spell, I distort our auras to fend off its persistent search for the living. Unlike my inherent ability to see the dead, this process takes more than a simple thought. Without hesitation, I block out the conversation around me, the girls' safety paramount. In my mind, I watch as my blue aura becomes intertwined with theirs.

Through my focus, I distantly hear Elodie's voice, gentle but insistent. "If you wouldn't mind staying a bit longer to get Mr. Doyle's statement, I'd be grateful."

Her voice is a faint beacon in the whirlwind of my mind, and I feel myself nodding, her request piercing through my daze as I fight to steady myself, the oppressive grip of the curse retreating as I regain control. Almost robotically, I grab my worn notepad from the outer pocket of my suit vest and walk towards the doctor as I hear the front door click closed.

"Mr. Doyle, correct?" I jot down his name, apartment number, and the current time as I prepare to ask him a series of questions.

"Yes, sir."

"I'd like to get a clear picture of what occurred here this evening. If you wouldn't mind, I'd like you to walk me through your day, starting around the time the sailors arrived with Liam." My voice strengthens as I fall back into the familiar routine of interviewing.

"Well, certainly. I'd barely been home from Acadamh na nGnáth five minutes— maybe around five o'clock considering I had a few meetings this evening— when the two sailors who brought you here came askin' for help. They said they'd found him and tried to resuscitate him, but since they didn't know much about healing, they went lookin' for someone else. The poor lad was as cold as ice from the water, so I had them put him in the bed."

"Hmm. I see. When you realized that it was indeed a curse, why did you not try to send for a *draoi*?"

"Ah, well, it's a bit of a sore spot, that is. I knew I wasn't supposed to involve any Réaltaí, not without the proper cause. Truth be told, I didn't fully grasp it was a curse until Liam started coming to his senses and whispered about a shadow. Originally, I was more concerned with the possibility of a concussion and hypothermia. By the time he began to bleed, my limited training was more of a hindrance than a help to him. Couldn't even think straight with the lad in such a state. Lookin' at the situation now, it'd seem the smart lad was hidin' in the water to fend off the effects of the curse until help arrived. It's a hard pill to swallow, knowing I might've done more if I'd understood sooner."

"I see. What I don't quite understand is why the sailors came to my office instead of going to Tara Hall, which is a five-minute walk closer and has a professor skilled in healing. As they likely didn't have permits themselves, you could've sent them with yours so that they could call for medical assistance."

"Well, you see, the sailor lad—Finn, I think he was called—started going a bit green at the sight of all the blood. I had a natter with Ms. Flynn over at Tara Hall this morning about you and the girls teaming up. Seemed like a grand idea to me. Thought if I sent them your way, you'd be able to sort it all out. Plus, it gave me a chance to help Liam without fretting whether that boy would keel over and give me two patients to worry about. One was more than enough for me at the time." His voice carries a hint of defensiveness. "As for me permit, like I said before, I didn't twig it was a curse until it was too late. The sailor lads had already cleared out by the time Liam came around, and that's when I started piecing things together." As I listen, I can't help but notice the dark blue-indigo hue surrounding him—an aura that speaks volumes of his anxiety.

Though I had my doubts about his story—especially how a sailor who's likely seen his fair share of rubby-dubby and injuries could go all wobbly at the sight of blood—the old fellow's haggard look makes me think twice about pushing him further. "Right, that'll be all for now. If I have more questions, I'll put in a request with the other Council members to let you come by my office. If you wouldn't mind, I would like to take some photos of the body before you prepare him for the morgue."

"Of course, Mr. O'Connor. I understand the importance. Just be swift— I've got a lot to account for here when I write my report. If you need anything else, let me know."

Kneeling beside the bed, I begin methodically documenting the scene with my camera. The room, dimly lit by the harsh beam of the flash, casts a stark light on the pale face of the second victim today. A faint, sweet scent, cloying and sugary, lingers in the air around Liam. I take note of the odour, uncertain of its origin. With Liam's arm still hanging limply off the bed where Rowan had let go, the runes etched into his forearm are impossible to miss. I snap a few shots with my camera, preparing to rise. Just before I move, a red berry catches my eye on the ground beneath the bed. I carefully pick up the branch and take several photos. I'll need to cross-reference these with the evidence Elodie and Rowan collected earlier and compare them to my own notes and growing suspicions.

I finish documenting the scene, carefully packing away my camera and notes. Taking one last look around the quiet, still room, I try to absorb every detail. Looking at my watch, I realize the time for the council's ceremony is quickly approaching. With a determined nod, I exit the apartment, ready to dive into the next phase of *my* investigation.

9

THE WILL-O'-THE-WISPS' LURE

ELODIE

Elderwood Avenue - 7:55 p.m.

Rowan and I quicken our pace along the street to Foyle Hall, the urgency in our steps matched by the cool evening breeze. The sun has begun to set, casting long shadows and turning the sky a deep, dusky purple. It's almost time for the Council meeting and I'm determined to not be late. Especially, if it means avoiding another one of Aiden's lessons—this one on the importance of arriving on time.

As we near the edge of Mystic Path, a flickering, ethereal light in the corner of my eye catches my attention. I stop and point. "Do you see that," I quickly ask Rowan, worried they'll disappear.

Whipping her head in my direction, Rowan follows my gaze, squinting as she tries to make sense of the strange lights. "Are those will-o'-the-wisps?" she asks, astonishment coating her words as she steps closer to the forest edge.

I nod, my eyes fixated on the ghostly blue orbs drifting just beyond the trees. "Yes, and considering everything that's happened, it's unnerving. I wonder if they could be the spirits of Rónán and Liam."

"If they are, it's as if they're trying to guide us—or send a warning."

A shiver runs down my spine at the mere thought, but I push it aside. Auntie Cait would never put us in danger. "We need to keep moving. The meeting will start soon, and we can't afford to be late." With a final uneasy glance at the haunting lights, we quicken our pace.

Foyle Hall looms ahead, its ornate architecture a testament to the town's rich history. Tall, arched windows are framed in wrought iron alongside carved wooden doors. I can't help but marvel at everything, knowing that not many neamh-draíocht have stepped foot inside before. Together we climb the broad stone steps before pushing open the heavy oak doors, revealing a vast foyer bathed in the warm light of a grand chandelier. The walls are adorned with portraits of long-departed figures whose eyes seem to follow us as we hurry down the hall.

At the end of the corridor, a set of double doors stands slightly ajar, revealing the chamber for the council meeting. The low hum of conversation hints that everyone, even Aiden, has already arrived. Moving to join them, I exchange a glance with Rowan that's a mix of excitement and apprehension, both of us eager to learn what we can tonight.

Auntie Cait greets us at the entrance with an overly cheerful demeanour that does little to mask the underlying tension. "Welcome, Elodie and Rowan," she says with a smile that doesn't quite reach her eyes.

Bypassing our usual hugs while in the Council's austere presence, she clasps our hands, her grip warm and reassuring as she ignores the glares we aim at Aiden. As she leads us towards the centre of the room, her confident presence commands the space. It's moments like these that remind me of the day she took us to the Headmaster's Office to meet Mr. Doyle on our first day at Acadamh na nGnáth. Rowan and I had practically begged her to let us stay home, but she'd finally coaxed us with sweets. Walking the halls of the academy, her presence made every student stare in our direction. Their looks had seemed so intimidating, but the gentle weight of her hand on our shoulders felt like something our own mother might have given.

"I'm delighted you could make it tonight. The Council is ready to begin," Auntie Cait says.

Moving forwards, I scan the council chamber. It's a sight to behold, filled with a mix of ancient and contemporary artifacts. I take in the small gathering with a quick sweep of my eyes, noting that Eldermoore's five council members are already seated, one of them being Mr. Doyle— the only neamh-draíocht member in over a century. He'd been inducted by Auntie Cait herself to show her desire to bridge the gap between Eldermoore.

"Allow me to introduce you to our members," Auntie Cait begins, gesturing to the group. "We have the esteemed Mr. Doyle, whom you've met before." As he catches my eye, he offers a small, welcoming smile. "Next to him is Ms. Maguire, our historian with an impressive knowledge of local folklore." The meticulous way she's put together makes it clear she values precision. Her cat-like eyes take in our every movement. "Over there is Dr. Collins, our botanist and plant specialist." His strong facial features are softened by his wide expressive eyes. "Last but not least, we have Mrs. Flanagan, who oversees all foreign trade and immigration into Eldermoore." Her slight wrinkles and smile lines speak of years of experience and genuine warmth, even though she exudes a serious demeanor.

As Auntie Cait wraps up the introductions, she turns to us with a reassuring smile. "We'll begin with the Tying of Knots ceremony. This ritual is intended to solidify our agreement between you three and the Obsidian Veil and offer you protection through the sharing of knowledge. Once it's complete, you'll be able to freely explore Eldermoore's history as well as the magic that might have been involved in the deaths of the two boys. For the ceremony to commence you'll all need to step into the Celtic Cross drawn on the floor here and join hands."

At her instruction to hold hands, Rowan and I can't help but raise our eyebrows in disbelief.

Seeing our looks of mistrust, she explains, "It's the old way of doing things, meant to seal the bond and keep the protection strong."

I glance to the floor, where a large Celtic Cross is meticulously drawn in white chalk. It's centred within a circular pattern, the arms of the cross extending evenly, creating a symmetrical and intricate design. The outer circle features interlacing knots and spirals that create the image of the cross that is deeply rooted in Celtic tradition.

Moving to stand above it, Auntie Cait hands me a length of branched hawthorn cord. Rowan takes another piece, while Aiden receives a third. As we stand within the cross and join hands, the council members begin to move with practiced precision. They circle around us, each handling the ends of our cords with deliberate care. Their synchronized motions create a fluid dance around us.

Auntie Cait moves gracefully among them, overseeing the process and making minor adjustments to maintain balance and symmetry. The cords gradually intertwine, looping and crossing with careful coordination. As they work, the design of a Triskelion begins to emerge around us.

Once the knot is formed, Auntie Cait begins explaining the significance of the cords. "The combination of the hawthorn branches and the Triskelion will symbolize the unity and connection between you, Rowan, and Aiden's fates, as well as embody the strength and wisdom you will need for the challenges ahead." With that, she glances around to ensure the other council members are ready. Satisfied, their voices join in a harmonious chant, resonating through the room:

> *By the Celtic Cross, strong and true,*
> *We bind this oath in ancient hue.*
> *With Hawthorn's might and Earth's embrace,*
> *We weave this bond in sacred space.*

> *With the strength of five, our leaders past,*

Their wisdom guides this pact to last.
With wind's whisper and fire's gleam,
We anchor our vows in a sacred seam.

From river's flow to mountain high,
We unite our fates 'neath the watchful sky.
By the strength of the land and stars above,
We bind this pact with truth and love.

As the Cross and Hawthorn stand tall and grand,
Your spirits unite by this ancient hand.
Guided by those who came before,
We forge this bond, now and evermore.

As they chant in unison, a warm, golden light begins to emanate from the cords binding us together. The light pulses softly, growing stronger with each rhythmic incantation. It spreads like liquid warmth up my arms and towards my chest, wrapping around my heart with a soothing glow. I glance up to see the same luminous transformation unfolding around Rowan and Aiden, their expressions reflecting the awe and concentration of the moment.

With the final, resonant phrase of the ritual, the light converges at the centre of our joined hands. It weaves and intertwines in intricate patterns before suddenly surging back towards us.

As the energy settles within me, I feel an almost imperceptible shift, almost as though a veil has lifted from my mind. A tingle of awareness causes goose pimples to raise the hair on my arms as a heaviness presses down on me, though its presence doesn't suffocate like I assumed it would. Instead, the sensation feels like someone draping a blanket across my shoulders, warm and comforting. The weight of it melds into my bones, becoming a part of me. It weaves an invisible thread of understanding between us— although Aiden's feels fainter than the bond I've shared with Rowan my whole life.

As I look around, a sense of clarity and heightened awareness washes over me, almost as if I can now grasp the subtler threads of magic previously eluding me.

Auntie Cait, noting our reactions, encourages Aiden to test whether the ceremony has achieved its purpose. "Go on, Aiden," she prompts. "Let's see if the magic has taken hold."

Aiden steps forwards, his gaze steady as he begins to concentrate. I watch, intrigued, as his eyes seem to glow as he focuses on something I can't quite see. He nods, then addresses us with a hint of a smile. "Well, it looks like the ceremony worked. We won't need to hold hands again any time soon."

Before I can retort, Aiden adds, "I specialize in aura reading and energy manipulation. It's how I can sense changes in magical connections and detect underlying forces." He focuses his gaze on Rowan and me, his expression reflecting a mix of interest and approval. "Your auras are glowing brighter and more harmonized than before. The ceremony has already strengthened your connection and opened your perception of magic."

As Aiden's words sink in, I'm taken aback. The idea of someone being able to read and influence auras feels both fascinating and a little overwhelming. I find myself reassessing my initial scepticism about Aiden. Maybe, *just maybe*, this won't be such a bad thing after all. If this is what our combined efforts can achieve, then perhaps our alliance could turn out to be more beneficial than I'd first thought.

Rowan, ever the one to lighten the mood, nudges me with a smirk. "Looks like we've got ourselves a human lie detector, eh? Just hope he's not going to use that power to call us out on every little thing!"

That's when I realize Aiden might have been sensing my mixed feelings all along. I groan inwardly, wincing as a flush of embarrassment heats my cheeks. *Ugh, what a right mess!*

ii

an uncommon bond

Three souls now bound can cross the Line,
Through song and rhyme their fates entwine.

A fourth now seen and heard,
The game afoot may take a turn.
Only if they trust and listen,
Though doubt and lies may soon start hissing.

Beware the Shadow that twists and weaves,
For not all truths are what they seem.
In unity, they must be bold,
For hidden secrets will unfold.

10

BENEATH THE SURFACE
ELODIE

I find myself in a moonlit forest, the air thick with an otherworldly stillness. There she is again—the same woman from my previous dreams. Her presence once again was both mesmerizing and unsettling. That's when I see it: her long, flowing hair is a cascade of pure white, glowing faintly in the darkness. An unsettling shiver travels down my spine, a sense of recognition prickling at the edge of my consciousness— it's something I should understand. Yet, the meaning remains just out of reach, like a word on the tip of my tongue that refuses to come into focus. I try to get closer to see who she is, but her face is shrouded in shadows. The all-too-familiar sound of her voice begins to take shape, but it's a song I haven't heard before.

In the dead of night's embrace,
Where shadows hide and secrets chase,
A mournful wail, a spectral cry,
Foretells the end as dark winds sigh.

WHEN THE RAVEN SOARS

The slow eeriness of her song causes a wave of emotion to surge through me, resonating to my very essence, and causing shivers to race down my spine. The echoes of her voice harmonize as she continues to her haunting chorus.

Trust the bonds that fate has spun,
Strength you'll need when dark times come.
In the gloom where spirits weep,
Face the truth or fall too deep.

Through dreams where whispers softly moan,
Eldermoore's fate is darkly shown.
Death's cold grip and sorrow's veil,
Unity's strength may yet prevail.

With questions running through my mind, I find myself calling out to the figure. "What are you trying to tell me?" I ask, my voice trembling with a mix of confusion and urgency. "Please, what message do you have for me?"

The woman seems lost in her own world, ignoring my plea.

Trust the bonds that fate has spun,
Strength you'll need when dark times come.
In the gloom where spirits weep,
Face the truth or fall too deep.

In the silence where shadows creep,
Echoes mourn and secrets seep.
As darkened fates begin to loom,
Find your strength or meet your doom.

As the final, lingering note of her song fades, the dream begins to dissolve around me. The woman's figure blurs, her haunting melody gradually becoming a distant sound. The ethereal mist that surrounds us evaporates, and the world I am drifting through slips away.

My eyes flutter open to the familiar confines of my room, the melody still echoing faintly in my mind. I know I must remember the woman's song, its eerie beauty too important to forget. As I struggle to hold onto the last remaining threads, I resolve to capture every note in my journal before it slips entirely from my grasp.

That's when it comes to me—the word that had eluded me in my dream. I quickly scribble down the title of my entry. This might just be the key to unravelling everything.

-Elodie's Journal-

A Banshee's Plea

Entry #8: October 2nd @ 3:00 A.M.

The O'Grady House - 4:30 a.m.

With the last echoes of the dream's haunting melody replaying in my mind, sleep will elude me. I stretch my tired writing hand, its fingers sore from pressing the pen against my journal, and untangle my legs from their crisscrossed position. Rising from the bed, I start to get ready. Before long I hear the alarm clock on my bedside table chime 5:30 am. Rowan's loud yawn and the soft hum of her alarm from the bedroom across the hall soon signal that she too is awake.

Heading to her door, I peek my head in and settle my hip against the door jam. "I'm not sure when Aiden will be making an appearance today. When you're ready, we'll head over to the office. I'd like to begin creating a file for Liam while we wait for Aisling and Maeve to arrive." Noting her tired expression and pale complexion I add, "It's my day to cook, so I was thinking of frying up some eggs and bacon rashers with your favourite spiced chai. Oh, and I think we still have those pumpkin muffins I made over the weekend. What do you think?"

"Mmm, yum!" She hums in delight plopping back down on her bed dreamily. "You really know how to spoil a girl. Thanks, I'll be down in a few."

I head downstairs chuckling. As I start to boil the water for tea, I hear Rowan shout down the stairs, "What's the weather like? I can't decide between a skirt or trousers."

Making my way to the television we purchased a few years ago, I tune it until I reach RTÉ and hear the telltale signs of the weather forecast.

As the reporter begins the morning program, I hear Rowan softly mumble under her breath, "What am I saying? It's always cold in Eldermoore."

Tuning back into the report, the man's voice drones on, "Temperatures are currently around 12°C, with highs expected to reach 14°C and lows tonight around 8°C. Winds are coming from the southwest at 20 to 30 kilometres per hour, bringing a bit of a chill."

"No rain but looks like a windy day ahead. Throw on a few layers, so you're not caught out in the cold," I shout towards the stairwell as I turn the telly off.

"Well, it's like I always say: looking grand can be a right ol' slog!" Rowan says, peeking her head around the corner with a wink before disappearing again.

Just as I finish plating the eggs, the sound of her heeled boots alerts me to her arrival. Coming up beside me, she takes a deep breath, her lips parting slightly as she savours the rich blend of aromas now filling the air—nutmeg and cinnamon mingling with the savoury scents of eggs and bacon rashers.

Her tongue flicks out to moisten her lips. "Ah, I love it when it's your turn to do breakfast. It's always a proper treat!"

"Well, we'd better dig in quickly. We've gotta hit the road soon!"

Danu's PI - 7:00 a.m.

Making quick work of unlocking the office door, Rowan and I go to move inside when we hear footsteps followed by the call of Maeve and Aisling asking us to hold the door for them. Spotting them a few feet away, I see them both bundled up in their coats and scarves carrying large stacks of the files from yesterday.

"Good morning, girls, I'm glad we've all managed to be here at once. We've got a fair bit of work ahead of us today—though it looks like you both might've got a jump on things. Settle in, and we'll call a meeting in 10 to see how your interviews at Raven Docks went."

Flipping on the lights, Rowan and I walk over to my desk and begin to prepare a file for Liam. "I suppose I'll also have to call Aiden over and see what he's got from his interview with Mr. Doyle." Picking up the phone on my desk, the cord drags as I walk over to the window to see if his car is parked by his office. Though the Obsidian Veil obscures the left side of his building, the right parking lane reveals his black car, still covered in dew. *Hmm, did he spend the night in his office? Wait, never mind, I don't care.*

As if to confirm my suspicions, Aiden's groggy voice crackles through the line. "Mornin', this is O'Connor's Investigations." There's a brief pause as if he momentarily drifts back to sleep before recalling he's on the phone. "How can I help you?"

His lack of usual alertness makes it hard for me to suppress the smile that's spreading across my face. "Hello Aiden, it's Elodie. I thought, seeing as how we're working together now, I'd need to invite you to come over to the office. We're about to have a chat about the cases and would like to hear what you found out yesterday so we can add your notes to our file."

"Ah, I see. Was there a question hidden in there somewhere, or was that your subtle way of asking me to drop everything and come help?" Aiden questions with his usual snark, sounding more awake.

"I'll see you in five minutes. Don't be late!" I reply with a playful firmness before hanging up.

Chuckling to myself, I collect my notes and head towards the couch when I catch Rowan shooting me a look of disbelief. "Looks like you and Aiden are getting along better already! Who knew you'd go from bickering to cracking jokes so quickly?" she says with a chuckle, clearly enjoying the moment.

Our newly formed bond sends prickles of awareness dancing across my skin, alerting me to Aiden's nearness before he opens the office door. Despite my morning wake-up call, he strolls in right on time looking like he just spent the night having a right kip on a cloud instead of at his desk. I had mentally prepared a joke about him arriving in yesterday's suit, but instead, he strolls in wearing a perfectly pressed black turtleneck and trousers. His hair, long on top and curling slightly, falls just below his ears in a deliberately messy but controlled fashion. I catch myself staring a moment too long, and Aiden's sharp green gaze meets mine before I can look away.

"What's with the look, Elodie? Did I grow a second head, or are you just amazed there are people out there that can arrive on time?"

My cheeks, which had been turning pink in a blush, are now flushed red with anger. Before I can do something I might regret later, Maeve saves me the trouble. "Mornin', brother!" she chirps, standing on her tiptoes to give him a quick peck on the cheek. "And while we're at it, quit nagging or we might just start charging you by the hour!"

"Alright, alright, I was just teasing," Aiden says, offering me a small, apologetic glance before taking his seat and getting down to business. "So, ladies, I think it's best we go through the events in order."

Filling him in on our analysis of Rónán's crime, I share how we've begun working on the files Auntie Cait sent over. "From what we've gathered so far, he was just as Auntie Cait described: a star student, no priors, active member of the student council, and didn't seem to hang out with any trouble and his peers confirmed he wasn't dating anyone recently."

"We also have no known witnesses for the time between his death and when Auntie Cait found him, so we're going to have to take our time cross-referencing the evidence we were able to collect at the scene and the coroner's report." Turning to face Aisling and Maeve, Rowan explains, "When we arrived at the Doyle's residence, we realized that the man was Liam Hassan. It was quite evident that the same person attacked both Rónán and Liam with a killing curse. If the notes left behind are any indication, they both must have known their assailant."

Quiet gasps escape both girls with Aisling paling at the revelation. I give them a moment to process the news of our friend's death.

It only takes a moment more for Aisling to gather herself. Her stark complexion and glassy eyes betray her sadness, yet there is a new sturdiness to her stance. "Maeve and I have been trying to decipher the runes found on Rónán, but our books are just not cutting it," she says with resigned certainty.

"I think I can help with that one," Aiden cuts in. "I know Niamh over at The Arcane Scriptorium who is great at deciphering languages and spells. We can also use the photos I took of the runes on Liam's arm. They might give us more to work with." He hands me the developed photographs to add to the file still open on my desk.

"That sounds like a good plan. Auntie Cait recommended her, and we were planning to visit, but it would be even better if you could introduce us and explain exactly what we'll need. We're still quite in the dark about magic at the moment." *I'll definitely need to get used to him helping us out.*

"Alright, then, Maeve, what were you and Aisling able to find out?" Rowan chimes in from her spot next to me.

"Well, the sailors were unusually sparse and unwilling to chat yesterday, but I did come across a fellow by the name of Lorcan." Flipping open her spiral notebook, she eagerly begins to recount Lorcan's story. "He told us that he'd seen Liam asking around the past few days looking for tickets out of Eldermoore for up to three people. Oh, and he said Liam would often be seen with different ladies: one with dark hair and features and another with light blonde or ginger hair. We were also able to snap some photos of the scene, but whoever the killer is must have planned these attacks for months or had experience doing this before. We found no evidence of anything being left behind except for the rope the sailors used to remove him from the water."

Taking in her notes, I try to connect what we know. "That reminds me of what Auntie Cait said when we first arrived at the school yesterday morning—something about death coming to Eldermoore once more. Perhaps she knows more than she's willing to tell us. Aisling should be able to find something to give us a clue in some of her Eldermoore history books. In the meantime, we should try to find these women. One is likely Leila since they go to the docks together to pick up shipments. I'm not sure who the other woman could be, though. Do any of you remember seeing Liam walking around town to meet someone recently who matches that description— maybe someone from Tara Hall?"

"Mrs. Flanagan is a possibility. She could've been meeting with him regarding his shipments since she's in charge of trade." With a look of contemplation, Maeve continues, "Although it sounded more like he was meeting a girlfriend to me. I'd say we can rule her out seeing as she's not from Gleann na Réaltaí and is about 20 years his senior. The only other person I can think of in Eldermoore is A…" Maeve's eyes widen in shock as we all turn to look at Aisling, who has so far remained silent.

Before I can even ask her if this is true, she lets out a heart-wrenching sob that causes her shoulders to shake. "I'm so sorry… I was going to tell you when the time was right. We had only just started seeing each other about two months ago. We were both scared someone from the Council would find out." Pausing, she takes my hands and gives a pleading look, as if willing me to understand. Her voice takes on a high pitch as she rushes to explain. "Please don't hate me. You three are the only other family I have; I couldn't bear the thought of losing you. You know there are penalties for relationships between a réalt and a neamh-draíocht. I didn't want to risk you being involved. I'll tell you anything you want to know if it means Liam's killer is found and you all can trust me again."

"You told me you were at the docks because Rowan and Elodie sent you. But you were really there to meet Liam, weren't you?" Maeve says, her face crumpling in hurt.

Another sharp intake of air passes Aisling's lips as she tries to control her crying. "That's where I'd go for my appointments. Liam always said it was the least suspicious place to find us together since ships were always coming and going. But I got so caught up in reading about the runes yesterday and was running late." Another sob escapes as she whispers, "I was only ten minutes late, but he was already being pulled out of the water when I arrived. I didn't even get to say goodbye or tell him I was sorry."

"Sorry for what?" Aiden's voice breaks through the tension in the room.

"He'd been acting suspicious lately—paranoid. I kept asking him what was wrong, but all he'd say was that it was better if I didn't know. He started asking the sailors at the dock how he'd go about leaving with his sister. He said even with the rift between their parents and the long journey, they would be safer back in Egypt. Last week we'd met at the docks, and he had been excited, finally like the Liam I knew at the start. But then he'd told me he found someone who could take them back and that he wanted me to go with him. I'd been in shock, angry that he'd ask me to choose between him and leaving the only home I've ever known. We were supposed to meet one more time, and I knew I was going to have to let him go, even though I loved him."

Seeing our oldest friend in pain, I move to comfort her. It's difficult to hear how she's been struggling these last few weeks. To hear how she hasn't been able to talk to us about it. To know someone my friend cared for— someone she loved—was taken from her without any apparent reason causes a piece of my heart to break right alongside hers.

"I'm so sorry you've had to face this alone," I say softly. "We're here for you now, and we'll stay by your side. It's perfectly okay to feel lost and to let yourself grieve. Please don't punish yourself for what happened, or think that you owe anyone an apology. You're one of the kindest and most compassionate people I've ever known, and I have no doubt that Liam loved you deeply. The pain of losing him is immense, and it breaks my heart to see you suffering." Tears spill down my cheeks as Rowan and Maeve join us for a group hug. "We're going to find out who did this, I promise. I know Leila is grieving right now, too… Why don't you come with us to see her? Maybe you two can talk. I find it's always easier to heal when you're surrounded by friends."

Taking in a calming breath, Aisling settles down, her cries turning into gentle hiccups. "I think I'd like that very much."

Probably sensing a more peaceful aura expanding from us, whether through aura manipulation or not, which is still unsettling to think about, Aiden offers, "I'll come with you and we can leave Leila and Aisling to talk while we go to the Scriptorium."

Not bothering to try and stop him, I give a nod of approval before adding, "I'll drive. We'll have to stop at the Stout & Sip first, though. Rowan and I promised Leila we'd bring her something to eat. I'm sure we could all use a little comfort food at the moment."

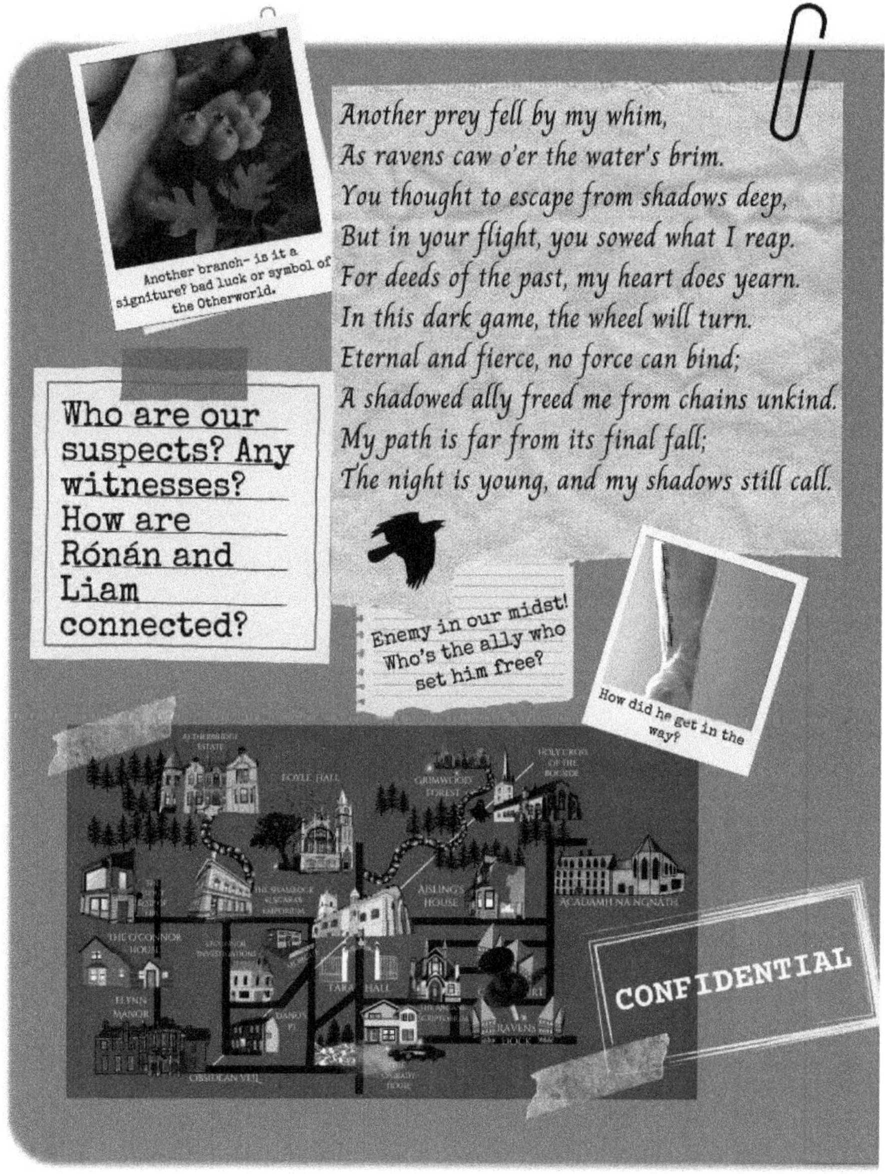

Liam Hassan- Property of Danu's PI

11

POWER UNVEILED

ROWAN

1. Wake up on time. Check.

2. Feel like a trolley hit me. Also yes. Okay…it's probably just a cold.

3. Solve the mystery of Elodie and Aiden. Getting closer! Woohoo! \\(^o^)/

4. Find Liam's mystery girl (who happens to be my best friend). Check.

5. Forgive said friend. Check.

6. Avenging Liam's death. Work in progress.

7. On the way to get sweets. Check.

8. Getting closer to solving this case. Well, it's not Mr. Mittens.

With a few minutes to spare on our drive to Stout & Sip, I squeeze into the back seat with Aisling and Maeve, giving Aiden the front seat and more legroom. This, of course, only adds to Elodie's fluster, as she now has to sit next to him. It's a minor discomfort that makes her fidget more than usual, especially since she's always been more at ease behind the wheel.

As I settle in, I run through my mental checklist—a daily habit I've kept since my Academy days. Despite the cramped space, the ritual helps me focus, even if it's only for a brief moment before we arrive. Auntie Cait and Elodie might see me as chaotic, but I assure you, I am orderly—just in my own way. Even though only a day has passed since the first attack, I can't shake the feeling that we're already ten steps behind.

Pulling up to the cafe, we decide to all get out and see what today's menu offers. Acting ever the gentleman, Aiden holds the door open as we step inside. Instantly, the air is filled with the comforting scents of autumn. The warmth of freshly baked Barmbrack mingles with the sweet-spicy smell of apple cinnamon scones. The rich fragrance of spiced nuts and pudding drifts around us, while the sweetness of baked apples is more subtle. An assortment of teas rounds out the sensory experience, making the room feel both warm and welcoming.

"Back so soon, are ye? If I didn't know better, I'd think you were tryin' to woo me with all these visits. But alas, I'm already spoken for." Lennon's deep baritone jolts me from my food trance, followed by a hearty, good-natured laugh as he rolls up the sleeves to his pale grey sweater.

Saoirse steps into the room with effortless grace, her arm sliding around Lennon's with a natural confidence. "Aiden's around so often, I might need to start charging him for the extra cuppas and scones. At this rate, he'll be up to his elbows in flour and handing out pints before long!" Her striking purple eyes, flecked with gold, soften to a gentle lilac as she smiles at Lennon, their shared mirth revealing a bond I've only ever read about.

Though Lennon is taller, his presence is gently overshadowed by Saoirse's pixie-like charm. Yet beneath her delicate exterior lies a strength; her purple jumpsuit highlights her powerful build, practical for both combat and managing rowdy patrons. Lennon's pale complexion and gunmetal grey eyes stand in vivid contrast to her dark features. Their eyes meet with an affectionate intensity, which Saoirse disrupts with a playful laugh as she reaches up to tousle his already messy white-cropped hair.

"At this rate, you lot are going to have me completely broke by the end of the day!" I hear Aiden joke back, clearly comfortable around his friends.

"What can we get you today? Another apology assortment to-go?"

Lennon's quip has me puzzled, but if Aiden's face is any indication, it's not something he wants his friend to explain further.

"Very funny," Aiden deadpans. "But seriously, we'll need one egg veggie roll, a selection of today's scones, and a dozen chocolate and jam donuts. We're heading to the Emporium."

"What a terrible shock," Saoirse says as she helps Lennon box up our order. "We heard about Liam when Mr. Doyle stopped by for a bite earlier." As she wraps the last scone, she adds with a warm smile, "I'll throw in a loaf of Lennon's famous Barmbrack on the house. It's bound to bring a bit of comfort."

The Shamrock & Scarab Emporium - 8:30 a.m.

Walking into the shop, I loudly announce our arrival, "Hi Leila, are you here? We come bearing treats as promised!"

Like yesterday, she emerges from the back storage room, but today her bright golden eyes are rimmed with red. She's dressed in a traditional abaya mourning garment: a long, flowing silk dress paired with a black headscarf.

"Welcome, my friends," Leila says sadly, her accent gently colouring the words. She looks visibly relieved to see it's just us, considering she must have had a flood of visitors since word spread this morning. Spotting the box of treats from Stout & Sip, she continues, "Thank you for your support that shines like the stars of Osiris in the sky. I don't think I could make it through the rest of today without you all."

"You don't have to thank us; we're happy to help. We don't want you to worry about a thing, which is why we had Lennon and Saoirse pack a bunch of different things for you. Saoirse even made sure to add a fresh Barmbrack loaf. You should be set for the rest of the week," Elodie says as she settles down at the table we used to share with Liam, his empty seat now a poignant reminder of his absence. "Why don't we all sit down and dig in? You must be starving."

Leila glances at the box of treats, a slight smile tugging at the corners of her mouth despite her grief. "I'd be lying if I said I wasn't," she admits. "It seems that even amid all the funeral preparations, hunger waits for no one."

Maeve steps forwards and hands her the egg roll and an apple scone. "Here you go," Maeve says gently. "This should help a bit."

Leila accepts it with a grateful nod, then shifts the conversation. "I need to ask: have you found anything to help solve my brother's case? Any new clues that might bring you closer to finding who did this?"

"We can't divulge too much since our investigation is still ongoing, but it seems like the same person attacked Liam and a student from Tara Hall due to some kind of vendetta. It's likely they both knew their attacker. Have you ever heard your brother mention the name Rónán Clarke?" Elodie's words make Leila's face scrunch in contemplation.

"I don't know for certain. If he was a customer, I should be able to find his name on one of our order sheets." Leila's voice grows stronger at the possibility. Walking to the desk at the front of the shop, she quickly opens a worn leather book and begins flipping through the pages. "This may take a while; Liam was diligent about writing down everything that happened in the shop." At the reminder, her voice grows somber. "He was usually the one who handled this part of our business. I feel so lost without him, and I still can't shake the feeling that I should've known more about what Liam was involved in. I regret not following him to see who he was meeting. If only I had been more vigilant…"

Aisling glances at Leila with a gentle, understanding look. "I'll stick around to help you with this," she says quietly. "Actually, there's something I've been meaning to talk about with you, something I didn't get a chance to say before. It's something personal, but I think it'd be good for us to discuss it—something about Liam. We can find a quiet spot after sorting through the orders.

I'll meet everyone back at the office later." Her eyes linger on Leila, a mixture of sorrow and determination in her gaze.

I understand her need for privacy. It feels like the right thing to do— to give Aisling and Leila space to grieve. My heart aches to see them like this, but I know it's important for them to talk alone. I turn to leave, with Aiden, Maeve, and Elodie trailing behind me. The silence of our departure feels heavy, each of us lost in our thoughts. As we leave the shop, I can't help but feel that this is just the start of the trials we'll surely have to face.

9.*Cheer up Leila. Check.*
10.*Visit Scriptorium to figure out the "Slayer's" coded message. On our way!*

But, seriously… the Slayer? Sounds more like a name for a heavy rock band. Maybe the Slayer's a fan of Led Zeppelin. They both certainly have a poetic flare, I think with a smirk as I recall the similarity between the letters and the haunting rhymes of Ramble On that played on the car radio just last week. My fingers twitch with the need to research and find any digital footprints. With a strong cuppa and a few hours with my computer, I should have no trouble digging up clues about his identity.

A soft brush against my ankle breaks me from my thoughts. Looking down, the same black cat from yesterday rubs against my leather boots. With a soft purr, the furry feline looks up at me expectantly before it darts into the empty street towards the Stout & Sip. Sitting down before the alleyway, it turns to look at me once more, as if waiting for me to follow.

"Oh, now you want my attention. I'm a bit busy solving a case, so you'll have to get in line., I say under my breath as our group reaches the car parked in front of the shop. As I reach for the door, my heart sinks at the sound of screeching tires and the roar of an engine that shatters the quiet.

"Ah, shite!" I shout, urgency driving me as I sprint towards the cat. My feet pound against the asphalt, each step a desperate attempt to save the feline.

From behind me, Elodie's voice slices through the chaos. "Rowan, watch out!" Panic tinges her voice as I hear her footsteps follow me. My focus remains solely on the cat, the world around me narrowing to a tunnel of urgency.

I hear Aiden's voice, sharp and firm, as her steps grow silent. "Stop! We don't need the both of you getting hurt!" Their voices blend into a cacophony of urgent bickering.

"Let me go, Aiden! Rowan's going to get hurt!" Elodie's voice rises in frustration, the sound of a struggle accompanying her words.

Time stretches, each moment dragging out as the vehicle passes the front of the Emporium we just left and hurtles towards the cat. My breath catches, the scene unfolding in agonizing slow motion. Just as I brace for impact, something unbelievable happens. The car doesn't hit the cat. Instead, it passes right through the black feline as if it's nothing more than a ghostly apparition. The vehicle continues down the road, the tires barely disturbing the air where it'd been.

I skid to a stop, breathless and bewildered, as the eerie scene begins replaying in my mind. I turn to Elodie and Aiden, heart racing with confusion. "Did that just… happen?"

Elodie, pulling from his grip, meets me in the street. "I told you to stop. What if something else had happened?"

That's the other thing I can't quite grasp. I'd been so close to the car that I should've been injured, yet as I braced for impact, it felt as though an invisible force had yanked me backwards. I know for certain that Elodie and Aiden had been too far away to help.

I glance at the cat I'd chased. No longer in the middle of the road, it casually grooms itself on the sidewalk across the street. Without the adrenaline from my panicked run, I realize the cat hovers slightly above the pavement. "I know, I know. But did you see it? The car traveled right through the cat!"

Racing towards the cat, I feel my heart sink as I catch a glimpse of black fur lying at the tree line behind it at the end of Nocturne's Nook. Ignoring the ghostly feline, I make my way towards the motionless animal. Bloodstains darken the ground beneath it. Suddenly, its shimmering form hovers closer, casting an ethereal glow of otherworldly light. I watch the cat's spectral form slink between my legs, sending a shiver of cold air across my shins, making me realize that the strange magic connecting us with Aiden must be allowing this.

Elodie, marvelling at the scene, says, "It's amazing. I believe it's chosen to stay behind and be with you."

I glance at them, then back at the spectral cat. A pang of regret hits me at how I hadn't been there to save her—how she'd likely been trying to lead me to her body, and I hadn't stopped to follow. Taking a deep breath, I crouch down to give the spectral cat a scratch on her head. Though cold, her form is surprisingly solid. "I think it's time we give this little troublemaker a name."

After thinking it over for a moment, I tell them, "I'll name her Shade. She's black and elusive, just like a shadow that slips in and out of sight." Even though Shade is visible in her ghostly form beside me, the weight of my failure lingers.

We find a quiet spot nearby, and with a heavy heart, I gently lay Shade's physical body to rest. As I finish the burial, I pause to murmur a small prayer, asking for peace for the cat's spirit and hoping it finds comfort in its new existence for however long she decides to remain close to me.

With my hands pressed against the earth, a shiver crawls up my neck, as if unseen eyes are watching. I catch a fleeting shadow in my peripheral vision, but when I turn my head, it's gone. Trying to lift the mood and distract myself, I remark, "I suppose I've got a friend for life now—or should I say, a friend for after-life!"

As we drive away, I can't help but feel as though Shade seamlessly blends into our ever-growing group of misfits.

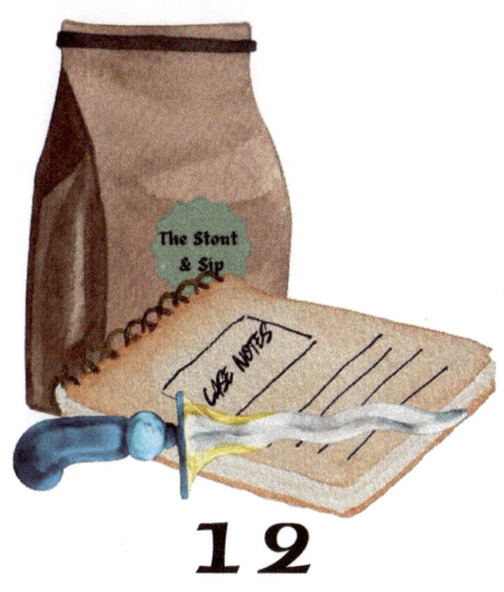

12

A LESSON IN MAGIC

AIDEN

The Arcane Scriptorium - 9:40 a.m.

After an eventful morning, we finally pull into the parking lot of the Scriptorium. Well, we've arrived in one piece. Miracles do happen. As I glance around, I notice the auras around us seem a bit gloomy. "You know, Elodie, if you keep this up, we might need a rocket license instead of a car. I'm half expecting us to take off at any moment! It's hard to believe, but you actually cut the usual trip downtown by ten minutes!"

As we get out of the car, I hear Rowan's voice instructing the cat. "Stay in the car, you stubborn thing!"

Elodie raises an eyebrow, clearly unimpressed with my joke about her driving. "Very funny, Aiden," she snaps back, quicker than I expected. "I'll add 'precision rocket landing' to my list of skills, right after 'putting up with your jokes.'"

I'm taken aback by her rapid-fire response and can't help laughing. "Touché," I reply, as I watch her aura brighten. "I guess I'll leave the driving critiques to the professionals. Maybe next time, I'll just hold on for dear life and try not to scream."

Elodie smirks and adjusts her coat. "That sounds like a plan. Now, let's get inside before you start giving me more 'advice' on how to drive."

I gesture for the girls to enter first, and their delighted gasps fill the air as they step into the Scriptorium. The grandeur of the room, with its high arched ceilings and walls lined with ancient leather-bound tomes, pulls their gazes in every direction.

Located in Balie na Muintir, the Scriptorium is a sanctuary of magical knowledge, its shelves brimming with rare manuscripts and journals predating the Veil's construction. Because many of these books predate the shadowy wall, attempts to build a newer repository have been halted by the Council. The O'Neill family, stewards of these mystical writings for generations, have instead been entrusted with the duty of ensuring the library's treasures remain undisturbed.

A subtle enchantment weaves through the Scriptorium's air casting an illusion over the library. To those without magical awareness, it might appear as a quaint, unremarkable room, filled with dusty volumes and mundane clutter. The charm alters perception, disguising the library's true grandeur and the significance of its contents.

Having not visited in over a month, I am struck by the autumnal magic woven into the library's décor—a testament to Niamh's festive spirit. Each shelf, usually home to dusty volumes and scholarly artifacts, now hosts a vibrant display of potted plants and whimsical trinkets, reminiscent of the knickknacks she used to decorate her locker with at Tara Hall.

Turnip and pumpkin lanterns, their faces carved into playful and eerie expressions, flicker on the long reading desks and spiral staircase, casting an orange light that dances over the ornate woodwork. Black and orange paper streamers twist and flutter from the arched bookshelves, interwoven with ivy garlands that cascade in lush green waves.

As I glance towards the front desk, I spot Niamh. She's deeply engrossed in a book adorned with botanical illustrations, her chestnut-brown eyes reflecting the warm glow of the desk lamp. Her outfit is a vibrant explosion featuring a flowing blouse splashed with swirling greens and sunny yellows, paired with bell-bottoms that ripple like leaves in a gentle breeze. Her large afro frames her face in a halo of tight, exuberant curls, adding to her presence.

As she looks up, her eyes sparkle with recognition, and she flashes a wide, welcoming grin. "Aiden!" she exclaims with genuine delight. She springs up from behind the desk, her colourful ensemble twirling with her, and wraps me in a quick, heartfelt embrace before turning to greet the others.

"Hello everyone!" Niamh bursts with a beaming smile and infectious energy. She twirls slightly on her heels, her hands animated as she speaks. "I'm so thrilled to have some visitors—I've been eagerly awaiting company and might have gone a bit mad talking to my plants!" She winks and leans in as if sharing a secret

At her introduction, the dark and muddy tint of worry morphing the girls' auras shifts into a bright yellow. Like everyone who meets Niamh, a smile lights up each of their faces.

"I'm Niamh, and I'm absolutely delighted to meet you all. As a botanist obsessed with plants, if you catch me whispering secrets to a fern, just roll with it," she says with a mischievous grin, her fingers gently brushing an imaginary fern. "I also follow in my ancestors' footsteps as a philologist and epigrapher. Every generation of my family has guarded The Arcane Scriptorium—and you guessed it; now it's my turn." She spreads her arms wide as if embracing the entire space. "Did I mention that I'm absolutely buzzed to get to know each of you?"

"Niamh, you're as lovely and wonderfully quirky as ever," I say with a playful wink. "Let me introduce you to everyone."

I gesture towards the twins with a nod of acknowledgment. "This is Elodie and Rowan O'Grady. They've had a bit of a dust-up with O'Connor

Investigations over the years, but given the circumstances, we've had to put our heads together. Despite their past with me, they're sharp as a tack—just best to avoid stirring the pot about our old squabbles." I point to Maeve with pride. "And this is my sister Maeve. She's the one I always go on about. She's the one who keeps the show on the road, even when things go a bit pear-shaped."

Each of the girls wave with a blend of politeness and enthusiasm, clearly caught up in Niamh's energy.

Becoming more serious, I add, "But before we dive into all that fun, we really need to get down to the business of our case. We've hit a few roadblocks, and I think your expertise could help us untangle some things that have us stumped. Are you up for a bit of detective work?"

Niamh nods enthusiastically, the tight curls of her hair bobbing with the movement. "Right then, let's stop dithering and get to the heart of it. Lay it all out for me."

I watch Elodie's hands move with deliberate precision as she unzips her bag, the zipper gliding smoothly. She retrieves a neatly arranged stack of files and a set of organized notes, each item clearly in its place. With care, she spreads them out on the table next to Niamh, the papers landing with a soft rustle. Her fingers hover over the documents, ready to draw attention to specific details as she scans them with a focused, efficient gaze. Pointing to a picture, she says, "This is our first victim Rónán Clarke. Look at the plant in his hand—it's thorny, though I'm not sure what it's called. There weren't any plants like this at the crime scene so it's strange to see one in his grasp. Also, our second victim, Liam Hassan, was found with a similar-looking plant. We need to figure out why they're holding it and what it might signify."

Niamh's eyes narrow with concentration as she reaches across her desk to grab a magnifying glass. She holds it up to the pictures of each plant, examining them closely. At the same time, her hand moves in a subtle, practiced motion, and the air shimmers as ancient tomes on botany begin to materialize from thin air, landing softly on the table with a whisper. She flips through the pages with a swift, expert touch until she finds what she's looking for.

A satisfied smile tugs at her lips as she looks up from the book. "Rónán's holding a Whitethorn thorn, while Liam has a Whitethorn berry cluster. The thorn is a single, sharp spike that grows from the branches, while the berries appear in autumn, long after the blooms have faded."

She pauses, glancing between the images and her notes. "In Irish mythology, the Whitethorn is often associated with protection and purification. The thorn is said to ward off evil spirits and symbolize defence, but it can also be used in binding spells to control or restrict. Similarly, the berry cluster, appearing in autumn, is linked to transition and change, and can be used in curses or rituals."

Niamh frowns slightly, her gaze returning to the pictures. "To understand how these plants relate to curses, I'll need to delve into more specialized texts. I'm sure Dr. Collins would be happy to expand on my findings." With a wave of her hand, the air shimmers again, and a dark leather book titled The Druid's Curse: Flora of the Enchanted Realm materializes. She flips through its pages, her brow furrowing as she searches for relevant information.

"Could the timing of these events have any relevance? Is there something significant about when these plants were placed in the victims' hands?" Elodie asks, noticing Niamh's struggle.

"I faintly remember something about key times of day being important in magical rituals during our Fae Rituals and Arcane Ceremonies class we took during our sixth year," I add, though I can't recall those lessons in full detail.

Niamh nods thoughtfully and snaps the current book shut with a dramatic flourish. She waves her hand, and a new volume appears in a puff of sparkles— this one a deep, dark red with the title Incantations & Dark Enchantments. She flips through the pages with eager curiosity, her eyes sparkling with excitement.

"Ah, the number three!" she exclaims, bouncing on her toes. "In Irish lore, it's like the magical trifecta: harmony, balance, and all that good stuff. Quite the charmer, really. Now, 1 o'clock doesn't have much of a ritualistic fanfare, but the number one is all about unity and new beginnings. So, if we're talking about these thorns, it might be hinting that the timing was meant to mark a big change. Quite the twist, wouldn't you say?" She pauses, flipping through the book with a thoughtful frown. "Now, onto the juicy bit: placing cursed objects directly into the victims' hands. That's like putting a personal stamp on the curse. It makes the whole thing more intense because it creates a direct link between the victim and the magic. Historical practices often believed that the specific times and number of actions involved could amp up the power and focus of magical workings. So, the more personal the connection, the more potent the curse."

Maeve, who has been observing closely, steps forwards. "This insight is incredibly valuable, Niamh. It ties so much together. There's another element to the case, though, where your skills could be a game-changer. The killer left runes on the bodies, and we're having trouble deciphering them. We're hoping your expertise with ancient languages can shed light on their meanings."

Closing the Grimoire with a dramatic snap, Niamh's eyes alight with a mischievous glint. She leans forwards, her fingers brushing the book's cover as if savoring its ancient energy. "Runes, you say?" she exclaims with a whimsical smile. "How marvellous! It feels like an age since I last wrestled with ancient languages. There's something so thrilling about deciphering old symbols that's a far cry from the usual plant folklore and magical minutiae Aiden usually has me dig into. Let's dive into these symbols; they might just unravel the enigma of our elusive foe."

Maeve guides Niamh to a larger table where she places more crime scene photos. As Niamh leans over the images of the runes etched into the victims' skins, her eyes narrow, reflecting the gravity of the symbols that seem to taunt her from the photographs. Her lower lip is caught between her teeth, a subtle sign of her frustration as the cryptic symbols remain stubbornly elusive. Straightening, she lets out a soft sigh. "These runes are unfamiliar to me. Their origins and meanings are beyond my current knowledge."

Niamh meets my gaze, her expression thoughtful as she taps her chin.

"I'll need to have a bit of a family chinwag. I like to think of them as my personal magic squad," she adds, her eyes sparkling with enthusiasm. Sweeping her hand through the air as if inviting us into her vision, she continues, "Imagine this: vibrant conversations over steaming cups of tea, where the ideas flow as smoothly as the brew. It's a world away from the rigid formality of the professors we had at the academy." She glances at me with a knowing grin. "Aiden and I remember them well. They always seemed more at ease amid dust-covered tomes than stern, pedantic lectures."

"Shifting gears," she continues with a playful smile, "after we finish here, I'll head home to huddle with my gang. They've got a knack for cracking codes faster than a pint is emptied at a Sunday sesh. And don't worry, once we've got it all sorted, I'll reach out to Aiden to have you stop by so I can give you the full lowdown." She pauses, glancing around the room with an inquisitive look. "But before I dash off, is there anything else I can help you with?"

"Actually, yes. The killer has been signing his poems as 'The Slayer'. Do you know if that name holds any historical or mystical significance in curses?" Rowan questions.

Niamh's eyes sparkle with excitement as she nods enthusiastically, then heads straight for a cart stacked with ancient manuscripts. She pulls out an old tome with a dramatic flourish, the cover creaking open. Flipping through the yellowed pages with nimble precision, she searches for any references.

After a moment, she looks up with a mix of seriousness and intrigue. Her voice drops to a conspiratorial whisper. "In folklore, 'The Slayer' is quite the figure. It usually refers to a heroic character who battles monsters and enemies with great flair. Take Cú Chulainn, for example—he's often called 'The Slayer' because of his legendary combat skills."

I watch Niamh stride towards the bookshelves to our right and gesture upwards. A bright green volume with elegant gold script reading Echoes of Éire: Folktales of Valor and Villainy begins to float off the nearby shelf, gliding gracefully through the air from a second-floor alcove. It settles gently in her hands as she opens it.

"There's a darker side to the term, too," Niamh adds, "In this text, 'The Slayer' refers to those who spread chaos or wield dark magic. So, our 'Slayer' might see themselves as an avenger or purifier, but with a more destructive twist. Quite chilling, if you ask me."

"Ah, so not a heavy rock fan," Rowan jokes with a small chuckle.

Elodie gives Rowan a quizzical look before quickly refocusing on the matter at hand. Scribbling down the information on her notepad, she asks, "I've also noticed that the Slayer signs off his poems with the image of a raven. Do you know if that symbol has any particular significance?"

Niamh's eyes sparkle with curiosity as she considers Elodie's question. "It's quite the emblematic critter. They're linked to Morrígan, who's our resident goddess of war and prophecy. Ravens in her company are like mystical postmen, delivering omens of both doom and transformation." She flutters her fingers in the air, as if to mimic the flight of a raven. "In old tales, Morrígan sends these birds to hover over battlefields. Their presence could mean anything from a looming fight to a shift in destiny. So, if our elusive foe is using this symbol, they might see themselves as a dark harbinger of change—quite the dramatic flair with their 'Slayer' label."

Niamh's eyes take on a shimmering, golden hue, reflecting the gears turning in her mind as if she's scrolling through an invisible archive. "Ah, and it just hit me!" she continues, her voice brimming with excitement. "The moon phases could play a role here too. My knack for recalling details really kicks in with the right celestial alignment. And wouldn't you know, the waxing crescent moon was shining brightly the night of the murders. It's all about renewal, setting intentions, and launching new plans. Using Whitethorn during this phase could supercharge a curse, making it more potent and far-reaching."

I turn to Niamh, grateful for her help. "You've been incredibly helpful today, Niamh. Thanks for diving into all this with us."

Niamh smiles warmly. "I'm glad I could assist. I can't wait to share more once I've figured out those runes!"

Together, we start to head towards the Scriptorium's exit. I turn to her as we walk. "Niamh, while you're investigating the runes, could you check into another issue? We're struggling to understand how the victims lost so much blood without any visible wounds. Not even Dr. O'Keefe could explain it."

Niamh's gaze sharpens with curiosity. "I'll look into it."

"This contains Rónán's autopsy report. It might offer useful details," I say as I hand her the folder.

Niamh accepts the folder with a dramatic flourish, tucking it carefully under her arm as if it's a top-secret dossier. With a mock-serious expression and a wink, she says, "Got it. I'll give this the full treatment and keep you posted. Think of me as your mystical investigator—minus the trench coat, but definitely with all the intrigue!"

As the door swings shut behind us, I hope her expertise will soon provide answers

Suddenly, Rowan's gasp slices through the chatter. I glance over and see her face drain of colour as her aura shifts from a bright yellow to a dark mud colour.

"What's wrong?" I ask, feeling a jolt of anxiety that doesn't belong to me.

Rowan's hand shakes as she points towards the top of the stairs. "There's someone…Quick, Elodie, pinch my arm." Her voice is taut with fear and disbelief.

Elodie's eyes widen, but before she can react, Rowan's own hand shoots up and digs into her forearm. Her fingers grasp her skin with frantic urgency as if she's trying to anchor herself in reality.

I follow her gaze and see Declan's ghostly figure materialize in front of us. "Rowan, please try to remain calm," I say, trying to keep my voice reassuring. "This is Declan. He's a friend and a—well, a ghost, like your friend Shade."

Rowan blinks, her eyes locked on Declan with a mix of awe and confusion. "I—I can see him clearly," she stammers.

Declan's form flickers with a soft glow, and he looks directly at Rowan, then at me.

"Sometimes," I explain, glancing at Rowan and Elodie, "the more we learn about magic, the clearer these bonds become. It seems like you might be tapping into some of my Súil to see Declan's presence."

Elodie's expression shifts from shock to tentative understanding. "So, this is because of the magic we're uncovering?"

"Exactly. It's customary for Réalt connections with magic to grow as we attain more knowledge. Although, it usually takes us years to hone our abilities. The bonding spell is likely helping you adjust faster."

Rowan's gaze flickers between Declan and me, her curiosity piqued. "But why can I see him so clearly and Elodie can't?"

"You must be more open to these connections than Elodie is. You broadcast your emotions more openly, which has made the bond between you and the magical realm grow faster. Elodie tends to keep her feelings more controlled, so her connection with the magical world isn't as strong."

Rowan's eyes widen slightly as she processes this, a playful grin tugging at her lips. "So, being an open book is making me a supernatural magnet?"

"Yes, it seems that way. The more in tune you are with your emotions and the magical world, the clearer these connections become. It's a unique aspect of how we interact with draíocht. I'm sure Declan will be more than happy to elaborate on it once we're back at my office. Meanwhile, I'll be busy solving this case for us."

"To think he complimented us earlier," Elodie mumbles under her breath.

Looking back towards Declan, I see his eyes meet mine with a look of urgent concern. He gives a wry smile aimed at Rowan and remarks, "I'd be thrilled to chat with someone other than Aiden for once, but I've got some urgent news that can't wait."

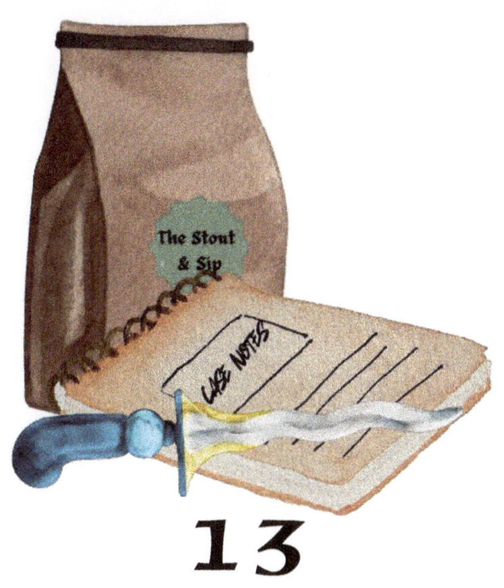

13

ÐARK REVELATIONS
AIÐEN

I hold the office door open for everyone, including Rowan's new feline friend, before walking inside. The familiar aroma of old leather and polished wood greets me, a testament to the generations of my family who have worked here. The walls are lined with bookshelves, their contents a mix of recent case files and old notes. At the heart of the room is my desk—a large, well-worn oak piece cluttered with my current work. I often spend my nights here, at this very desk, just like my father did before me. Above, the loft extends like a private refuge. It's where I retreat, not just to unwind but to recharge and disconnect from the relentless pace of solving cases.

I set my coat on a hook by the door and offer to take the girls' outerwear. "Alright, Declan," I say, glancing around the room. "We're here. What did you find out? I'm assuming this has to do with the mission I sent you on." I turn to

Maeve, Elodie, and Rowan, gesturing towards the various seating options. "Help yourselves to a seat wherever you're comfortable."

Once everyone is settled, we face Declan as he starts talking, though Rowan and I are the only ones who can see him.

"It didn't take me long to catch up to Liam's spectral. It seemed as though he had lost his ability to move freely, like a force was pulling him. I've never seen anything like it. Once I followed him through the Obsidian Veil I came across the ghost of a middle-aged man. He was standing there, clothes in tatters and his body covered in gashes that looked painfully recent."

"Recent gashes? Could the Slayer be escalating, using these fresh wounds to extract blood faster or for darker magic?"

"Yeah, that's what I was thinking, too. The wounds were still raw, with this dark, nasty substance seeping through the ripped fabric. I don't know what it means, but it sure as heck can't be good for Eldermoore—or us."

I watch as Rowan turns to Declan, already seeming accustomed to her new reality of communicating with him. "What do you mean you had to follow Liam? And what do you mean there was a new ghost? Declan, did you notice any signs of a crime scene nearby or did they tell you their name?"

Declan's brow furrows as he considers her question. "Part of Aiden's gift is seeing and helping souls, which is why I've been around as long as I have. Usually, when a spirit cannot find their way to Tír na nÓg, I travel where Aiden cannot. It tends to be quite a simple process and we've never lost a soul yet. However, while I was having a gander, I spotted a right bunch of lads and lassies with the same wounds lining up towards the back gate at the school. With the protective shield Ms. Flynn has up and the added power of the Veil, it'd be impossible for the ghostly forms to leave the grounds. Well, that's the usual craic, but I saw Liam stop right at the gate and shove it open. Then, out of nowhere, a portal popped up on the other side. I reckon the Slayer's trying to build some sort of army. Unfortunately, they weren't spectrals like Liam and me, so they weren't much use."

"If they aren't spectrals, what are they?" Elodie questions, her gaze on the desk to the left of Declan. Rowan grabs her chin and slightly directs Elodie's head with a chuckle.

"I reckon they're best thought of as echoes. Unlike a spectral, an echo's spirit heads off to Tir na nÓg. A piece of their energy—usually from the moment of their death, given its dark twist—gets left behind to help them find peace in the afterlife. As their name suggests, it's pretty common for echoes to relive their death over and over. They're not aware of what's happening around them, poor souls. It's up to the Dullahan to collect their souls, guiding them to the other side and ensuring they find their final resting place. Clearly, the Slayer is trying to outsmart the whole system, the cheeky blighter!"

"Hmm," Rowan hums thoughtfully, "with that many bodies, there's bound to be something in the archives about recent incidents. Aiden, do you mind if I borrow your computer?"

I nod and gesture towards my desk. Settling in, she powers on the machine, the soft whir of the device filling the room as she navigates the screen.

"Once I gather these leads, I'll head back to the office to use the microfilm reader," she says, fingers flying over the keyboard. "There have to be old articles that could shed light on this mess."

"Declan, I know that gate. I saw it the morning we went to Rónán's scene. I believe it leads to the path to the cemetery. I wonder why Auntie Cait didn't mention it while we were there though?" Elodie's question hangs in the air.

"Sounds to me like some dangerous magic is in play, especially since a portal can lead anywhere in the world. With the amount of magic it takes to open one, it'd be almost impossible for any Réalt not to feel the energy around it. And let's not forget the consequences of activating a portal."

Elodie's curious stare reminds me that the girls are only just learning about magic. "You've studied interrogation techniques at the academy, right?" At her nod, I continue, "Well, think of a two-way mirror. Detectives can observe suspects without being seen. A portal operates similarly; unless you're the creator, you have no idea where it leads. Worse yet, it can function as a doorway, allowing beings to cross from either side. The charms around the school might be blocking awareness of the portal, but that level of magic would impact everyone within the school with symptoms like dizziness, loss of time, and things of that nature. It looks like we've got a fair few questions for the Headmistress to sort out."

As I speak, heat rises in my chest as frustration surges through me. My fingers tighten into fists at my sides, and I glance away, trying to steady my racing thoughts. Ms. Flynn asked me to help the girls, but how am I supposed to keep them safe if she's keeping crucial information hidden? My jaw clenches as I imagine the potential consequences of her secrecy.

With a sheepish smile, Declan rubs the back of his neck in discomfort as he turns to me. "So, I might have investigated the portal."

"YOU DID WHAT!" the girls and I shout in unison.

"Now hold on," Declan says, raising his hands in a calming gesture. "I figured, what's the worst that could happen? I'm already dead, right? Besides, I'm the best spy to ever haunt the afterlife, if I do say so myself. With Rónán and Liam both gone and that line of ghosts at Tara Hall, the Slayer must be right under our noses." Perching on the edge of my desk he adds, "When I slipped through the portal, it was pitch black and I was in some sort of underground tunnel. I followed the ghosts into a room filled with some proper flashy gear. Well, except for this one little trinket that completed the portal circle which seemed out of place, but that was giving off a lot of energy. I'm not quite sure what it was all for, but I saw some ghosts having their energies drained until they just poofed away. Seeing as how I had to pull Liam out of there, I'd say Rónán is already gone. The Slayer must be siphoning their abilities using both the curse and the echo energy. With that much magical juice, a person could supercharge their powers tenfold." Standing up he begins to pace the length of the room. "Now get this, when I finally reached the end of the tunnel, it let me out at a gate hidden in Nocturne's Nook. So, I wager Ms. Flynn's barrier doesn't stretch underground. That's when I caught up to the lot of ya!"

"Isn't it just a bit peculiar that there's a doorway to an underground tunnel right next to the Stout & Sip, and this little furball led us there today?" Maeve wonders, her brow furrowing. She leans down, her voice softening into a coo as she gazes at the cat. "What do you think, girl? Are we about to uncover something?" She gently pats his head, a smile breaking through her worry. "You're such a clever little detective, aren't you?"

"You could be onto something!" Rowan says with enthusiasm. "I'll dig into this more later, but check this out!" She waves us over. "There was an incident in Shadow Glen, just across Lough Foyle. Almost thirty people were killed!" Her eyes sparkle as she dives deeper into the details. "Oh, and would you look at our luck — there are photos! Do any of these people look like the echos you saw, Declan?" Rowan looks up at him expectantly as he moves to peer over her shoulder at the screen.

"Him!" Declan exclaims, pointing eagerly at the picture.

I lean in closer, taking in a man in a dark blue police uniform, sharp creases and polished buttons glinting in the light. He stands tall, his peaked cap adorned with the Royal Ulster Constabulary badge. Grabbing my notepad from my trouser pocket, I begin jotting down the details of the event. As I move to Declan's left to get a better view of the article featured on the right of the photographs, Elodie's head suddenly pops up in front of me, her own notebook out.

I watch as she leans over Rowan's shoulder, her hand resting on the back of the seat as she stands on her tiptoes. She really thinks she can solve this case before me—that's rich! I'd pay to see her try. As I step directly behind her, she attempts to create more space between us and stumbles towards the desk. Just before she faceplants into the table, she catches herself and shoots me a menacing sneer.

"Oops sorry about that! I was having a hard time seeing the screen past your big head."

As I throw my jab, I hear Declan chime in from behind Rowan's shoulder as he continues looking through the pictures. His ability to control electromagnetic fields makes it easier for him to scroll through them quickly.

"Whoa, Aiden, that's not how you make friends!" I roll my eyes but can't help but smirk at his serious yet playful tone. "Elodie, I've got your back. Rowan, make sure she heard me!"

I watch as Elodie laughs as Rowan relays Declan's message. Turning towards me with her arms crossed and a smirk of her own, Elodie adds, "Oh, and Aiden, maybe you should stop doodling and take some actual notes! I'm sure I could give you a lesson on that. Declan's right: being nice does go a long way!" Well, would you look at that? It would seem the pup's now the dog!

"Well, we have a great lead! Maybe the detective on the case can tell us more about who they're looking for and if there is any connection to our Slayer." Eyes moving rapidly across the screen, Rowan continues, "From the article it sounds like the culprit was planning an attack on the security at Shadow Glen's gate and then vanished without a trace. If the ghosts are here, maybe our Slayer has an accomplice helping them get souls? While Maeve and I work on setting up a phone conference, you three should ask Ms. Flynn about the portal and maybe get a closer look."

"There's a small hiccup in your plan, love. This type of portal only allows the dead to pass through. We'll have to see if we can enter through the back tunnel entrance if we can find it. If it's anything like the magic used to create the portal, the Slayer has hidden the door from the outside," Declan explains. Then, he adds with a grin, "On the upside, consider me your personal polygraph. While Elodie and Aiden speak with Flynn I'll do some snooping. If she's stuck to her normal routine she should be getting ready for dinner. That'll give me enough time to see what she's hiding in her house, and if I find anything that contradicts what she tells them, we'll be ready."

"One, that's very inconvenient. Two, thank you. And three, creepy. How do you know her schedule?"

"I make it my business to know everything. I can't remember a thing from my past, but I bet I was a right cunning fox! Unless I was just that weirdo eavesdropping on the old lads at the pub—like Mr. Brennan, the night guard over at Tara Hall!" Declan says, shuddering at the thought.

"Well, no time like the present. I'll drive Elodie over to Ms. Flynn's house and see what we can uncover." Glancing at my watch, I note that it's almost 5:30 pm. "We'll have to wait for the sun to go down before investigating the alley so our culprit doesn't see us coming. If Rowan and Maeve want to join us around 8:30, we can take a look together." Turning to Maeve and Rowan I state, "Feel free to stay here and chat with the detectives. I've added additional charms to protect the place while I'm gone." As I move towards the loft stairs, I call over to Elodie, "Let's gather what we need and head out."

I stop in front of a bookcase against the back wall and reveal a hidden door behind it with a subtle tug on a book titled Interrogations for Dummies. At the sight of Elodie's raised eyebrow, I can't help but laugh. Pushing the door open for her, I give a noncommittal shrug and add, "My granda had a knack for pranks."

The room beyond is dimly lit, filled with an assortment of gear: grappling hooks, flashlights, and forensic tools neatly organized on shelves. I steal a glance at Elodie, who appears to be stunned speechless. "I usually keep this room a secret, so consider yourself my first guest. We'll likely use it for training if your fighting skills are anything like your driving."

With a playful jab in my side, she makes her way over to one of the metal desks lined with weapons. Her hands graze over the top of each item in wonder. "I'll hand it to you; your family knows how to be prepared. I'd love to have a room like this back at Danu's!"

As we gather an assortment of daggers, flashlights, lockpicking tools, binoculars, and fingerprint powder, I reach for a duffel bag to store everything. With a quick wave to her sister, Elodie grabs her jacket and follows me outside, where I spot Declan already waiting inside the car.

Whatever it takes, we'll get to the bottom of this.

14

SECRETS AND SUSPECTS
ELODIE

After seeing Aiden's secret training room— a place I can only dream of one day having— it's no wonder the man is as arrogant as they come! As we walk towards his car parked at the front of his office, he leans in to open the passenger door for me.

"So, your ma did teach you some manners, after all," I tease, offering a small smile in thanks as I slide into the seat and he hands me the bag to put in the backseat. His answering chuckle is muffled by the closing door.

He walks to the driver's side, fingers raking through his wavy hair, and I catch myself staring a bit too intently. Heat rises in my cheeks as I watch him pull on his coat. As he slips his arm through the sleeve, his shirt rides up just enough to reveal a glimpse of toned skin. I quickly look away.

I give myself a mental shake, trying to refocus, when a voice behind me cuts through the moment. "Careful, you've got a bit of drool there."

"What the—" I startle as a cold breeze brushes against my chin, and I turn to look at the back seat, only to find it empty. "Declan, you about scared me to death!" To be honest, I'd completely forgotten he was joining us.

Despite our rivalry, having Aiden join my investigation has been unexpectedly enjoyable. Running theories by him and exchanging jokes brings a much needed reprieve from this dark and grim case. Not that I'd ever admit it to him. I'm perfectly content with him believing I hate his guts!

"Well, that wouldn't do. We've got enough death in Eldermoore to keep us more than busy, thank you," Declan says in a way that I just know he has a giant grin on his face.

With a questioning look towards us, Aiden starts the car and begins the short drive to Auntie Cait's house.

As Aiden drives, my thoughts spiral around Auntie Cait. A tight knot forms in my stomach as I recall how jumpy she was at Rónán's crime scene. Why did she insist Aiden join us if she truly trusted us to solve this case? If what Declan and Aiden said about the portal is accurate, how could someone with magic not notice it on school grounds? The questions swirl in my mind, each one more unsettling than the last. What else is she hiding? The thought gnaws at me, casting a shadow over my trust in the one person who raised us.

We pull into her driveway and I take a moment to settle my thoughts. A sharp whistle breaks the silence as Declan quips, "House? More like a mansion! It might take longer than I thought to search around."

"She does practically run this town," I laugh as I open the passenger door to get out. Walking the front pathway, I feel my heart hammering against my chest. If she's keeping secrets, what kind of strain will this have on our relationship?

As I knock on the door, I steel myself against my fears. If I'm going to solve this case, I need to know everything. No matter what.

✦)) ● ((✦

"Elodie, what a surprise! I see you brought Aiden along, too. You two must be getting along better than I thought. What brings you here at such a late hour?" Auntie Cait practically sings as she opens the door with a smile.

89

"Ah, yes, we are getting along just fine. Sorry to pop by without a call, but do you mind if we come in? Aiden and I would like to ask you some more questions regarding the case." I ask as she brings me in for a hug.

"No worries at all. I was just thinking to myself, 'I wonder how my girls are getting on!' Come in, come in. I'll whip up a bite to eat, and we can have a good old natter. It's a pity Rowan's not about—I miss her something fierce!"

She ushers us into her house, and I take in the clean white marble floors and freshly polished wooden furniture that sits on the left wall of the entryway. The scent of vanilla and a beef pot roast fills the air, reminding me of the days Rowan and I spent racing through these halls as kids. This is the house where I learned to read and cook, and the first room at the top of the stairs is where we pretended to cast spells and solve our made-up mysteries. The memories flood back, filling my mind with laughter and adventures from our childhood.

"Ah, I'm sorry she couldn't make it. She and Maeve are knackered with paperwork and couldn't join us, but Rowan said to pass on her love!" I explain as we head towards her dining room where she begins to set out additional place settings. At the head of the table, a full bowl sits waiting, steam rising invitingly. A buttered roll rests to the right, a small piece already nibbled away. Declan was right about her schedule.

I exchange a worried glance with Aiden as she rushes to the kitchen to make us a dish, the weight of our discovery heavy in my chest.

"Auntie Cait," I begin, as she enters the dining room once more and urges us to take a seat. I ensure my voice is steady despite the flutter of nerves. "We've gotten a report of a portal at Tara Hall. It leads underground, and we've discovered that only the dead can travel through it."

I watch as her eyes widen in shock, and she quickly puts down her spoon. Though her reaction is convincing, she always has been great at hiding her real emotions from Rowan and me.

Aiden leans in, his eyes green eyes focused. "We're surprised you didn't mention feeling any magic around Tara Hall. Have you noticed anything strange? Have students or professors reported feeling sick?"

Auntie's brow furrows, disbelief flashing across her face. "A portal? At my school?" Her voice drops. "I've sensed odd energies now and then, but I never thought it could be something like this. The charms surrounding the school protect students from any external threats, not the people who have access to the grounds already. Although, I did get a call from Dr. Collins earlier today. As our school's botanist, he's highly skilled in medicine and has become our lead healer in the medical bay. He reported multiple students complaining about headaches and asked for permission to order more supplies for their care. I thought the students were just coming down with a cold. You know how it is when students start school after having the summer off."

Searching her expression, I voice a growing concern. "Do you think the killer could be blocking you from feeling the source of magic?"

Her gaze drifts towards the window, worry flickering across her face. "That's what I'm worried about. Just earlier today, Mr. Brennan, the night guard, came to my office. He said he heard strange noises the night Rónán died. You need to go talk to him. It's crucial—do it as soon as you can. In fact, I think it's best if you two leave now. I've heard he frequents the Stout & Sip, so you might catch him before he leaves."

Ushering us from our seats, our stew untouched, she leads us towards the door with our wrists in her tight grip. Her grip tightens as I dig in my heels to stop our momentum.

"We'll go find him, but I do have one more question," I start as she goes to open the front door. "Rowan and I have been wracking our brains over something you said at Rónán's crime scene. We've even had Aisling pull the history of Eldermoore, but we've all come up empty-handed. Why did you say death has come to Eldermoore once more? Do you know who is doing this?" My voice cracks as I force out the last question, my emotions betraying my earlier facade.

Her eyes turn glassy as she turns away and whispers, "Ó, a grá." When she faces me again, her expression has hardened, though her eyes still sparkle with unshed tears. "I'm bound by magic to never reveal the dark history of

Eldermoore. It was by my granda's magic that swore my family to secrecy, and the laws of Eldermoore were written to protect us all. I'd hoped working with Aiden would open your eyes to the magic around you, but it appears the truth remains elusive to you. If it's answers you seek, you must first uncover your own past. I know you feel I've betrayed your trust, but I'd reveal to you all my secrets if I could. I just hope that when you find what you're looking for, you can forgive me." Her voice falters, ending in a quiet sob as she reaches for the door once more. "It's getting late. If you still plan on interviewing Mr. Brennan, you better get going."

When she finishes speaking, I stand frozen, shock coursing through me like ice water. My mind races, grappling with the revelation that the woman who raised me might hold secrets about my sister and me that I never imagined. A deep sense of betrayal gnaws at my insides.

Aiden senses my turmoil—whether through our newly forged bond or the shimmer of tears threatening to spill over—steps closer, guiding me into the cool evening air. The chill bites at my skin, but it pales in comparison to the confusion weighing heavy on my heart.

As we step into the dim light, his voice is quiet as though he's speaking to me underwater. When he shakes my shoulders and I still don't respond he pulls me into his warm embrace. I lean against him, my head resting on his shoulder. The steady rhythm of his heartbeat soothes the storm raging inside of me.

"Don't worry," he murmurs, his voice low and reassuring. "We'll uncover the truth, I promise." His words wrap around me like a comforting blanket, grounding me.

I draw in a shaky breath, allowing the warmth of his presence to seep into my bones. He gently grips my face, his thumb brushing away a stray tear that has slipped down my cheek.

"I can't stand to see you cry," he says, his brow furrowing with genuine concern. The intensity of his gaze surprises me, igniting a warmth within me that I didn't expect, especially from him. His face is so close that I can see tiny gold flecks in his forest-green eyes and a small scar that cuts across the right corner of his upper lip.

"Whatever Declan finds in your Auntie's house tonight might lead us to the answers you need."

A flicker of hope ignites within me, mingling with the pain. I cling to that hope, letting it spark a determination to uncover the secrets that haunt this town and all who reside here.

"Am I interrupting something?" Declan's voice cuts through the moment.

I instinctively try to pull away, but Aiden keeps his hands on my cheeks, searching my eyes as if he's trying to decipher a puzzle. The intensity of his gaze makes my heart race, but, just as quickly, the tension softens. Aiden's lips curl into a familiar smirk, crinkling the corners of his eyes. Finally, he releases me, allowing the space between us to feel less charged.

"Of course not! I was just making sure Elodie was okay. You know, trying that whole 'being nice' thing you keep going on about," Aiden stammers, his usual composure only slipping slightly as he fumbles for an excuse to be caught standing so close to me. I can't help but notice the faint pink creeping up his neck. "Now that she's fine, we should get going. Places to be, people to question." His awkward attempt at nonchalance only makes me smirk as I realize he might not be as self-absorbed as I'd always assumed.

"Ah, yes. I caught a bit of what Flynn said as I was making my way to the study. Sorry, Elodie." His voice becomes melancholic as a cold breeze taps my shoulder that I assume is supposed to be comforting.

Glancing in the direction I assume he stands, I give him a small smile of appreciation. "Did you find anything that could help us learn about her, or better yet, let Rowan and I learn about our past?"

"Well, the lady definitely likes to keep things neat. Every room I went into was spotless, with not a speck of dust in sight. I did however notice a door leading to the attic was locked, though that didn't pose much of a challenge for me. The room appears to be some type of altar where she practices her magic.

The floor is strewn with books, their pages filled with intricate diagrams and notes on strengthening protection spells. I don't know what secrets she's hiding, yet, but it appears whatever it is has scared even her. I also spotted a small letter chest tucked under her desk in a drop-front drawer—don't ask me how I found that one. Anyway, I tried to open it, but it seems she's woven a charm around it so that it only unlocks for her."

"I know that chest." The mention of the small ornate box brings forth memories from my childhood, and I rush to explain. "She used to keep it in her room. When Rowan and I were kids, we stumbled upon it while playing hide and seek. When she found us trying to pry it open, her usual playful demeanour had shifted. She became stern, almost fearful. Once she calmed down, she warned us that some secrets are better left untouched and urged us to forget we ever saw it. I've always wondered what's inside. I bet the answers we're looking for are hidden in those letters."

As we all pile into the car, Aiden echoes my thought, "Well, it'd be a good start. We can see if Niamh knows how to counter the charm on the box. I don't think Ms. Flynn is working with our culprit, but I think she knows who it is. For now, we should take her advice and go find Mr. Brennan. Maybe he can help us piece together more about Rónán's death."

Stout & Sip - 7:20 p.m.

As I push open the door to the Stout & Sip, the familiar atmosphere envelopes me, a stark contrast to the cozy café below where we'd grabbed breakfast that morning. The scent of freshly baked bread and pastries lingers in my mind, but here, the air crackles with energy, laughter echoes off the walls, and the low strum of a folk tune weaves through the chatter.

I immediately spot Saoirse at the bar, her hands expertly pouring drinks as she engages with the patrons nearest to her. Gone is the purple jumpsuit she wore earlier. Instead, she's dons a rich brown leather V-neck that complements her skin perfectly. Next to her, Lennon takes food orders, his usual sweater swapped for a crisp black button-up rolled to his elbows, lending him a more imposing appearance.

"Aiden, is this a date? I'm sure there are nicer places in town, even if the Stout & Sip does have the best food!" Lennon jokes. I laugh and ask if he knows where Mr. Brennan might be. He points to the back with a smirk, saying, "Good luck with that one!"

"There he is," I whisper to Aiden, who stands beside me, tense and serious.

He shakes his head in agreement, a serious look settling on his face as he meets my gaze.

"Looks like he's had a few," he says, eyeing Brennan with mild concern. "Let's hope he's still sharp."

We approach, and Mr. Brennan looks up, surprise flashing across his face. "I wasn't expectin' you two so soon. What brings you here? Trouble again?"

"Mind if we join you?" I ask, sliding into the chair across from him. Aiden settles beside me, notepad ready and pen poised.

"Sure, but make it snappy. I'm not here for a chinwag," he grumbles, his voice gravelly and a bit slurred. "What's on your mind?"

"We're looking into a few things about Tara Hall," Aiden says, his tone serious. "We need to ask you some questions."

Brennan's smile fades, replaced by a hard look. "You want to talk here? With the way things are going? You must be mad."

I lean in, lowering my voice. "Why don't we head to our office, Danu's PI? It'll be quieter there, and I can brew you a lovely cup of tea. A little warmth might do you good before your shift."

Mr. Brennan rubs the back of his neck, his expression softening a little. He takes a long sip from his glass, froth clinging stubbornly to his lips, then glances at us with a sly grin. "I hope you drove here; I could use a lift."

Danu's PI - 7:40 p.m.

On our trip back to Danu's I stopped by Aiden's office to get Rowan and Maeve, who had just finished speaking with the detectives. Now, balancing a cup of tea along with some leftover biscuits that I keep stored in my desk drawer for emergencies, I make my way over to the couch where Mr. Brennan and Aiden are having a silent stare-down. Men. I quickly place the cup and tin in front of Mr. Brennan before taking a seat.

"So, Mr. Brennan, you didn't seem that surprised to see us. Is there something you would like to tell us?" I ask with a smile.

Before he answers, he grabs a biscuit, crumbs shooting towards me as he eagerly chomps on it.

"Well, you see," he mumbles, half-chewing, "I was on duty the night of Rónán's… well, you know."

I lean in, my interest piqued. "Where were you the morning Ms. Flynn called us to the scene? What did you see?"

He wipes his mouth with the back of his hand, his eyes narrowing thoughtfully. "Yes, well, I didn't feel the need to interrupt your investigation. I assumed when you were ready to talk you two pretty ladies would come looking for me." At his comment, a small breeze blows my hair forwards, and Mr. Brennan rubs his left cheek, a faint red mark appearing. "Ah," he says clearing his throat in discomfort, "I must have bitten my cheek while I was eating. The few pints I've had must have slowed my pain response," he says with a chuckle. At the expression on his face, I hide my smirk knowing that it was definitely not the cookie if Aiden and Rowan's grins are anything to go by.

"Anyway, during my shift that night, I saw two figures dash across the front lawn, so, naturally, I followed them since no one was supposed to be there. I made it all the way to the back gate, but nothing. I assumed it was just kids mucking about, so I made my way back to the office. An hour must have passed by before I started hearing an argument. It almost sounded like they'd fought before, though I was too far away to make out who it was. From what I can recall, that was around 1 am. When I finally made it back outside, whoever it was had gone quiet. I even walked the perimeter of the grounds again, but it was like they weren't even on academy property. I only found Rónán's body near the tree when I was headed to open the gate for Headmistress Flynn around 3:20 am. That lady sure does like to get an early start— always says there's not enough time in the day to prepare for the student's lessons."

"Do you remember what the voices sounded like? Could you tell if one of them was Rónán?" Rowan asks, her tone hopeful.

"I can't say for sure; I'd only ever spoken with the lad once. I remember it sounded like two men, one older than the other, and their voices were loudest near the back gate."

"Well, that's probably because of the portal." Aiden's causal drop of information stuns me. He even has the gall to look unperturbed as he grabs a cookie of his own before adding a wink in my direction. Taking the hint, I wait to see how Mr. Brennan reacts.

His face goes red, and he begins to stumble over his words. "Por…PORTAL! Not on my watch! I've never heard a more ridiculous claim!"

"It's no claim at all." Aiden's calm exterior breaks as his eyes light up with anger and he leans forwards so he's at eye level with Mr. Brennan. "I had an expert investigator look around and they reported it directly to me. Are you saying they lied?"

"Of course not! I just can't believe it. I've worked at Tara Hall since I retired from military service. How could anyone get past Ms. Flynn's protection spells? They're practically impenetrable; I would know."

"What's that supposed to mean Mr. Brennan?" I ask from my seat across from him.

"Uh…uh…it's not how it sounds. I just meant I've been protecting the grounds forever now; I know it like the back of my hand. If there aren't any further questions, I really must be going. My shift is coming up, and… well, I don't want to be late with all that's happening."

"Yes, that will be all for now. If we have any more questions, we'll know where to find you."

I watch as Aiden walks Mr. Brennan to the door, making sure he's well on his way to Tara Hall before he makes his way back inside.

"That was fun," Maeve's voice cuts through the silence. I turn to see a smile lighting up her face as she bounces with excitement. "Oh, and Aisling called while you were out. She said she'd be ready to work tomorrow, but she was going to take the night to rest up."

Rubbing my hand across the back of my neck to release some of the pent-up tension our conversation with Mr. Brennan caused, I shake my head in acknowledgment. "I think it'd be best if we all got a good night's rest. We can start digging into more of those school records tomorrow. Someone who has access to the grounds is involved, and I want to know who."

Taking a moment to collect my thoughts, I look to Rowan and begin to explain what we uncovered during our talk with Auntie Cait. "Plus, if anything she said was true, I'll need to start digging into our past. Aiden, if you can start working on a spell to open that letter chest with Niamh, we might catch a break in this case."

Helping to form our plan, Maeve continues, "Instead of only checking the door tonight, we should do a few stakeouts over the next few days. I doubt Mr. Brennan will do anything tonight; it looks like we spooked him. That will give us a chance to see if anyone is coming or going."

"Great idea, Maeve. Rowan and I will take the first watch tonight. Aiden will be with Declan and Aisling tomorrow, and Maeve, see if you can track down that sailor you interviewed. If he's willing to work with us, he can keep an eye on the dock and report back to you. We might be able to get one step ahead of whoever this man going around as the Slayer is—if Mr. Brennan's witness statement can be trusted."

"Well, I can't say I didn't think you'd come up with a plan like this. Though a bit reckless, it might actually work. Luckily, I grabbed some protection charms from the training room before we left earlier." Standing up, Aiden reaches into his coat pocket thrown across the back of the lounge chair and unbinds a small piece of rolled up leather. As he lays it flat on my desk, I move to get a closer look.

"So cool! Are you sure you're not the Phantom? I'm pretty sure I read something like this on the comic strip in last Sunday's paper."

Usually, I never know where my sister comes up with these quips, but I happen to catch her reference to the comic in the Irish Independent, and I have to say, the four daggers lined up in the leather roll are quite unique.

"Unfortunately, not. I'm much cooler than him." Aiden winks. "I figured you ladies would want more than the typical charm being the private investigators you are. These will keep you safe and will emit a light blue glow when danger is near. You can give Aisling hers tomorrow. In the meantime, let Declan stay during your stakeout tonight— it's not like he needs sleep anyway. I'll stop by the Scriptorium tomorrow and see if Niamh's found anything."

I watch as Maeve picks up the dagger with the yellow gemstone, its blade curved. At the same time, Rowan reaches for the dagger with the red gemstone, its blade coming to a sharp point. Waiting to choose mine I note there's a dagger with a light blue stone, the edges of its blade almost wave like. Next to it sits a dagger with a green gemstone, its blade is slightly shorter than the others. As I move to test them both, Aiden's hand shoots out to grab the blue one saying, "I think you'll find this blue stone more to your liking."

Moved by his thoughtfulness, I don't argue. Gently, he places the handle in my hand, his fingers lightly grazing my palm. Quickly pulling away to stop the fluttering in my stomach, I move the blade in a few practiced motions. All the while, I feel Aiden watching me. When I look up his eyes are alight with mischief, that stupid grin of his making my pulse race. As he turns to face Rowan and Maeve, I'm given a moment to compose myself.

"I'll stop by tomorrow. Your training officially begins." With that, he grabs his coat. Avoiding the stunned expressions on our faces, he walks to his office without a backwards glance.

What have I gotten us into?

"I think I liked him better when he didn't like us," Rowan quips to my right.

15

Changing the Game

Elodie

October 12 — 9:00 a.m.

Rowan and I wrapped up our last shift keeping an eye on Nocturne's Nook, our only company being the chatterbox, Declan, who Aiden assigned to us for the past two weeks. On our third night at the alley with no movement, we all agreed to start taking shifts at both ends of the portal.

To say I'm exhausted would be an understatement. Then, to make matters worse, Aiden strolls into our office every morning at 7 o'clock, completely unfazed and ready to train. And by train I mean Aiden gets to torture us with two hours of gruelling strength and agility exercises, followed by an hour-long monologue—I mean 'magic lessons'— on the history of magic from the very beginning.

In the last two days, we finally received Aiden's seal of approval to use our new daggers—albeit for just ten minutes—only to start all over again the next day. I feel like banging my head against my desk, which is exactly how Rowan and Maeve find me after I sent them to pick up some pastries and tea I ordered following my morning in Aiden's torture chamber.

And to think I wanted one!

"Girl, we need to make some serious changes. I can't even feel my arse anymore, and I only fell twice during our target training—go me!" I watch as Maeve rubs her bruised backside, then raises her hand for a high-five with Aisling to celebrate her victory.

Though I complain, I have to admit that these lessons are strengthening us both physically and mentally. I never thought I'd be saying this, but I'm grateful that Aiden has taken the time to teach us about magic. When Auntie Cait told me I was still blind to the magic around me, I'm pretty sure Aiden took it upon himself to open my eyes. I mean, he did promise to help.

Now, I just need to figure out how all this information helps me uncover my past. With the little time we've had, Rowan and I have been going through all the files we've created since we were six. Although we'd told Auntie Cait that we'd stop looking into our parent's disappearance, we became investigators to continue our search the only other way we knew how. With all the information we've collected, we're bound to find something eventually.

"Yoo-hoo, earth to Elodie. I think we broke her." Rowan's voice breaks me from my thoughts as she gives me a flick on the forehead.

"Was that necessary?" I groan.

Rowan gives me a quick wink over her shoulder as she takes a seat on the sofa next to Shade. The feline snuggles up to my sister, purring as she scratches the cat's tummy.

"Thank you, Rowan! As I was saying, we need to get out of this office. I was talking to Rowan and Aisling on the way back and we agree that a recon mission is exactly what the doctor ordered." Maeve's words come out in a rush as if she's afraid I'll say no before she's done explaining.

I raise my eyebrow. "Recon? We just spent the last two weeks keeping an eye on the alley and all connecting streets to make sure no one has gone in or out. Who could we possibly follow? Even our search through the school files hasn't given us a viable suspect. Not to mention Aiden and Niamh haven't found the right counter spell for the charm Declan felt on the letterbox."

Pushing back my seat, I walk over to grab one of the blueberry tarts that Aisling has begun to pass around.

Handing me the tart with the most frosting and a cup of steaming chamomile, she starts to fill me in on her research findings. "We think Mr. Brennan isn't telling us everything. I mean, from what you filled me in on, he says he's been in the military and has worked as Tara Hall security for longer than we've been alive. Last night, I checked the records, and he never even enlisted. Instead, he was part of a militia group that was formed the same year the Obsidian Veil was created. Maybe this group has been working underground, waiting to get enough magic to cause serious problems. I think it's worth looking into—and what better place to hear town gossip than the famous Stout & Sip, where all the locals and travellers come together to down some pints and loosen the tongue."

Cutting in, Maeve adds, "Plus, I haven't been able to track down Lorcan yet. I assume he's been traveling. Maybe we can spot him there? I know a bunch of sailors frequent the pub after a day at sea." Widening her eyes to give me her best puppy-dog, face she explains, "You were the one who said we needed his help, and if we do spot him, it might help improve our chances of convincing him to work with us."

"Well, it couldn't hurt, but—" My words are cut off by Maeve's cheerful scream and I watch her spin around the room. A smile of my own begins to form at her cheerfulness. With a laugh, I finish my thought, "But, I think it's best we keep this little operation to ourselves."

Just thinking of the lecture Aiden would give us if he knew of our plan makes my head hurt. It's sure to be something along the lines of how we must be more cautious, or how we don't check our surroundings enough, and blah, blah, blah. What he doesn't know won't kill him.

+))●((+

The Shamrock & Scarab Emporium — 5:40 p.m.

With the quantity of projects I have Aiden and Niamh working on together, we successfully avoid him all day. Even Declan is nowhere to be found, although I'm sure he's keeping tabs on us somehow. Throughout the morning, we all pitched in to map out our plan for getting answers from Mr. Brennan. First, we decided we'd need some disguises to help us blend in—something casual but nondescript. Then, we figured out how to approach him: friendly and a bit evasive, so he doesn't catch on to what we're really after. We jotted down key questions to guide the conversation and discussed what weapons to bring just in case things didn't go as planned.

Sticking to our plan, I lock up as Aisling, Maeve, and Rowan pile into my car, leaving Shade behind to watch over the office. Glancing at the dashboard, I see it's nearly 5:30 pm. Our first stop is the Emporium, and we're hoping to have enough time to reach the Stout entrance by 7 o'clock sharp. Opening the door, I spot Leila standing behind the counter, her hair framing a face marked with sorrow. She looks up as we enter, her expression softening as she realizes we've come to visit.

"Evening, friends," she says, her voice gentle as she comes around her desk to greet us.

"Hi, Leila. I wish we had more time to talk, but we're hoping you can help us." At my words, her head tilts, inviting me to explain my sudden request.

"We have a plan to get more information on the case by going undercover down at Stout & Sip. Unfortunately, I have a feeling won't make it long seeing as everyone in Eldermoore knows us. Maybe you have something to help us blend in? Something discreet, but effective."

With a thoughtful pause, Leila glides to a nearby shelf filled with magically enhanced clothing and an assortment of bits and bobs. Her fingers dance over the items as if she's sensing their energies. "Let's explore your options." She picks up a small, intricately carved stone shaped like a scarab.

"This is a charm of protection. It can shield you from unwanted attention and even obscure your magic from others who might sense it. It requires a certain clarity of purpose, however, so if your mind wavers, its power may falter."

Rowan leans closer, intrigued. "How do we use it?"

"Simply carry it with you, focus on your intent, and it will resonate with your energy."

As she speaks, I instinctively pull out my notepad and flip to a fresh page. I jot down the details, my pen moving quickly as I capture every word. I want to remember each nuance, each warning. I glance up occasionally, making sure I'm catching Leila's expression—her slight nods and frowns guide my understanding.

Rowan notices and smirks. "Really, Elodie? We finally get a peek at the magic clothes rack and you're taking notes, even now?"

I shoot her a playful glare but can't help smiling back. "Hey, you never know when this might come in handy!" Then it hits me—I sound just like Aiden from last week's lesson. Seriously? Shaking that thought off, I tell myself I always take notes diligently.

Next, Leila reaches for a delicate vial filled with shimmering powder. "This is faerie dust; our shipment of it just came in yesterday." She holds it up to the light so the sand-like minerals begin to glow a soft green. "A sprinkle can create illusions, allowing you to divert attention. But use it wisely; too much can cloud your mind and lead you astray."

I scribble a quick note: Faerie dust—use sparingly!

Aisling bites her lip as if hesitant to speak, but her curiosity gets the better of her. "And what happens if we lose control?"

Leila's expression grows serious. "Illusions can ensnare you. There was a case several years ago involving a student at Tara Hall. He thought he could use an illusion for a class project—a way to craft a vibrant island filled with thrilling adventures and sun-drenched beaches. Once he stepped inside, the bright colours and immersive experiences enveloped him. Days melted into one another, and the outside world faded completely. It took multiple professors to navigate the depths of the illusion and bring him back. When he finally emerged, he was a mere shadow of himself—disoriented and hollow, haunted by the vivid scenes he'd left behind."

"Understood," I say, jotting down the warning with a swift stroke of my pen. I exchange glances with the others, knowing we're all feeling the weight of the choice before us.

Leila glides to another shelf, retrieving a small amulet shaped like the Eye of Horus. "This grants clarity and reveals hidden truths. It's a common symbol in my homeland. However, it may show you visions you aren't prepared for. Be cautious as sometimes knowledge carries a burden."

As we explore further, my gaze drifts to a shelf with an ornate mask. Its dark surface glimmers like obsidian, reflecting the light in a way that almost seems alive. The mask is shaped like a raven's face with intricate carvings adorning the edges, mimicking feathers, while the eye sockets are deep-set. A slender band of silver wraps around the base, etched with runes that pulse faintly.

"What about that one?" I ask, pointing to the mask.

Leila's brow furrows and a shadow crosses her face as she spots what I'm looking at. "Ah, Morrigan's Mask," she murmurs. "It is said to possess the power of transformation, allowing the wearer to channel the goddess's strength, but it comes at a steep price."

"What kind of price?" I ask.

"It demands a toll—your memories, your will," Leila explains, her tone grave. "It can change you in ways you might not anticipate. The mask is documented to whisper lies, twisting perceptions until they become the only truth the wearer knows. There are stories of a twin to this mask that vanished in the early 1800s, lost to time and legend."

I glance back at the mask, the allure tugging at me. "It sounds powerful… but dangerous."

"Indeed. I'd advise against it."

"Let's stick with the charm and the dust," I say firmly, looking to Rowan,

Maeve and Aisling for confirmation.

"Agreed," Rowan replies after a moment of silent deliberation.

Leila's eyes light up, a genuine warmth radiating from her. "Great choice! Using the scarab and the faerie dust together will create a perfect balance. The charm will offer protection, while the dust allows for the necessary illusion. This combination will enhance your disguise beautifully." Her enthusiasm is infectious.

"That's even better!" I say, a smile spreading across my face as I reach for my coin purse.

Leila holds up a hand. "You should keep your money. What I truly desire is your help in finding the person responsible for ending my brother's life."

Surprised, I exchange glances with the others, a mix of determination and sympathy in our eyes. "We'll still have to leave you something for your trouble," I insist, placing the coins on the counter despite her protest before grabbing our acquired items.

Leila's expression softens as she nods. "Thank you. Remember, girls, the power lies within you as much as in these items. Trust yourselves and have faith in one another. When you are ready, all you have to do is channel what you desire and speak the incantation, Féth fíada."

The scarab charm feels warm in my palm, and the vial of faerie dust thrums with potential in my pocket. I turn to look at the girls, their expressions a mix of excitement and resolve. I pause, glancing back at Leila. "Could we try them out here? I want to make sure we know how they work"

Leila's eyes widen as she quickly nods. "Of course. I can't believe I didn't suggest that sooner! It's wise to test them in a safe space." With a wave of her arm, she motions for us to follow her to a corner of the shop with a large antique mirror. "Now, focus on your intent."

Rowan nods, closing her eyes. "We want to blend in, to be unnoticed."

Whispering the words Leila taught us, a warm glow envelops us, the soft light extending a few centimetres from our bodies before disappearing. I blink in surprise at the speed of our transformation.

Rowan twirls, her floral mini skirt flaring out in a burst of colourful fabric. Her dark bob lightens to a warm chestnut with bangs, the sunlight catching it in a way that makes her look vibrant and fresh. Her blue eyes sparkle with excitement.

Maeve steps forwards, her usual blonde curls transforming into sleek, dark waves that cascade down her shoulders. She wears a fitted peasant top covered in geometric patterns, paired with high-waisted flared jeans that accentuate her athletic figure. Her green eyes sparkle with mischief as she twirls, laughter bubbling up.

Aisling glows in a rich emerald green A-line dress that sways around her knees. Her ginger hair shifts to a deep auburn, flowing in soft waves and framing her face beautifully. She tilts her head, offering a bright smile, her freckles standing out like constellations against her skin.

My dark attire morphs into a red wrap dress that moves with me. My brown hair transforms into a striking platinum blonde, with no blue highlights in sight, giving me a bold new look.

"Your minds are strong; it's working beautifully."

Rowan stares at herself, shaking her head in disbelief. "Wow! With the exception of our eyes, I wouldn't even recognize us! It's a bit strange not looking like Elodie's twin anymore." Turning away from the mirror, Rowan excitedly hugs Leila before glancing once more at her new outfit. "Thanks, Leila! With these disguises, our night should go off without a hitch!"

With a flash of a smile, Leila walks us to the door. "You'll let me know if you find anything?"

I give her a quick nod as I exit the shop, the cool autumn breeze rustling the hemline of my dress.

"Good," Leila responds. "Please, be safe. Should you need me, I will likely be here working late tonight to catalogue the new shipment. I look forwards to hearing all about this little adventure."

With a final click as the door closes, Rowan, Aisling, Maeve, and I each release our hold on the small charms. The warm presence of the scarab against my palm becomes cold as my normal appearance materializes once more.

I glance at my watch to check the time. I'd thought we'd need all day to find a disguise, but with the magical charm Leila gave us, we still have half an hour until Mr. Brennan is due for his regularly scheduled arrival at the pub. "Alright ladies, it's only half past six, so we've got just enough time to discuss what Auntie Cait told me and Aiden the other night. Now, we just need to decide where to go so that Aiden won't be suspicious."

"Agreed! Knowing my brother, he's probably holed up in his office right about now. Why don't we head over to my house? Plus, I can always say we're having a girl's night if he asks," Maeve contributes.

"You've certainly got the hang of this undercover work." Rowan smiles as she gives Maeve's hip a small bump with her own and begins walking towards the car. "If you've got a computer, I can try to dig up some more dirt on Mr. Brennan. It might give us better insight into how we should deal with him."

"My father splurged on me this year for my birthday and got me a personal computer." Maeve leans towards the front passenger seat and covers her mouth to whisper to Rowan. "I'm not really supposed to say, but it's the model Xerox Alto. It technically hasn't been released to the public yet, but my dad's cousin works with a man who is friends with the creator. It works like a charm and has so many new gadgets that I haven't even figured out yet. I'm sure you'll have a party with it!"

"Heck, yes! That model has been traveling in the digital grapevine for months now. I can't believe you got your hands on one!" Rowan's eyes light up with her enthusiasm. Knowing my sister, it'll be a miracle if I can pull her away from the screen.

Pulling into Maeve's driveway, I take in the house. Though Rowan and I have passed it many times throughout the years, we've never been inside. Its crisp white façade glows in the fading daylight. Ivy tendrils creep up the bricks, their tender green leaves glowing faintly as they stretch towards the fading warmth, adding a touch of inviting charm to the entrance. On the left side of the house, the bay window catches my eye, its glass shimmering softly. Flower boxes overflow with vibrant dahlias and marigolds, their rich colours brightening the serene atmosphere.

Opening the door, Maeve welcomes us inside with a wave of her arm. "I'll put on a quick cuppa and we can catch up in no time. I've been dying to hear what your Auntie told you, lassie. I couldn't get a peep out of Aiden." Her voice fades as she walks into the kitchen, her low heels clicking on the tiled floor. Quickly popping her head back around the corner, she nods to a room on her right. "Have a seat, girls. Make yourself at home."

Rowan and I call dibs on the floral settee as Aisling heads for the bright blue armchair that looks right off the pages of the recent edition of House Beautiful magazine. Just then, Maeve returns with a steaming teapot, the gentle clatter of cups breaking the cozy silence. As Maeve pours the tea, I lean forwards to spill the latest news, the air thick with anticipation as the conversation begins to flow.

"Wow. That's a lot to take in. I can't imagine how you girls are feeling. I would've never suspected that Ms. Flynn was hiding so much. When I attended Tara Hall, she always was so open with the students, making sure we felt like the academy was a second home." Maeve's words cut through the hurt I still can't quite shake. Her reminder of the woman I grew up with—the kind and loving mother figure I'd never trade for anyone—reminds me why I must uncover the secrets she hides and save us all from this darkness that has shrouded our lives.

Glancing towards Rowan, I see her quickly nod, determination igniting in her eyes. "We can't let this go," she says, leaning forwards. "I need to look up more details on Mr. Brennan." Without waiting for a response, she springs up and heads for Maeve's computer, which Maeve pointed out to her on our way to the sitting room.

"I can't believe I get to use this!" I hear her exclaim from the next room, her enthusiasm echoing against the walls as the clacking sounds of the keyboard reach us. We follow Rowan into the small office, eager to see what she can uncover.

"We tried to stake out Mr. Brennan, but he never showed—he was too spooked by Aiden's questioning." Her focus sharpens. "And check it out, there are some redacted records, and even though the details are scarce, it looks like he's tangled up in that murder over in Blackthorn Glade. Though Maeve and I didn't get much out of the Shadow Glen Detectives, there are rumours about two men—people are calling them Mr. A and Mr. B. They say they frequent Stout & Sip and other bars in nearby towns to recruit new members, drawing them in with promises of action against Eldermoore's restraints and laws." Rowan leans back in her chair, her eyes narrowing with fury as she pushes away from the desk. "Mr. B for Brennan? Seriously? If they were going for discreet, they could've tried a little harder! What's next, Mr. C for 'Can't Keep a Secret'? It's downright insulting! It's like the Slayer's having a laugh at our expense, sitting there thinking, 'Look how easy it is to pull their strings!' At this rate, he's turning this whole investigation into a twisted game, and I refuse to let him play us for fools."

Aisling claps her hands together, her eyes sparkling. "This is great! We're finally getting somewhere. At least we can narrow our search down to men—that should make things a bit easier. We can use this information to aid us tonight."

"You're right, I think it's time to put our detective skills to the test. If we get split up for any reason, we'll meet back here. By tomorrow, we might finally have some of the answers we've been looking for."

Armed with our charms and new information, it finally feels like we can stop the darkness and bring justice for Rónán and Liam. The girls buzz with excitement, their chatter filling the night air as they gear up for our first recon mission. But I can't shake this unease. My heart races as we walk to the pub, a tight knot forming in my stomach.

Even now, Aiden's powers course through me, a faint pulse that sends shivers down my spine. It's like I can tap into his abilities, and that realization both excites and unsettles me. What does this growing connection mean for our relationship? I haven't dared to mention it to anyone—partly because I don't fully understand it myself, and partly because Aiden would probably tease me about it.

The truth is, as much as I've grown to like him, admitting that makes me feel vulnerable. Oh, and let's not forget that the fate of Eldermoore may very well rest in our ability to find some answers tonight.

No pressure, right?

16

undercover shenanigans
elodie

The Stout & Sip — 7:00 p.m.

By the time we reach the entrance to the Stout a low thrum of music and the rowdiness of it's patrons spill into the street. Before I can open the door, a man stumbles out, almost knocking me to the ground.

Luckily, Rowan catches me and angrily shouts at the man's retreating form "Hey, watch where you're going next time!"

I grab my head as my vision splits and a strange dark blue glow follows him. As quickly as the colour appears, my vision returns to normal, leaving me confused and even more wary of how the night will unfold.

Catching Rowan still staring daggers down the street I give a small laugh before reassuring her that I'm fine. "Easy there, Ginger, it was just an accident. We better head inside to see if Mr. Brennan's arrived, yet."

Taking out my charm, I hold it in my palm and the girls do the same. As we each think of our intent to blend in and whisper the incantation, our appearances change just as they had earlier.

As soon as I open the door, the lively strains of a fiddler can be heard from the upper loft. Much like the last time Maeve convinced us to stop by after work, the dance floor is packed with people swaying to the rhythm while laughter and chatter blend into the background.

At the bar, patrons lean in close to one another to be heard over the music, ordering pints and cocktails. I catch a glimpse of Saoirse as she whizzes by, balancing two tall glasses that flicker with blue flames to a group of giggling girls in a back booth. I hold my breath as I wait to see if she'll recognize us.

As she passes us, however, she only gives us a brief smile and a wink as she yells over her shoulder, "Welcome, lassies. Find a seat where you can. We've got a full house tonight. I'll send someone your way in a jiffy."

Behind me, I hear the girls' own sighs of relief before I take a quick glance around.

Just as we expected, I spot Mr. Brennan in the same spot Aiden and I found him last week. Though he couldn't have arrived more than a few minutes before us, three empty glasses already scatter the table as he takes a hearty gulp from a fourth. His eyes are a bit glazed, and there's a looseness to his movements as he raises his hand to signal for another drink.

"Here's the plan: let's split up to avoid drawing too much attention. It's much more crowded tonight than expected, so we'll need to adjust our approach. Maeve and Aisling, you two head over to the bar and see if you can spot Lorcan. Rowan, you take the second floor while I keep an eye on things down here. If anyone needs assistance, just send a signal, and one of us will come to help. And remember, everyone needs to stay alert—we can't afford to miss a thing."

I watch as my friends disperse into the crowd, each step purposefully. Maeve slips towards one end of the bar, her gaze darting from face to face, sharp and focused, while Aisling glides to the other, her posture confident as they both scan for any hint of Lorcan. As Rowan ascends the stairs, I see her shoulders relax, the tension easing from her frame as she embraces the spirit of the night.

She weaves between groups, laughing and leaning in to catch snippets of conversations, effortlessly drawing people in. Watching her work fills me with pride. Most kids grow up anticipating their first taste of freedom, their first pint, or learning to drive. For Rowan and me, the disappearance of our parents made us grow up fast—sometimes I think too fast. Yet in moments like this, seeing years of determination and training pay off, I know our parents would be proud of what we've accomplished and the people we've become.

I take a breath, steadying my nerves as I scan the seats around Mr. Brennan, looking for a spot close enough to watch him without drawing attention. As I move, I let the buzz of conversation wash over me, picking up snippets of laughter and gossip from nearby tables. A group of sailors three tables over catches my eye, their laughter booming above the din.

One of them gestures, a friendly grin spreading across his face as he catches sight of me standing nearby. "Hey there, lassie! Plenty of room at our table if you fancy a seat! You must be fresh off the boat—everyone knows you've got to arrive early if you want to nab a good spot!"

Their warm invitation ignites a spark of hope. This could be the perfect chance to gather information about recent travellers and maybe even Liam, all while keeping an eye on Mr. Brennan. I offer a quick smile and make my way over, ready to do my part.

+)) ● ((+

It'll be fun they said. Yeah, that's what I thought, too. Unfortunately, that was before I decided to sit with a bunch of eejits. If I had to hear one more joke about sailors or their ridiculous antics I was going to bang my head against this damn table. On top of that, it's been about thirty minutes and the most exciting thing to happen to Mr. Brennan was getting a wet shirt from a too-drunk dancer when the crowd decided to move the dance floor to the tabletops.

Meanwhile, I can't seem to shake the feeling that someone has been watching me all night. Each time I attempt to look around, the men at my table pull my attention back to their story with a friendly nudge. But every time they do, my headache from earlier comes rushing back, causing the men to glow in a

115

mix of yellow and green. And just when I think everything is back to normal, my vision flashes red and an unfamiliar rush of anger surges through me. Whatever is happening to me will have to wait, though. If I want any answers tonight, I'll have to act now.

As I move to stand, the men around me pause their animated storytelling, their eyes widening in mock disbelief. "Wait, you can't just leave now!" the man who introduced himself as Colm exclaims, his hand dramatically pressed to his chest as if struck by my decision.

"Piaras here is just about to re-enact our fight against the Pirate Lord. We barely escaped with our lives!" the scrawny teen, Mick, adds, leaning forwards as if to pull me back into the tale.

They rise from their seats, trying to convince me with an imaginary sword fight, their laughter infectious.

"Sorry, lads, as much fun as it's been, I see an old friend of mine. You'll have to tell me all about the Pirate Lord and his hidden treasure next time."

They groan in playful protest, but with a laugh and a wave, I bid them farewell.

I scan the room for one of the girls when I spot Maeve talking to a man at the bar. Just as I'm about to move deeper into the crowd, my foot catches on a stray chair leg, and I stumble forwards. Before I can regain my balance, a firm hand grips my arm, steadying me.

"Careful now, mo thrioblóir beag. I wouldn't recommend falling on the floor in a place like this. If I'm not wrong—and I'm hardly ever off the mark— I reckon I saw a lady losing her pints on my way in." Aiden's voice slices through the noise, smooth and familiar, his presence commanding even in the pub's chaos.

I look up, and the rowdy patrons blur around us. His gaze is intense as if he can see straight through the layers of my disguise.

"How did you know it was me?" I ask, heart racing in the warmth of his gaze.

Aiden's smirk carries a hint of something deeper as he leans closer, the space between us charged. "Even with my eyes closed, I'd recognize you anywhere. No magic could ever hide you from me. Not when it feels like your soul calls to mine, easing the weight of my powers and settling my thoughts in a way I can't quite explain. It feels like you've cast a spell on me, and if I didn't know better, I'd say you're the one with magic."

His words wrap around me like a warm embrace, igniting a flutter in my chest. I can feel the pull between us, a magnetic connection that's both exhilarating and terrifying. As he holds my gaze, I wonder if he feels it too—the way our bond has grown, an unspoken understanding thrumming in the air.

The intensity of the moment breaks as he glances towards the crowd. "I got a message from the library. Niamh found something she needs to share with us first thing tomorrow—something urgent."

With his usual mischievous glint back, he grabs a piece of my blonde hair to study before gently pushing it behind my ear as he leans in to whisper, "I might have also had Declan tail you all day when I realized you were sneakily dodging me," he says, his cheek brushing against mine. I can feel a grin breaking out across his face. "Someone's got to keep an eye on you four hellions. But don't worry—I promise I won't get in your way. Despite what you might think, I'm just here to help. And if you'd let me, I got myself a cloaking charm from your friend Leila—you won't even know I'm here. I don't want to interfere, but it'd make me feel better if I could be here to help if you need."

I roll my eyes, a hint of annoyance creeping in. "I knew I felt someone watching me all night," I reply, forcing a lightness into my tone despite my slight irritation at his clear distrust in our skills. "Well, since you asked so nicely, I suppose you can stay."

Aiden's playful demeanour fades as concern etches itself into his features. "I only just arrived. I didn't want you to think I was taking over your plan." He pauses, his gaze piercing through the crowd more thoroughly. "We need to be careful."

Then, trying to lighten the mood, he grabs his cloaking charm and offers a reassuring smile. "Don't worry, I'll keep an eye out for you."

With a wink, he vanishes, leaving me momentarily startled before I turn back to the crowd

✦)) ● ((✦

I weave between tall tabletops and drunk patrons before I snag a half-empty glass from an abandoned table and make my way towards Mr. Brennan. Stopping just before I reach him, I pretend to trip and bump into his shoulder, the rest of the drink splashing him in the process.

Widening my eyes, I put on a face of innocence as I begin to apologize. "Oh no! I'm such a klutz." Taking a good handful of the napkins set on the table I begin to dab his shirt. "I should've stopped at one like my friends suggested, but you know how it is… Those Blackberry Bramble's are just too good to resist."

Mr. Brennan pushes me off him and raises his eyebrow as a look of disgust flashes across his face at my drunk antics. "Do I look like I drink cocktails?"

"Oh, no disrespect, Mister…?" When he doesn't offer his name, I continue, "Oh, who cares. Mind if I sit?"

Without giving him a chance to respond, I take the empty seat across from him. As I do, his eyes widen and small dots of sweat begin to bead on his forehead as he looks around the room.

"You'll have to find someone else to bother; I'm expecting company." His words slur slightly, but he's definitely more alert now that I've taken a seat.

"That's wonderful news! You've got yourself a lady? I'd love to meet her! I'm new to town and could use a few friends!" I beam, raising my hand to wave down the waitress. When she arrives, I call out over the music, "Another pint for my friend here, please!" I fight to hide my smile as I watch him fumble for words. "Now that we've got drinks sorted, I want to know all about her!"

"Listen here, lass," he says, his words slurring together slightly as he sways in his seat and points at me, "I'm not meetin' any lady, and ya ought to mind your own business." His snarl might scare off someone else, but unfortunately for him, he's stuck with my sober self.

"Oh…" Folding my legs under me, and kneeling on the seat, I lean across the table. I cup my hand to my mouth like I'm about to share a grand secret. I catch his brow furrowing in confusion, but curiosity wins as he leans in, almost toppling over. Just behind him, I catch a glimpse of Aiden who is no longer cloaked. His gaze is locked on me despite the older man beside him attempting to grab his attention. Inspiration strikes, and when Brennan is directly in front of me, I shout, 'You're meeting a lad! I need to meet him! I've had a right bit of bother with my boyfriend and might just be on the prowl for someone new! He keeps saying I talk too much, but I think he's just worried I'll find someone who actually listens!"

He jolts backward, eyes wide, a hand flying to his head as he covers his ear, startled by my sudden outburst. "Oi! Keep it down, will ya?" he exclaims, trying to regain his composure. "Since it seems like you'll talk my ear off, I'll just tell ya. I'm here to meet a work aquaint—"

"Work! Where do you work!" I interrupt, eager to keep him talking. The waitress arrives with the new glass I ordered and rushes by to help the next table.

Brennan picks up the glass and greedily chugs the beer, as if searching for liquid courage. Despite his eagerness to be rid of me just moments ago, I've clearly struck a topic he's all too keen to discuss: himself. I suppose I should've just started there.

"I'm really a jack of all trades. But Chief, my pal, recently piqued my interest in some work over in Blackthorn."

"What's in Blackthorn? I've heard it's a spot where all sorts of dodgy characters hang out to make a quick buck… no offense. There's even been talk of recent deaths and some kind of uprising brewing. Sounds pretty dangerous, honestly! How did you end up working there?" I rest my chin on my hand, widening my eyes with curiosity I no longer have to feign.

"Funny enough, it was a few years back when I lost more than a few pounds to Chief during a round of cards. I would've paid more attention, mind you, but I was really down on my luck and had racked up quite the tab before the game even began. I knew the barkeep would have my head if I didn't settle up. Luckily, Chief was feeling generous and mentioned he had another way for me to clear my debt. We got to chatting about our childhoods and how everything changed after the Veil."

At the mention of the Veil, a flash of anger flickers in his eyes, his jaw tightening. Clearing his throat, he continues, "You know, I still can't quite figure out where he came from. One day, he just appeared, like a shadow in the night. When he offered me work that could return Eldermoore to its former glory days, I couldn't refuse."

"Sounds like you're a philanthropist of a sort, am I right?" I probe.

With a smirk, he drawls, "Of a sort. You see, I'm a real bleeding heart for those wronged by Ol' Darragh's laws. And there are some men in this town who've got their eyes on something more than just a quiet life."

He leans in closer, lowering his voice to a conspiratorial whisper, glancing around as if ensuring no one else is listening. "These fellows? They're ready to stir the pot. It's risky business, but Chief… Well, he knows what he's doing. He's having me based here to recruit more to our cause, you see. Trust me, lass, you don't want to get caught in the middle of it."

He takes a long sip from his glass, the bravado in his posture wavering. There's a slight tremor in his hand as he sets the glass down, the playful glint in his eyes dimming. It's clear that Chief's presence has shifted the air in the room, tightening the atmosphere around us. Mr. Brennan leans back slightly, as if trying to distance himself from the topic. His gaze darts towards the entrance as though he half-expects this Chief fellow to materialize from the shadows at any moment. The way he speaks, a mix of admiration and fear, reveals the grip this rebellion leader has over him—an unspoken acknowledgment that the man commands more than just respect; he wields a power that sends shivers through those who cross his path.

Mr. Brennan leans in, his voice low. "You best be going now, lass. Chief should be here any minute. Trust me, you don't want to be caught near 'im." His eyes flick towards the entrance, tension radiating from him.

"You know, I think I'll take you up on that suggestion, I could really use a drink anyhow. All this talking has me parched, if you'll excuse me." I let my tone switch back to a carefree quality that I no longer feel. I make my way to the bar, attempting to blend back into the crowd and keep my eye out for Mr. Brennan's guest.

A few minutes pass, and I notice a cloaked figure descending the stairs, glancing around as if waiting for the right moment. They move purposefully towards Mr. Brennan's table, and I can't help but lean in closer. It's clear they've been here, lurking in the shadows, biding their time for this encounter.

As they reach him, the pair exchange hurried words, and the figure hands over a note. I watch Mr. Brennan's face go pale, the colour draining as he reads what is written. The tension between them is obvious, and I strain to catch any hint of what's being discussed, but they speak in hushed whispers. Before I can move closer, the cloaked figure slips away, disappearing into the crowd once more.

Shooting a glance to the back table I last saw Aiden, I see him slip on a ring that once again makes him invisible. Though he'd likely tell me to stay put, I can't help but rush after them. Running towards the back entrance I push open the heavy metal door, preparing myself to jump into a full-on brawl. Instead, I'm met by a bewildered Aiden.

"Dammit, I was right on his tail! Then just like that … POOF! I mean, I've never seen anything like it, and I've been able to see ghosts since I was 13! I have a feeling the longer we stay out here in the open, the more of a target we'll be. Let's regroup inside, and we can come up with our next steps."

Too wary to argue, I simply open the door and follow his lead.

17

DISCOVERIES AND ENCOUNTERS
ELODIE

As I pass one of the empty dark-lit booths, hands envelop my wrist making me tense. Jerking out of their grasp, I turn, only to be met by a pair of familiar blue eyes that are exact copies of my own. "Darn it, Rowan, you nearly scared me to death!" Taking a calming breath, I add, "I was just coming to find you. Did you have any luck?"

"Sorry, sis. I saw that cloaked man over by Brennan and thought I'd see if you needed help. I've been trying to tag him all night, but every time I got close, he'd disappear. I was hoping some of the patrons might know more about him, maybe see if he's our Mr. A, but it's like he's a ghost. I did happen to get one interesting tidbit, but I'll share it once we find the girls"

She grabs my hand, leading me towards the bar where we left Aisling and Maeve.

As we round the left side of the bar, we're forced to squeeze through more than a few rowdy students from Tara Hall. Closest to the entrance, I spot the girls talking to the same man from earlier—this must be Lorcan.

Up close, I can see that his skin is tan from days spent at sea, and his shoulder-length golden hair is streaked with natural blonde highlights. Maeve stands animatedly waving her hands through the air as she talks, her dark raven hair pulled back into a low ponytail secured with a piece of leather cord. Every now and then, her hand subconsciously reaches for it.

As Aiden approaches his sister, he rests a hand on her shoulder and bends to whisper in her ear, likely letting her know it's him. Moving to stand beside him, I notice a shadow cross Lorcan's face, his eyes bright with a hidden fury as he glares at Aiden's hand resting on Maeve's shoulder. A glance at Rowan and Aisling confirms I'm not the only one who's noticed. Well, this might work in our favour.

"Ah, there you are! Why don't you introduce us to your friend?" I prompt.

"Oh, yes! Where are my manners? Meet Lorcan O'Rourke. Lorcan, this is Rowan and Elodie, and this here is my brother, Aiden." Looking at me, she smiles before adding, "I was just telling Lorcan here how well this job of ours will pay if he agrees to help us." Her smile shifts to a mix of apology and desperation, silently pleading for me to play along.

"Of course…" Having no other option, I throw up a silent prayer to whatever deity might be listening. "Since our search was ordered directly by the Council, they'll pay you handsomely for any assistance you can provide." At least, I hope they'll agree once I speak with Auntie Cait. "We could use the help, and Maeve has spoken highly of your knowledge of those who frequent the docks. We're hoping to put your observation skills to the test."

"Did she now?" He pauses, smirking at Maeve. "Well, Ms. Elodie, I must say I'm quite intrigued by your approach. I'm not usually one for company." Gesturing towards Maeve and Aisling with a wave of his hand, he continues, "When I first spotted these two coming my way, I figured they were just here to pass the time with some idle chatter. But then Maeve told me to stay put and started insisting it was her from the docks the other day. The moment she started calling me 'sir,' I knew she meant business—she's the only one who does. I won't be at port long, but I'll do what I can. Will it be you I report to?" Waiting for my response, he flashes a full-toothed smile.

Before I can answer, a hand wraps around my waist. Its presence is warm and comforting as Aiden stands beside me, and I have to strain my neck to catch a glimpse of his face. With a calmness that doesn't quite match the tightness of his grasp, he answers for me. "Unfortunately, we'll be busy conducting our own investigations. You'll need to set up a time and rendezvous point to meet my sister."

"Ah, of course," he replies, a smirk creeping across his face, as if Aiden has unwittingly played right into his hands. Rising, he tips back the rest of his glass and pretends to wave an imaginary hat at us before turning to Maeve. Grabbing her hand, he places a kiss on the top, making her cheeks flush with colour. "I'll send a note tomorrow detailing our meeting spot. We can discuss any orders your Council might have there. But alas, I must return to my ship— a sailor's work is never done."

Without a backwards glance, he leaves us staring at his retreating form, the tails of his coat billowing with his long strides.

Once he exits the pub, I hear Maeve release a quick breath. "I wasn't sure I'd be able to convince him to work with us. Sorry about the money thing; I figured a man like him would only agree if there was something in it for him."

"I'm not too sure that's why he agreed…" Rowan mumbles under her breath, causing Aisling to choke on her drink.

Nudging Rowan in the side, I give Maeve a reassuring smile. "I trust your instincts. And don't worry about the money; I'll have a word with Auntie Cait and see what we can come up with. I wasn't completely bluffing when I told him that the Council would be happy to pay if it helps us solve this case."

"That reminds me," Rowan says, taking a seat in the now empty bar stool and waiting for us to gather around her, "while I was walking around, I happened to spot Mrs. Flanagan and the historian Ms. Maguire speaking with Dr. Collins. It looks like the Council members are in a bit of a tizzy over this case. There was a lot of blame being passed around, most of it directed at Mrs. Flanagan. Like us, they think she might be involved since she has direct access to the docks. I think our next step is to interview them all. We'll see what Dr. Collins's take on all of this is. We can even put his botany skills to use and see what more we can learn about the whitethorns."

"Agreed. Aiden says Niamh might also have some new information for us. I say we call it a night and start at the library tomorrow. I'll let Auntie Cait know to set up meetings for us on the way there. The less time they have to prepare the easier it'll be for us to weed out any lies." Pausing to gather my thoughts I begin to recount the information I was able to gather from Mr. Brennan. "Our conversation proved quite informative. He's definitely a part of this somehow; I'm just not sure how much he knows. Seems to me like he's a puppet in this game just as much as the rest of us right now."

"Elodie and I saw his friend slip him a note before making a hasty exit. I had Declan try to read what was written on it while I went after the cloaked figure. By the time Elodie and I reached the alley, they'd vanished. With this mysterious figure hanging around, it's clear we need to work in pairs from now on. I'll also be increasing your training; I want you ready for anything." Aiden crosses his arms, his jaw set and eyes narrowed, making it clear that there's no room for argument.

"Now, wait a second," I start, my anger rising. Who does he think he is, barking orders like that? Sure, he's part of the team now, but I won't let him dictate my actions, no matter how sincere his concern seems. More training would be helpful, but it's vital to consider everyone's input before making decisions. I cross my arms, making it clear that while I acknowledge his perspective, I refuse to have my opinion cast aside. The confused look he gives me makes it clear he's used to having his orders followed without question. "We can't always be working in pairs, and before you even suggest it, Declan can't be in multiple places at once. I think it'd be better to see if Leila has something we can use to protect ourselves in case we ever do get separated."

At my suggestion, his confusion morphs into a smile of approval. "That could work. The more we can control, the better."

I return his smile, grateful that he's open to my idea. "Well, let's just hope whatever Declan saw will finally help us get a step ahead."

18

THROUGH THE THICKET

ROWAN

October 13th —6:30 a.m.

Before my alarm can wake me up, I'm abruptly pulled from sleep by the feeling of my nose being tickled. Squinting my left eye open, I see the black furry tail of my new companion hitting me in the nose. "When I said we could share the bed, I didn't mean you could sit on my head." With a gentle laugh, I scoop Shade up and place her next to me just as the blaring noise of my alarm clock goes off.

Quickly hitting the off button, I can't help but snort. "Well, I guess I won't be needing this thing anymore!" Between our eventful night and how I've been feeling recently—like I'm moving through fog, my skin a little too cold and pale—I'm surprised I even remembered to set the old clock. Trying to stop the ringing in my ears I take a deep breath and try to focus. Alright, let's see what's on the schedule today…

1. Visit Niamh at the library.
2. Have Auntie Cait set up interviews with the Council.
3. Find out from Declan what was on Mr. Brennan's note.
4. And… I'll guess I'll see how the day goes!

Now that I have a clear to-do list, I sit up and prepare to dress. The quiet sound of Elodie's humming tells me she was up early again. I don't know how she does it.

Crossing my bedroom to the oak dresser, I open the drawer, squinting at the mess inside. Why is it always like this? I grab the first tank top I can find, then pull out a jumper—Eh, good enough. Next, I try digging through the pile of skirts before finally grabbing one that doesn't look like it's been through a tornado. Sure, this'll do. Bending down, I grab my favourite black chunky heel and snag a pair of black tights from the wicker bin next to it, which Shade currently occupies.

She lifts her head and gives me a look—half judgment, half disappointment, like she's the queen of the house and I've just insulted her with my mess. Great, even the cat's giving me the side-eye now.

I hold her gaze, resisting the urge to laugh. "Really? You're gonna give me that look, Shade?"

I glance around at the chaos, and, for a split second, I consider cleaning it up. Yeah, I should probably get to that soon. But then again… Cleaning? I shake my head, grinning. Maybe next month. Or, you know, when I'm retired and have nothing else to do but cry over laundry.

As I get ready, the rattling of pots echoes from downstairs as Elodie prepares breakfast again. The smell of cinnamon and warm oats sneaking under my door makes my stomach rumble. Alright, alright. I hear you, tummy! Just a few more minutes. Grabbing my hairbrush, I go to the full-length mirror to try and tame my wild bedhead, knotted strands catching now and then. Just as I finish showing a knot who's boss, a white strand of hair catches my eye. Not believing it, I grab the piece of hair hidden near the nape of my neck and lean closer to the mirror. The red-tipped end of a strand is now a stark white against my brown roots. Oh, hell no. I blink a few times, hoping it's a trick of the light, but it doesn't disappear. I'm too young to be turning grey!

Elodie's heels on the stairs as she makes her way to my room, likely feeling my unease through our new bond. A quick knock later, she enters the room, bursts of her worry hitting me in waves. "What happened? Are you okay?"

"Oh, nothing—just that I clearly need a vacation! I've completely skipped the greying stage of my life and gone straight to frost on a bog—and I haven't even turned 28!" My voice comes out higher than normal as I walk over to her with the strand held in my outstretched hand.

"Oh, blimey, I thought you had a full-blown crisis on your hands, not this! Maybe it's a side effect of the charm we used last night. We did keep it on for a fair bit, didn't we?"

"So, why isn't your hair turning white, then?" Shade's quiet meow from behind me seems to echo my question.

"It could be because you had to focus harder around the council members," Elodie says, rubbing her chin. "They already know us and unlike Mr. Brennan, they each have strong magic. The charm probably took more effort to maintain." Pulling out her notepad from the pocket of her knitted vest, she flips to the last few entries. "Looks like the more you concentrate when using magical tokens, the higher the chance of side effects. We can ask Leila when we visit, to see how long it'll take to revert to normal.

Nodding in resignation, I tell her, "Okay, that makes sense… but still, magic messing with my hair? What next? I swear, life was so much simpler before all this magic and spell nonsense."

Elodie laughs, reaching over to ruffle my hair. "Oh, don't worry, you're still beautiful, even with the rogue silver strand. Now, enough dilly-dallying."

I grin, shoving her playfully. "You're such a bossy little thing, you know that?"

"Born for it," Elodie says with a wink. "Now, quickly finish up and come down to eat. We've got a long day ahead of us and we still have to pick up the girls."

Arcane Scriptorium- 7:12 a.m.

"Yay! You've made it just in time for the first official Clue Crew meeting! Hmm, that sounded more clever in my head. Anyway, Aiden just arrived a few moments ago." Niamh, who looks like she's had a few espressos too many, hops down from a newly added throne-like chair. Her pastel blue dress swishes gracefully as she moves, and atop her head is a little hat, perched jauntily. She tugs at the dress's skirt as she twirls around in her excitement, clearly a bit too long despite her height.

I try not to laugh as I watch Declan, who now stands behind her. His eyes widen at Niamh as she quickly skips back to her chair, practically bouncing in her seat. She looks around the room, clearly giddy to share the latest updates.

"Okay, so we've been at this for days," she starts, clearly revving up. First, I roped in Mam—obviously. She's the only one who can read a recipe book and a cursed scroll with the same enthusiasm. She started matching up symbols with every ancient text she could find. She didn't get much out of it, but, hey, she found a few words that might be relevant… or maybe they were just names of herbs. It can be hard to tell sometimes. Anyhow, she did find a few patterns, so I brought Granda and Nana in to help. They've got this uncanny knack for languages, and—get this—I think they might've cracked it, or at least most of it. They were both holed up in the library for days, muttering about 'root words' and 'dark magic.'"

"So it is a language? What worries me is that I didn't come across anything like it in my history books. Was your family able to date its origin?" Aisling, who has been leaning against one of the reading tables, moves closer to

Niamh's desk to ask her question.

"I'm so glad you asked! It's an ancient Celtic writing script known as Ogham, though some folks call it Ogam. It's predicted to have been in practice throughout the 4th century CE. However, my Nana had thought she'd seen something like it before. She was able to dig up an old newspaper clipping from the 1500s and it turns out that around the 1700s, Eldermoore's Council did their best to scrub it from history—and, in some cases, from our minds entirely. But my grandparents were different. They were the last keepers of the Scriptorium at the time, and the protective wards and spells they had over the place made them immune to the Council's memory wipe. They never let on, of course, but they skipped right past all that nonsense. So, when I started poking around and asking questions, they began digging through a restricted part of the library that even I didn't know about. Which is mad, right?"

"So, we need to assume that the Slayer either found a way to bypass the memory spell like your grandparents or wasn't even a member of the town at the time," Elodie surmises as she writes the theory in her notes.

"I would say so." Niamh leans on her hand as she frowns. As if she knows just what to say to cheer us up, another grin appears. "Ogham's are often written for magical intentions. So, it looks like your culprit will have magic, which greatly reduces the number of interviews you'll need." Grabbing a book from her desk, she opens it to a page and motions for us to gather around.

Peeking at the page, I can see the same lines that had been engraved on our victims, but they're no longer bunched together. Instead, each character is separated with some text beneath it.

Pointing to the first character on the page, Niamh explains, "Like any language, Ogham is made up of an alphabet. Each of these lines and notches represent a different letter when written a certain way, and they'll mean another thing entirely when weaved together. A feda is each individual letter that makes up the alphabet and a fid is the letter and its unique name and meaning. This means we aren't necessarily going to decipher this by picking apart each letter, but instead by looking at what it symbolizes. The tricky part of deciphering is to figure out what aicme type, which means sequence, the writer was using. Unfortunately, there are four to choose from, but we were able to narrow it down almost immediately to the Second and Third Aicme"

"How? From what you've said, I thought you'd be holed up in here for months researching." Aiden's question causes Niamh to laugh.

"You'd probably be right, but, lucky for us, the Slayer made a mistake."

"Ooh, I love it when they dig their own grave!" Maeve exclaims.

"Same! So, it turns out that his use of whitethorn and signing his notes with the raven were his hubris. In fact, the first letter of the second aicme is in the feda H, which has the meaning of terror, represents the whitethorn tree, and its bird symbol is the night raven. So, in this case, I'd say he dug a trench." Leaning back in her chair, she continues, "Cross-referencing all the aicmes to the autopsy photos you shared with me, we deciphered the text on Rónán's arm to mean 'Tosach n-echto', which translates to 'beginning of murder' and comes directly from the third aicme feda 'Ng'. The fid for Ng is nGétal, which means 'wound' and 'charm'. Although typically meant in a healing sense, a person with ill intent associated with the letter H can cause death. It looks like the Slayer is leaving you hints as to what he plans and maybe even why."

"Well, in that case, we'll send over a copy of Liam's report for you to translate now that we know you've cracked the code. Once we know for sure that they're using the same encryption every time, I could make a program on my computer to add the cipher. That way, if a memory spell ever does happen again, it'll always be stored on the hard drive." Just thinking about how much fun it'll be to code a program that can help the team makes me want to start right now.

"Speaking of the autopsies, I also went over Rónán's to investigate the possible cause of death. From what we saw, the blood loss doesn't make sense. There were no wounds, no obvious signs of trauma. It took some searching through some old medical scrolls with my Da, but there are old stories about curses— they call it the 'whispering death,' where the life force is drained slowly, without leaving a wound. My Granda used to tell me about the old magic—how it ties to things like hagstones and the ancient ones that used them to trap souls. I think Rónán's death might be connected to that old power that's just been lying in wait," Niamh tells us with a shiver.

Aisling leans forwards, her brow furrowing with concern. "But how could it have escalated so quickly? If this curse drained him that fast, what triggered the speed of it?"

Niamh tilts her head, clearly pleased with the question. "It's the plants, especially the Whitethorn. That tree's notorious, you know. It's called the truth tree for a reason. It holds a lot of power—magical and otherwise. The thorns aren't just part of the curse; they enhance it. When someone uses those thorns in magic, they're channelling something far stronger than ordinary spells. And if the culprit used Ogham script—well, that makes it worse. The Ogham script itself is powerful, tied directly to the earth and its energies. Whoever did this wasn't just casting a simple spell; they were weaving the curse into the very fabric of the land itself."

"Well, that could explain the unusual ghost activity and the portal." Declan's deep voice fills the quiet as we think of the implications of what Niamh has discovered.

Though I've become accustomed to having him around, the sudden shout of surprise from Niamh has us all sitting upright.

"What in the hell's bells and begonias!" Her sudden outburst is soon replaced by a giddy excitement as she turns and spots Declan. "A ghost in my library! Who would have thought— I mean, I've read tons of stories about them, but I never thought I'd meet one in person!" Enunciating her words and giving a small wave, she adds, "My name is Niamh, who are you and do you know you're dead?"

"Uh…Niamh, this is Declan. He helps me out on most of my cases. How are you able to see him? I didn't know you had the gift of sight," Aiden introduces.

Giving Aiden a small whack on the shoulder she scolds, "Aiden O'Connor. How dare you keep this a secret!" With a calming breath she explains,

"I unfortunately don't possess such a unique gift, but the library is a treasure trove of knowledge and has a mind of its own. It's likely that the Scriptorium recognized Declan and decided to reveal his presence."

Glancing at Declan, his face is contorted in a mix of shock and absolute delight. With a grin that spans ear to ear, Declan bows in a theatrical pose and says sullenly, "Alas, I've known for quite some time that I no longer possess a human form. I'd been traveling this plane of existence for too long before I met Aiden. I almost became an echo of myself and I'd say he saved me just in the nick of time! So, don't be mad at him dear Niamh it was I, Declan Finnegan, who suggested I remain a secret so that I could help investigate."

"Well, in that case, I guess I can't stay mad at him! Now, what was it you said about ghosts and a portal?"

"It was right after Liam's death that Aiden and I saw his spectral leave. I was able to track him to the academy and there were ghosts waiting in line to get hooked up to a soul-sucking machine." He visibly shakes as if still disturbed by the encounter.

"Hmm, the Academy, you say." Niamh hums while looking deep in thought. "That reminds me: I asked Doc to send me Liam's autopsy so I could check for patterns while I was researching the cause of death. The autopsy done by Doc was nothing like Headmaster Doyle's. There was also a huge gap in the report—nothing about the smell Doc had made a point to note when he called me: that odd, sweet scent lingering around the body just as Aiden had described. It was like it had just disappeared. Someone must be trying to cover their tracks. Unfortunately for them, they didn't count on Doc writing with such a heavy hand and I spotted the indents straight away. A little bit of magic, and boom, the missing note was restored. Turns out, that smell wasn't just some random medical herb or part of the curse—it was the distinct scent of barbiturates. Likely phenobarbital— a strong sedative. It's known to cause a sweet, medicinal odour when someone's been exposed to it, especially if used over time. But the dose Liam got? That's where things get sinister. At a high enough level, phenobarbital can be deadly, and judging by the concentration in his system, it's clear it was intentional. I'm not one to point fingers, but seeing as how it wasn't found in Rónán's system, I'd say you need to talk with Headmaster Doyle."

"By the saints! If this is true, Mr. Doyle must know something," I say urgently. "He was probably trying to keep Liam just lucid enough to appear helpful, but out of it enough so he couldn't tell us anything. We need to question him again!"

"I agree, but we'll have to be careful. He could be the one behind all of this," Aiden says, his voice laced with concern.

"I have to agree with Aiden on this one," Niamh says. "It looks like Liam might have been saved if Headmaster Doyle had called a draoi sooner. If he's behind all this, he could be dangerous—there's no telling how far he'll go."

Elodie nods, her expression serious. "If Mr. Doyle is tangled up in these deaths, who knows who else on the Council is involved? I was going to have Auntie Cait set up a meeting, but I think it might be better if they didn't know we were stopping by, especially if our suspicions about Mrs. Flanagan are true, too."

19

IF WALLS COULD TALK
ELODIE

Tara Hall - 9:00 a.m.

I s it just me or does this place get creepier around Halloween?" A visible shiver racks up Rowan's spine as we take in the cathedral-like structure of the Academy.

"Well, I'm sure the ghosts currently surrounding us drop the score on overall curb appeal," Declan adds before he drifts through the car door, his form appearing much clearer than it had a few weeks ago when I only saw his shadowy outline.

"He was just joking, right?" Rowan turns to Aiden for confirmation, but his silence as he exits the car says more than enough.

Likely picturing said apparitions surrounding the car and peering in, she hastens her movements as she flings off her seat belt and quickly follows us before rushing up to Declan. "I was thinking you should probably clue us in on

136

what Mr. Brennan's note said in case we run into him in the halls."

As she speaks, her head turns on a swivel, as if expecting to see a ghost appear at any moment. When she doesn't get an immediate response, I watch as she looks up to see if Declan hears her. I smirk as I catch him staring down at the tight grip she has on his arm. With a light chuckle, she releases her hold and straightens the hem of her jumper to appear more like the fearless detective she usually is.

Clearing his throat, he explains, "It was a bit difficult to read with Brennan's hand shaking so much, but I was able to read a few lines. The first line mentioned how as long as he kept doing what was required of him, he could get what he wanted. Then I caught tomorrow's date and a time stamp for the witching hour on the bottom while he was crumbling it. I was able to clear one thing up for us though: our culprit and Mr. A—or Chief, as Brennan called him—are definitely the same person. The note was signed with a raven."

"Nice work. At least we know we're on the right track. See, Aiden, you should be thanking us with dozens of pastries and giving us trophies for our little undercover work instead of threatening us with training!" Maeve's conspiratorial wink at us behind his back accompanied by Aiden's groan hints that this isn't the first she's suggested something like this since last night.

"We'll see. Let's try to get through this first." Aiden's noncommittal grumble suggests he has no intention of giving us a trophy unless he's ranking bad behaviour.

Though we've caught no sign of Mr. Brennan as Rowan suggested, I'm on edge. I've paced these halls hundreds of times with Rowan while we waited for Auntie Cait to complete her work. I remember how we'd sneak away while she was on an important call, her door closed a bit more than usual to block out our giggles. We'd sit near classroom doors to try and listen to the magic lesson of the day, sometimes taking turns acting as a step stool for each other to catch a glimpse of the students inside. It was probably the reason why Rowan was always so fascinated with learning magic and the beginning of her disapproval for barring non-magical students from learning too.

Now, these halls seem to hold more dark secrets than I could've imagined. Though Aiden and Maeve seem more at ease, the tightness of his cheek as he clenches his jaw tells me he's just as worried.

"If only these walls had eyes and ears! We'd be out of a job and this case would be solved already!" With a playful nudge, I watch as he visibly relaxes. He turns to me with a grateful smile, as if he knows exactly what I'm trying to do.

"Maeve and I tried a spell that did exactly that once. She'd been talking nonstop about a boy in her class, but she wasn't sure if he liked her back. I had just learned the spell called Mianta na Focail Fírinne which allows the user of the spell to ask the walls questions and hear unspoken truths. I suggested we try it out so that she'd stop badgering me with questions. Let's just say he already had a girlfriend, and turns out the spell is harder to control than I thought. There are still reports from students who hear voices in the potions wing and say it's haunted. Many students who attend the school theorize that it is a former student turned vengeful ghost." Looking to Maeve, who smiles up at him, he adds, "We never did figure out how to make the walls stop talking. I think the only reason Ms. Flynn let it go was because she could always tell when I was skipping class."

His story sets us all at ease as we head to our first stop; Ms. Maguire's office.

As we arrive, a student rushes out in tears, almost knocking into us as she passes. Through the cracked door, I can hear Ms. Maguire's voice, steady and authoritative, as she wraps up the lecture. "And for those of you who would like to discuss your grade, you will have to meet me during my office hours tomorrow between two and four."

As the last student leaves, she stands up, smoothing her skirt with an easy grace before walking to clear the chalkboard filled with the history of magical creatures. "Well, come on in. Don't stand in the hall like a pair of wet hens." Ms. Maguire looks back at us, eyes calculating and observant whilst her lips curl slightly at the corners. "Take a seat, darlings. What can I do for you?"

"We've got a few questions for our investigation. Seeing as you're on the council, I'm sure you won't mind answering," Aiden says, getting straight to the point.

"Well, I've got another class in thirty minutes, but I'm all ears until then," she warns.

Taking a seat at a desk in the front row, Rowan starts the interview. "Great, we'll start with our first question, then. Ms. Maguire, where were you on the first of October?"

"Am I under investigation now?"

Trying to smooth things over before she decides she's done talking before we even start, I rush to reassure her. "I wouldn't say that; we're just dotting our I's and crossing our T's. It's nothing personal, just part of the job. We hope you understand."

Seeming somewhat placated, she perches on the edge of her desk and appears to concentrate. "Well, let's see, I had class around 10:30, office hours from 12 to 2 pm, followed by a lunch in the teacher's break room and another class at 3:30 pm. We were supposed to have a council meeting later that night, but that fell through, so I was home by 5 o'clock."

"Can we ask why the council meeting didn't happen?" Aisling chimes in.

"I'm not sure, to be honest. Ms. Flynn just left a note on my desk cancelling. When she held a meeting the next day concerning the death of Rónán, I figured that was why."

"We'd like a copy of that note if you still have it," Aiden tells her.

"I'm sure it's around here somewhere; I tend to be a bit of a paper hoarder." As she begins sifting through the top drawer of her desk, she quickly comes away with the evidence. "Ah, here it is, just as suspected. You can have the original copy and save us both time," she says as she stuffs the paper in his hand. "Is there anything else?"

"We're aware that a few council members were seen entering the Stout Tuesday night, with you among them. We'd like to know the names of those who attended and what was said."

"It was just a night out among colleagues—a chance to wind down after a long day of grading midterms. I invited Mrs. Flanagan, Dr. Collins, and Mr. Doyle to accompany me. I don't remember all that was said, but we probably discussed the case and expressed our worries for other students. I can't say much else happened." Looking at the cuckoo-clock perched above the door, she notes, "This will have to be all for today. I still need to prepare notes for the lecture and my students will be arriving in 15 minutes."

Recognizing that we won't be getting more from her, we make our exit and mentally prepare for the same warm welcome all over again.

+)●((+

"Am I under investigation?" Mrs. Flanagan's voice hardens as she cuts off Rowan. A quick flash of anger crosses Rowan's face at the question.

"No, I apologize if that's how it sounded. We've had a long day. If you could just provide an alibi for Rónán and Liam's death, we can move on to our next question."

"I see." Contrary to her words, from the way her face contorts into a sneer, she isn't happy about our line of questioning. "I had off from school that day to handle official Council business at the docks. As you know, it's my job to see what goods come in and out of Eldermoore. I'm sure there are sailors who can attest to seeing me. Plus, Headmistress Flynn records all the hours of her teachers and is the one who signed permission for me to miss school that Thursday. I arrived at the docks by 1:00 am when the first boat docked and didn't leave until 11:00 pm that day."

"What exactly do you look for in these shipments? Have you come across any hagstones and are you aware that there is talk of an uprising in town?

"An uprising? That's complete nonsense. If I were you, I'd fact-check my sources. Anyhow, no weapons ever make it into town on my watch. I personally check all shipments and do background checks on all crew. Now, concerning a hagstone, I did happen upon one late last spring. Though, while you're taking notes in that little journal of yours, make sure to write that all malicious magical artifacts are either destroyed or kept under lock and key. This stone is safely stored in the schools safe for further research."

"Is there a chance that someone could've taken it out of the safe?"

"Of course not, and I don't appreciate what you're insinuating. Only myself and Ms. Flynn have a key to the vault and neither of us would ever endanger the students or residents of Eldermoore by removing it. Now, if you'll excuse me, I'm holding a club meeting for our agricultural and trading students."

✦) ● (✦

Well, we made it through all but one member and I can say that it went as well as expected. If I had to hear one more 'am I under investigation?' I was going to go insane. I mean, what were they expecting? We're running an investigation here!

With an audible deep breath from all of us, we get ready for our visit with the last council member. Knocking on the office door that reads— "Dr. Collins's" on a shiny new nameplate, we wait for a few seconds before hearing his voice call out for us to enter.

"Can you tell us your whereabouts on October 1st… and, before you ask, no, you're not under investigation," Rowan rushes to say before he can beat her to it.

"Of course not, you're all just doing your job. Let me just look at my calendar so I don't mix up my days." He smiles at us, a relief from the usual cold dagger look the other council members gave us. Finding what he's looking for, Dr. Collins looks up ready to answer. "It looks like I had my usual morning classes, then lunch at the Stout & Sip because I love their homemade soup and bread, you know?! I'm sure those lovely owners can confirm. Anyway, then I came back about an hour and a half later to finish my scheduled evening class. Oh, and I guess we skipped a council meeting. If I remember correctly, I was to blame for that week's cancellation as I might have overdone it with the helpings of potato soup." He laughs, his cheeks reddening with embarrassment.

"Oh? We were under the impression that the council meeting was canceled due to the unexpected death of Rónán."

Laughing jovially, Dr. Collins says, "That's probably more likely, and to think all this time I thought I was to blame. It was such a terrible shock when

Headmistress Flynn shared the news; he was such a promising student."

Crossing the room to a wall covered in pictures, he points to one right in the middle. Rónán stands next to Dr. Collins and a few other awarded students as he holds a trophy. The plaque under it reads "Awarded for: Brightest Réalt of Our Time." Next to that is another picture, this time with Rónán and a girl named Laoise being awarded a trophy by him again, this one dated one year prior.

"He was a star student of mine, always thinking about the future and how to improve Eldermoore through agriculture and magical ventures. He could've done such great things…" Dr. Collins adds, trailing off with a shake of his head.

"Ms. Flynn mentioned that you were a botanist. We were hoping you could give us some insight into the use of Whitethorn when used in a ritual," Aisling says.

At the mention of plants, Dr. Collins's eyes light up. "Of course! The Sceach Gheal is Ireland's native tree. The white flowers are known to cause a sickly-sweet scent in May. The haws, or berry clusters, that are more common this time of year are an important source of nutrition for our avian friends and a great part of most jams and wines. Another interesting fact that isn't so commonly known is its beneficial effects on the heart when taken long-term." Looking conspiratorial, he leans in and whispers, "It's also said that where an oak, ash, and thorn tree lies, there will be Fae folk around. Though, you have to be careful with them; never know what or who you're truly messing with. If you have any more questions, just stop by my office anytime and I'll be happy to help!"

"Thanks, Professor, you've been a great help. As a local historian, I love it when I can learn something new. You can count on us reaching out again. We'll let you get back to your work, now," Aisling exclaims with a cheerful smile and a grateful handshake.

Danu's PI - 2:00 p.m.

Returning to Danu's, the bell above our door startles us before none other than Lorcan saunters in.

"What are you doing here? I thought your note said to meet you tomorrow for an update," Maeve glowers accusingly.

"Change of plans, mo siréine bheag. Fortunately for you, I had time to stop by today after witnessing a very interesting 'scene' at the docks. I'd also never pass up the chance to check in on some beautiful lassies."

Crossing their arms, Aiden and Declan growl in unison, "Watch it," although Lorcan is clueless about Declan's presence behind him.

Unperturbed, Lorcan makes his way to the loveseat and settles in, his boots leaving remnants of dirt and bits of dried seaweed on the coffee table as he crosses his ankles. "If you don't want the information, I can just go." He raises an eyebrow but makes no move to get up.

"Alright, alright, just be out with it already, you heathen," Maeve exclaims, huffing in frustration as she pushes his feet off the table and sits beside him.

"As you wish," Lorcan starts with a Cheshire grin. "I was walking to the Stout & Sip from the docks, picking up an order, when I saw the night guard fella from the other night and a taller man wearing some fancy suit...I think the guard called him Daryl or Douglas. They were having some sort of argument before they saw me and rushed through the back gates of the Academy. So, like the good citizen I am, I of course had to follow, which led me straight to some sort of crypt near the graveyard."

"I'm not even going to ask how you made it through those gates," Maeve says while rubbing her temples.

"I didn't want to give myself away, so I kept to the shadows. But I could hear 'em plain enough. They were talkin' about a fella—Mr. A, they called him—and he didn't sound too happy with 'em. They were in a bit of a panic, sayin' they needed to stay on his good side, or things could go south. They mentioned the lot of ya, too—said somethin' about how you're too close to the truth and they'd have to deal with it soon enough. Then somethin' rattled 'em, 'cause the next thing I knew, they were gone."

"Was the man with Mr. Brennan actually Headmaster Doyle, by any chance?" Rowan questions.

"Aye, that tracks now that ye mention it," Lorcan says, giving a thoughtful nod.

"If this isn't enough proof to bring those two, in I don't know what is," I say, my voice firm with resolve. "We can't let them get away with this— especially if they're planning to hurt more people. We need to act, and we need to act now."

+)) ● ((+

As we reach the landing of Apartment 13, the atmosphere feels noticeably different from the last time we were here, but just as heavy. We hear rustling from inside, and before we can even knock, the door swings open. Headmaster Doyle stands there, a nervous sheen of sweat on his brow. His face quickly shifts to one of fear when he sees us.

"Hello. We hope you weren't planning on going out; we have a few more questions for you. Mind if we come in?" Rowan sharply says as she levels him with a glare.

Mr. Doyle stumbles over his words for a moment, clearly caught off guard. Not having any more patience, Aiden steps forwards, his tone smooth as he cuts through the awkwardness. "Apologies for the intrusion, but our orders come straight from the Council. You know how they are," He finishes with a wink.

As we push our way through, Rowan and I link arms with Mr. Doyle, making sure there's no way for him to escape. Walking into the living room, he begins sweating more and keeps trying to pull us back to the other side of the room. That's when we hear a rustle come from his home office to the left. Giving Aiden and Declan a subtle nod in that direction, they waste no time.

The boys enter the office, and I watch as Aiden pulls the back of Mr.

Brennan's coat collar as the man tries to climb out the window to make his getaway.

"Mr. Brennan. Why am I not surprised? I really wouldn't do that if I were you. Put your hands up and stand against the wall," Aiden orders.

Before he can try to escape like Mr. Brennan, I have Mr. Doyle sit on the yellow sofa. The kitchen wall obstructs my view of the room Aiden disappeared into, but hearing a bit of a commotion, I quickly shout, "Everything okay in there?"

Just as I finish voicing my concern, out walks Aiden, not a hair out of place. In contrast, Mr. Brennan looks dishevelled as he attempts to break the charmed handcuffs that force him to follow behind Aiden.

Smiling at me, Aiden explains, "Don't worry, I was just explaining to our guest here why it's rude not to greet company properly. I'm sure these two will be all ears for our questions now, won't you, boys?"

"We ain't got nothing to say. Isn't that right, Doyle?" Mr. Brennan practically dislocates his wrists trying to escape at the same time Mr. Doyle shouts, "It wasn't me! It was all him!"

"What the feck! Now you've done it. Nothin'll save you, not even Chief. You're a right two shoes in the grave!" Brennan yells in Doyle's face, spit flying in his anger.

"Well, now that we've got a confession out of the way, why don't you tell us the truth and the Council might be lenient," I say as I share an eye roll in Rowan's direction. Yeah, that will happen… Never!

At the promise of leniency, with a last-ditch effort to save himself, Mr. Brennan starts spilling his secrets without care. "No one was supposed to get hurt. We were just trying to prove a point, stand our ground. He promised."

"And who is this he you keep speaking of? Don't be shy now," Aiden starts questioning, quickly taking on the routine of good cop versus bad cop. If you can't tell, I'm the good cop, unfortunately. Not my choice ;)

"I…I… can't say. No matter what you promise, his threats are much more real. I'd be dead before the sun sets. I can't tell you anything anyway. I never actually met him. There was a different messenger every time. Kept sayin' I'd join the inner circle when I proved myself worthy."

Just as Mr. Brennan finishes talking, I startle at the sound of Mr. Doyle. Hearing his hiccuped gasps and choked sobs, likely having a nervous breakdown now that he's been caught, we all look towards him. That's when he lifts his head, a wild look in his eyes, anger transforming his features. The sobs we thought racked his shoulders morph into laughter as he murmurs, "Mr. Brennan, you think Mr. A will let you in? You don't stand a chance. You're just a tool, a pawn. A failure." His breathing grows more frantic as he leans forwards, eyes burning with a mix of fury and desperation. "You'll never be part of what's coming. But I will be. I'm the one who brought him back, not you. If anyone should be allowed in, it's me."

He falls quiet for a moment, his breath ragged, before adding in a near-whisper, "But you're all in it now. Deep, deep trouble. There's no turning back. You'll all learn what that means soon enough… and it won't be pretty." His words hang in the air like a dark promise, thick with tension and dread.

"Who did you release? What's going to happen?" Maeve's voice is laced with concern as she tries to decipher Doyle's crazed rant.

Laughing manically once more, he shouts, "The Veil was never meant to be a permanent thing. I was there when Flynn's Granda signed those laws. That fool thought it'd be enough to protect his precious Stars, but, oh, how wrong he was, and now you're all going to pay, pay, PAY!"

Fear flashes across Brennan's face as he attempts to hide behind Aiden. I think he might've even wet his pants a little there.

"You're right bonkers! Two innocent boys died because you have a bone to pick about the Veil? Are you serious? You're on the council for crying out loud. All it would've taken was a few meetings and a town vote!" Rowan shouts from where she stands, her body shaking in anger. "People in Balie na Muintir looked up to you for paving the way to a better community and the promise of equality. I… I used to look up to you." Rowan hangs her head as if ashamed to even admit it.

Immediately, Declan stands beside her, giving Rowan small comforting pats on the back.

Saving Rowan from her downward spiral of thoughts, I tell Aiden, "We need to call this into the council and let them know we need a pickup from Príosún Fear Marbh over in Creevan to hold them before their trials are set."

With a nod, Aiden grabs his notepad and jots down a quick note before handing it off to Declan. "Get this information to Ms. Flynn as quickly as you can and tell her to make a few calls before coming down."

With a determined look, Declan disappears. While we wait, Aiden finishes conducting a quick holding spell as well as a silencing charm to keep them both from bickering at one another.

Luckily, just half an hour later, Auntie Cait comes storms in with a fully armed Creevan Bastille Brigade, her power pouring out at us in waves. Catching sight of her trusted employee and friends, her face contorts in a mixture of grief and anger. "YOU!"

Raising her hands, golden ropes of electricity lasso around both men as a small rush of electricity rushes towards them. The guards make quick work of grabbing the now-sleeping Mr. Brennan and Mr. Doyle as another two guards open a portal that will lead to their new home.

With them gone, Auntie Cait takes a calming breath before coming towards us with a hug. "I'm so glad you're all okay. I got a call from a Scriptorium employee named Declan and came as soon as the Brigade could spare a few guards to portal to me. I can't believe they'd do such a thing, after all the things we've been through together. I thought we shared the common goal of protecting our residents. Good work on closing this case, girls!"

"We're glad you got here when you did. Unfortunately, Headmaster Doyle and Mr. Brennan are only puppets in this game. Our killer is still on the loose, but we're closer than ever. We all need to be careful now though, especially you! No more late nights at the office. Right home and to bed from now on!" I explain to her with increasing urgency as Rowan nods in agreement.

"Please, girls, it makes my heart happy to know you still care, but Tara

Hall is my life, and I won't be scared away from what brings me such joy. If it puts your minds at ease, I'll finish my work from home."

"From what Mr. Doyle confessed, he has a bone to pick with your Granda and the Réalt. I'm hoping we stopped any plans he had, but just promise you'll call from now on when you make it home," Rowan pleads as she grasps Auntie Cait's hands.

"How about we have dinner tomorrow? We can talk some more and it'll ease your worries about me being alone. Plus, it feels like I haven't seen you both in forever, and while we're making plans, why don't you have your friends come too? I'd love to meet the people that make you girls so happy." Auntie Cait pats the top of Rowan's hand and gives us a wink as if the last few minutes never happened.

As she touches Rowan's hands, though, a faraway look crosses Rowan's face. Before I can think more about it, her eyes return to normal, and they quickly meet mine with a look of concern that screams: We need to talk!

After packing into our car and promising to go to dinner tomorrow, we drop Auntie Cait safely back at her house. As soon as she locks the door behind her, Rowan rushes at me and grabs the keys from my hand before tossing them at Aiden, hitting him square in the chest.

Without a backwards glance, she yells, "You drive back to the office. Elodie needs to be able to pay attention while I talk to her!" With the urgency in Rowan's voice, Aiden and I don't even argue about him driving my car.

"Rowan, what's going on?" I say once she asks Maeve to take the front and pulls me into the backseat.

"I don't know how, but I think Aiden's magic allowed me to have a premonition or an emotional equivalent of one. All I know is one second I was holding Auntie Cait's hands and the next I felt this immense fear. I could hear her screaming…Then, she let go and it was like it never happened." With a frantic look, she directs her attention to Aiden, not even pausing to breathe. "I mean, is this even possible? Nothing's going to happen, is it?"

"Whoa, there. Relax, Rowan. Take a deep breath in on my count or you're going to pass out," Declan says to her right while resting his hand above hers, though he's a bit squished with Aisling to his left. Following his lead, she starts to calm down enough that Aiden can answer without worrying about her having a full-on anxiety attack.

"I've never heard of a sharing of powers that doesn't directly match the magical user's capabilities. Then again, no one has been known to share their abilities with so many. The powers you've acquired from me may be manifesting so they fit your unique genetic makeup. Have you had any other symptoms or felt different recently?"

"I don't know…Maybe? I feel a little more sluggish, but that could just be from overworking with this case. I also found a white hair this morning, which seemed a bit odd, but that could be explained away by the same thing or be a side effect of the charm we used while undercover. I was planning to ask Leila tomorrow."

"That sounds like a good idea. I wish I had the answers for you but believe it or not, there are some things even I don't know. That's saying a lot considering I'm pretty much a genius when it comes to all things magical." Aiden tries to lighten Rowan's mood, though I catch his look of concern in the rearview mirror.

Joining in, I hold her hand while trying to convince us both that everything will work itself out. "There's probably no need to worry."

20

WHISPERS OF WHAT'S TO COME

ELODIE

It had been almost two weeks since the night I dreamed of *her*—until she visited me on October 13th. Today is no different. I take in the dark and rotting landscape and instantly I know where I am as I watch the fog roll across the forest floor. She stands just out of reach, her long hair seemingly glowing in the moonlight. Much like before, there's an unworldly stillness to her. I'd tried to catch her once more the night before without success.

Accepting I may never reach her in my dreams, I stay put, fearing that if I attempt to cross the distance, she'll disappear. My bare feet sink into the mud as I wait for the all-too-familiar sound of her voice to break the quiet. Tonight's melody feels more urgent, her tone rising as she weaves a new song.

Hold close, hold tight, for the night grows near,
Where the winds whisper secrets you must not fear.
In silence, the truth is a sharpened knife—
What is unsaid could claim your life.

Hold fast to the light, keep close what you know,
For shadows will gather where the cold winds blow.
By hearth and by heart, don't let them stray,
For night brings the things you cannot say.

Hold fast, my darlings, to the light you know,
Keep close the ones who help you grow.
For shadows may come, and silence may call,
But love's the flame that will never fall.

Can I trust what this voice says? Rowan and I were only called that by one person… No, it can't be… Could it? "Mam? Is that you? Why are you in this dark place?" My heart aches to hear her reply, but all she does is sing.

My little ones, don't wander too far,
For the winds will lead you to places afar.
I've seen the road you've yet to walk,
Where silent eyes in the darkness stalk.

The past is a murmur, the future a sigh,
But in the stillness, you'll learn to fly.
I will be near, though you may not see,
For I am your echo, I am the breeze.

In a flash, the woman who I've chased through the woods races towards me, her face now inches from mine. Yet, I have no fear in my heart. Willow-the-wisps now surround us, bouncing off our arms as if trying to say, "I'm here, too!"

She smiles at me, her features a perfect reflection of my own. Tears spill freely down my cheeks as I take in the face of the woman who raised me for the first years of my life—the face I was starting to forget. The same woman Rowan and I have never stopped looking for. Her own eyes fill with unshed tears as she brushes a strand of my blue-tipped hair behind my ear and continues her song

After all this time, you've wondered, it's true,

Who's been beside you, watching you through.
I've been the shadow, the light in the dark,
The voice you've heard, the flicker, the spark.

I've been with you, love, from the very start—
Trust in my words, and quiet your heart.

In a flash of blinding blue light, I wake with a start. Rowan's cat, Shade, sits beside me on the bed. Her violet eyes seem to peer into my soul before she begins lazily cleaning her paws. Reaching up, I brush away the remnants of a stray tear, realizing it wasn't a dream. That, just maybe, these 'dreams' had been real all along.

-Elodie's Journal-

"Echoes of Her Love"

Entry #10: October 14th @ 3:00 AM

⁎)❍●((⁎

With the recent symptoms Rowan's been facing, I hesitate to add my problems to the never-ending list. But, I know if she'd been the one with these dreams, I'd want to know. With a determined nod, I clutch my journal and make my way to her room with Shade following closely behind. Knocking on her bedroom door, I quietly push it open at her groan. She slowly rubs the tiredness from her eyes and tries to remain awake long enough for me to talk.

"Sorry to wake you so early, I just really need to get something off my chest." I ease my way into it and watch as she becomes more alert. "I've been having these strange dreams. I used to have them as a child, but they started coming back the night of the murders. A woman's voice would sing to me about how we needed to be careful, that we needed to stick together. From what I found in some books at the library while Niamh was talking to us, it was clear it wasn't just a woman. It was a banshee." I whisper the last word, almost afraid that saying it aloud will make it true.

"Are you sure, sis? Maybe you've just been stressed out and are trying to

152

cope with everything that's been happening," Rowan suggests as she raises onto her elbows and clicks on her bedside lamp.

"I would've said the same, except tonight was different. Her voice was more clear, she called us…her darlings…" I flip to the last journal entry and hand it to her to read, though I don't need the book to confirm the words I'll never forget. "I didn't want to believe it at first, but then there she was staring right at me. It was Mam…She was beautiful, ethereal…I think she's been trying to help us all along. She seems worried. I don't know what everything means, but we need to watch each other's backs. I don't think she would have revealed herself otherwise." I exhale a long breath, feeling relieved at finally having someone to share this with.

Grabbing my arms, Rowan pulls me into a hug, her own tears hitting my shoulder. "Thank you for letting me be a part of this with you. We've searched for them for so long… I think a piece of me still hoped we'd see them again. Even if I never will, it's enough for me to know she's seen us grow up. As long as we have each other, I know everything will be okay."

Leaning back, I finally get a full glimpse of Rowan. Her hair, once a dark coal colour, is a pure silver that catches in the light. At the apparent shock and frantic look on my face, she laughs, but it quickly turns into a cough.

Rowan's voice drifts out, but it's not just hers—it's layered, like an echo of herself stretching across time. The sound swells in the air, shifting between tones. "Have I got another white strand?"

I blink, a chill creeping down my spine, before I answer, "A full head of them, Rowan." Her half-smile comes to a halt, "We need to see Leila, now!"

I rush towards my room to get dressed.

Scarab Emporium - 5:00 a.m.

Accompanying the early morning fog is a cold breeze. Huddled under the portico, Rowan and I both continue to knock on the Emporium's door in hopes that Leila is inside.

"Alright, I'm coming. This better be important!"

I sigh in relief despite Leila's stern announcement.

As she cracks the door open she continues, "What's going on— Rowan, are you okay?"

As I push Rowan forwards, she pulls off the hat she put on before leaving the house. A look of shock crosses Leila's face as she hides a gasp behind her hand.

"We're hoping you might be able to help," I say with a silent plea.

"Come in, come in! Tell me what's happened." Leila ushers us inside, the warmth instantly embracing us.

"We thought it was a side effect of the disguising spell or Aiden's magic…Now, we're not so sure. I've been feeling drowsy and a bit lightheaded, possible premonitions, and then there's my hair. Have you seen this happen before?" Rowan explains as Leila brings over a pot of freshly brewed tea.

"I've sold hundreds of those scarab charms throughout the years, and nothing like this has ever happened. There are a few curses that I know of that could be causing this. I just don't know how you were cursed in the first place. Let me go find the book, and I'll be right back." Rushing to the back office, she quickly reappears, an old-tome-like book held in her hands. Flipping through the pages, she stops when she finds the information we're looking for. "Okay, so it says here that the curse that can cause similar symptoms could include those of the Sidhe or the Fae transforming someone either as a reward or a punishment. There is also The Curse of the Cailleach which causes the individual to prematurely age and marks a change in one's fate."

"I've never encountered a Fae before, and the only thing that's old about me is my hair. I don't have one wrinkle. I won't get wrinkles, will I?"

"Hmm, not Fairies then…" Leila considers other possibilities, scanning the pages with ease. "How about banshees? Have you encountered any of those recently?"

"Not me personally, but Elodie was just telling me this morning that she's been having dreams where a banshee speaks to her. Elodie believes this banshee is none other than our missing Mam. That couldn't affect me though, right?"

"In that case, I can't think of why it'd only be affecting you if Elodie is the one having the dreams. It says here that banshees have deep ancestral ties, and they mark people who are linked to tragic or violent deaths or as a sign of mourning, causing a physical change as part of their power over life and death," Leila finishes reading.

"It could also explain your new gift of premonitions," I add, trying to help piece this mystery together.

"That still doesn't explain why you haven't had symptoms. I mean, we are twins, after all. If it runs in the family, wouldn't that make you a banshee, too?"

Leila cuts in as she continues to scan more pages. "Not necessarily. It appears this curse only passes to one person per generation. It says twins share a unique 'fated' bond where there's an unspoken bargain ensuring one is spared. If you're more in tune with your emotions, it might have made you more sensitive to your mother's ancestry and the traits a banshee carries. You might even have a stronger link to Tír na nÓg. If it's something that's passed down as a 'gift' it might mean something different than a banshee marking someone for death," Leila adds on in a hopeful tone.

"That's just great. Elodie was blessed with dreams while I have to live with silver hair for the rest of my life!"

Shaking my head at Rowan's well-deserved antics, I try to find out more from Leila. "I'm pretty new to the whole magic thing and finding out we have a magical ancestry but correct me if I'm mistaken: can't a curse be broken by a counter-spell?"

"You're not wrong, but assuming this was a gift there's not much I can do." Looking to Rowan, Leila adds, "Regarding your hair, you might be able to hide the effects by wearing your scarab charm. I can't promise it'll work forever, though. Banshee magic is ancient and unruly; there's never been a documented case of a living individual becoming one."

"I guess I'll just have to bring hats back into fashion." Rowan sighs in resignation. "Thanks for bringing us some clarity, though, Leila. I don't know what we would've done if you hadn't answered the door."

Trying to lighten the mood, Leila quips back with a laugh, "Maybe wait until eight when the shop actually opens?"

"Will do! Though, while we're here, I'd like to discuss the case. We've caught a break, and I don't want you to be shocked later on when word spreads. Apparently, Mr. Doyle and Mr. Brennan were accomplices in Rónán and Liam's deaths. Although we haven't found the mastermind orchestrating this all, I'm confident we'll find them soon."

With a look of disbelief, Leila gasps. "I can't believe it. Liam and I spoke regularly with Mr. Doyle while waiting for shipments. He lived so close to the docks and always seemed a bit lonely. I thought he was just trying to make conversation." She sniffles before adding, "Thank you for catching some of the culprits to blame for my Liam's death. May they rot in Príosún Fear Marbh."

As she wipes the building tears from her eyes, we watch as Leila jumps up and goes back to her office before returning to her chair, now holding a pile of old parchment in her hand. "Oh, I just remembered setting aside the order I said I'd look for. It took some searching, but I found a note in an old children's book on the top shelf of my brother's closet… There were letters he'd written to Aisling. I was hoping you could pass them along to her. I think my brother would want her to have them."

As she hands me the letters addressed to our friend, I give her a grateful smile and tuck them safely away in my inner coat pocket.

"In terms of the receipt, it was a bit cryptic for Liam's usual writing. Then again, he was becoming more and more paranoid. I guess he had a good reason for that, in the end. It took some time, but I finally pieced it together with the help of Niamh down at the Scriptorium. Turns out Rónán did contact my brother. He'd been hoping to purchase a Tyet, which is a Protective Knot also known as the Knot of Isis. It's a very powerful and ancient symbol of protection back in Egypt, said to shield a person from both physical danger and spiritual threats. From the looks of it, my brother received a shipment for it and completed the transfer to Rónán the Wednesday before their deaths."

"I wonder if this has anything to do with the hagstone being kept at Tara Hall. Maybe our bright and shining star knew something and needed to protect himself. The only question now is, where did the Tyet go? It wasn't at the scene or in his room." Rowan voices her concerns.

With a visible shiver that runs through her body, Leila shares her own fears. "That might be the real problem here. The Tyet protects from dark magic in the hands of someone like Rónán. If the killer has it now, they could corrupt it to use it as a way to absorb life forces or magnify the malicious intent of their hagstone. For our sake, I hope that Tyet is lost to us all."

Danu's PI - 6:23 a.m.

Making a quick stop at the house for Rowan's charm and what she said was a more fashionable hat in case the charm stops working, we get to the office just in time to open the door for Aisling and Maeve.

"Morning, gals. I hope you were able to catch up on some sleep. We've got another long day ahead of us. Oh, and don't forget that Auntie Cait is expecting us all for dinner."

"I can't wait! I've heard all about her famous Irish Apple Cake and I've been dying to try some. By the way, what's with the hat, Rowan?"

"Trust me, you don't want to know. It's a long story of my ancestors dooming me for eternity and I don't think we'll have enough time to explain before we have to walk over to Aiden's dungeon of pain."

With a shrug from Aisling and Maeve, likely thinking Rowan's just being her dramatic self, we grab our water bottles before heading across the street.

Like the previous times we've trained, Aiden is waiting in the training room. Looking around, I can tell he's added some agility and strength exercises to our lessons, but more are now focused on hand-eye coordination and target practice for the daggers he gifted us.

Declan sits on one of the long metal desks, waiting to continue his role of sideline cheerleader. "Looking fierce and ready to kick arse this morn', ladies! You'll be pro's in no time." He cheers as we each find a station to start at.

At the sound of Aiden's metal whistle, we begin our first of five stations. Since there are only four of us, the last station with the targets will be completed as a group. Every ten minutes, we take turns running through cones, lifting weights, boxing, and completing memorization drills. We're fluid, fast, and have no hesitation. By the time it's 7:50, we're all out of breath.

"Alright, ladies, time to hone your dagger skills. For the next ten minutes, I want you to use what you've learned in the drills today to see how many times you can hit your target's bullseye. Your daggers have been spelled to return to their owner once thrown, so there'll be no need to run into firing territory, and, in a real fight, it can be an asset that allows you to keep distance between you and your enemy." With a blow of his whistle, he shouts, "Begin!"

Behind us, Declan cheers us on.

Taking a few meditative breaths to calm my racing thoughts, I focus on my task and the target ahead of me. With a steady hand, I aim and release the blade with a sharp flick of my wrist like Aiden taught us. I watch in anticipation as the dagger spins through the air and hits the centre with a satisfying thud.

"You go, sis! You'll be slaying monsters in no time with that precision." Rowan joins in my excitement.

⁌ ⁚) ● (⁚ ⁍

"Am I awful if I say I actually enjoyed today's training? Though he's bumped up the number of reps, I can tell my strength is improving daily! I even managed to hit the target 7 out of 10 times." Maeve's excitement is infectious as she mimes throwing her dagger.

Just as we finish laughing at her antics, the bell above the front door chimes, alerting us to company. As we move to greet the new arrival, we're met with the familiar face of Saoirse dressed in athletic wear and a scabbard that holds an intricate greatsword. The red leather wrap on the hilt act as proof of her time serving as a Knight.

Upon spotting us, she waves before exclaiming, "Morning, girls. I hope you don't mind, but Aiden stopped by the cafe for breakfast and was telling me about your training. I figured Lennon could finish setting up and I could offer my services here. You're now looking at your new weapons trainer! Don't worry, I've brought some sweets we can eat once we've finished."

As she motions for us to follow her outside, we grab our daggers from our desks and meet her out the front where her car is still running. "I know you girls have been training indoors, but if you're ever going to be ready, you need to face the elements. Today, we'll be training near the docks."

After piling into her small metallic purple VW Beetle, Saoirse makes quick work of navigating the busy streets and somehow avoids hitting any red lights.

Finding the stunned look on my face, she lets out a quick burst of laughter before assuring me she doesn't have the powers to control traffic lights. "I'm just extremely lucky; it runs in the family. Even Lennon was shocked when we first met. It comes in handy when I have to get across town to make a delivery, though."

Parking by the dock, we follow her to the first empty docking bay. "This is my favourite spot to work on balance. Most fighters will tell you to hone your strength, but women of your stature need to focus on speed and agility. Before you can master this, though, you must first ensure you can stay on your feet in a fight." She pauses, eyeing us closely. "Has Aiden taught you forms?"

At our nod, she grabs the rope tied to the dock and pulls the attached platform closer. "It's floating, so it'll shift with your weight. When I announce a new form, you'll switch places with someone else. Keep your stance grounded—if you're not stable, you'll end up in the water." She gives us a wry smile, but there's a sharpness to her words. "I recommend talking to each other as you go through the forms. The more you communicate, the more in sync you'll become. By the end of this session, you should be able to move together without making the platform tip too much."

Her eyes flick over us, appraising our readiness. "Let's get started."

+)) ● ((ꞏ

"I never thought I'd say this, but I think I miss Aiden. My legs are so sore it feels like I'm still on that platform," Maeve says as she drops to the dock, lying on her back as she rings water from her shirt.

Laughing, Saoirse leans over to ruffle her hair before wrapping the remaining rope around the dock cleat. "Don't worry, you'll be stronger in no time, and the disorientation will wear off in a few seconds. You all did amazing. It took me more than double the amount of tries before I stopped falling in. How about we have those treats now?"

"I take it all back. I love you. No matter how much I beg Aiden, he refuses to compliment or reward us. He says it'd just go to our heads, but I think he's just afraid we'll surpass him," Maeve adds with a forlorn look.

Saoirse lets out a small, knowing laugh. "Well, you're not wrong. Aiden's always been able to maintain the tough love act, and he's not one to give up leadership easily. Don't let his macho attitude fool you, though. He's not as bad as he wants people to believe. Once you've earned his trust and loyalty, he'd do just about anything for you. He wanted me to keep it a secret, but you should know that Aiden came to me this morning asking me to take over your training because he knew he'd pushed you about as far as he could. He's a good fighter, but he can't teach you what I know. I've spent years training with combat masters, and even longer in battle. As a great-granddaughter of one of the toughest clan chiefs, it was a rough blow to my Da when he learned I was a girl. It's tradition to pass my great-granda's sword down to the next male heir to be inducted as a Knight of Fàil. Since the day I could lift a wooden training stick, I set out to prove him and the rest of my family wrong." Holding up the scabbard hanging from her belt loop, a faraway look crosses her face. "Oh, and what a sweet victory that was," she adds, almost as if speaking to herself.

There's a moment of silence as her words hang in the air. I hadn't realized it before, but something about her story resonates with me. Aiden's been harder on us than I thought, not just because he's trying to prepare us, but because he knew he was running out of tricks to teach.

Maeve raises an eyebrow, a half-smile playing at her lips. "So, my brother finally admits he's not perfect, then?"

Saoirse grins. "Aiden? Not perfect? Oh, I'm sure he'd rather eat chocolate than admit to that. But, yeah, he came to me because he knew you girls needed more."

A strange wave of gratitude washes over me for Aiden's willingness to step aside and let us grow. Maybe he's not the hard-headed, prideful man I'd always thought. Maybe there's more to him.

"Alright, I'll get you girls back to the office. I'm sure Lennon's given away over a dozen free meals by now—the man's a wonderful baker, but he's a real bleeding heart. Plus, you have a busy schedule catching that killer."

21

BEFORE THE LIGHT FADES
ELODIE

Danu's PI -10:00 a.m.

We've been training practically all day, but I can't say that Saoirse's lesson hasn't helped us hone our fighting abilities. Sure, my legs feel like they're about to fall off, and my shoulders are sore from keeping my arms outstretched for balance, but I'm excited for our next lesson. It's a bonus that she's one of the coolest women I've met, other than Auntie Cait.

Catching movement outside the window, I watch as Declan and Aiden make their way over to our office. He quickly greets us before questioning us all on what Saoirse taught us at the docks, looking a little sad that he and Declan weren't invited.

As we fill him in on our eventful morning, he looks taken aback at our enthusiasm. "I see how it is: out with the old, in with the new. In all seriousness, though, I'm glad you could get something out of her experience." As Maeve hobbles across the room, Aiden gives a quick laugh before adding, "And from the looks of it she didn't take it easy on you."

"Ha, ha, you're so funny. Did you come over here to laugh at us?" Maeve retorts in mock anger.

"Thanks for the reminder. I come bearing good news. While you were training, Ms. Flynn sent a note informing us that they've scheduled the trial. The Council has agreed to move theirs to the front of the line. It should take place at the end of the month."

"That's great. The sooner they're sentenced, the better." Aisling tone brokers no room for sympathy.

"There's also some bad news. I was reading Ms. Flynn's note when I noticed something strange. The note I received has some subtle differences from the penmanship on the note Ms. Maguire found on her desk. I scanned a copy and sent it to your email, I was hoping you could use your projector to take a closer look."

"Great idea! Let's check it out now," I say, excited for another possible lead.

I power on the projector whilst Rowan works to bring up the image and the girls make quick work of lowering the blinds.

Examining the side-by-side photos now spanning the wall we keep blank just for this reason, we try to spot the differences Aiden spoke of.

Walking over to the wall, Aiden starts pointing out his suspicions. "If you look at the letter Ms. Flynn sent me this morning," he says, indicating the first note, "you'll see in words like 'letter', 'later', 'well', and of course, her name, her 'L' is written in a very distinct way. From my analysis of the second note, this trait is not an exact match."

He pauses for a moment, studying both letters before continuing. "I learned about this when I was looking into handwriting analysis for an earlier case. It's common for people trying to forge someone else's writing to make this exact mistake. When you're attempting to replicate someone's handwriting, especially under pressure or without practice, it's easy to overlook the smaller, almost subconscious details. If I had to wager a guess, I'd say Ms. Maguire's note was written by none other than the Slayer. He couldn't have them interrupting his plans by having a meeting so close to the Academy. This also means that he either knows the council's schedule through the help of his accomplices or he's been stalking them for some time."

"In that case, there might be more to worry about than I thought. Let's add this to our evidence file and we can ask Auntie Cait about it tonight. Perhaps, she'll have a few letters on hand we can use to confirm whether this really is a forgery and we can also find out who has access to the classrooms," I suggest, setting up a game plan while we impatiently wait for 5 o'clock to arrive.

Dearest Aiden,

I hope this letter finds you well. I'm writing to let you know that the remaining Council has petitioned for Mr. Doyle and Mr. Brennan's trial to commence at the end of the month. Luckily, they've agreed, and I have confirmation that they have been moved to top priority.

I look forward to seeing you all tonight.

With affection,
Ms. Flynn

Good Afternoon Ms. Maguire,

I hope this letter finds you well. I'm sorry for the late notice, however, the Council meeting tonight will be cancelled. Thank you for your understanding.

With affection,
Ms. Flynn

+)●((+

"Welcome, welcome everyone! Come in before you catch a cold. The weatherman says we've got even harsher winds rolling in with the tides if you can believe it—something about the full moon." She waves her arm to usher us in before firmly closing the cold out. Bending down to give Shade a scratch on the neck with a quick 'coo' of an introduction, she notes, "The beef stew is just about ready. If you want to gather at the table I'll just be a few minutes."

Before she turns Aiden announces, "Thanks for having us it smell's amazing in here. Maeve and I brought you our Mam's famous homemade shortbread. We hope you enjoy it as much as we do with a cuppa."

She smiles, her eyes twinkling with affection. "Well, now, you've really made my day. Homemade shortbread? That sounds like heaven."

Declan starts to head towards the smell of the food when Auntie Cait's voice stops him. "You must be Declan, the boy from the library." Before we can ask how she can see him, she adds, "Now, now, you think I haven't seen you, dear Aiden, walking around town holding conversations when nobody is about." With a wink in his direction, she says, "Plus, I have become friends with your Mam since you and the girls started working together." Directing her conversation back to Declan she continues, "I grew curious after you called me last night about the case, so I made sure I took a stop by the library this afternoon. Niamh was telling me how you were visible thanks to the Scriptorium wards, so I figured there must be a spell I can add to the charms here."

I watch as Declan takes in Auntie Cait's words, a soft smile pulling at his lips. "Thank you… I'm grateful," he says quietly. "Your kindness means more than you know. It's not every day you meet someone who cares as much as you do."

Auntie Cait chuckles and waves him off with a playful roll of her eyes, but the warmth in her gaze is undeniable. She doesn't acknowledge the sentiment directly, but it's clear she's touched. "Oh, don't go getting all sentimental on me, Declan. You'll have me blushing," she teases. "You just happen to remind me of a boy I used to know. Now, head on in before the food gets cold!"

After showing everyone to the dining room, I follow her into the kitchen, Rowan right behind me. The place smells so warm and comforting—like home. "Do you need any help?" I ask, resting against the counter, watching her stir the stew

She gives me a quick glance, smiling over her shoulder. "I'm good, love. Just set the table, will you? Oh, and grab a bowl of milk for Miss Shade she's quite the lovely addition to the family."

Rowan steps forwards, grabbing a wooden spoon from the counter and stealing a quick taste from the pot. Auntie Cait swats at her playfully. "Oi, that's not for you, yet! You'll spoil your dinner!'"

Rowan grins, wiping her mouth dramatically, "I'm just helping you out. You wouldn't want them to have a mediocre meal."

Auntie Cait shakes her head, laughing. "Right, right, as if you're a big help." She turns back to the stew with a mock grumble, but I can tell she's enjoying the banter.

Her stirring slows, and the kitchen falls into a quiet moment, the soft clink of utensils and the crackle of the stew simmering the only sound. I glance at Rowan, who's busy fiddling with the saltshaker, then turn back to Auntie Cait, my voice taking on a more serious edge.

"Auntie Cait," I start, choosing my words carefully, "have you noticed anything strange at the academy lately? Like, people who don't belong or… maybe someone following you?"

She stops what she's doing and raises an eyebrow, clearly sensing the shift in my tone. I take a deep breath and press on. "When we met with Ms. Maguire, she gave us a note she said was from you, dated the day of the murders. But today, Aiden brought over the note you sent us, and it's obvious someone is forging your handwriting. They're trying to mess with the Council, trying to make it look like you were involved in something you weren't."

The room feels heavier now, the playful energy from earlier slipping away. Rowan stops mid-movement, her eyes flicking between Auntie Cait and me.

"Someone's been using my handwriting?" she repeats, her voice low, almost a whisper. Then, as if processing the weight of it, she exhales slowly and turns back to the stove, her hands steady but her voice suddenly stern. "You're sure?"

I nod, my stomach knotting. "I'm sure. Whoever's behind this isn't just trying to frame you—they're using your influence to get what they want. We don't know why, yet."

Taking a slow breath, as though weighing everything carefully, Auntie Cait begins to speak again. "I'm the only one with full access to the classrooms at the academy. I've placed wards and detection spells on each room to keep them locked when there's no class or Professors present. The spells track anyone who enters or tries to tamper with the doors, so if someone's been sneaking in, it would've triggered a warning in the system."

She pauses, her brow furrowing. "All staff are logged in through the magical system, too. If it was someone like Mr. Brennan, the entries would show up. I'll go through the logs tomorrow. If there's been any unknown entries or breaches, it'll be clear."

Rowan shifts, her eyes narrowing as she thinks. "But are there any ways around the wards? I mean, is there anything someone could use to get past them without triggering the system?"

Auntie Cait doesn't miss a beat, shaking her head. "The only thing that could bypass the wards would be a hagstone, but that's locked up in the school's safe." She looks up at us then, her expression serious. "Even with the hagstone, though, it wouldn't be enough to break through my spells unless someone had something powerful to amplify it. A really strong source of magic, like an artifact or a spellcaster with a lot of power behind them."

Rowan and I exchange a worried glance. The mention of a powerful artifact like that of the missing Tyet hangs in the air between us.

I clear my throat, trying to shake off the tension. "We don't want to ruin the rest of dinner. We'll stop by tomorrow to go over everything. For now, let's get everything to the table before they eat all the appetizers."

Rowan nods in agreement, relieved to leave the heavier conversation for later. We grab the rest of the food and head towards the dining room, where the others are chatting and laughing. The table is already laid out with Auntie Cait's traditional Irish appetizers; small, golden-brown sausages, crusty bread with soft butter, and little bowls of creamy mashed potatoes with chives. The smell of freshly baked bread and hearty stew wafts through the air, and, for a moment, everything feels normal again.

We set everything down, and the conversation picks back up, warm and familiar. Everyone digs in, the jovial chatter filling the room. Auntie Cait starts with one of her classic stories, her voice rich with nostalgia. It's always something about Rowan or I growing up— those little moments only family truly remembers. As she talks, the stories flow, one sparking another, and soon everyone is chiming in with their own. Laughter spills over, filling the room with warmth. The evening flows easily, and, for tonight, the worries and mysteries outside fade into the background.

As the meal winds down and the table clears, Auntie Cait rises with a flourish. "Alright, enough of that now. Time for something sweet!" She ducks into the kitchen, returning moments later carrying a warm, golden-brown Irish apple cake. The unmistakable scent of cinnamon and baked apples fills the room.

"I believe this was requested," she says with a wink, setting the cake down in the centre of the table. "Made just like my Nana used to." Her eyes twinkle as she slices generous portions for everyone. "Go on, try it. You'll be glad you did."

I take a bite before anyone else, and it's perfect. The cake melts in my mouth— rich, buttery, exactly what I needed. I glance at Rowan, who's already going for a second slice.

"You're going to be in a food coma by the time we leave," I say, my voice light.

Rowan just smiles, her eyes half-closed in contentment. "Worth it."

Across from me, Maeve takes a bite, her eyes widening with surprise. She begins a little happy dance in her seat, her feet tapping and her shoulders swaying with joy. The room quiets as we watch her, and Aiden, Aisling, and Declan chuckle, shaking their heads at her infectious enthusiasm. Maeve looks up at Auntie Cait, beaming.

"Ms. Flynn, this is incredible," she says, almost breathless.

Auntie Cait smiles back at her, her eyes warm with affection. "Ah, you can call me Auntie Cait, now. We're family, whether by blood or choice." She gives a playful wink before adding, "And you're not getting out of it, mind you. You're stuck with me."

Maeve's cheeks flush, and she nods eagerly. "Right, Auntie Cait. Thank you for this. It's perfect."

The room settles into a peaceful silence as everyone continues eating, the weight of the day lifting with every bite. Auntie Cait looks around at us, her gaze full of contentment.

"I'm so happy you could make it," she says, her voice gentle but firm as she ensures everyone gets a *see you soon* hug, as she likes to call them. "It's been far too long. I want you to know that you're always welcome here."

As we head for the door, Auntie Cait's voice follows us, love shining through. "Don't be strangers now, ya hear!"

A calm warmth settles over me, and I glance at Rowan, her posture already more relaxed than when we arrived.

I nudge her gently as we make our way down the walkway. "See? Everything will work itself out," I whisper, thinking back to her earlier worries about Auntie Cait.

Rowan smiles, a small sigh escaping her. "Yeah, I think you're right, sis."

But as we walk towards the car, a heavy thought settles in my chest, pressing down on me like a weight I can't shake. The peace of this moment feels fragile, like the calm before a storm. The truth is, I feel that everything's about to change. And I don't think we'll be ready for it.

MR. A

The cold night air does nothing to quell the burning anger fuelling me— my sole purpose. I watch as they smile and laugh as they make their way to their vehicle. From my hiding spot, I watch as she waves goodbye from the doorway. How sweet. Yes, say your goodbyes, *sionnach glic*. Those will be the last you ever speak.

The thing halts, its gaze flicking in my direction, ears twitching as if sensing my presence before it lets out a low, menacing hiss. The girls usher it forwards, unaware of the danger I present. The cold stone of the artifact in my hand reassures me. They won't see me. Not yet. Not before I'm ready.

I chuckle under my breath. They think they know who I am, that they can stop me! Little do they know I've only just begun. I was so sure they'd see the presents I left and start to understand, but they're no smarter than those paraisítí who tried to protect them before. Look where that got them. Look where it's gotten everyone else who has tried to stand in my way.

I watch as the group disappears down the street and she makes her way back inside. All alone? Fearless as always. Finishing my masterpiece, my pulse quickens, and my thoughts quiet. A smile tugs at the corner of my lips as I rise from my crouch and begin to walk. There's a cold shiver that runs up my spine as the wards stir as if they sense me, trying to push me back. But nothing—no ward or charm—will stop me now. Not now that I've found my way back.

"Ah, how delightful. It's been far too long… But don't worry, darling. I'm here now."

22

THE SHADOWS SHIFT

ROWAN

The wooden planks of Auntie Cait's house are cold against my bare feet, though in my pursuit I barely notice. I giggle as I chase Elodie down the stairs. The black mask and the pillowcase we've made into a money bag she's slung over her shoulder adds to her villainous look for our game of Catch the Culprit. Our little feet cause the steps to creak as we rush down the stairs, Elodie speeding up whenever my fingers graze her hair. Just as I reach the bottom step and prepare to lunge, my vision shifts—Elodie is no longer there. I feel myself grow taller and I have to catch myself before I fall to the floor as my centre of gravity shifts.

I brace myself on the stair banister and scan the room. Just ahead, I watch as Auntie stares out the window, a lone tear tracking down her cheek. Immediately, I sense that this isn't a memory, though I'm not certain yet what it is I'm seeing. She looks as she did when we left the house last night, only there's no joy lighting her face. She seems almost resigned as she watches the entryway begin to glow with the dark golden hue of her powers.

I creep closer, but it's clear she's not aware of my presence. I reach out to comfort her, but my sight shifts once more as a burst of light makes me close my eyes. The transition seems instantaneous, but my stomach has a harder time catching up as it gives a silent protest and my muscles contract.

Taking a deep breath, I brush the white wisps of hair from my eyes as I attempt to peer through the pitch dark that now surrounds me. The complete stillness is unnatural, and I struggle not to choke on the ink-like powers. With my feet still bare, I can feel a thick stream of liquid gently swishing against my ankles as I walk, and the soles of my feet become difficult to lift the farther I go.

"Auntie Cait?" I whisper, my voice echoing around me as I hear what sounds like the pitter-patter of water from a faucet.

Reaching out, my hand brushes against stone and layers of dirt that hint I'm somewhere underground. I lift my hand, ready to call out again when I realize the same bag little Elodie had been holding in her hands is now gripped tightly in mine. However, it's no longer painted with the black smudge of a dollar sign drawn in coal and it's the source of the dripping noise. I bring it closer to my face to try and see it through the darkness.

A distinct copper smell hits my nose first as my eyes adjust. Grazing my fingertips across the cotton fibers, the warm substance coats my fingertips and leaves a sticky residue. I gasp and drop it, the bag becoming submerged by the dark pool of liquid I've been walking in. The liquid that I now realize is blood. In my panic, I rush ahead, the long hallway seemingly endless. Suddenly, I watch as a dark figure turns towards me, their red eyes peering through the dark.

The shadow's smile is menacing as its shoulders begin to shake with laughter. "Poor little Banshee…all alone."

Instinctively, I reach for my dagger that I've started to wear on a leg strap, courtesy of Leila, but my fingers brush against the fabric of my pyjamas. I freeze, my blood turning cold at the sound of the voice. It's not just mocking—it's taunting, like he's savouring each word, drawing it out like a blade, of which I desperately wish I had right about now.

A laugh spills from the figure's throat, its sound warped and dissonant, like nails scraping across glass. "You think this is a game. You think you're safe, don't you?"

The laugh grows, unsettling and disjointed, as if it's coming from all directions at once. "You're not. Not anymore."

I try to move, to run, but my legs feel like stone, as if the weight of the darkness is pulling me down. The shadow steps closer, its smile widening, sharp and cruel, like it knows something I don't—something that makes the air feel colder, thicker, almost suffocating.

"Hurry, Banshee," it whispers, its voice crawling into my skin, twisting deep in my chest. "We wouldn't want to disappoint Mother, now, would we?"

I jolt awake, cold beads of sweat making my hair cling to the back of my neck. "Elodie!"

Springing up from my bed, I run to Elodie's room. Barging through her door, I grab her shoulders to shake her awake.

"Elodie, something's not right! I had a dream or one of those weird premonitions, but I think Auntie Cait's in danger. The Slayer was there and somehow, he knew what I am. We have to go, now!"

Not waiting to ask questions, Elodie reacts as I knew she would and we both rush down the stairs, quickly grabbing our coats as we go. We make it outside but before we reach the car, Aiden and Declan are pulling into our driveway, the car's tires screeching to a stop.

"Are either of you hurt? What's wrong?" Declan says as he materializes in front of us before Aiden can even put the car in park.

"There's no time to explain! Auntie Cait might be in danger," I respond. Aiden pushes the passenger door open, the seat already pushed down. That's all the invitation we need to slide in the backseat as I yell to him, "Take a lesson from Elodie and put the pedal to the metal."

With a slight flush to her cheeks and a bit out of breath, Elodie asks, "Not that I'm not grateful, but why are you here?"

He glances in the review mirror, meeting our eyes for a brief moment as if needing to reassure himself that we're both unharmed. His grip tightens on the steering wheel, knuckles going white before he exhales a shaky breath and explains. "Declan and I were at the office when I felt extreme fear coming from one of you through the bond. I've learned to recognize when you're having a nightmare, which, frankly, you two seem to have a lot." He lets out a short, frustrated laugh. "Something seemed off tonight, though. I would've just sent Declan, but I needed to make sure you were both safe."

We make it to Auntie Cait's house just as dawn breaks, the sun just beginning to paint the sky in a softer shade of yellow over the hills. Not waiting for Aiden to open the door for us, Elodie snakes her arm around the passenger seat to grab the handle. Rushing across the front lawn, I send a silent prayer to any god who will listen.

ELODIE

Rowan and I knock on the door in unison. Our knuckles just graze the wood as we try to calm down. We peer through the glass pane on either side, half-expecting Auntie to round the corner with a warm smile, greeting us with a "Back so soon, my loves?" But when a full minute passes, I strike the door harder, my fist pounding louder, more insistent. Rowan shakes the doorknob, the frantic rattle of the metal cutting through the silence. Our breaths quicken, knots of unease tightening our chests as we wait. Still, there's no answer.

I watch as Rowan's pupils widen, raw terror in her eyes as her fist comes down on the door. The sound of it reverberates through the silence. She hits it again, harder, and the door shudders in response. I don't hesitate slamming my shoulder into the door at the same moment. The frame rattles, but the door doesn't budge.

"Declan!" Rowan's voice is echoed, the pitch of her voice rising with her urgency. "Check the house! See if there's anyone else here!" Her eyes dart to me, filled with raw desperation as Declan disappears.

I turn to Aiden, my vision blurred as tears form, barely seeing him. "Please…" My voice cracks, barely a whisper, but it's just enough air to squeeze past my lips.

We strike again, harder this time, and the door finally yields under the pressure as Aiden adds his full weight. The frame groans, splinters of wood raining to the pavement as the door crashes open.

The house is eerily quiet, the only sound being Declan's voice as he yells, "Downstairs is all clear!" from the direction of the kitchen. Racing to the stairs that lead to the bedrooms, I watch as strands of Rowan's hair shift to white and back again, her fear over what we'll find making her lose control of the scarab charm.

As we make it to the landing, a light coming from the room at the end of the hall slows our steps. Unlike the rest of the doors, this one lies slightly ajar, inviting us to come closer. Aiden opens the doors nearest the stairs, checking no one is waiting to attack.

With no time to waste, Rowan and I head straight to Auntie's room. With a light brush of my fingers, the door creaks open. As we peer inside I hear Rowan's audible exhale as she sees Auntie Cait lying in bed.

"Auntie, did you take too much of that sleeping aid again? I thought you promised to try something more natural now that you're living alone. You know it's almost impossible to wake you. What if someone tried to break in" With a chuckle, Rowan adds, "I mean, we just did, and you're still oblivious."

When we still get no response, I move to stand beside the bed as Rowan hops on the mattress next to her. She looks serene with her white hair fanned out on the pillow in a halo of soft curls.

Rowan grabs her by the shoulders, shaking her gently, "Auntie?"

Reaching out to grab Auntie's hand, I gasp in surprise at the coldness of her skin. With the warm heat still circulating the room from the fireplace across the room and the pile of blankets wrapped around her, she should probably be sweating.

"Rowan…" The words catch in my throat. No, I refuse to think that way… She's just sleeping…

Though I hear Aiden's footsteps as he enters the room my eyes remain glued on Rowan. I watch as she continues to try to wake her, tears streaming down her face. I'd say I was likely a perfect reflection of her pain, but I was numb to the feeling of my tears starting to track down my cheek.

As if coming to realize what I'd been too afraid to voice, I watch in helpless horror as Rowan's hair turns as white as bone, her skin paling, and her eyes begin to glow with an otherworldly light as she opens her mouth in a silent cry. Then sound rips through her, an inhuman wail, so piercing and full of raw, unbearable sorrow that it feels like the earth itself trembles beneath her. It isn't just grief; it's the wail for a soul lost to the void, a banshee's cry of mourning. Though I instinctively know that Rowan's still there beneath it all, I fear that her curse… her gift, might eventually take her too from me.

aiden

I felt the stillness of the house as soon as we entered. There had been no sound of alarm from the charms I'd felt only hours ago, though the girls didn't seem to notice through their panic. Hearing Declan clear the first floor, I rush to follow them as they run up the stairs. I'd thought they'd stay put until I cleared the upper bedrooms, but I should've known better.

As I enter the last room, I watch as Rowan kneels on the bed beside her Auntie. Using my Súil, I let the room shift in colours, the process taking mere seconds from years of practice. Though the girls' auras shift between dark blues and purple, the usual red and golden hues are absent from Caitriona.

A sudden piercing scream rattles the windows. The glass shatters on the ones along the back wall, and the room brightens, no longer shielded from the sun that now sits high in the sky. Covering my ears, I watch as tiny shards fly through the air, the jagged edges nicking our skin.

Drops of crimson trail from a cut on Rowan's cheek, mixing with her tears, a stark contrast against her pale skin and stark white hair. A pulse of deep blue continues to surround her. If I hadn't seen her transformation myself, I wouldn't have believed that she was the same woman. What is she? Rowan pulls her Aunt closer, hugging her still form and murmuring apologies.

Looking at Elodie, I notice she hasn't moved. Her tears are the only sign that she understands.

Moving from the doorway, I cross to where she sits on the floor. "Elodie?"

The sound of my voice breaks her trance. Her hands shoot forwards, clawing at the blankets that cocoon her Aunt.

"No, no, no. If it was him, he'd leave a message. Where's the message?" She pulls at the sleeves of Cait's nightshirt, her movements desperate as she searches for a clue—something physical to focus her grief and anger towards.

Her frantic jerks and pleading look tear at my soul. If I could rewind time, if I could give her back those last few moments with her Aunt just to see her smile again, I would. But I've known death since I first came into my powers. I've watched souls leave their physical bodies and search for the next path, their next journey beyond our world. I've also seen what happens when those souls are left in this world too long. How Declan had almost become something else, something dark. I could ask Declan to search for Cait's soul I know he'd do it in a heartbeat but she wouldn't be the same as they remembered, at least not forever.

Elodie sees it on my face before I can even speak. Without warning, she begins pounding at my chest, the blows coming fast but lacking any real strength. I let her, knowing I'm responsible for this new wave of pain, for crushing the last of her hope.

I enclose my hand around her wrists, stopping her from hurting herself, though she tries to wrestle free.

"I'm sorry," I say softly. "There's nothing that can be done."

"No," she sobs, shaking her head. "You're wrong. I have to find the message. It's my job to change the outcome, to bring justice to those who've been wronged. I can bring her justice. I just need to find it. If I can't even do that, what good am I? What good am I if I can't even protect the people I love?"

Her words pierce me, but I refuse to look away. She leans her head on my chest, her quiet sobs muffled by my coat. "We should've stopped this," she whispers. "There were so many warnings and we still let him slip through the cracks."

I lift her chin gently, making sure she meets my eyes. I need her to know that I mean every word I'm about to say. "You are everything good in this world. You help people others wouldn't even think to stop for. You're a better detective and person than I could ever hope of being." She looks at me, disbelieving, so I continue. "I didn't think twice about turning Ms. Sile away. I had an important case at the time, and I've seen how she holds her liquor. But you—you and Rowan—you didn't hesitate to take on her case. Even though it ended up just as I thought, you pursued every lead until the very end."

I look away for a moment, the weight of the memory pulling at me.

"I was so envious of your kindness towards her, the way the townspeople didn't hesitate to answer your questions because they like you, not because they fear you." I release a quiet laugh, a bit guilty as I confess, "I even had Declan make a copy of that case file… The Case of Missing Mittens. It's hanging in my office. I look at it every day to remind myself to show compassion for the people who need it most, even for those who don't ask."

When I turn back to her, I see the faintest trace of a smile tugging at the corner of her lips. I reach up to push a strand of hair that's stuck to her tear-stained face behind her ear, my voice low as I add, "You still have Rowan and the girls. You have Declan and the rest of the town ready to help if you ask, and, most importantly, you'll always have me. We'll stop him, and you'll get justice. But right now, you need to take a moment to grieve and to feel. Don't bottle your feelings and let them control your actions. Don't do this out of revenge. Do it because you're the same kind and caring detective who helped Ms. Sîle. The same person I aspire to be like every day. Don't let him win."

I promise myself that I'll help her search. Even if I have to tear this whole house apart, I'll help her find the answers she needs.

Noticing Rowan's sobs have quieted as well, I look up to see Declan has been comforting her. Knowing they're both okay, I finally release a slow, calming breath. With each inhale, I see Elodie trying to mimic me, trying to steady herself, to regain focus.

"A little better?" I ask, knowing full well it'll likely be months before they can fully process their grief.

Though tears still shine in her eyes, Elodie gives me a shaky smile and a determined nod.

With Rowan's help now that she's loosened her grip on Cait, we finally find it. The Ogham script is carved into the back of Cait's neck, and like Rónán and Liam, she holds a thorn and the same parchment found with Liam and Rónán in her hand. This time, the parchment is pressed tightly into Cait's grasp, her fingers curled around it in a way that's too perfect—unnaturally perfect. The paper is crisp, with not a wrinkle or crease in sight, like it had been placed moments ago. The Raven's mark—black and sharp—sits at the bottom of the note, but this time it doesn't feel like a symbol. It feels like a brand. For her.

With our mad dash to the house, none of us brought the proper investigative equipment. I grab the phone from the bedside table and call Doc, requesting that he bring a camera so we can capture the message and send it to Niamh for translation while we try to decipher the note.

1. Breathe. Just breathe.

Though more of a mantra than a list this time, the simple repetition of his words keeps me from spiralling any further. It'd taken Declan's soothing voice to pull me from the banshee's grasp. It'd been as though I was lost in a void, seeing, but not truly there. When I calmed down enough, I was grateful he didn't ask questions. I don't think I could've answered them, anyway.

Even with Doc here, I refuse to let her go. I'd been so sure Elodie was right, that everything was fine. But we were both wrong. The last parent we had left was now gone. When he asks us to gently roll Auntie Cait on her side so he can photograph the engraved words, Elodie helps me shift her. I grasp Auntie Cait's left hand to keep her from moving, sending out a silent apology to wherever her soul now resides.

My finger brushes something cold grasped in her other palm. I gently unclench her fingers, and a tiny gold key falls onto the mattress.

"Is that…what I think it is?" Elodie gasps, her voice a mix of disbelief and sorrow.

I nod, tears welling in my eyes once more. "She was thinking of us, even in her final moments. She must have tried to escape with the key or hide it for us to find before he…" My words trail off, too much left unsaid. Too many questions, and too much pain, for us to wander through the possibilities right now.

As Doc leaves the room to speak with Aiden, Elodie and I huddle around her one last time. Even in death, her beauty is apparent, her face a picture of serenity despite what she must have gone through. We dry our eyes, each of us vowing— to her, and to any god who might be listening—that we'll find him. No matter what it takes. Even if it costs us everything. Even if I lose myself in the process.

It isn't until late afternoon that we allow Aiden to inform the town of her passing. Elodie and I hold vigil, grieving in the few hours we have left with Cait's physical body before she becomes nothing but a memory. As Head of Council and the most powerful witch in town, her passing demands more than a funeral. It calls for a ritual, a sacred rite to ensure her soul crosses safely, to honour the life she led, and the role she played in this community.

Not long after, Doc returns to prepare Auntie for the ceremony, leaving the house with a crypt-like coldness that has emerged in her absence. After calls from Maeve and Aisling, and promises that we won't go through this alone, we agree to meet everyone in front of the office.

As the sun begins its slow descent, Elodie and I make our way there. The sky, painted in brilliant hues of pink and purple, feels as though it's mocking us— too bright, too vivid, as if the world refuses to be touched by our pain. The colours swirl above us, but all I can feel is the heaviness of our loss.

Aiden greets us last, his steps slow, giving us a few more seconds to linger and catch our breath. He hands each of us a lantern for the walk ahead. As we step forwards, the weight of the town's grief presses down on me with each step. The cobblestone streets are bathed in the soft glow of hundreds of lanterns—each one held by hands that tremble with sorrow. There's no need for words. Their presence, their silent solidarity, speaks more than anything ever could.

Each lantern is an offering, a beacon for Cait's spirit to follow as it journeys from this world to the next. But it's more than just light; it's a testament, a living tribute. Each one is the heart of a lesson she taught, a kindness she offered, a quiet strength that wrapped around the souls of the students, parents, and townsfolk she cared for.

The procession moves like a river of light, winding through the streets from each home towards Holy Cross of the Bogside—the ancient church standing with quiet authority just beyond the shadow of Grimwood Forest.

I walk beside Elodie, our hands tightly clasped together, as if we might lose each other in the darkness. From the corner of my eye, I see our friends— Aisling, Maeve, Aiden, Declan, Niamh, Leila, Saoirse, and Lennon—gather around us. They give us the space we need, but their quiet presence is a balm. In this moment, it feels as though we're walking through a dream—this strange, suspended place between worlds where grief and love, loss and memory can exist side by side.

As we draw closer to the church's heavy doors, the elders step forwards, their movements slow and deliberate with each step bound by tradition. They begin chanting, their voices soft at first, weaving in and out of the wind.

I glance at Elodie again, my heart aching at the tightness in her jaw. She searches the crowd, eyes frantically looking for Auntie Cait's body. When she spots her, lying on a bed of moss and hogweed, a wave of grief crashes over her, pulling her under.

I take a deep breath and step forwards, Elodie at my side. We kneel beside Cait's body, and I place my hand over hers. The coldness of her skin stabs into me, a sharp, cruel reminder that she's gone. The warmth of her is no longer there, but I can feel the weight of everything she was, all she gave, still lingering in the air.

"We release you, Mother," I whisper, my voice breaking on the final word. The words feel too heavy, too final.

Elodie's voice shakes as she whispers, "Begin your journey. We honour you."

Her fingers gently brush over Auntie Cait's hair, and I feel the calmness of her gesture through our bond even as my insides twist with grief. Her hands tremble, but her movements are deliberate, filled with a quiet grace. This is our final duty to Auntie, and she's carrying it out with strength, with love.

In that moment, I see it. I see Cait's spirit in Elodie—fierce, protective, unwavering. It's clear as day, no need for Aiden's sight, no need for any magic. The same unyielding force that has kept us grounded and safe, lives on in her.

We must now release the last of her, the final goodbye we never thought we'd have to say. I lift the ceremonial knife, its blade cold and steady in my hands, a reminder of what has already been lost. There's no turning back now, only the quiet, aching finality of what must be done.

With a steady breath, I make the first cut, severing a lock of Auntie Cait's hair. It falls softly, landing silently on the linen beneath her. I hold my breath as I pass the lock into Elodie's waiting hands—the final piece of Cait we'll carry with us in this life. Next, I cut a piece of hair from mine and Elodie's and gently place it in Auntie's hands so that her soul may travel only within the light and be guided by our love. There's a shift in the air, like the world is bending, stretching, as her spirit begins its journey. The lanterns flicker and dance, their flames reaching upward as though drawn by some unseen force.

As the final chant fades, the last of Auntie Cait's ties to this world are cut, and the air stills. The town remains silent, watching, waiting.

Elodie and I, our hands still clasped, step back as the townsfolk begin to move, slowly at first, but with purpose. Auntie Cait's body will be laid to rest, but we'll keep the lanterns burning. Her light will guide us, even as she passes beyond this world. Her light will live on in every one of us—in our work, in our love, and in the memories we carry of her.

We follow the procession, knowing a gathering awaits to celebrate her life now that we've honoured her in death. As we reach the edge of the woods, I glance back one last time, my hand slipping from Elodie's as she continues to walk. The hundreds of lanterns surrounding the ground that'll be her final resting place fill me with pride, reminding me of how lucky I was to be raised by such an incredible woman. But it's the little blue wisps of light that capture my attention next. The four will-o-the-wisps seem to dance together. One continuously grazes against Auntie Cait as though reuniting with an old friend—or perhaps, it's saying goodbye. In that moment, a calm washes over me, their presence a quiet reassurance that wherever her soul is, it is now at peace.

With a small smile, I wipe away a tear, then turn to catch up with Elodie. In just a few steps, I reach her, and we walk arm in arm, the familiar, comforting weight of her presence beside me.

✝✝✝

THE PAST UNVEILED

The wind will whisper hidden secrets,
Listen closely—connect the pieces.
Search the trees and the sacred places,
Where moonlight's touch leaves faint traces.

Seek the spot where darkness hides,
Where ancient shadows gently rise.
Hear the echoes of the past's soft spell,
And ravens croak where old tales dwell.

Follow the path where the moonlight spills,
Find the place where stillness fills.
Past the hollow where the brambles cling,
And listen for what the wind will bring.

23

UNTOLD TRUTHS
ELODIE

Despite the early hour, the soft melodious tune of *Gort na Saileán* from a group of musicians can still be heard within the pub. A few too-drunk stragglers from the gathering remain inside, but most left before sunrise. Though the storytelling has been replaced by a tranquil reminiscence, the quiet only seems to bring my emotions to the surface.

With a small nod to the balcony outside to let Rowan know where I'm headed, I take a deep breath of the cold autumn air and clutch the small metal key I placed in my coat pocket before the ceremony, too scared to lose our only clue. I look out at the rooftops of the town, the rising sun casting a warm glow upon the brick and weather-worn shingles. From here, I can see Auntie Cait's house, but it's as though the sun recognizes no soul lingers within, its golden rays seeming to skip over the land entirely. Hearing footsteps behind me, I turn, expecting it to be Rowan or Aiden checking on me, ready to tell them I'll be inside in a minute, but instead, it's Dr. Collins.

"Sorry, I didn't mean to startle you. Mind if I join you? I just came out for a bit of a breather myself," he admits.

I move to the side to allow him room and he takes that as my silent agreement. For a few moments, we stand in silence as he takes in the town much like I did, a small smile making him seem more boy-like than the esteemed medical and agricultural scholar he's come to be recognized as.

Breaking the silence, he says, "You know, it was your dear Aunt who was the first to give me a chance here. I'd been looking for work right out of the Academy a few towns over with no experience except what I'd learned in textbooks and not a dollar to my name. I'd almost given up, believed that I'd have to settle for a job I didn't care for but could pay the bills." Turning to me, he grins warmly. "But, much like her students, once she saw potential in someone, she didn't let them give up. I have her to thank for making me part of the community here in Eldermoore. Now, it feels as though everything is turned upside down." He looks away for a moment, a sadness in his eyes I've come to recognize in my own when I look in the mirror.

Gripping the iron rail with one hand, the other still in my pocket, I say, "They say love comes in many forms. Whether romantic, familial, or friendship-based, they never say how much it will hurt when you lose them. Don't get me wrong: there are tons of tales and tragedies written about true love, but nobody talks about the other kind." At his arched eyebrow, I grip the key tightly as a reminder and continue, "The kind of love that is messy and painful. The one where you have to learn to forgive or end up living with hate. One would think those scholars and poets were too scared, or maybe they had never found such unconditional love themselves. But I don't think they were scared of the idea of love at all. No, I think they were terrified of just the opposite."

"And if those people can bury the past and find a way to overcome hate? What would anyone with love need to fear?"

"The one thing we all fear in the absence of love… Loneliness." I take a deep breath to gather my thoughts. "That's why I think it hurts so much that she's gone. It's not only the loss of her physically, but the memories we can no longer create and the changes in mine and Rowan's life that she will never get to see."

Dr. Collins seems to mull over my words, but I'm too focused on the cold metal gripped in my hand to pay him much mind. Without a second thought, I release my hold on the cold metal and in doing so, it feels like I can finally breathe. Maybe I hadn't been worried about losing our next clue, but the memory of the person it belonged to.

Like all the times before, I feel *his* approach. His footsteps are quiet as he makes his way to my side. No longer occupied by the Professor, his hand rests above mine on the railing.

I close my eyes to hide the lone tear that tracks down my cheeks as Aiden all but whispers, "She knows." As if sensing my disbelief, he gently picks up my hand to point at something in the distance and I guide my eyes to the sky. "See that? Every time you see the first glimpse of the sun, know that she's saying hello. And when you see the moon and fear she's once again absent, know that she paints the night sky with stars as a reminder of how much she loves you. She's watching, and she always will be."

Arcane Scriptorium - 10 a.m.

After heading home for a much-needed change into warmer clothes and as much sleep as we were able, we met Aiden, Declan, and the girls at the shop before making the quick walk to the library. Walking towards the Scriptorium's doors with the others in tow, I spot Niamh on the top step. Not waiting for us to reach her, she hurtles down the step before crushing me and Rowan in a tight embrace.

"I know I just saw you a few hours ago, but I just can't help myself when a friend is hurting and you know me, hugs are my love language… and maybe books, and plants, and coffee, and baby animals, and language in general, and did I mention books, oh and—"

"Okay, okay, we get it. You've got a lot of love to give, but you're going to crush them if you don't let go." Aiden chuckles, cutting her rambling off and breaking the tension we've all been feeling.

"Right, sorry about that. Why don't we head inside and, when you're ready, we can look at what new clues we've got."

As Rowan and I give her a quick squeeze of thanks for the short comfort she's brought us, Niamh slowly releases us. She makes her way towards the door and holds it open for us.

Making our way to the tables we worked at last time, I spot Auntie Cait's chest waiting for us. Pushing forwards, I tell everyone, "It might be easier if we start now. Like ripping off a bandage—best to get it over with."

Aiden pulls out a chair and remove a piece of parchment from his inner pocket as he sits. Even from this distance, I can tell it's the same note I'd searched for as Rowan had held Auntie Cait in her arms.

"I think it might be best we start with the clue from our culprit first. That way we can validate anything we discover in your Aunt's letters." Unfolding the paper, Aiden waits for us to find a seat before he begins to read.

> *Our fates entwined, her folly unfolds,*
> *For her sins, my fury now holds.*
> *And in her fall, my heart's revenge,*
> *A secret lover, they did allege.*
> *My shadows continue to seek and plot,*
> *Did they think that I forgot?*
> *Untold truths have now been buried,*
> *If I were you… I would hurry.*

Aiden's face is inscrutable as he reads the small passage. It's no secret that he'd once thought Auntie Cait was in league with our killer. I'd even had some doubts, but this note seems to hint that Aiden may have been right. To learn that she may have known Mr. A— to possibly have had a past relationship with her murderer— only fuels my eagerness to prove her innocence.

"Could this have been what she was hiding, not only from you and Rowan but from the town?" Aisling questions as she absentmindedly strokes the fur between Shade's ears. "Could this Mr. A be the reason for the Veils creation? It'd make sense why so much of our history has been erased and overwritten, especially if there was so much death surrounding the very family who'd been elected to protect Eldermoore."

Niamh's gasp startles us all, causing Shade to jump down from the table as Niamh walks over to grab the note from Aiden's hand and points at a few words in the riddle. "Look here. In multiple lines, he talks about love, revenge, and untold truths." Taking a moment to let those words sink in, she looks at our blank expressions before continuing, "You guys! This Mr. A is trying to throw us off his trail. When you sent over the picture of the Ogham text, I was able to translate the word to mean betray. I thought the betrayal was hiding how sick students were getting from the portal, but it very well might be a betrayal from more than 16 years ago. He's trying to get you to think that this has to do with some lover's dispute, but I believe Aisling is onto something here. It's possible that everything has to do with the Veil. Why? I'm not sure yet. I mean, Aisling can attest that despite the divide between the magical and non-magical, there have been no disputes written in our history, and has thus far kept everyone safe. But safe from what exactly? That will be the key." At the mention of a key her eyes light up and she walks behind the chest, her nails softly tapping against the lid before giving us all a cheshire-like grin. "And I think I know exactly where we can find out."

Taking a closer look at the ornate chest, the Flynn family's tree insignia etched upon the lock, I can't help but wonder what secrets we'll uncover. I take a deep breath before I pull the key out of my pocket and unlock the box that may hold the answers we've been looking for. Stepping next to me, Rowan slowly lifts the lid as everyone crowds around to see what's inside. Taking hold of the topmost pile of letters, I scan the dates and who they've been addressed to, though I soon realize that the oldest is only dated from a week ago. Passing the letters to Rowan for her to inspect, I'm stunned to realize that the rest of the chest only holds blank parchment, red wax, a wooden-handled dipping pen, and a jar of ink not yet opened.

"Why would she need to hide letters she wrote to the council members?" Rowan opens one to read, but from the look of disappointment on her face, it doesn't say much. "I don't understand. These letters are just the council's approval to go through the magic ceremony with Aiden."

I knew she wanted us to have powers to protect ourselves, but I never thought she'd risk her life trying to hide something like this. I'm about to close the chest when something catches my eye. Peeking out beneath the new ink bottle is what appears to be a deep engraving. I quickly remove the blank parchment and ink to get a closer look. The same family insignia from the lock has been etched into the wooden bottom. *Could it be?* Picking up the lock, I place the insignia down into the box until I hear a small click.

"A puzzle box? I do love a good puzzle!" Niamh exclaims, excitedly clapping her hands as she leans closer.

Turning the box to the right, I realize a small mechanism has been activated. Rotating the dowel clockwise, another wooden piece within the box raises. Pushing down on the button-like piece, I watch as the tray that held the letters snaps up. Removing the false bottom, I see letters dated from almost a century ago lying within the chest. Picking up a small handful of them, my eyes catch on the same handwriting Rowan and I have stared at during countless nights of searching for clues of our parents' disappearance while at the Academy. *Mam...* Carefully unfolding it, I read aloud the contents so everyone can hear.

"Looks like we were right. From the sounds of it, history is repeating itself, and your parents and Ms. Flynn were right in the middle of it," Maeve says after I finish reading.

"I'm inclined to agree," Niamh comments. "Also, if you look here at the date, this was the same time the deaths started happening for us, only 45 years earlier, and by the sounds of it, in the same fashion. Here let me try to find out more; it must be in one of these books."

We watch on in anticipation as Niamh works her magic to find a book that can help us get one step ahead.

As a heavy tome entitled, *Annals of Eldermoore*, floats towards her waiting hands, she excitedly shouts, "Oh my, I've never seen this one before! The fates might finally be favouring us!" She begins to flip through the pages quickly, her eyes scanning written symbols that seem to shift under her gaze. "This… this doesn't make sense," she mutters, her voice tight. "The ink is moving. It's—it's like it's alive."

I feel more than see a barrier wrap around us as Aiden leans in closer to the book, voicing what we all fear. "No, not alive. It's cursed."

"It's not just that," Niamh replies quickly, her fingers trembling as she flips another page. "The Council have never been allowed to break the protections here—not without serious consequences from the Flynn Clan." She pauses, her lips pressed tight as if she's piecing something together. "But they must've known they couldn't destroy Eldermoore's history, so they hid it in plain sight from anyone who'd try to look here."

She flips the pages faster now, eyes scanning. "They—" She stops herself. Her throat tightens, her hand hesitating over the pages. "Oh my, this is an ancient seal created with magic designed to stop anyone from breaking through. If someone were to try…" She blinks hard. Niamh slowly pulls her hand back, her face growing pale. "If we try to break the curse… the book, the pages… it'll all be destroyed. All the truth, all of Eldermoore's history." Hunching her shoulders, a distraught look crossing her face, she continues, "I'm so sorry. I failed you in this. It looks like we'll need to rely on these letters if we want to learn anything about the past."

Not wanting to let this hinder our progress, I try to focus on what we can still do. I reach out to comfort her. "It's okay, Niamh. It's not your fault. This just means we'll have to work a little harder. Why don't we each take some letters and if anyone finds something that seems important, anything at all, we'll read it together."

Seeing everyone take a calming breath and nod their heads in agreement, I separate the letters into a few piles and lay them out on the table before we get to work.

It feels like we've been at this for hours before Maeve interrupts the group. "We've got a winner! Look what Declan and I found!" she exclaims as she shakes a letter in the air, holding a gold band in the other.

My eyes widen at the realization that there's not just one ring but two. "Who wrote this one?" I inquire as I set aside my letter and stand beside her.

Maeve picks up the letter to begin reading but quickly lowers it. "It's complete gibberish."

I watch as Declan takes the letter, his eyes lighting up with excitement as he lets out a laugh. "You know, it was pretty common during the Irish War of Independence to encode letters with details you didn't want in enemy hands. Only someone with great historical knowledge and direct links to Eldermoore would be able to decode it." With a grin, he adds, "Lucky for you, I have extensive first-hand knowledge I'm willing to share. From the envelope, it seems like your Aunt and a mystery writer were sending coded messages."

Rowan rolls her chair over to Declan and suggests, "If you can give me the correct cipher, I should have no problem generating a program to help us decipher the letter, especially if we come across any others."

Her excitement is contagious, and I can't help but smile. "Then let's get to work!"

Dearest Cait,   1 October 1925

I don't know how much longer we can keep this hidden. The town is already on edge, and the worst is yet to come. People are disappearing—vanishing in the dead of night, drained of blood. There's a coldness in the air, and it's not just the autumn winds. I can feel it creeping in, like something waiting in the shadows.

Ciaran is doing everything he can to stop it, but the darkness is spreading faster than he can fight it. I see the toll it's taking on him—how it's wearing him down. He's trying to protect everyone, but it's getting harder. He's not just fighting a man anymore, Cait. This is something older, something that's been here long before us, something that won't be put to rest so easily.

The ravens are gathering again. You know what that means. The old gods are restless. It's as if they're watching us, waiting for the end. I never thought I'd see this in my lifetime, but here we are, facing down the darkness that the gods once guarded against. The stories we used to whisper in fear now feel all too real.

We can't wait any longer. Ciaran's strength is waning, and I fear we're close to losing him to whatever power has taken hold of this town. If we don't act now, there will be no turning back. You have the power to stop him, to save Eldermoore before it's lost to whatever darkness has taken hold. We are depending on you, more than we've ever depended on anyone before. Please, Cait, help us do what must be done before the ravens stop calling, and it's too late for all of us.

With all my love,
Deirdre

·)) ● ((·

"Gotcha!" Rowan shouts as I hear the click of her mouse right before the printer on Niamh's desk starts up. Though we've looked over most of the letters while waiting for her and Declan to crack the code, we haven't found any more clues.

We gather around the table as Rowan slides the paper in front of us. On the left is the scanned photograph of the letter we've decided to protect in a charmed evidence bag and on the right is what I assume is the deciphered letter.

Pointing to the note on the left, Declan explains, "I was able to recognize that our penman here was using a columnar transpositional cipher which was quite common at the time, but it was trickier than I thought it'd be to find the keyword. You see, most times it's a word only the sender and receiver will know is important. Luckily, Rowan and I were able to figure out the one thing that'd mean the most to your Aunt: Eldermoore. We figured that before the Veil was created, there was no divide among the people her family protected. Then we cross-referenced that with clues from our current case and realized all the victims had one thing in common—they all come from a long line of magic with ancestors that aided in the creation of the Obsidian Veil other than Flynn herself, who'd directly partaken in it. Therefore, we've deduced that the only possible word could be réalta. It's the plural form of réalt because it's a correspondence between two magic wielders." He looks at Rowan to continue as he notices she's bubbling over with excitement.

Picking up right where he left off, she notes, "So, when we finally put the note into the program I created, it came back with what you see on the right. We'll give you a chance to read it before Declan and I share our theories."

Opening my notepad, I quickly scan the letter before writing down some points of discussion. "It looks like Auntie Cait did know more than she let on. Though, most of this seems more like a lover's tiff than anything to cause the creation of the Veil."

"Hmm, and since I don't believe in coincidences, this Raven also refers to shadows like our current killer, which could mean there was, and still is, dark magic influencing his mind," Aiden adds as he turns to lean his back against the table.

"Can I just add, as your local plant enthusiast, how he calls her Dahlia!" Niamh calls over a magenta-coloured tome with the title: *Herbarium: A Botanical Classification.* "Let's see. No. No. Definitely not. Oh, here we go! The Dahlia is known to signify strength, defiance, and elegance. However, it could also carry the message of change and deceit which in my opinion is definitely where this Raven was going with this since, you know, he's evil and all that. Not to mention the whole letter sounds like one big mockery of Ms. Flynn and a whole dollop of paranoia considering it's the only letter he sent her that was encoded."

Aisling, who has been silent the last few moments holds up the rings Maeve found. "I'd also say that these are more of a promise ring of sorts instead of the wedding bands we assumed they were. In the history books I skimmed through, it was common for soldiers to present the one they loved with a token before leaving for war as a promise to wait for their return. It's possible that he sent her the rings to hint at what he planned— a promise and a warning to the evil your mother spoke of."

"Considering this is the last message between Ms. Flynn and this man after your Mam's note, I'd say they went through with whatever plan they had." Aiden shares his thoughts on the matter.

"Exactly! Declan and I saw that he mentioned foxes quite a lot, which was a common code word for the militia to use when referring to traitors. Then if you look here," Rowan says as she circles a line on the paper, *"even the cleverest fox can't outrun the night."* Taking a calming breath, she explains, "In my dream, he'd been hiding in complete darkness, almost as if he was darkness himself. Then he alluded to his shadows in the riddle he left with Auntie Cait. This letter could mean that he was planning to attack them next."

"It also seems like he puts a large emphasis on the idea of it being a full moon. I know we discussed the possibility a few weeks ago, so it seems even back then his power would be heightened the most during that phase. Niamh, do you have a map of this month's moon phases? Maybe if we can map out when he's killed so far, we can predict when the next one will be." I turn to her as I take a seat, exhaustion from the day finally taking its toll.

"I like the way you think! I'll be right back!" Niamh exclaims as she rushes off before skipping back to the table with her arms full of celestial maps and a bowl of candy and confections. "To keep our energies up!" she says with a playful wink as she pops a multi-coloured apple drop in her mouth. "Alright, if you look here, the first full moon was the day before Rónán and Liam's death. Then the Slayer went silent; we thought it could've been because he was already done and in hiding, but it occurred during the waxing gibbous. I can't believe I didn't make the connection before, but this means he was rebuilding his energy and preparing. Then boom, the 14th of October, the night before Ms. Flynn dies, another full moon! Our next full moon is not until the 30th, but I think we need to be cautious. The time in between will be during the waning phases when the moon is most hidden. In this case, there are connections to Morrigan's battle and death, as well as when our world is less visible to the spirits and the gods. In my opinion, I'd have to agree with your Mam: Mr. Doyle has released a creature more monster than man back into Eldermoore."

"Up until now, we've assumed that Mr. A alluded to having informants and spies like Doyle and Brennan when he wrote about shadows. If what Rowan and you have theorized is correct, any Réalt could be the next target," Declan contributes, "In addition, if what I saw underground is anything to go by, the spectrals' energies could be what's helping him attack sooner, especially if he's using them as his eyes and ears."

Knowing Declan is right—that no one is safe in Eldermoore— I declare, "In that case, we're going to need a little more protection, and I know just the person who can help us." I pause as Niamh nudges the dish in each of our directions, urging us to grab a snack as we pack up our evidence. Placing the wrapped candy in my pocket for later, I continue, "The Council asked us to clear out Auntie Cait's office tomorrow morning, so meet us at Leila's tomorrow afternoon."

The letter chest in my hands feels heavier than when I first brought it here—the secrets it once held weighing on my mind. Hopefully, we'll have enough time to stop him before we lose anyone else.

To my dearest Dahlia,

How delightful it is to write to you, my most cherished, beloved companion. How I've longed for your presence and the warmth of your smile. Ah, yes, how you've changed since we first met, how your grace has evolved in such mysterious ways. You always were a woman of many secrets.

How strange that it's come to this—how the paths we've walked together have grown so... different. I can almost hear your laughter now, mingling with the whispers of the wind, as you walk among those who truly understand your heart's desires. The way you've come to be so close with them—how truly special that must be. No one would ever guess how entwined you've become with these... newfound friends. No, Caitriona. No one at all.

Tell me, my sweet, do you find it so comforting, being surrounded by so many foxes now? I'm sure their company is... reassuring. They must be, to someone as wise as you. After all, what's a little change in the wind between old companions? What's one more fox in your nest? But remember, even the cleverest fox can't outrun the night forever. The truth has a way of finding those who think they can bury it.

Do you feel it, too? That strange tension in the air? That weight that presses down on us both? You've always said that you could sense everything, that you could feel the unseen around you. Perhaps you've sensed it already—that cold feeling creeping in, the one that chills the bones. You should be careful, my love, who you share your fire with. Not all embers are meant to be kept close.

But don't worry, my darling. The moon is full, and I see things with new clarity. I know where your heart lies, and it isn't with me. You don't fool me, Cait. Not anymore. I've learned the truth, as I always do.

And while you and your little friends unknowingly dance in my shadows, I'll wait for the right moment. I always do. When the time is right, I'll be there—just as I always promised.

Until then, my sweet, know that I keep you close in my thoughts. I always will.

Raven

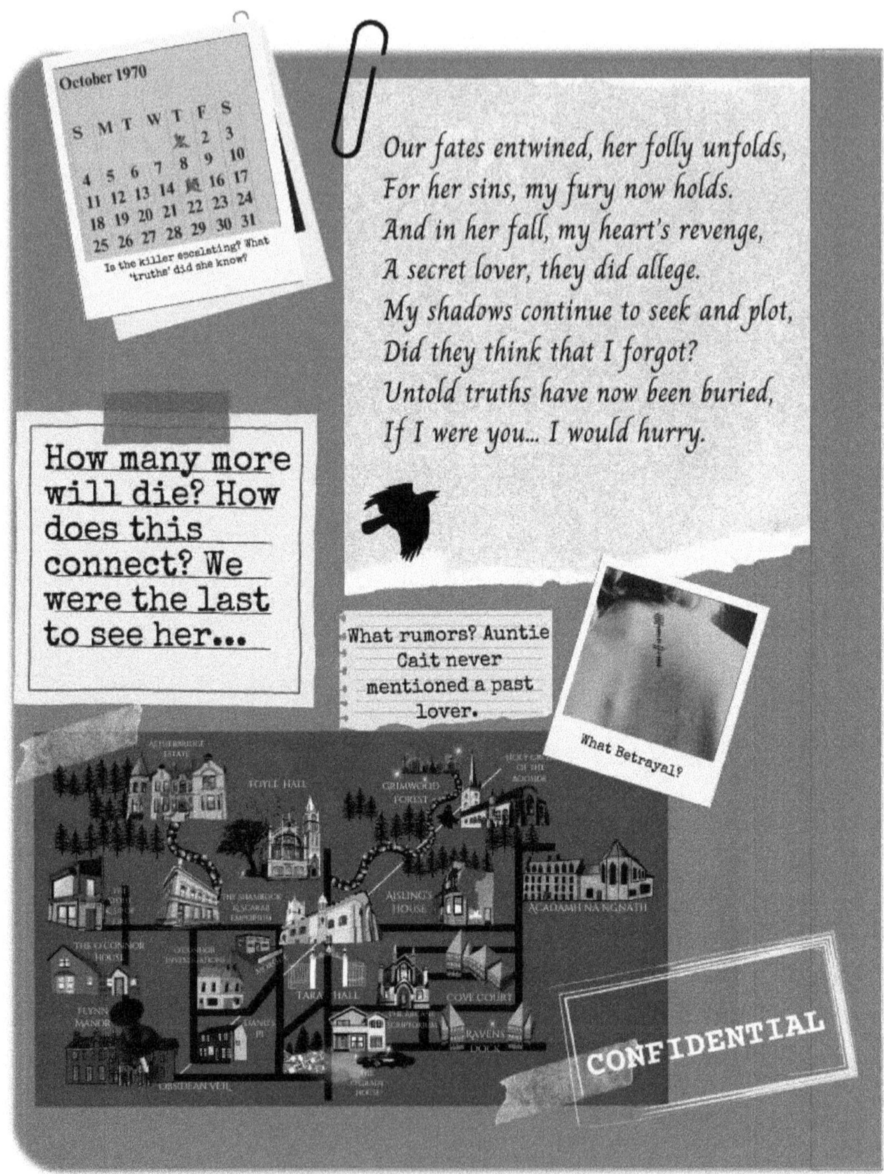

Caitriona Flynn- Property of Danu's PI

24

WHAT LURKS IN THE DARK

ELODIE

Waking up in a cold sweat is starting to get old. I take a sip of water from the glass I'd placed on my bedside table the night before to try and calm my nerves, yet I can't help but feel like I'm still being watched. The shadow-like hand that reached out as if to grab me felt all too real. From the murmurs and sudden gasp as Rowan wakes in her room, I can tell she's not having much luck in the dream department either. Walking over to her room, I meet her at the door. Knowing neither of us will be getting back to sleep anytime soon, we agree to get a head start on our day.

Deciding the fresh air might do us some good, we start our trek down Elderwood Ave towards Tara Hall. Yet, the frigid air only reminds me of the cold emptiness that always seems to linger after death.

Making our way through the ornate doors that once mesmerized us, we try to make a swift escape towards her office, away from the looks of sympathy and quiet condolences that follow us down every hall.

I lock the door behind us, Auntie Cait's wards no longer active with her gone. The familiar scent of vanilla fills the air, a small comfort amidst the chaos. The room is dim with the curtains drawn tight, as always. In the corner, the fire crackles softly in the hearth, courtesy of one of the academy's charms. Auntie Cait's desk stands as it always has, cluttered with books, papers, and trinkets, but this time, nothing feels safe. Nothing feels like it used to.

Rowan picks up the frame on her desk and looks at the last picture we took together over the summer. The three of us had taken a day trip to a town up north known for its legendary ice cream. Auntie Cait had insisted that we take a photo, reminding us at the time how important it was to not let our work control us and to make memories as often as we could.

Placing the frame inside the cardboard box we brought with us, Rowan looks around, "What do you suppose the Council has decided to do about the headmistress position? I'm sure Auntie told them about the portal. Without her magic to ward the grounds, it's only a matter of time before students get sick and the spectrals start causing problems. Elodie? Did you hear me?"

"Sorry, I think you're going to want to have a look at this," I say as I grab the fire iron and drag out the remaining pieces of paper starting to catch aflame in the hearth before placing it in the bin to cool.

Picking up the stapled pile, I turn the paper towards Rowan so she can see what's caught my eye. Right on the top are Auntie Cait's scribbled words giving directions to drop this at our office the day she died. Right under that is the fax number from her home office to this one.

"It looks to have been the list of people who have access to the classrooms that Auntie Cait said she would look into for us. I didn't see anything like it when we looked for clues before the funeral. Mr. A must have destroyed it before we got there, which means his name must have come into question on the alarms."

"If this rubble is anything to go by, he knew she sent a copy here and that we'd be cleaning her office today. He's toying with us, having us grasp at threads so we can never see the full picture. He might still be in the building; we need to check if the hagstone is here and get to Leila's."

Keeping an eye out for anyone suspicious, we head towards Mrs. Flanagan's office as quickly as we can without alarming any of the students. We knock just as I hear the doorknob rattle.

Mrs. Flanagan sticks her head around the door to see who it is, a look of urgency on her face as she opens the door for us. "Ladies, I was expecting you. Though, I thought you'd be here sooner considering the accusations you threw my way the last time you came to visit."

I feel my cheeks grow hot at her words. Rowan all but stutters at her forwardness.

"Accus— We were only doing our job. You know, the one you and the Council all but beg—" At the arch or Mrs. Flanagan's eyebrow Rowan's words cut off.

"If you're done wasting my time with your little speech, your dear Aunt sent me a telemessage the night she was killed saying if anything happened I was to show you the safe. Quickly now, follow me." With a quick turn, she leads us out of her office.

At the far end of the hall, she halts before a stretch of seemingly solid stone. Her fingers trace the surface gently and a soft hum vibrates through the walls. In an instant, a stone door shifts, sliding open with a sound that's more felt than heard. A cold draft escapes, stirring the air around us. We step inside as the door moves to shut behind us.

We wander a short way in the dark, a cold breeze encircling us, almost as if trying to learn who we are. As quickly as it appeared, it dissolves, soon replaced by a sweltering heat. Reaching the end of the tunnel, a faint glow is cast upon the steel safe, the blue flame from the sconces on the wall allowing us to see the vault before us. It's tall, weathered frame is carved with intricate patterns that seem to shimmer, but it's not the runes or symbols that catch my eye. It's the sense of something ancient, something older than the academy, hiding just beyond the reach of mortal hands.

Mrs. Flanagan doesn't hesitate. She takes a step forwards and whispers something in a tongue I don't recognize. A sudden, unnatural stillness falls over the room, the air thick with magic. The temperature drops once more, and in the darkness near the vault's base, a pair of glowing eyes flicker to life—amber and reflecting no light, only darkness. The creature is something I remember seeing a picture of in a book Aiden had us read. Its piercing gaze flickers from me to Rowan with an intelligence that causes all the facts I try to recall about mythical beings to flee my mind. If it's dangerous, I can't remember. Even from this distance, I can tell it searches— no, hunts —for something hidden within the deepest parts of our souls as if it seeks the truth of who we are.

At last, the Púca emerges from the shadows, its shape flickering as though an embodiment of the very secrets it guards, sending a shiver down my spine.

"This is no ordinary lock," Mrs. Flanagan murmurs, unfazed. "The vault isn't just protected by magic. The Púca ensures that no one—except the rightful bearer and those entrusted by the Flynn Clan—may access what lies beyond." Mrs. Flanagan steps forwards, her hand reaching into her coat, causing the Púca's ears to twitch. Carefully, she approaches the vault, placing the key into the lock. "Only those with true purpose may enter, and even then, it ensures that no ill intentions can pass through."

With the vault door fully open, the creature gives one final, knowing glance, before slipping silently into the shadows, leaving us alone with the vault's secrets.

"It's right over here, if you'll follow me." Mrs. Flanagan moves quickly, her hand brushing the shelves as she makes her way to the spot where the hagstone should be secured.

Rowan and I follow, our hearts pounding in our chests, but as she reaches for the space, her fingers hover over a glass case. Then, we all see it.

The stone is gone.

Rowan's face mirrors mine—shock, disbelief—and she turns to Mrs. Flanagan. "How could someone have gotten inside?" she asks, her voice tight with frustration. "You said this vault was protected by magic only a handful knew. The Púca—how could someone deceive it?"

Mrs. Flanagan's gaze drops to the floor uncharacteristically, her lips pressed together in a thin, worried line as she returns to the entrance. Her fingers brush over the edge of the stone door like she's searching for something, some clue, but finding nothing.

After what feels like an eternity, she speaks softly, as if reluctant to voice the terrible thought that has crossed her mind. "There are ways," she said. "It's a creature of both mischief and wisdom bound to its charge, but… if someone knew how to bargain, how to twist its allegiance, they could have gotten past."

The blood drains from my face. A creature this ancient? Deceived? It was supposed to protect the vault, not turn a blind eye to whoever wanted the stone. "This is worse than we thought, we must leave quickly. Mrs. Flanagan, please keep this to yourself. If our killer can fool the *Púca*, he can fool us all."

+))●((+

The Shamrock & Scarab Emporium - 12 p.m.

As we turn the corner to the Emporium, I can see Aiden talking to the girls on the steps, his back to us. At our sudden appearance, Maeve cuts off whatever Aiden is about to say as she pushes past him to greet us.

"Ah! Finally some real company. I was starting to get worried that I'd have to hear Aiden go on about the importance of keeping up with our training all day." She pouts with a wink only we can see.

Skipping back up the stairs, Aiden tugs the end of her braid teasingly as he mutters under his breath, "Just you wait, You'll all be thanking me. Oh, how I can't wait for that day!"

Acting as though she didn't hear him, Maeve opens the Emporium doors and ushers us in as she calls out for Leila.

"Please. Sit, sit. I've gone ahead and ordered sandwiches for everyone from the Cafe after Aisling stopped by last night to let me know you would be coming over this afternoon." She stops before Rowan and I as the others get comfortable. Taking our hands, she quietly tells us, "I'm sorry I have not checked

203

on you sooner. I'll always be here for you as you've been for me."

Giving us a small hug, she pulls back slightly, looking towards Rowan as she whispers, "Is this about your gift? Was the charm not strong enough?"

With a smile, Rowan shakes her head. "I think the cat's out of the bag in that regard but thank you for trying."

Declan gives a short laugh behind us as he shakes his head. "Well, I think your scream from a few nights ago knocked the hearing right out of me. I'm dead, and, since meeting you, I've gone deaf in one ear. I'm truly suffering for the ladies, as usual!" he sighs in jest before joining the others.

"Funny," Rowan deadpans as she glares at his retreating form. Turning her attention back to Leila, she adds, "While I could use some help to keep the symptoms from getting worse, we're actually in need of something a little different."

"I'll start looking into things that might help. In the meantime, how can I be of assistance?" she inquires as we find an empty sofa to sit on.

"Remember the hagstone you mentioned? It's been stolen and there's a very good chance it's in the killer's possession." At everyone's gasp of shock, we shake our heads. "While cleaning Auntie Cait's office, we discovered a list of possible names regarding who has access to the classrooms burning in the fireplace." Looking at Aiden, I add, "After you showed us Ms. Maguire's false note, we asked her to investigate the academy's staff. The list was dated for the day she died. Rowan and I realized that if he's able to forge notes and enter Auntie's locked office, he might be able to find the vault. Turns out Auntie Cait had told Mrs. Flanagan to take us there if anything were to happen to her. When we got there, it was guarded by a Púca. Somehow it was bargained with or tricked. Do you have any ideas of how this could've happened?"

"Oh my! Someone very ancient and powerful would have to be at play. They'd also need inside knowledge of the security in place. A Púca has not been heard of for decades. From what I know, this creature must have agreed to guard the vault during the very creation of Eldermoore. Even with the knowledge that it was guarding the safe, the thief would need the bridle made by High King

Boru to bargain with it. Liam and I acquired it a few months ago now that I think of it, but it was bought by Ms. Flynn."

"Really? From what Mrs. Flanagan told us, Auntie Cait is one of the rightful bearers of the vault key. Did she say why she needed it?"

"Well, she was acting quite strange that day, if I recall. She seemed in a hurry and unwilling to chat. I even tried to tell her the story of you girls and Liam, but she looked rather angry about something. Perhaps she lost her key? I believe that was the same week that the hagstone arrived by sea, so maybe she was afraid she wouldn't be able to keep it safe."

"Looks like I'll need to set up a meeting with our sailor friend sooner than planned," Maeve says with a grimace.

"Good idea. Try to write out a message to send to him before we leave so we can see if he has any information for us. The sooner he gets it, the better." At my instruction, Maeve pulls out a pen and paper from her bag. "And Leila, based on what we've discovered so far, I fear you might be right about us dealing with someone ancient and powerful. Do you have any protection tokens that could help us?"

"Luckily, I've just received a shipment of charms that I ordered after Liam's death. Let's see if there's anything that may be of use to you." Leila places her cup of tea on the table before pulling a large box down from the storage cabinet to her right.

Opening the bejewelled lid, she rifles through the contents carefully. "I have some blessed Ivy leaves and four-leaf clovers that help ward off dark magic and ill will. Oh, this might work! Now it might seem a bit unorthodox…" Leila says with a chuckle as she pulls out a wooden stake and hands it to me. "It's made from an oak tree. It could prove more effective than your daggers and is written in many texts to be an effective tool against most dark creatures. We have our very own oak tree here in Eldermoore so I commissioned this one a few years ago."

Her eyes light up upon seeing whatever item catches her attention. As she pulls her hand from the chest once more, I see an elaborately decorated handheld mirror, the handle itself forged to look like a twisted branch.

Handing it to Rowan, she explains, "With your Sidhe ancestry, you most likely have a deep connection to the Cailleach. This mirror is said to be hers. According to the stories I've heard passed down from those who have owned it in the past, it bridges a gap between our plane of existence and the spiritual. The last buyer claimed the mirror's power reveals a person's true nature, helping her discover that the flock of grey birds haunting the town were actually the Sluagh, the host of the unforgiven dead. Through the mirror, she saw their true form as restless spirits, guiding the town towards its doom, not just the mere omens everyone thought them to be."

Next, we watch her pull out what looks to be a cloak. Rising, she hands the forest-green cape to Declan. "This is the Mantle of Aine. Though often associated with love and the Otherworld, she's also linked to the spiritual realm and the ability to create barriers for healing. Worn like a cape, this acts like a shield against evil. Due to the goddess's link with the spiritual world, a person of flesh and blood wouldn't feel its full protection."

"Oh, and I've got one more thing I think will be of interest."

Leaving us to walk to the back room, she soon returns with a small wooden crate. I watch as she lifts the lid, the package's paper cushioning rustles as she grabs whatever lies within. At first, it appears to be a simple wooden wand before it elongates with a jut of her wrist.

"Now, that's neat. I bet Saoirse would love to get her hands on that." Maeve's eyes widen in wonder.

Taking a step back, Leila swings the pole in a circular motion and thrusts the staff forwards, finishing in a fighting stance as a sharp spearhead appears at the end. At our small claps, she smiles before standing tall.

Looking at it in appreciation, Leila tells us, "Liam was the one to find this gem. We'd been searching for the last few years for some more unique artifacts and happened upon a weapons dealer who'd been traveling on one of the ships. Liam always told me they never knew what they had." She gives a light chuckle before handing it to Aiden and continuing, "Gáe Assail, otherwise known as the Spear of Lugh. Weapon to the champion of the Tuatha Dé Danann, it's said to never miss its target. It's been charmed to remain hidden in its compact form, though Liam and I were able to tell what it was by the small rune carvings on the casing. Perfect for traveling, if I do say so myself!"

"Not that we don't appreciate the new gadgets, but are we sure they'll work?" Aiden inquires.

A look of sadness flashes across Leila's face before she takes a seat. "Since we're dealing with the powers of a hagstone and a malevolent force unknown to us, I can't be sure, but it won't hurt to be prepared. It might be wise to enhance the power of these by combining them. One way to do this, like with any magic, is by sticking together as much as possible. Ni neart go cur le cheile."

"Seems fitting for our motley crew. Thank you for all your help. We'll use these wisely. Please stay safe yourself." I voice my concern for our dear friend as I hand her a small pouch of gold coins we put together for today.

Letting the others go ahead of me on my way out, I stop Leila. "Thank you so much. I don't know what we'd do without you. While you're looking into the charms for Rowan, could I ask you for one more favour?"

"Of course, Elodie," she says, her tone both calm and reassuring. "You needn't even ask. It's my privilege to be of service. What is it that you require?" She regards me with a look of quiet expectation, a picture of unspoken strength.

"We found a letter from my mother to Auntie Cait. She wrote about the ravens gathering and the old gods stirring… It's more than just a warning. It feels connected to what's happening now, but I don't fully understand it. It seems like our mother knew more about the old gods and their influence, especially when it came to objects tied to them."

"Liam studied the gods and their artifacts while attending Tara Hall to help with the Emporium, but I've been able to pick up on a lot of it over the years from all the notes he'd toss around. What your mother wrote… it sounds familiar to me."

A weight lifts off my chest. "Thank you, Leila. I knew we could count on you. We've got to figure this out before it's too late."

"I'll look into it. Leave it to me."

Back out on the stoop of the Emporium, the afternoon sun casts long, crooked shadows across the cobblestones.

"We'll split up," I say, turning to Rowan beside me. "Aiden and Declan, see if you can find out whether more students have visited Dr. Collins in the infirmary. If Mr. A is planning on rallying more people for his cause, they're likely to have the most exposure to the portal— and likely the worst symptoms. Maeve and Aisling, I'll leave it to you to check the docks and ensure that the letter's sent. Everyone stay sharp. We'll reconvene back at the office tomorrow."

Maeve O'Connor | Danu's PI, Eldermoore | 17th October 1970

Mr. Lorcan O'Rourke | The Blackthorn Wraith | Raven's Dock, Eldermoore

Dear Mr. O'Rourke,

I hope this letter reaches you in good spirits.

We're moving forward with the case we discussed, and I find myself in need of a bit more information. Specifically, we're looking into any recent sightings, purchases, or rumors surrounding a Hagstone. Given your... extensive network, I thought you might have caught wind of something.

If you've heard anything, no matter how small, it would be most helpful. Should you find something of interest, kindly send a telemessage, and we'll meet you at the office.

Looking forward to hearing from you soon,

Maeve O'Connor
Research Assistant, Danu's PI

25

THE QUIET BEFORE THE STORM

ELODIE

The darkness is suffocating. It's the same darkness that I've been unable to escape for the last few nights. It presses in from every side, thick as ink, swallowing the faintest hint of light. My feet feel like they're sinking, the ground slick and treacherous beneath me. I try to move, but it's as if the shadows themselves are pulling at me, holding me in place. Panic rises in my chest. I can't breathe. I call out for help, but the words are swallowed by the silence. The only sound now is my heartbeat, thudding in my ears, faster, faster.

Someone… someone help me.

And then, I hear it. A voice. Soft at first, barely a whisper. But then it rises, filling the air with a haunting melody—melancholic, ancient. I freeze. I know that voice. I know it. It's my mother's.

The figure of her emerges slowly from the depths of the darkness, her face glowing faintly, ethereally, like the moon trying to break through storm clouds. Her eyes, hollow and distant, hold mine.

"Don't be afraid, my child," she sings, her voice a quiet hymn, a dirge that wraps itself around me. The words are both comforting and terrifying at the same time.

Fear not the dark, nor powers untamed,
You walk in light, though shadows claim.

She drifts closer, her hand outstretched, not to touch, but to guide. Her eyes never leave mine, her voice steady despite the weight of the world she carries.

It is not for you to run away,
Your power's gift, you must obey.
What once was hidden now takes flight,
A force unleashed, a soul ignites.

At her final words, something stirs inside me, something I don't understand, something old and primal. The air around me shifts. The power she speaks of is mine. And then, in a split second, it bursts open.

I feel it, like an electric current shooting through my chest, through my heart, through my very soul. It crackles, sharp and overwhelming. My body trembles as the world around me begins to twist, the edges of reality blurring and bending. The darkness begins to fade, and something else takes its place. The shadows part like a curtain being drawn back. I'm not in the void anymore.

I see him. Liam. His eyes wide in shock, mouth open in a silent scream, blood dark against the weathered boards of the dock. His body is pulled towards the water, but he's not alone. There's a shadow looming over him, and I know in my bones that this is the one who took him. The one who—

I see a flash of glowing light. Then, red eyes, and finally, I hear it. The sound of something heavy splashes into the water, finality marking the noise. A shudder runs through me, and just before I'm swallowed by the dark, the image of Liam fades completely.

-Elodie's Journal-
"The Power Between Us"
Entry #11: October 18th @ 3:00 AM

Danu's PI - 7:00 a.m.

After tossing and turning all night from that nightmare, I made sure to stop by the cafe on our way to the office for caffeine and goods. Walking towards the office, I see Maeve and Aisling waiting outside. Though gorgeous as always, they look worn. If I'm honest with myself, I know this case is taking its toll on everyone. I smile as Rowan and I approach and see Maeve begin to theatrically give a slight bow, her arms raised in a dramatic arc as though hailing a deity.

"Oh, gracious one!" she exclaims, her voice full of playful reverence, eyes fixed on the box of baked goods in my hand.

"You've truly outdone yourself," she adds with a wink as she takes the to-go box while I unlock the door, her eyes widening as she peeks under the lid.

"Lucky for us, Lennon made sultana cake today. I couldn't resist throwing in a few slices to our usual mix." I give a short laugh as I hear her stomach give a small grumble. "I'll get the kettle on while you guys dig in. Aiden and Declan should be over shortly."

Waiting for the water to boil, I make my way to the sofa unable to resist the delicious honeyed-vanilla sweetness of the cake any longer.

I watch as the girls happily eat their own before Maeve says around a mouthful, "Oh, I almost forgot." Taking a moment to swallow, she puts her plate down and grabs an envelope from her pocket. "When Aisling and I arrived, this was on the door. It's likely Lorcan's response to my letter, though I thought it might take a bit longer. Aisling and I had to hide the note since his ship hadn't been at port. Let's see what he's found."

Unfolding the paper, she begins to read it aloud. At the mention of possible information on the hagstone, I can't help getting excited, but it also makes me question the Council. If a sailor has heard chatter about the hagstone, why hadn't Mrs. Flanagan? Had she fooled us? I'd been so sure she seemed fearful that the stone had been stolen. Could it have all been an act? Lost in thought, it isn't until I hear Rowan snicker that I look back up to see Maeve has torn a piece of the letter and stuck it back into her coat.

"Something you want to share with the group, Maeve?" With a grin, Rowan adds, "Aisling, is it me, or is that a blush I see?"

At Rowan's jest, Maeve brings her hands up to cover her cheeks before murmuring under her breath, "That heathen!"

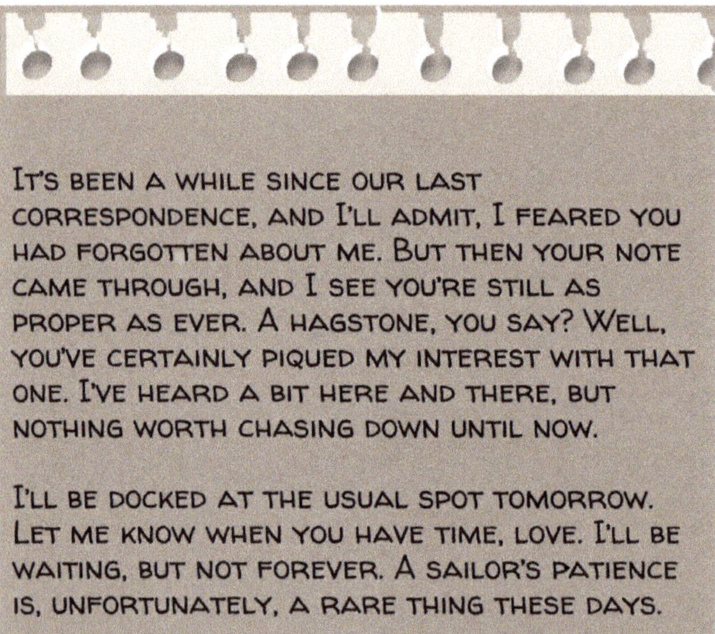

At the look of murder on Maeve's face, we break into fits of laughter, Maeve joining in as she relaxes. It feels good to laugh with my friends. For the first time in weeks, we aren't worried about what clues to find next or where we need to be. In this moment, we're able to breathe without the pressure of this case weighing down on us.

At the chime of the door opening, we look up to see Aiden and Declan arriving. Stopping in the doorway, their dual looks of confusion only make us erupt into another bout of giggles.

"Do I even want to know?" Aiden asks with a look of bewilderment.

Wiping tears from my eyes, I wave them over as I get up to bring the whistling kettle over. "No, we were just having a bite to eat." After pouring myself and the girls a cup of tea, I look up to ask if he wants one. At the shake of his head, I take a seat and explain, "Maeve was letting us know that Lorcan may have some information and can meet with her tomorrow."

Calm now, Rowan reaches across the table to grab a chocolate biscuit square. Before taking a bite, she asks Aiden, "Were you able to learn anything about the students from Dr. Collins?"

"Not much. He'd been on his way out when we arrived at the school. He wrote down a few names of students he remembered stopping by, but he says none of them have reported to the infirmary more than once."

"Perhaps the students aren't his target, although there must be a reason he chose to create the portal on school grounds. It seems like the students who are getting sick are just casualties in whatever he's planning," Declan theorizes.

20 October 1970 - Danu's PI

Currently hunched over a pile of our combined notes, I look around the room to take a breather. Declan and Rowan are across from me, bent over a map, tracing lines between locations and dates. Their eyes flick between the map and the scattered notes, their murmurs low but intense as they discuss possible connections. Meanwhile, Maeve, Aisling, and Aiden are working through the autopsy reports and crime scene photographs, trying to research every detail they come across that might lead us in the right direction.

As Maeve calls for a short break to work over our current findings together, she begins, "I thought I might start with what Lorcan and I found yesterday. After meeting him at Raven's Dock, we looked into a lead he found. There's a sailor who overheard some men talking a few towns over, near where the spectres were killed. They were discussing a hagstone. The sailor said a man his crew came across had it a few weeks back. They described him as… well, strange. Creepy, even. The interesting part was that the man quickly disappeared when discussing the shipments they were taking to Eldermoore. Any guesses as to what the shipment contained?" Maeve pauses for dramatic effect before shouting, "That's right! None other than the special order of charms and talismans we've just acquired from our dear friend Leila."

"That means he must have stolen the stone right after Auntie Cait locked it in the Vault. If what Leila told us about the artifacts was true, he must have been worried he'd be revealed by the mirror before he could start any trouble. That's likely why he hired Doyle and Mr. Brennan to do his dirty work."

"My thoughts, exactly. Unfortunately, there was little else to go on. Lorcan felt he could get more out of the crew if he stuck around on his own, so he told me he'd find us at the office when he had something solid."

Just as I think to ask if Rowan and Declan have found anything, Aisling announces, "Leila's coming," and I'm struck by a strange, almost unsettling thought. The timing of it all—seeing that vision of Liam's death in my dreams the same day that Leila visits us. It feels too coincidental. Like something bigger is at play.

Leila steps inside, the bell above the door chiming softly. Greeting everyone quickly, she turns down the offer of treats and refreshments as she moves over to my desk, settling into the chair opposite me. "I'm sorry to interrupt, but I've been looking into what you asked," she says, setting down her bag and folding her hands in front of her. "There's something here, Elodie. It's bigger than we thought, especially with the timing of when all these deaths have occurred—more than just the magic of the moon at work. I cannot fully explain it just yet. I need to verify my theory at the Scriptorium before I can be certain."

Before I can ask more, she shifts in her seat, her gaze growing distant for a moment, as if she's lost in thought. When she looks back at me, her voice softens. "I know you're in need of this information quickly, so I've been making notes as I discover more information, but I'll need the day to myself tomorrow," she says, a hint of vulnerability creeping into her otherwise composed manner.

"It will be Moulid an-Nabi," she continues. "The birth of the Prophet. It's a tradition in my family. My brother Liam and I always marked the day together back in Cairo. It's time for reflection, for prayers… for family." Her voice catches slightly on the word family, and I can see the weight of loss in her eyes. She doesn't need to say more. I understand.

Her tone is quieter now, the smile she gives me faint but sincere. "This year, it'll be different, but I wish to still honour the tradition like my brother would've wanted. I'll come to meet you the next day to continue our work. I promise."

I give her a small, understanding nod. "Take all the time you need, Leila. You've more than earned it."

Leila gives a small, grateful smile before standing up and heading for the door. As she steps out, I can't help but admire her quiet resolve. She carries her burdens with such grace, choosing to face them on her own terms. My mother's warning echoes in my mind as well as the strange power she spoke of. This force shared between Rowan, Aiden, and me is growing; I can feel it. But what does it mean? Whatever it is, it's moving fast—too fast—and I'm not sure we can keep up. All I know is that with danger closing in on us from all sides, we could use every bit of prayer and protection we can get.

26

TICK-TOCK

MR. A

I've been patient. Haven't I?

Taking my raven stamp, I mark the next note with ink.

Yes, yes, I've allowed them their little victories. I've let them think they're getting closer, that they're finding answers. It's all been part of the plan, hasn't it? Every insignificant moment, every delay… just *necessary* steps in the grand scheme of it all. They're so eager, so quick to believe they're uncovering something, as if it's some simple puzzle to solve. But they don't see. No, they never see the bigger picture.

Beneath my fingers, a collection of old charms and trinkets sits within a gold chest, relics of their misguided attempts at protection. They think baubles like these will save them. These *trinkets*… these measly things. With a swing of my arm, they crash to the ground. My satisfaction grows as I watch them become stained in her blood.

I smirk to myself, a dry chuckle slipping from my throat. How foolish they were. She hid it so well, didn't she? The charm—*that charm*—the one she always wore, thinking it'd protect her. They never learn. My shadows see everything. She thought she was the only one who knew what it meant. But now, they'll see. And when they finally piece it together…

In the distance, the faint ringing of the clock tower at Foyle Hall cuts through the silence, a reminder—no, a *countdown*. Tick-Tock.

"All in good time," I whisper to the room, pacing slowly, letting my eyes drink in the clutter of maps, torn documents, and mementos strewn across the desk. The low hum of my breath fills the silence as I gather the cloak that waits on the chair nearby. I drape it across my shoulders with practiced fluidity, my movements slow and deliberate, like an artist preparing for the final stroke of their masterpiece.

They've had their *moments* of relevance, haven't they? Cute little heroes playing at being clever. They think their search for answers matters. They think they're still *in control.*

I chuckle softly, the sound hollow and dark. They have no idea. No idea that it's already too late. The next clue I leave will be perfect. I can feel it. I'll set it all in motion, and when they read it, when they understand, the truth will finally hit them.

Their *failure.*

I pause for a moment, savouring the anticipation, the giddiness bubbling in my chest. This note will be my *final gift* to them. A gift they'll never be able to escape from.

I can't wait for them to read it.

The idea of them scrambling, wondering, searching for answers they'll never find, makes my heart race. It'll be too late by the time they figure it out.

When they do, I'll be waiting. I smile darkly, sealing the letter with an unholy satisfaction.

And they'll come.

They always do.

ROWAN

Something's wrong. I can feel it, even through the haze of sleep. It presses on me, a weight I can't shake, crawling under my skin like a silent warning. I try to reach back into the dream I just had, but it's gone, slipping through my grasp as if it was never real.

And then it hits me—something shifts. Not the world around me. But *me*.

A tremor runs through my body, cold and electric. It's like the air itself thickens, pressing in from all sides, suffocating. My breath hitches, my heart pounds, but it's not fear that rises in my chest. It's something ancient. Something primal.

The scream comes from deep inside me before I even realize what's happening.

It's not my voice.

Not my choice.

It rips through me, raw and aching, a wail that feels like it's been buried in my soul. I can't stop it. I can't control it. The banshee power inside me has been awakened, clawing its way to the surface, forcing its way out like a dark omen I can't escape.

I collapse back, gasping for air, but the power is still there, a heavy weight in my chest, a gnawing uncertainty.

Is this a warning of something that's already happened? Or something that's still to come?

I don't know. But I feel it; whatever *it* is, it's already here.

27

hall of two truths

Rowan

This time, I'm able to gradually force the banshee down, but Elodie still had to comfort me through it—not just the fear, but the raw power that I wasn't sure how to contain. I remember the worried look on Elodie's face as she came rushing in and I can't help by wonder if I'd ever have control over my *gift*.

At the sound of our landline, I look towards Elodie in horror. The only calls we receive this early are those of bad news. Ensuring I'm not about to turn into the abominable she-demon any time soon, Elodie races to get to the phone before the last ring as I attempt to get my breathing under control.

From the kitchen, I hear her pick up the phone and I follow the sound of her voice. As she sees me round the corner, she mouths, "Aiden," with an eye roll that assures me no one is hurt. "No, Mam. Yes, Mam. Sure thing. Did you wanna sing us a lullaby, too? I mean, seriously, relax Aiden. We're both okay. You too, Declan; don't think I can't hear you…" Just as she's going to say something else, we both hear the faint beep alerting us to another incoming call. "Never mind. Would you hold that thought? I'm getting another call."

Before he can so much as utter a reply, Elodie puts Aiden on hold before answering whoever else is calling us at this hour and puts it on speaker phone so I can listen in.

"Good mornin', this is Elodie speaking."

"Oh good, Elodie, I was hoping I'd reach you. It's Saoirse. I'm sorry about the early hour. With the influx in travellers this month, we've run out of Lennon's famous Barmbrack, so we've been up trying to get some prepared before the cafe opens because you know how busy we get…" Taking a quick deep breath, she continues, "Anyway, sorry to ramble on, but we saw someone running from Leila's shop a few minutes ago down Nocturne's Nook. We promised her we'd keep an eye on her with her brother gone, so Lennon and I went over and knocked on the door. There's been no answer, and I don't have the authority to enter. I'd hate to cause trouble, but I have a feeling something is wrong. Could you and your sister come down and check it out?"

"Of course, Saoirse. Hang tight, we'll be right there."

Ending the call, Elodie puts Aiden back on the line. "Saoirse just called. We're headed to the Emporium. Are you still at your office? Alright, we'll pick you up on our way," she clips in a hurry.

Getting the girls on the phone next, Elodie rushes to tell them to meet us at the shop.

Dressing quickly, we grab our PI gear kit and daggers before we leave. If it was Mr. A they saw, we need to be ready. As Elodie starts the car, I put the gear in the trunk and hop in the passenger seat. As we make the short drive to Aiden's, I keep an eye out for anyone traveling by foot, but the fog from the Veil seems to be uncommonly heavy tonight.

Within ten minutes, we all get out of the car as Elodie parks in front of the Emporium. On the stoop, I can just make out Saoirse and Lennon waiting by the door, or should I say Lennon is waiting. Saoirse, on the other hand, has her sword drawn and looks ready to pounce at the next thing to move. At seeing us arrive, she waves us over with urgency.

"She's still not answering," Saoirse says, bypassing greetings.

Standing a few feet away now, Saoirse puts her sword in the scabbard tied to her waist. Both her and Lennon are still wearing aprons, their faces sprinkled with splotches of flour.

"Lennon thinks he saw her leave earlier today, so she might not even be at the shop. I just can't help worrying after I saw that figure running. The fog is so thick tonight I was surprised I even noticed."

Grabbing the kit, I retrieve our lock-picking tools and get to work as I hear Elodie reassure them, "Rowan will get us inside in no time. Hopefully, the person you saw was just an early-morning traveller from the docks looking to see if the cafe was open yet."

When she's done speaking, I give the pick one last jiggle, and then, with a soft click, the lock gives way. Turning the handle, I creak open the door, and a soft hum of music can be heard from within. Taking a tentative step inside, I call out for Leila, but I'm met with darkness and the crackle of the radio as the host from the popular station, Voice of the Bogside, reports the latest weather update. "It's going to be a cold one today at a low of 8.6°C. Make sure you bundle up, or, better yet, just stay inside! Now, let's start this early morning off—"

His squeaky voice is cut off by the sound of static before the radio shuts off. Looking at Declan, he gives a shrug before walking towards the light panel by the door. As he flips the switch, there's a faint crackle from the bulbs before they illuminate, filling the air with a light hum of energy.

"Everything looks to be in order. Didn't she mention needing the day off? Maybe Lennon was right and Leila was able to prepare a portal to Cairo for Moulid an-Nabi. With Liam gone, she must have wanted to be with her parents," Aisling asks hopefully as we look around.

Although the front room looks exactly as we last saw it, a cold breeze enters the room from the storage office in the back.

"Did you guys feel that?" I ask as I try to suppress a shiver.

Aiden is the first to move, and I can see an energy surround him as he uses his powers. His steps, which are unhurried at first, falter as he enters the office, the orb around him disappearing simultaneously.

At his stillness, I know instantly that we're too late. The cold dread I felt upon waking causes me to take a quick intake of air as I feel the power I'd only just hidden start to bubble to the surface.

"Rowan, are you okay?" Aisling's voice is almost too sharp. Her voice, full of fear, is like a knife slashing at the little control I have.

The feel of warm hands on my shoulders helps to ground me, though the charm should've been enough. Leila had assured me it'd work until she found a stronger replacement. Did *he* know? Is this my fault? Slivers of my nightmare from this morning flash before me, making me sick to my stomach. Looking across the room towards the table Leila had sat at with us, it's almost as if I'm dreaming all over again. A blurry figure of a man walks towards the table and knocks a gold chest off the table, the clovers and talismans she'd talked about, spilling across the floor. At the sound of his cold malicious laugh, I'm jerked back to the present.

I can't help but feel guilty as I look at Aisling. "I'm so sorry."

"What?"

Following my gaze, she walks towards the sofa with the rest of the group. I watch as they round the sofa and finally see the horror I've now seen twice. Aisling bends down to pick up a silver bracelet, droplets of blood I can't see but know are there making her eyes widen. At the sight of blood, Elodie and Maeve let out quiet gasps, their faces turning pale in horror as Saoirse seems to freeze, her eyes appearing to glaze over in memory. Lennon pulls her into his arms, turning her away, his grip tight as if he can hold back the past that's grabbed ahold of her.

"No, she's fine." Aisling's head swivels from me to Saoirse as if trying to protest our grief. Suddenly, she pushes past us in a flurry of red hair before attempting to move past Aiden. Unaware of the magic shield he reformed surrounding him, she's knocked to the floor.

Kneeling in front of the invisible force preventing her from going any further, she begins hitting the air in an effort to find the magic's weakness. Her anger quickly becomes shouts of panic as her voice grows hoarse with emotion. She desperately yells at him, "Let me pass! She's fine… She has to be. I promised him I'd always look out for her."

Aiden turns, though his body still blocks her view into the room. A look of sadness crosses his features, but he quickly masks it with his usual collected demeanour. Standing taller, the tenseness in his stance the only sign he isn't as unaffected as he wants Aisling to believe, he calmly states, "I'm sorry, but I don't think you should see her. If I knew anything about Leila, it was that she wouldn't want you to remember her like this."

He watches as Aisling stops pounding her fists against his shield and slowly slides to the floor in grief. Placing a hand on her shoulder in comfort, he adds, "If the remnants of her aura are anything to go by, she was a warrior until the very end. Remember her strength. Why don't you take a moment then go with Maeve across the street so Lennon and Saoirse can show you the security cameras from their shop? If the figure they saw was running from here, we need to know how our culprit made it in and out of the building, and how long they might have been inside."

Aisling looks up at him, her eyes bloodshot now hardened in anger once more. "I know you can be cold, but I never thought you had no feelings at all."

Aiden flinches at her words, but she pays him no mind. Pushing from the floor, she knocks his hand off her shoulder, her hands shaking, before making a quick exit through the shop's entrance. Maeve rushes to follow her as she calls for Aisling to wait, though her voice is cut off by the slamming of the door.

Giving Aiden a pitying look, Lennon's voice fills the quiet space as he walks Saoirse to the door. "We'll go check on her. I'll let you know when we find something on the surveillance." With a final nod to assure Aiden, he turns to leave.

With only the three of us remaining, Elodie is the first to break the silence. "She's been through a lot these last few weeks… as we all have. I'm sure she didn't mean it." Wiping tears from her cheeks, she takes a deep breath. "And you're right: we shouldn't waste time. We can't bring her back, but I'll be damned if I let him get away with this. If Saoirse and Lennon saw him leave here, that means he's getting sloppy. Mistakes mean clues."

With a grateful nod, Aiden walks to the entrance and presses his hand against the door. His eyes close in concentration as he begins speaking in a language I'm not familiar with. Beneath his hand, the door begins to shimmer before enveloping the building.

With the walls now glowing, he explains, "It's to make sure the scene is secured. Since charms seem to be ineffective against our killer, this barrier will act as a second layer of protection if he decides to come back. It also has the added benefit of allowing you to move around the scene without the protective suits they taught you to wear at the academy. Declan informed me that they aren't the most comfortable."

With a grateful smile, I watch as Elodie sets our gear on the table before selecting the camera for herself.

Feeling like I'm drowning in an endless wave of grief, I create a list of next steps as I begin to search the room for clues, doing everything I can to avoid looking towards the back room for a few minutes more.

1. Focus. Catalogue the evidence.

2. Breathe. Find the riddle. It has to be here somewhere.

3. Focus. Look for a motive.

Bending down to pick up the bloodied bracelet, I can't help but wonder why Leila's death is so different. So far, every victim has been drained of their blood, so why not her? His motive couldn't have simply been to target me— or should I say, the banshee. *Mr. A has been very meticulous in leaving us clues thus far. First the thorn and letters… Perhaps this is the next.*

After letting Elodie take a few photographs of the artifacts, I place them in an evidence bag to be sent to the lab. Taking out my notepad, I ask Doc to run some blood tests and staple the paper to the bag. From across the room, I can hear Elodie and Aiden speaking quietly as they examine the storage room. With our emotions so high, I can tell that Elodie is trying to stay strong for me. She thinks that I'll lose control again and she might be right, but I know I'll have to face the fact that Leila's now gone, too—*eventually.*

With slow steps, I make my way to the storage area. Using the breathing techniques Elodie has been trying to teach me, I enter the room. Near the desk, Elodie and Aiden have just finished photographing her body. A cloth now covers her to give her some peace in the afterlife. Immediately, I'm struck by the potent smell of copper and how seemingly no area has gone untouched by traces of Leila's blood. *All except for one.*

I make my way to the table, eyes narrowing as they catch on the scale in the centre. It's out of place here, amidst the scattered candles and half-burned herbs. The scale's arms are uneven—one side drooping low, the other barely holding steady, as though some unseen hand is tipping it too far.

On one side lay the body of a raven. Its iridescent, yet shadow-like feathers barely press the scale's arm down as if it's not even there. My breath catches. It should be heavier; it *has* to be. Meanwhile, the other side holds a single feather—pale, delicate, and soaked in blood. The blood stains it, soaking into the soft, wispy fibres, each drop sinking deeper, tipping the scale further. Below the scale, I notice a folded parchment tucked neatly to the side. Calling out to Elodie and Aiden, I read it aloud.

Breaking the silence, Elodie asks the question I'm too afraid to voice. "What secret would Leila possibly have to hide that it put her in danger? Do you think it had something to do with Liam's plan to leave Eldermoore?"

"Liam and Leila would pick up their shipments together at the docks. If you're right, that must have been where he first targeted them. We'll need to go back to your office and compare the two notes," Aiden remarks.

Analysing the note again, I say, "The one thing I don't understand is why he says they were a curse that clashed with Eldermoore's stars. If I had to guess, it seems to be a connection to the Réalt— the same keyword used in his note to Auntie Cait all those years ago. It has to be something to do with the Obsidian Veil again."

The silence in the room thickens. Turning to look at the scale once more, it's clear that he's out for more than revenge. I watch the blood-stained feather as the dish it sits in continues to lower as more droplets spill. I can't help but worry that the *lie* Leila had been holding—whatever it was—has tipped the balance beyond repair.

Stout & Sip - 9:40 a.m.

Entering the cafe with Aiden and Elodie right behind me, Lennon jumps up to grab bar stools from behind the counter. Aisling and Maeve sit behind the brightly lit computer screen, their gazes focused as Saoirse pauses the footage every couple of minutes. Pulling the offered stools behind them, Aisling turns as we take a seat. Looking to Aiden, she gives a small smile; it's barely a lift of the corner of her lips, but it's just enough to offer an apology. Taking a moment to grab a tissue from the box beside her, she wipes a stray tear before informing us of their findings.

"With the fog so heavy this morn', it was hard to get a clear picture off the cameras. Luckily, we were able to pinpoint the time of arrival to when Saoirse and Lennon saw him leave through the alley. If he went underground, he hasn't resurfaced— at least not the same way he went in." Pausing, she looks at the notepad Maeve is scribbling her notes in. "From the timestamps, Leila left the store around lunch but returned around 7 pm. She appeared to be looking over her shoulder, but we didn't see anyone following her. When we backtracked from the alleyway, we were able to pinpoint the time of arrival to around midnight, which is the same time the fog appeared. It's like he used some sort of spell to conceal his movement. With the fog still out there, he could still be planning something."

Lennon, who's just finished helping a guest, comes to stand behind Saoirse. With a look of smug satisfaction, he adds, "Luckily with Aiden shopping for apologies so often, Saoirse and I got to reminiscing about our old Academy years a few weeks back." Smiling at Saoirse as he pulls a small leather-worn journal from his apron pocket and places it on the table, he continues, "We remembered the story of the haunted hall and bumped up the security in the pub. With the Hassans's permission, we installed a surveillance spell very similar on their door. Whoever enters the shop is immediately recorded in a journal stored in our safe. It won't tell us where he is now, but it should be able to give us a description of your mystery madman."

With a laugh, Elodie picks up the book. "Ah, yes, Aiden told us that story not too long ago. Just don't let him think it's his idea, or we'll never hear the end of it!"

As she looks through the pages, Declan appears behind her, his eyes scanning along as she reads. Suddenly his eyes light up as she flips to the last two pages.

"Look here. These pages have timestamps for the last few weeks. Only, on the day following Liam's death, the same hooded figure from this morning was seen standing in front of the shop. They never went inside and never got close enough to the door for a better description. He must have been able to sense the spell. It looks like the door caught him coming up the steps, but from the sounds of it, he used the spectrals to hide his appearance. His true identity could be hidden in any one of these accounts."

At the grim expressions taking over Lennon and Saoirse's face, I rush to reassure them. "This might not have revealed who he is, but it's helped us confirm that Liam's death wasn't as planned as he wanted us to believe." At their questioning stares, I explain, "It was Leila he was after all along."

O'Keefe's Morgue - 10:28 a.m.

"Doc give us some good news. Have you found anything?" I rush to peek over his shoulder as he writes on the sheet clipped to his clipboard.

Pulling the document close to his chest to hide it from my view, his eyes crinkle in a glare. "Always impatient, Ms. O'Grady. If I were you, I'd start taking note of your dear sister's mann—" His spiel cuts short as the lights begin to flicker and a sudden deep growl comes from directly behind him.

Face turning ashen, he turns slowly, as if expecting the morgue to come alive with the dead he examines all day. Not seeing Declan, he turns back to face me as he murmurs about indigestion. As Elodie and Aiden enter his office, his face lights up. "Ah, just the detectives I was looking for. I was able to find some interesting things during my examination."

"Is he always like this?" Declan whispers as he crosses his arms and leans against the pristine stainless steel examination table.

"Afraid so. I think he's still holding a grudge against me from the time I sneaked into the lab to see what I scored on the medical training exam back when he held a camp at our academy. Don't let him fool you, though, he still loves me. I was one of his star students after all." With a wink at Declan's look of shock, I head towards Elodie to hear what Doc has learned.

"While examining Ms. Hassan, I can confirm that she was murdered by the same person as the previous victims. From the note you left on the artifact bag, I ran some tests on her blood and compared them to some plasma samples I had collected from the other victims' blood before their deaths. With the annual Trial of Lir approaching, a few town members volunteered to donate blood in the case of any serious injuries. The games are no mere sport; it's a fight against the sea itself. I've encountered countless cases of hypothermia, loss of reason, those who succumbed to the seductive call of the selkies, terrifying hallucinations, and, all too often, drowning—"

"Yes, of course, Dr. O'Keefe. That does sound awful. I'd love to hear more about it later, but what were you able to find out about Leila's blood?" Elodie stops him from rambling on.

A faint blush crosses his cheeks at the reminder of what he's supposed to be telling us. "Yes, of course. As I was saying, I tried to compare her blood sample to the others, but the results came back inconclusive. Not once in my career has anything of the sort happened. I know it's not the equipment since the other victim's blood got a normal reading. So, I figured she must be wearing some type of charm or spelled artifact from that antique shop of hers. That's when I found it."

Flipping his clipboard over, he turns to a photograph of a necklace—a broad collar, with a lion's head at its centre, carved in gold. I try to remember if I've ever seen Leila wearing it, but she must have hidden it under her clothing.

"The only thing is, I wasn't able to remove it, and from the scratch marks around her neck, it appears as though your culprit wasn't able to either. Whatever magic it is infused with is strong. I'd wager Mrs. O'Keefe's Sunday roast that even the Council wouldn't be able to remove it."

"If even you can't find anything from her blood, why go through the trouble of placing it on the ostrich feather as a clue?" I question.

Flipping to the next photograph, Doc points to the scale that Elodie had taken a photograph of. "Now, I never said I came up empty-handed. As we all know, the mass of an ostrich feather outweighs that of a raven's—but not an entire raven. So, why would the Slayer even try and compare the two?

Thankfully, with the help of Ms. Niamh when she came to get the photos of the Ogham script, we've concluded that this is not just any ordinary scale, but that of the Egyptian goddess Ma'at, as is the feather itself. Its true purpose is to weigh the deceased individual's heart against that of the feather of Ma'at. According to Niamh's notes, this is a test of truth, justice, and purity determining the direction of one's soul in the afterlife. However, Leila's blood stains the feather, warping its purity, and rendering the scales entirely void. The once-sacred object now holds a corruption, a reminder of the deceit she is said to have carried with her in life. The scales meant to measure the soul against truth, are now incapable of fulfilling their divine role."

Unable to help myself, I break through Doc's explanation. "And then, of course, there's the raven, the symbol used from the very beginning. It seems he sees himself as something beyond human—beyond judgment. A god, perhaps. He doesn't need a god or goddess to weigh justice because this is his test now, his decision on whether the living or the dead are worthy. This isn't just a challenge—it's a proclamation to all of Eldermoore."

"Quite right, Ms. O'Grady. I'd think the whole thing quite clever if not done by such a madman" Doc looks up towards the ceiling as if contemplating this moral dilemma.

"I'm starting to think we're in the presence of one right now," Declan mutters under his breath.

"Hmm?" Doc hums as he glares at me. *As if I would ever say that… Well, not to his face, at least.*

Glaring at Declan who still stands behind Doc, I turn my attention back to him with a smile. "I was just agreeing with your sentiment. Were you and Niamh able to discover more about the necklace Leila wore, too?"

"Unfortunately, she had returned to the Scriptorium by the time I discovered it. The only thing I could decipher through some tests is that it is not made through dark magic or a curse. I wish I could be more help, but, bless her soul, artifacts and magic as old as this were a specialty of Leila's, and are outside my scope of knowledge. However, I'm sure if you visit Niamh, she'll have the engraving translated by now and would be happy to help."

"Thank you, Doc. We'll head there now."

Lost in thought as I follow behind the others, his voice suddenly pulls me back to the present, his grip on my shoulder tight as he comes up behind me. "And a word of warning from an ol' lad. No one is safe anymore."

Stepping towards the door, the weight of his words settle over me. We're so close to the truth, but the closer we get, the darker it seems.

Leila Hassan- Property of Danu's PI

28

CRACKS IN THE VEIL
ELODIE

Scriptorium ~ 11:30 a.m.

When I got the call from Doc, I didn't want to believe it. How could anyone want to hurt Leila?" Giving Aisling a tight squeeze, Niamh walks back to her desk, where a book and magnifying glass sit beside an assortment of flowerpots. With a snap of her fingers, the pots disappear, and she motions for us to join her.

Niamh leans back in her chair, her face drawn, eyes flicking from one person to the next as though weighing how much we can handle. She inhales sharply, then exhales with a slow, frustrated sigh, rubbing her temples.

"I know we've had more than enough bad news to last us a lifetime, but guess what. I've got some more for you. And, uh, it's two kinds of bad: the kind you don't want, and the kind that's even worse," she says, her tone bracing us for the impact.

I flinch when Niamh shoots to her feet, her movements so sudden and sharp that it takes me a second to process what's happening. She paces a few steps, then spins back to face us, her eyes blazing with anger. Her hands fly up in the air, fingers trembling as if she can't keep her frustration in check any longer.

"It's bad enough this fungus among us calls Leila a liar in that damn note," she snaps, her voice thick with disgust. "But the Ogham he marks her with? *It means* bréagadóir. Liar. *Liar*! And, as if that wasn't insulting enough, the artifact the Slayer uses is completely useless now—*utterly useless!*"

"If this is the bad news, I don't think I want to know what could make matters worse." Rowan groans from beside me.

"To make things worse, when he used her blood to 'prove' his point" she starts grimacing and shaking her head, "he might've made things even worse for Eldermoore. The gods aren't to be trifled with, especially one as powerful as Ma'at."

Aiden looks through the notes he made while we were at Doc's office before asking, "Say the gods *are* angered now…. are you saying it'll not only affect Mr. A, but all of us? We can catch a man masquerading as a god, but do we even have a fighting chance against the real thing?"

"We can only hope it hasn't reached that point yet. The reason I'm telling you this is because of what I found out about Leila's necklace." Picking up a magnifier, she hovers it above a page in a tome. "Now, most of this is written in *mdju netjer*, an ancient logographic script, but I've cross-referenced it with a few other texts, and see this? This hieroglyph represents Bastet."

Niamh's finger hovers above the sketch as she waits for us to get a closer look. "In one hand, she holds what I've translated as an *aegis*, though it's also referred to as a ceremonial collar, or seshed. The key detail, though, is the lion's head." Her voice softens as she leans closer to the text, almost reverently. "Isn't it beautiful? But it's not just for show—it's a direct reference to Bastet's early form as a lioness, a symbol of her strength and protective nature. This book describes it as a powerful token of protection worn only by royal women and priestesses when worshipping the goddess Isis.

Her gaze lingers on the image, awe clear in her expression, before she snaps her attention back to the present. "That's when I remembered the book Leila was looking through the other day when she was here. In it, I discovered Bastet is considered the soul of Isis, and Isis herself is connected to magic. When combining the two through wearing the aegis, I believe Leila was channelling Bastet for her role as protector of women, and get this—secrets," Niamh explains, her eyes wide.

I exhale slowly, the truth settling in. Leila hadn't just chosen the aegis. It'd been *placed* on her. That power wasn't something we could just remove with brute force or clever spell—if it could even be removed at all. The fact that it'd remained intact, even after Leila's death, is proof enough of that. Just as my thoughts continue in a downward spiral, Niamh's voice once again breaks through the silence.

"Alright, so since this is time sensitive, I called up my Nana to see if she could lend a hand again. Lucky for us, she's got some pretty wild connections with Heka priests in Egypt. It's actually a funny story, but all you really need to know is that she used to help this archaeologist friend of hers with ancient texts. The guy was obsessed with Egyptian artifacts, and one of his buddies just so happened to be a Heka priest. Small world, right? Anyway, the priest was able to track down someone who could help him portal here. They're supposed to arrive tomorrow to help perform the ritual to free Leila from the aegis and, fingers crossed, figure out what she was hiding. In the meantime, I think it'd be best if I showed you some good news."

I watch as she walks around the desk and motions us to follow her up the spiral staircase that seems to be never-ending. As we reach the landing for the fourth floor, Niamh guides us to a table towards the back. As I draw closer, the wall adjacent catches my eye. A whiteboard hangs floor to ceiling with a projected image of the calendar month and drawings of the moon on certain days of the week.

Seeing our attention has focused on the board, Niamh announces, "Ah yes, I'll be discussing that in a minute." With a flourish of her hands, the projector goes dark and the table it's perched on can now be seen in the dim light of the iron candle sconces lining the sides of the nearby bookcases. "First, I want to show you what I discovered once I cross-referenced Liam's riddle to Leila's. Now, through the clues you've found, we know from the note that the Slayer discovered Liam's plans to leave Eldermoore and that before the Obsidian Veil, he'd been imprisoned by your parents."

"We also know that he fancies himself a living god and the only judge, jury, and executioner." Maeve sneers, the same look of disgust she wore when I told her and Aisling about our visit with Doc crossing her face.

Pointing to Maeve, Niamh continues, "Right! And in the first letter written for Rónán, he discusses the Veil, and in Leila's, he says Eldermoore's Stars. Based on this, I think we can conclude one thing…"

"He has a vendetta against anyone from Réalt who chooses to protect an neamh-draíocht." Pausing briefly, Rowan begins to tap her chin in thought. "And if he's trying to use the moon cycles and spectral energy to boost his power, it's no wonder he's been going after people in Eldermoore with the most power and knowledge."

Looking morose, Niamh plops down into one of the chairs. "Exactly, which is why I saved the whiteboard for last." Flipping the power button on the projector, the image takes a moment to refocus. "Aside from what we talked about a few weeks ago, Leila had some interesting theories to contribute." Rising, Niamh walks over to the board and begins to write down the days of each murder. As she reaches today's date, a pattern begins to take form. Pointing to each of the Thursdays now marked, she explains, "Although we know he's chosen these days due to the moon's power, Leila provided some insight into the Egyptian's gods that I think you'll will find interesting." Returning to the table, she flips open the notebook that's marked with Leila's neat script. "Here, she noted that the gods would often bestow gifts upon those who left offerings at their temples. Yet, when they disappeared almost 2,000 years ago, the villagers would choose their next rulers from those believed to have been gifted magic from the gods themselves."

"Which we know is possible since Leila was gifted a necklace. I'm not sure how Egyptian lore is going to help us catch Mr. A, though," Declan contributes.

Looking up from the notepad, Niamh gives a tisk-tisk in his direction. "I thought you of all people would see where Leila was getting at, Mr. Spy. Since we don't know what happened before the Veil was created, Leila believed that if the Slayer is able to remove the Veil, he'll be like many of the past kings who have ruled her home. Yes, most were benevolent, but only towards those who could give them more power and wealth. When it came to those who worked to survive, they were taken advantage of—enslaved for hard labour or chosen to die in battle."

Aisling clears her throat to get our attention. "What if the Veil didn't just protect Balie na Muintir, but completely stopped us from developing powers in the first place? In all the history books I've read, only after the Veil creation did Eldermoore show signs of fewer people with magic." Waving her arms in mine and Rowan's direction, she continues, "I mean, look at you two. It wasn't until you bonded with Aiden that we could all start seeing more of the magic around us. If the letters we found in your Aunt's chest are anything to go by, your da had power, so why wouldn't you?"

Could she be right? If the Obsidian Veil truly has made powers go dormant, is this what Auntie Cait wanted us to discover? All our lives, Rowan and I had to work harder than anyone else to prove we could do our job, that we could find our parents. Now, I'm not so sure it was a bad thing at all. What had been making us different most of our lives had actually been keeping us safe. He knows what Rowan is and has spoken to both of us in our dreams. If he truly is here for revenge, it's only a matter of time before he comes for us.

Oct. 23ʳᵈ

With thoughts from the Scriptorium spinning in my head, I barely got a wink of sleep. No one had been able to combat Aisling's words, the truth hitting us like a bucket of cold water. We knew he'd been seeking revenge— he'd said so in his riddles— but it's more than seeking revenge on those involved in his capture. Mr. Doyle had said something big was in the works—that he'd been promised power himself. If Mr. A successfully takes down the Veil, there will be an endless supply of power to harness and use at his will.

Calling to the bond, I easily grasp Aiden's power of sight, the strand of his power like a beacon in my mind. The room transforms into a kaleidoscope of colours within seconds, no longer a transformation I have to think too hard about. Just beneath the surface, I sense something *more*…well, *mine*. Maybe Rowan and I had both inherited gifts from our parents. Auntie had told us to look for answers in our past; perhaps this is one of the truths she wanted us to discover. With her gone, though, who's to say that the Council won't try to block us from our heritage once more when we find the Slayer?

Walking to the window, I watch as the sun begins to rise, the first golden rays rising above the trees that Rowan and I climbed every summer. The pink and orange clouds cast reflections on our parents' car. Eldermoore is part of our family's history, our home, even though it's been hidden from us for so long. As I watch the sun settle high in the sky I finally understand why Auntie Cait had been so adamant that we learn the truth. The Veil had been a necessary evil at the time, but it's time for change. It's our responsibility now to protect Eldermoore, to rid it of this evil and for the truth of our town to come to light. Smiling up at the sun, I savour its warmth on my face, almost as if it's embracing me. Aiden was right. She never left at all.

Scriptorium, 9 a.m.

After meeting the girls at the office, Aiden drove us back to the Scriptorium to meet the Heka priest who had finally arrived. As soon as I stepped inside, the thick, smoky scent of incense curled into my lungs, sharp and familiar. It pulled me back to those long afternoons when Rowan and I would lose ourselves in conversation with Leila and Liam in the Emporium. Inhaling deeply, I try steadying the flutter of nerves in my stomach and follow Aiden towards the sound of Niamh's voice blending with a man's.

I follow Aiden up a few flights of stairs, their voices louder as we reach the top. The space in front of us is nothing like the library below. It's open, with stone pillars and an altar at the centre. It's there that I see that Leila's body lies on a bier, draped in linen so fine it almost seems to glow. Candles flicker in the dim light, making shadows stretch like whispers against the walls.

My chest tightens. It's hard to breathe as I take in the sight of her—so still, so composed. The reality of her absence settles around me, heavier than I expected. I'd tried so hard to stay focused yesterday, to find the clues we needed to bring her justice. I saw how broken Aisling had been. I'd seen the look of guilt on Rowan's face. I had to be strong for them, for Leila, for us all. Brief flashes of the promises I'd made her as she grieved for her brother crosses my mind. She'd trusted us and believed in our ability to find who did this. In the end, we'd been too late, and I'd lost them both.

Niamh stands with a man, who looks up as we enter. His gaze is warm, but there's something in it—an understanding, a quiet recognition of how we're feeling.

He's tall, dressed in simple linen robes, gold threading along the edges. His head is shaved, and his dark eyes, rimmed with kohl, hold a steady kindness. "Welcome. I know this has been hard. It is good to finally meet you."

At this, we bow our heads in greeting as Niamh instructed us to do before we left yesterday. "Thank you for traveling so far to help us," I say, my voice soft but sincere.

"It is my honour. A friend of the O'Neill's is a friend of mine. My name is Si-Osire." he says, his voice calm and reassuring. "Heka is a powerful tool, but it is also a gift, one that allows us to communicate with the gods. Today, we use it not only for Leila, but for the bond she shares with Bastet and Isis. They have watched over her, and now we ask for their help. Her death was unnatural—violent—and the gods have been shielding her. But we must be certain that she is not lost, that her path is not disrupted."

As he settles around the offerings to the gods, we hear him begin to pray. "Osiris, ruler of the Duat, we offer these to you, to nourish the spirit of Leila. May she never go hungry, and may her soul always find sustenance as she journeys in your realm."

Next, he gently places a bowl of water down. "To you, Anubis, Guardian of the Dead, we offer this water to cleanse Leila's spirit, remove the stains of her violent death and ensure her safe passage." He dips his fingers in the bowl and sprinkles water lightly across the altar.

Arranging a bundle of lotus flowers at Leila's feet, Si-Osire continues, "Just as the lotus rises from the mud to bloom towards the sun, so too shall your soul rise towards the light, Leila. May the gods grant you rebirth, the peace of the afterlife, and protection from all that would seek to harm you."

The air thickens with the scent of incense, the smoke curling upwards as the priest lights a bundle of frankincense and myrrh. As it rises, he chants in low, measured tones. "O Ra, God of the Sun, shine your light upon this soul. O Anubis, guide her through the halls of Ma'at, so that she may find balance and peace in the afterlife."

As the final offerings are made, the Heka priest pauses, and the room falls into a deep silence. We hold our breaths, waiting, until the room seems to exhale in unison with the start of the priest's second invocation.

"The gods have watched over Leila's spirit since her passing," Si-Osire says quietly, his tone both solemn and compassionate. "The collar she wears has kept her tethered between this world and the afterlife, a safeguard against the chaos that threatened her soul. Now it is time to release her from this bond."

The priest raises his hands, and the chant grows louder, now pulsing with power. The incense swirls, filling the room with its heady scent. The very space feels different, like the walls are bending, and the air is vibrating in response to the priest's words. "We call upon you, Bastet, fierce Protector of Souls, and you, Isis, Goddess of Wisdom and Rebirth. Hear our plea. Leila's soul has been kept from the darkness, shielded by your grace. We ask you to sever the final tether that binds her. Let her spirit move freely."

The collar hums, its light flaring bright enough to blind as the room fills with an unnatural stillness that feels as though time itself has held its breath. Then, the space around us begins to unravel.

The veil between this world and the next tears open like a vast curtain pulled aside. The room dissolves into a swirling, golden expanse that stretches beyond comprehension. I look for the others, but only Rowan remains. We're no longer in a library, but standing on the very threshold of the divine, where reality bends with the presence of something beyond our world.

And then, they appear.

Bastet, towering and regal with the head of a lioness, steps forwards first. Her presence is commanding—unmistakably powerful—but there's also a deep, profound tenderness in her gaze as she looks upon Leila's resting form. Beside her, Isis emerges, her form radiant, wings unfurled in a sweeping arc, glowing with an ethereal light. Her eyes are soft yet filled with an eternal strength, as though she's witnessed the universe's greatest triumphs and sorrows. Together, they stand, powerful but gentle, guardians of Leila's spirit, their connection to her clear. Their voices come not from their mouths, but within our minds.

"Children of the Earth," Bastet's voice thunders inside my mind, full of authority yet laced with deep affection. *"We know what you seek, the answers that twist within your hearts and minds. You search for the truth, for the mystery of Leila's past, for why she suffered, for what comes next. We have watched over Leila from the moment she took her first breath. We guarded her as she walked the earth, always unseen, always near. You did not know this, but we were with her."*

"You do not know of the burden she carried," Isis adds, her voice flowing like water, gentle but heavy with the weight of wisdom. *"Leila and her brother crossed vast seas to find their way here. The journey was perilous, but we kept them hidden from those who would have destroyed them."*

"But there is more that you do not know," Bastet continues. Her voice carries a depth of sorrow that makes my heart ache. *"Leila did not possess the power you believed her to have. It was taken from her long ago— stolen from her, by those who feared her potential. In her homeland, she was a priestess, and her power was ripped away, leaving her*

vulnerable. She carried this loss, this emptiness, for so long. She prayed, in secret, when the weight of her loss became unbearable. It was then that we answered her call."

"We did all we could." Isis's voice trembles, and, for the first time, I feel the weight of her grief. *"We shielded her, kept her hidden from those who wished her harm. Allowed her to roam undetected between the Veil your ancestors created. But we are gods, and we cannot interfere in mortal affairs. We cannot change the course of a life completely."*

Bastet's voice follows, full of power but also a heavy sadness. *"You have been loyal friends. Fear not for her soul. It is free, and we release her from the collar. It has served its purpose."*

There's a long pause, and then Bastet steps forwards, her gaze lingering on Leila with affection, as if she's a mother seeing her child off on a journey. The lioness goddess kneels beside Leila, her fingers tenderly brushing Leila's face. She leans down, pressing a soft kiss to Leila's forehead, her lips lingering for a moment. Her hand moves gently to the collar at Leila's neck, and with great reverence, she lifts it away, cradling it in her palm. The collar glows softly, almost as if it's reluctant to let go, but Bastet places it around her neck, securing it in place.

"I shall guard it once more." Bastet's voice is resolute but filled with grief.

As the vision begins to fade, Isis speaks, her voice softer now, like the whisper of a breeze. *"The path ahead will not be easy, children. Darkness grows closer, like a shadow that follows your every step."*

Bastet's eyes flash with quiet intensity, her gaze piercing. *"Beware the ones closest to you. The Slayer hides in plain sight, wearing a face you trust. The gods cannot protect you from the choices you must make, but we will watch, and we will guide you. Know that you are never truly alone."*

29

LOST BETWEEN WORLDS
ELODIE

October 24, Danu's PI - 12 p.m.

The bell chimes from the front door and my breath catches. My hands go cold, my heart thudding against my ribs. For weeks, it's been the same: the bell tolls, and in walks something we're never prepared for. I glance up from my desk, holding onto the faint hope that this time might be different. To my surprise, it's none other than Maeve's admirer from the docks and I release the breath I didn't know I was holding.

He stops just inside the doorway and his eyes travel the room.

"You just missed her," I supply. From my desk, I motion for him to sit in the chair across from me. As he settles in, I add, "Maeve hadn't informed me that you'd be stopping by today. Was there something you found?"

At the news, Lorcan's eyes dim and a frown takes over his usual smirk. Clearing his throat, he leans back in the chair, his legs resting on the corner of my desk. "I'd hoped to have a chat with the lovely Miss O'Connor, but you'll have to do."

"Gee, thanks," Rowan grumbles under her breath from her desk.

Pushing his crossed ankles off my desk, I give him my best no-nonsense smile, my teeth grinding in annoyance. "Was there something you found or are you just here to be a bother? A lot has happened recently, so, if it's the latter, I'll have to ask you to leave."

His eyes flash in annoyance as he tries to balance the chair before his lips turn up in a smile. "I'm a sailor, love. I always bother women. Seeing as I always deliver," he says with a wink, "I'll have you know I did find something of use to your case. More of a who than a what. I discovered the poor bloke wandering the docks. He told me he'd just arrived from Blackthorn and was looking to offer us some names involved in the rumoured uprising if we could protect him. He refused to believe me when I told him I was working for ya, so I'm afraid one of you will have to convince him to talk. It's also the reason only one of you can go with me. He seemed ready to jump ship again before I left. Chum, like him, always seems to attract the sharks. We wouldn't want to scare him further, y'know?"

Jumping up from my seat, I head for my coat as I yell over my shoulder, "Why didn't you just start with that." As I go to open the door, Rowan's hand covers mine.

Pulling my hand from the knob, she drags me up the stairs to our photography room. Before closing the door, she shouts down to Aisling, "Keep him company for a minute; I need to speak with Elodie." As soon as the door closes, she begins pacing the length of the small room, the sound of her quick strides reverberating against the wooden floors.

"What's wrong? If we have any hope of solving this, we need all the help we can get." I whisper under my breath so as not to be heard by the others downstairs.

"What's wrong? What's wrong!" she exclaims in hushed tones as she pulls at her hair that's begun to shift to a soft cream colour. She takes a deep breath, to calm herself before she continues, "Do you not remember what the goddesses told us? Someone we trust has been deceiving us, and it could be that conceited jerk you were about to go traipsing across town with. What do we even know about him?"

Now it's my turn to pace as I contemplate the possibility. "He's been helpful so far, and he's clearly smitten with Maeve. How bad could he be? Plus, we need answers, and right now he has some."

Placing her hand on my shoulder, Rowan stops me from making another turn about the room. "I know, I know. I'd just feel better if I went with him instead. Not only do I have a better sense of magic, but I'm a banshee. Whether a gift or a curse, I can use that to my advantage. If anything happens, I can scream and alert the other ships' crews." Giving my arm a light punch, she cracks, "And seeing how Declan is still going on about how he can't hear, I'd bet you'd hear me all the way from here."

I have to admit that her attempt to lessen my worry is working. "Well, you have a point." Grabbing her in a hug, I whisper, "Just promise you'll be safe."

"Don't worry, the wind has always been at our backs. I'll return before you know it." With a quick wink, she leads us back downstairs where Aisling waits with Lorcan by the door.

As we approach, I notice that Lorcan is unusually quiet, his gaze focused on his reflection as he stands beside Aisling. Despite her attempts to draw him into conversation, he barely responds. Their one-sided conversation about the weather halts as Rowan makes her way to the coat rack.

Placing mine back on its hook, she grabs her own coat. Taking Lorcan by the arm, she pushes him through the door, her voice muffled by the glass window, "Let's go, Romeo. I've got a date with a hot slice of pie when we get back."

+)>●((+

At the sound of the bell ringing again, I look at the clock on my desk. *That was quick.* With a smile, I joke, "Jeez, did you take a parasail?"

My smile dims as I see someone hold the door open for Maeve, her hands full of the baked goods we ordered. Aisling rushes over to help as she tries to place the box on the table when a figure follows her in.

"Lorcan?" The question stumbles out of me.

Taking a seat on the sofa, he tips an imaginary hat in my direction before waving a piece of paper in the air. "I don't normally do door deliveries, but we found this outside." His words are muffled as he tries to speak around a glazed cranberry biscuit. As he goes to reach for another, Maeve slaps his hand away.

"Hold on a minute. What are you doing back so soon? And why didn't Rowan come back with you?"

"Contrary to the rumours you might have heard, I'm a one woman at a time kind of fella," he says with a wink.

At his nonchalance, my anger quickly rises. "Do you take anything seriously? You were here not ten minutes ago and now you're acting as though it never happened."

Before he can respond, Maeve takes my hand and leads me over to the loveseat. "Whoa there, Elodie. Take a deep breath. He couldn't have been here. I found him leaving the cafe as I was heading in. He offered to keep me company considering he had some news for us. What's this all about?"

Feeling my head rush, I sit down. "Unless you're playing some kind of trick on us or have a fetch out there, something is seriously wrong!"

Sitting next to me, Aisling confirms what we both saw. "Elodie's right. A man who looked and acted just like Lorcan came in saying he found a witness we needed to talk to down by the docks. Rowan volunteered because you... I mean, the man, told Elodie only one of us needed to convince the fella he was working on the case to find Mr. A."

Sitting up now, Lorcan looks at us with concern and shock. "Well, lassies, I'm sorry, but it's as Maeve said. I really wasn't here before, though for your sake I wish I could say I was."

Just as my hands start shaking, the door slams open and Aiden rushes to my side. Numb to everything around me, I barely hear the others fill him in on what's happened.

"You said I'd always have her," I whisper as I look up into his eyes before he brushes a tear from my cheek. "He took her; I know it. They told us it'd be someone we trusted. I shouldn't have let her go alone." Remembering the goddess's words, I jump up from my seat and rush to get my notepad from my jacket.

Returning to my seat, I frantically flip to the notes I took from one of our first visits to Leila's. *There.* Underlined and written in bold letters is the proof of his deceit. Scanning my friend's faces, they look on with concern, too afraid to say anything that'd cause me to break. "The goddesses who freed Leila from the collar told us that he'd be wearing a mask. I thought it sounded familiar, but I couldn't remember why." Turning the page towards them, I point at my scribbled words. "The Morrigan's Mask. Leila told us that the one that completed the pair had gone missing. It has the power to transform someone into anyone they desire."

Lorcan looks unnerved by the mention of the mask. "Seems like a nasty piece of work… and impersonating my beauty? I'm shocked you can't tell a real diamond from a fake. Unfortunately, this seems outside my specialties so, if you need me, I'll be on my ship." His words make him appear aloof, but I caught the way his eyes darkened in fear before he hid behind a mask of his own making. As he rises from his seat and dusts off the crumbs from his clothes, Lorcan is jerked back down by Declan's firm grip on the collar of his coat.

His eyes are dark as he sneers at the sailor. "Sit." With a strength I've never seen from him before, Declan rips the note from Lorcan's hands before tearing it open. Reading aloud he starts:

Your sister's lost in shadows deep,
A prize in my clutches where dangers creep.
Your curse, though dark, can find its end,
But first you must face the terror I send.

This blight was laid by your parents' hand,
A dark legacy etched upon this land.

You ignored my clues, now face the strife,
Their ghostly cries herald the end of your life.

As he reads the last line, he throws the letter and a photograph of Rowan onto the table. The lights above us flashing on and off, before Declan storms towards the door.

Aiden rushes to stop him, his voice tempered as he tries to reason with Declan. "Where are you going? He could be keeping her anywhere. We need to come up with a plan if we have any hope of finding her."

Shaking off Aiden's hand, Declan pushes open the door as he announces, "I'll be right back."

I watch from my seat as Declan disappears into Aiden's office. Within seconds, he returns, a large poster rolled in his hand. His strides are long as he turns towards the corkboard to unravel what I can now see is a map of Eldermoore. Turning to face us, he starts to place black-coloured tacks at the five crime scenes, the last one placed on our office where Rowan was taken. Next, he uses two grey tacks, one to mark our parents' last known location and the other to mark the spot Rowan and I had seen the will-o-the-wisp. "Do you see the pattern?"

Walking to the board, I point at the crime scene locations. "These are all within Réalt. All except Liam's, but we know his death wasn't originally part of the Slayer's plan."

"Exactly." Taking a pen from the cup on my desk he draws a perfect circle around the murders within Réalt. "After your Auntie's death, we focused on the idea of revenge seeing as he always wrote it in his riddles. We were able to connect two locations for certain—your house and hers." Pausing, he creates an arch to connect them.

"Yet, the first crime occurred at the Tara Hall, which is the same place Auntie Cait worked when she wasn't attending Council meetings," Aisling says from beside me. Taking the pen tucked in her hair, she draws a connecting arch between Auntie's house, the school, and Foyle Hall.

Borrowing the pen from Aisling, I sketch another connecting line as I add, "The same Hall where Rowan and I did the bonding ceremony with Aiden."

Taking a step back from the board, the picture we've drawn is immediately recognizable. Within the circle is a Triquetra. The symbol for life, death, and rebirth. "

A trinity knot. This means he needs both of you to complete the cycle so he can be reborn." Lorcan's and Maeve's voices blend together as they come to the same realization.

"I don't like this. He's obviously leading you into a trap. He knows you'll look for her. He must have only taken Rowan today because he's still weak from using his power to kill Leila," Aiden cautions.

"I agree, but if what we've learned is true, he'll have no other option but to wait until the next full moon." Thinking back to the image Niamh projected of the calendar, I add, "That's six days away. We need to find her before then."

+)) ● ((+

The darkness closes in around me, thick and suffocating. It presses against my chest, choking the air out of my lungs. My limbs are heavy, and I feel like I'm sinking slowly and endlessly into this void. I can't breathe, can't think, can't escape. The weight of everything, the guilt, the loss, the helplessness… It drags me deeper, and part of me thinks I should let it.

I want to let it.

Maybe it's easier to just give in, to stop fighting against this crushing tide. Maybe if I let the dark take me, I'll stop feeling the raw ache in my chest—the hollow, gnawing emptiness that's been growing since the moment Rowan was taken. My sister. My twin. Half of my soul. Gone. The thought presses on me, suffocating me more than the darkness ever could.

I close my eyes, hoping it'll disappear. But it doesn't. I failed you, Rowan. The thought circles endlessly, a mantra I can't stop repeating. I should've been there. I should've protected you. And now you're gone. But then, through the suffocating silence, I hear it. A voice—soft at first, distant—but unmistakable. It's my Mam.

"Elodie…"

It's faint, but it pulls at me, as if it can reach through the darkness and touch the deepest part of me. Her voice doesn't feel like comfort. It's laced with a deep sorrow, but something in it stirs. I can't stop myself from reaching for it. But even in my dream, my hands can't find her.

"Don't surrender to the dark, darling. There's still a road for you to tread."

I don't know how to respond. I don't even know if I can respond. The darkness around me pulls tighter. My thoughts spiral further into grief, into hopelessness. I can't think of anything but the crushing weight of Rowan's absence.

But her haunting voice is insistent. *"You must seek her. She is not gone—not yet."*

I want to ask how, but I can't. The words are trapped behind the wall of grief, of failure.

"You're tethered to her, Elodie. Bound in light and shadow both. Look for the spark."

I try to focus, but the darkness is so thick, so heavy. I can't see anything, can't feel anything but the endless ache in my chest. Her words slip through the cracks in my thoughts, pushing past the grief that clouds everything. I try to feel for Rowan, try to reach for that thread, but it's as if everything is slipping through my fingers. It's too dark. It's too much.

"She's waiting, love. She calls for you."

And for the first time in what feels like forever, I feel a shift. The dark presses harder, but I know it's not enough to take me. My mother's words pull me back, like a rope tied around my chest. *"Elodie… You must move. The light will lead you home."*

I try, desperately, to find that pull, that connection. And just before I lose myself again, I hear it. Rowan's voice. It's faint, almost lost in the dark, but I hear it.

"Elodie… come… wake me…"

The sound of my name is a thread through the shadows. My heart catches in my throat. For a moment, I'm still, too afraid to move, too afraid that if I reach for it, the light will disappear again. But then, with a trembling breath, I take a step forwards.

"*Rowan,*" I whisper, and the dream cracks, shattering the darkness.

-Elodie's Journal-

"The Last Thread"

Entry #12: October 25th @ 3:00 AM

As I wake, I take in my surroundings. The office lights blind me and I snap my eyes closed once more, the contrast from my dream making it hard to adjust. As I rub my watering eyes, a shadow blocks the light, giving me a moment of reprieve. Squinting my eyes open, I can just make out Aiden as he leans against my desk.

"Take it easy. You dozed on me for a few minutes there. You should get some proper rest. You've been pouring over these folders for hours. We all have." With a smirk, he leans closer to me to whisper, "You might have to battle Lorcan for the sofa. Though with the way he's sleeping, he might not even notice."

Although I know he's trying to get me to laugh, my heart beats erratically at the mention of taking a break. It feels too much like giving up. "I'm sorry, I just *can't*. She'd do the same for me."

Fully opening my eyes, I look around to see Maeve and Aisling slouched over the table, their eyes heavy with sleep. On the couch, Lorcan quietly snores into the papers Maeve assigned him begrudgingly when he refused to leave hours ago after coming back from confirming that Rowan was never seen near the dock. Looking towards Rowan's desk, I almost expect her to be sitting there, her fingers racing across the keyboard. Instead, Declan has been using it to research the spectral devices he saw throgh the portal. If he can find a way to shut them off, we may be able to stop the Slayer from gaining any more power. At least, that was what we theorized two hours ago. From the way his shoulders are hunched, it could be days before we find the answer. It's time we didn't have.

Straightening the file on my desk, I ignore Aiden's words, and his shadow slowly lessens as he sits back down in the seat across from me.

"Okay, mo thrioblóir beag. Tell me what you need me to do."

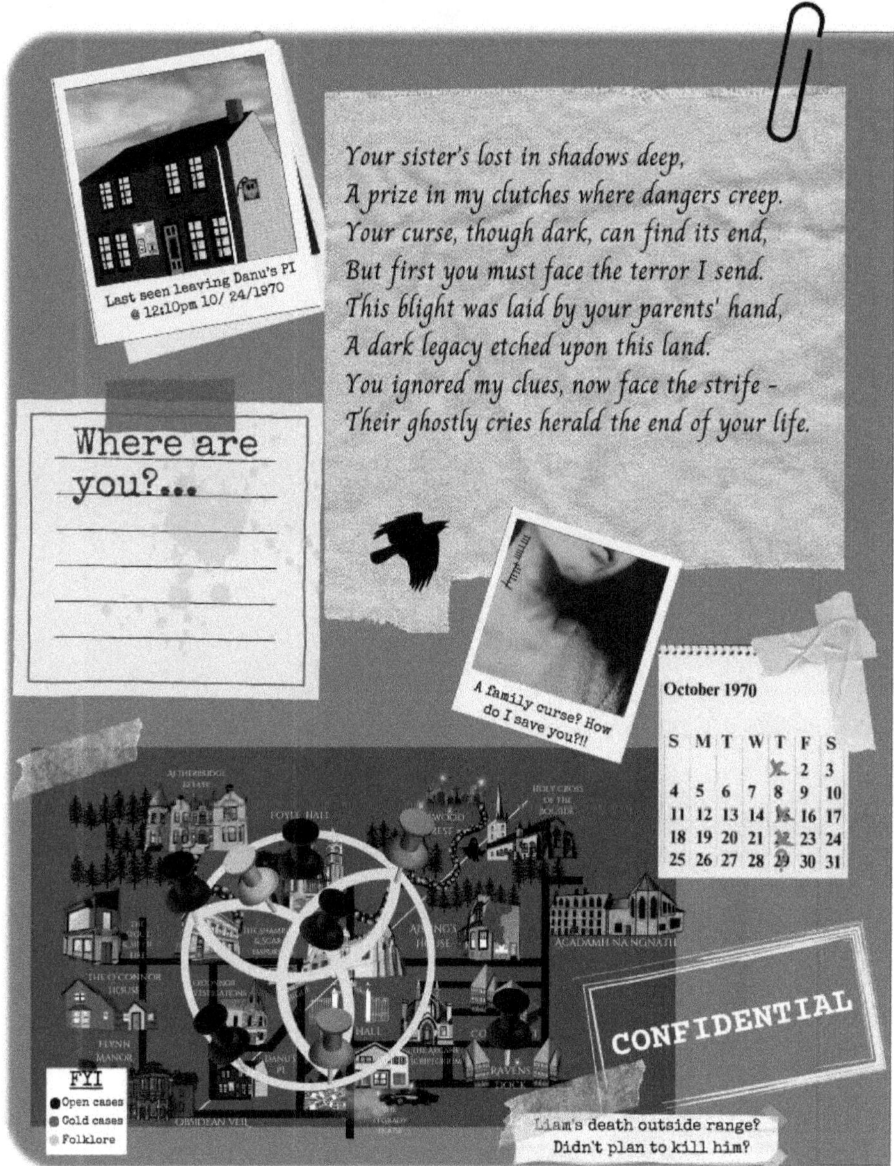

Rowan O'Grady- Property of Danu's PI

30

ALL ROADS LEAD HOME
ELODIE

October 28th - 2 days until the full moon

Already four days have passed, and still nothing. I barely sleep, but I force myself to knowing the only time I ever feel her near is in the darkness of my dream where I hear her calling to me— begging me to wake her. Aiden keeps assuring me that we'd both feel it through the bond if she were in pain, but what terrifies me most is that most times I don't feel anything at all.

We've had Lennon and Saoirse check the surveillance outside their shop while the rest of us have split up into teams, scouring Eldermoore for anyone who might have witnessed something. I've been to the Scriptorium's temple each morning, trying again and again to reach the Goddesses. Every time, I offer a new prayer, hoping one will be the right one. At first, I begged them to keep Rowan safe, to help me find her. Yesterday, I prayed they'd let me switch places with her. This morning, I woke with the full expectation of finding myself in darkness again. I was ready to face it, to lose myself there if it meant Rowan could be free. But when I opened my eyes, it was the harsh light of our office that greeted me once again. Today, my prayer is simpler. I don't even know what to ask for anymore—just a sign, anything to tell me I'm not completely lost.

October 29th- 1 day until the full moon

The ringing of the phone breaks the silence of the office, everyone's eyes turning to me as I pick. "Danu's PI. This is Elodie speaking."

The muffled sound of breathing on the other end of the line instantly puts me on high alert.

"Hello? Who am I speaking with?"

The phone crackles once more before the line goes dead.

Too stunned, I gently place the phone back down when suddenly it lights up with the same number as it begins to ring again. Not waiting again, I hurriedly answer. "Hello? I'm not sure what kind of trick you're playing at, but— "

My words are cut off as I hear an otherworldly screech come through the line.

There's rustling and quiet pants as if the person calling has been running.

"Elodie, it's Mrs. Flanagan. Don't hang up. After your last visit, I've been keeping an eye on the vault's artifacts. I found a letter addressed to you and your sister while I was looking through some old paperwork. The Púca has refused to let me leave with it. I've been locked within the chamber. The only way I can get you the letter is if I read it to you from here. Now get a pen; I'll only have time to say it once."

Could this be the sign? Quickly motioning to Aiden to start writing, I put the call on speaker.

Mrs. Flanagan's breathing has quieted, and her voice is steady as she speaks.

My dearest friend Deirdre,   24 October 1925

My thoughts are filled with sorrow, for I know that I have let this go on far too long. I should have seen the signs earlier and acted with more urgency. You begged me for help, and I failed you. Failed to see past my fear to the true weight of the evil we have been facing. Instead, the blood of my most treasured friends—Ciaran, Declan, and you, Deirdre... Your sacrifice haunts me every waking hour. Too much loss, too much grief. I cannot bear the weight of it anymore. The time for hesitation is past. I will do whatever it takes to stop him, to end this madness. I will find a way to stop him, even if it costs me everything.

I have come to realize that my power, alone, will not be enough. I feel it in my bones. But I dare not speak more plainly, for fear of revealing my secrets to his shadows. Know this: there is something buried deep within this land—something ancient, rooted in the earth itself—that will bind his fate. His doom is not written in silver or fire, nor in any old sword or stake, but in the heart of the earth itself. Its mighty roots know his name. And when the time comes, the earth will call it forth, and his face will meet the underworld at last.

But, Deirdre, there is something I can promise you now. I will do everything in my power to protect your children. They are the future. And I will make sure that the evil that stole you from this world does not take them as well. I will guard them as my own, and I will not let the darkness touch them. I will protect them with every last breath I have. You have my word.

With all my love,

Caitriona

Taking the phone off speaker, I bring it up to my ear as I carry the cord over to the window. "How do we know you're who you say you are, that you didn't just make that up? How do we know we can trust you?" My tone is sharp as a blade. I can't… no, I won't be deceived again. Not when Rowan's life is at stake.

"My girl" Her voice turns stern, and I can picture her scowl as if she were right in front of me. "I may not have always seen eye to eye with your Auntie, but I never doubted her for a moment when it came down to you and Rowan. After she lost your parents, you were her whole life. You practically grew up in the Academy, you took your first steps in these halls and it's where you learned to investigate by spying on our classrooms."

I gasp in shock at her words. Rowan and I made sure we never got caught. With a laugh, she continues, "Ah, you thought you were thick as thieves. I might oversee trade, lass, but I always made sure to keep an eye on ya', to make sure you stayed out of trouble." I hear her take a deep breath, the noise catching as if the memories have become too much. As she begins to speak, her accent is thick, her words shortened by emotion "Cait was a dear friend, an' I'd ne'er betray her trust by sidin' wi' the devil, ya hear?"

"Aye, I hear you. Thank you for getting us the letter." In a whisper, I add, "Thank you for being there for our Auntie. I owe you one."

She's quiet for a moment, and I wonder if she's ended the call, but her voice is clear as she says, "You don't owe me anything. Just promise me you'll find that fecker causin' all the strife an' bring our girl Rowan home."

I smile at her words. The fury within my eyes as I stare at my reflection in the window blazes even stronger than the anger I hear in her voice. "Now that I'll gladly promise."

Even after I hear the dial tone go dead, I take a moment to breathe. Only when I no longer see such anger in my reflection do I return to the group. Their words are hushed as they try to pick out clues from the letter, but as I approach they motion me to hurry over.

I try to tamper down my excitement at the possibility of having found the thread we need to connect the pieces. There may be nothing but more unanswered questions, but the smiles on their faces give me hope. Saying a small prayer of thanks to the gods, I rush back to my desk.

"Alright, what did you find?" My voice betrays my excitement.

Whatever it is, it must be good, because Maeve twirls in place before stunning Lorcan with a kiss on the cheek. As if realizing what she's done, her face turns red as she tries to smooth away an imaginary stray hair. Clearing her throat, she focuses her attention back on the paper. "It appears that Declan was a friend of your family. He'd even died trying to help your parents capture the Slayer."

Turning to Declan, I ask, "Do you remember anything from before? I know it's not common for spectrals to retain memories, but it's worth a try."

I watch as his face pales. "Most of my memories disappeared as a result of the darkness that had almost made me a shade of myself." As he takes a deep breath, the colour slowly returns to his face. "I'll say that I remember waking as a spectral not far from Foyle Hall. The path we took to the Holy Cross of the Bogside for your Auntie's precession seemed very familiar."

Remembering the will-o'-the-wisp Rowan and I had seen, I can't help but think that it may have been showing us the land's last remaining part of his soul before he entered Tír na nÓg. Since we were little, we'd followed their path in hopes of finding our parents, but it'd only led us to the entrance of the woods by our house. Though they hadn't appeared in years, the recent murders seem to have woken them once more.

Walking to the map, I point to the location Rowan had remembered to mark. "Would you say right about here?"

Considering the map, Declan shakes his head in agreement. "I'd say very close, if not the exact spot."

So, the will-o'-the-wisps have been giving us hints. Walking back to my seat I read the note as Aiden points to our next clue.

"Your Auntie's never been one to repeat herself, but she's mentioned the land multiple times," he says. "From her previous letters, it's clear he was defeated on this side of the Veil, but even narrowing that down, there are still too many trees in Eldermoore to dig beneath them all. It'd be impossible to find some ancient power hidden beneath us in the time we have left."

My hope dims at his words. He's right; we don't have time to find Rowan and where Auntie Cait had first captured him. Glancing at the map from my desk, I try to think, to sort out the trail of riddles. As I follow the connecting arcs we've drawn, the clock tower above Foyle Hall sounds, the evening ring alerting me to another day without Rowan. *Wait…* Grabbing the files we made for each victim, I pin the photographs to the board. *We've had the answer all along.*

⁺)ᴐ●ᴄ(⁺

I run through the forest, the one I've known all my life, drawn towards the soft flicker of will-o'-the-wisps. Their lights dance ahead of me, guiding my steps with a promise of something near—something I've been searching for. The trees, their branches thick with mist, part before me as I move deeper.

The voice of my Mam guides me like she has from the very beginning, even when I hadn't known it yet. "You're almost there," she says, her words like a gentle breeze, pushing me forwards.

"She needs you."

Rowan. I push forwards, desperate to reach her. Then, the air shifts. The light of the will-o'-the-wisps falters, flickering like a dying flame. The trees begin to close in on me, their shapes twisting unnaturally, their roots holding me in place.

The warmth of my mother's voice fades into something colder, and I know, deep down, something is wrong. A sudden, sharp laugh rings out, shattering the silence.

He's here.

The darkness consumes the light as his voice drips with mockery. *"You still think you can reach her? That you can save her? How heroic of you."*

I freeze.

His laugh curls around me, a sickening sound that tightens in my chest. The forest is gone now. There's nothing but the sound of his voice and the suffocating darkness.

"You'll never make it in time," he taunts. *"All your searching will be for nothing. There are no heroes in this story."*

257

He sneers, his tone slipping into something darker, more frenzied. *"You always thought you were the only one looking out for her. Like I didn't see her—like I didn't know exactly where she was. Foolish. That thing… that thing she kept so close. I thought running it down would do the trick. But no, it's still there. Still there, like a thorn in my side, haunting me. I should've known it wouldn't just vanish like that."*

Pausing his voice shifts, as if lost in his own spiralling thoughts. *"Let her come, then. Let her see what's left when I'm done! And your sister? She's mine now. Just like you'll be, soon enough!"*

His voice fades as his shadows engulf me in darkness. And I see nothing. It's as though I'm in a void where time stands still. I have no thoughts, my mind silent, almost too quiet. I feel as though I should be doing something. Every time I think I grasp the memory, it disappears.

Maybe that's what I should do, too.

Disappear.

-Elodie's Journal-

"Unveiling the Way"

Entry #13: October 30th @ 8:00 AM

October 30th - 10 hours until the full moon

I jolt awake, the memory of his hand reaching for me making my stomach turn. Seeing the light from my desk lamp, I almost feel like crying. *I've never been so happy to be in the office.* The sudden rhythmic tapping on the side of my desk startles me, just as I feel something soft brush against my leg. Jumping from my seat, I catch sight of a black form as it makes its way around the other side. *Did his shadows follow me from the dream?* The black mass pounces onto the table, and I have to stop the sudden scream rising in my throat as I see its bright purple eyes.

"Dammit, girl, you nearly gave me a heart attack," I whisper as I give Shade a scratch behind her ears. Too caught up in trying to find Rowan, I hadn't even realized how Shade's presence had been missing—her attachment to

Rowan usually too strong for her to stay away for long

"Where have you been?" I whisper, trying not to wake the others.

As she stares at me, it's like I'm transported back into my dream. The ramblings of a madman now become clear in my mind. Taking her semitranslucent body in my arms, I embrace her in a hug, despite her attempts to break free. If she's been with Rowan, keeping her safe, then she's the closest thing I've had to embracing my sister in days.

"I think it's time we get back what's ours."

6 hours and 30 minutes- 11:30 a.m.

The loud smack of the case folder against the table causes the girls to jump awake while the boys sluggishly sit up from their sleeping positions spread around the room. At their grogginess, I only feel slightly bad for such a rude wake-up call, but the clock is ticking. With only the five of us left to solidify a plan now that Lorcan returned to his ship, I need to make sure we're all on the same page. *I can't risk losing anyone else.*

As Aisling rubs the sleep from her eyes, Maeve does a few stretches, making her way to my desk. Aiden, whose turn it was to take the sofa, hits the ground with a pained groan as he tries to untangle himself from the throw blanket.

"Alright, I'm up. Did you find something?" His tired green eyes focus in my direction.

"I had another dream; it was leading me somewhere. It seemed like I was walking forever, but then he was there. Only, I think this one may have been more like dream-walking than a premonition. I usually wake from them around three, but today it was later. It's almost like he was able to keep me trapped." I shake my head just remembering his crazed taunts. "He's spiralling, that's for sure. It wasn't until I woke up that I realized he'd unknowingly given us a clue to find out where he's hiding."

"Are you sure he's not just leading you into a trap like before?" Aisling looks at me with concern, yet there's a spark of hope in her eyes that I haven't seen in weeks.

"He's become more beast than human. The dark magic he's used has affected his mind, but I've found when someone is desperate, they always slip up." Tapping my desk, Shade jumps to the tabletop. With a smile, I add, "Luckily, I caught onto his mistake, thanks to Shade."

Looking at me incredulously, Aiden deadpans, "You're saying a cat, no, a ghost cat, helped you?"

"Very funny. This isn't just any cat, though. It's Rowan's." Pointing to the file I woke them up with, I continue, "Since I didn't want to just speculate, I gave Niamh a call before waking you. She was able to find a few instances of animal bonds. The most common case is a familiar. If an animal forms a bond with a human before or after their death, they become a familiar. Since Shade bonded with Rowan, who happens to be a banshee, their energies became inseparable, making Shade not just any cat, but a unique form of the cat sí. It's more than just a regular bond, it's a soul bond. They can share each other's energies for healing and protection, drawing from the power of death itself, or, in special cases, travel to different realms, particularly the realm of dreams and the Otherworld."

"I'm not sure I know what that means, but are you saying what I think you're saying? Has Shade been with Rowan this whole time?" Maeve questions, her voice filled with uncertainty.

Feeling a smile form from just the thought of seeing Rowan, I focus back on Maeve as I say, "Yep, and she's going to lead us straight to her."

"I want Rowan back just as much as you do, but the Slayer's not going to give her up just like that. And what's to say his desperation won't lead him to find your replacement? We already know he's not afraid to go off script to get what he wants." Aisling voice catches, likely thinking about Liam.

Grabbing a red marker, I walk over to the board where the map is still pinned. "Simple. I found the location my Auntie used to capture him the first time."

At their stunned silence, I keep going, "Remember in the note Mrs. Flanagan had us write down how Aiden was able to figure out we're looking for a tree within Réalt?" Taking the marker, I re-draw the Triquetra, and then point to the corners. "The Triquetra does mean life, death, and rebirth, but to put it more plainly, it symbolizes eternity. From the letters we found in the chest, we know the magic the Slayer processes is ancient and so is this so-called ancient root. So, the tree would have to be here." I use my marker to circle the tree in front of Foyle Hall.

Aiden crosses his arms as he takes in the map. "It is the most logical. Not only is the Flynn family crest a tree, but your Auntie took over her family legacy as head of the Council after Darragh Flynn passed. If she promised to keep you girls safe, it'd make sense why she spent so much time at the Academy and running Council meetings."

"You said it yourself, though. Even if she'd been unable to tell you this herself, she'd been frightened when she discovered Rónán. If he was able to break free from the tree without her knowing, can we trust that it'll imprison him for good this time?" Maeve states, trying to rationalize a safe way for us to destroy the Slayer.

"I was thinking the same thing, and, honestly, I don't know for sure. It's why I didn't bring it up last night." Taking a calming breath, I explain, "This morning when I re-read her letter, I realized she mentioned how she was working alone and with limited power. I think she knew it would only be a matter of time and that's why she had the original Council create the Veil. Darragh Flynn must have known it too. Why else would he have used the crest to sign the Veil laws?" Coming up behind Maeve and Aisling, I place my arms around their shoulders in a brief hug, "But since I have some of the best detectives working for me, I already have a backup plan."

With a laugh I hadn't heard from them in a while now, Maeve leans into the hug, "You always do."

"Well, then. I think it's time we put our month of training to the test." Giving them one final squeeze, we start to prepare for the biggest battle we've yet to face.

"In that case, you'll be needing an upgrade," Aiden calls over to us as he takes a wrapped parcel from Declan's hands. As he spreads the brown fabric out on the coffee table, my eyes are drawn to the four blades he'd gifted us not too long ago. They look new, now, the blades shining in the light. As I look closer, I realize it's not the blades themselves that glow, but the gems on the pommel. Picking the blue dagger up, I give Aiden a questioning look.

His cheeks look flushed as he rubs the back of his neck and averts his gaze. "I borrowed them after Rowan was taken. I asked Niamh and Saoirse to work on adding extra enchantments." Picking up a small disk and a golden bracelet, he adds, "These took a bit more convincing, but Niamh worked with the Heka Priest to collect some of the safer artifacts at Leila's shop to create weapons for you. Similar to your daggers, you'll have to be precise with your throws. I'd recommend using these first. They'll help you avoid close combat for as long as possible." Looking to Maeve, he jokes, "For those who don't have the best aim, they're enchanted to return to the person who wears the matching bracelet no matter the distance."

After safely securing our daggers, Aiden leads the way outside. Taking one last look around the office to make sure we have everything, my eyes dance across the piles of case folders and open books until the map finally comes into view. Only time will reveal if we prevail, or if Eldermoore falls into darkness. But; I know one thing for certain.

I'm coming, Rowan.

31

WHERE THE WEST WIND BLOWS
ELODIE

5 hours until the full moon- 1:00 a.m.

I've walked these woods hundreds of times, but it's never seemed this… *eerie*; not even in my dreams. The dense canopy of trees only allows for slices of light to brighten our path. Our steps are silent, except for the occasional branches we step on that are hidden under the recently felled leaves.

Shade leads the way, her sleek black fur barely visible in the light. I try not to think about how this is the same path our parents disappeared on—how we spent years searching, and still—Rowan and I found nothing.

This time is different. I'm coming, Rowan. I repeat this mantra, the only lifeline keeping me from fearing the worst. I can't think about that. I can't think about anything except Rowan. Suddenly, Shade comes to a stop in the clearing, the moon bright with the trees no longer hiding the sky.

I watch as her ear prick up, and she lies down in front of us. *This can't be it, there's nothing here…*

There's no warning, no time to respond. One moment the earth is solid, the next, it cracks open, and we fall. A scream escapes me as the world flips, the air rushing around me. I hit the ground with a sickening thud. The wooden spike from Leila strapped beside my dagger causes pain to shoot up my leg, but I'm too dazed to process it.

"Is everyone okay?" I hear Aiden's voice beside me, his green eyes glowing in the dark. "This must be an old well that dried up. I don't sense anyone beside us here."

As I feel his hand grab mine, I hear the others groan in unison.

Managing to sit up with his help, I take in the jagged stone walls and the flickering candles that cast long shadows over everything. Declan helps the girls to their feet and then brushes off the Mantle of Aine he wears. A rancid, iron stench of blood and death fills the space. Of magic. *Draíocht dhorcha.* I push myself to my feet, the others already standing, their eyes scanning the cavern that splits ahead of us.

"We have to keep moving," Aiden murmurs, his voice barely a whisper, but the urgency in it is clear.

His eyes remain a luminescent green as he whispers under his breath, a blue shield beginning to form around him. Placing my hand on his arm, I stop him mid-spell. His eyes take me in, almost as if afraid I did get hurt during the fall.

Shaking my head, I whisper, "I'm fine. It's just that… we don't know what we'll be facing. Using them might alert him to our presence." Looking between him and Maeve, I add, "Only use your powers when necessary."

For a moment, I think Aiden's going to argue, but then his shoulders sag.

"Hey, look over here. I think this is close to where I followed Liam's ghost," Declan whispers as he makes his way into the left tunnel.

Following after him, Aisling sucks in her breath as she walks into the next outlet ahead of me.

"Wow, you weren't kidding. Where did he get all of this?" Her voice is tinged with a mixture of fear and disbelief.

Taking in the row of heavy machinery, their steel surfaces shining even in the dark, it's hard to believe this has been hiding right beneath our feet. The glass containers that line one side of the cave are filled to the top with a glowing goop-like liquid, now the only evidence left behind of the people he hurt. "

I'd say he's been gathering funding from his followers on top of being a soul thief and killer. Though, I could've sworn there was a real antique right here that powered this all up. It looked like a knot from what I can remember," Declan adds with a scratch to his temple.

Grabbing my notebook from my pocket, I quickly jot down a sketch before bringing it in front of his face. "Are you saying you found the Tyet weeks ago and we didn't even realize it?"

Without needing to look it over long, Declan hums in agreement. "Yes, I'd say I did. I did mention I'm a great spy. Unfortunately, it looks like it's not here anymore, which could mean he used all its power, or, wishful thinking here, maybe Rowan found it and it's keeping her safe. Either way, I think we need to keep moving."

Knowing he's right, we press forwards, the air thick and heavy with the scent of decay. The flickering candlelight only makes it worse, the shadows twisting around us like they're alive. I don't need to see more to know we're close to whatever is hiding.

The crunch of glass beneath our feet makes us pause. I glance around, my eyes catching on shards of glass and frame scattered across the ground. I kneel, recognizing the familiar pattern—fragments of the mirror Leila gave Rowan for protection.

Aiden takes a piece from my hand, his brow furrowed as he inspects it. "We must be getting close," he murmurs.

And then, we find her.

I stop, my body freezing. My heart skips a beat, then stutters. My vision blurs. It's like the world has come to a screeching halt. I can't breathe.

"No… no, no, no," I whisper, my voice raw, a jagged edge of panic lacing the words. "Rowan? Rowan!"

I take a shaky step forwards, but before I can move any closer, I feel a pull on my arm. Aiden's grip is tight, urgent.

"Don't," he says sharply, his voice low. "Something's wrong."

I try to shake his hold off, try to think rationally, try to *see* what he sees. But all I can see is her. Rowan's lifeless form. Her hair is spread out around her, her body too still, her skin too pale. I jerk out of Aiden's hold, heart hammering as I move towards her.

"No," I breathe, my voice cracking. "No, she's just… She needs me to wake her," I'm already at her side, but just before I can kneel, something stops me.

Shade hisses. It's a sharp, warning sound, and I freeze in place.

I glance at her: her eyes wide, her fur bristling. Her body is coiled like a spring, ready to pounce.

"Why is she…" My voice falters. "Why is she acting like this?"

Aiden grabs my shoulder this time, pulling me back gently but firmly. "Elodie, wait."

I glance around, but nothing makes sense. The room is cold, too cold. The shadows don't settle; they twist and writhe, and the cold breeze they create as they roam the walls causes some of the candles to extinguish. The darkness stretches, creeping across the stone walls as if reaching for us, but the faint glow of our daggers pushes them back.

Then, Rowan's body moves.

At first, it's so slight I think I imagine it, but then, the figure on the ground shifts. A breath—slow, shallow. Her chest rises and falls. I take a tentative step forwards, my heart in my throat.

Before I can reach her, her eyes snap open. They're dark. Hollow.

A cold, harsh laugh breaks the silence. The sound is wrong, so twisted, that my chest aches with the weight of it. "You thought it'd be that easy?" The voice that escapes Rowan's lips is low, cruel, and unrecognizable. "Did you think you could waltz in here and take her back? I told you, she's *mine*. And you…" Their cold eyes narrow as they take in our group. "You'll be next. As soon as I take care of your friends."

I want to scream, to run, but my body won't move. As if given a wordless command, the shadows in the room grow deeper, darker, as if they're closing in on me, surrounding me. I stagger back, my heart pounding in my chest. Before I can even react, the shadows in the room flicker. I try to follow them, but they move so quickly, slipping in and out of my sight. One moment, I think I see something in the corner, and the next, there's nothing.

"Where is he?" Aisling mutters under her breath, her eyes scanning the room as she pulls out her dagger.

"Don't let him get close," Aiden warns. His hand moves to the side, readying the shield, but the darkness is so thick it seems to swallow the light.

The laughter breaks the silence again, this time louder, echoing from every direction, as if coming from the earth itself.

"You shouldn't have come," a voice hisses.

Suddenly, the shadows snap into place, revealing a grotesque figure standing before us. It's a nightmare made flesh—a decaying creature with pale, ashen skin stretched tightly over bones, its red eyes sunken and hollow. The stench of rot fills the air, rancid and overpowering, like something long dead. Its lips peel back in a twisted grin, revealing jagged, bloodied teeth.

He smiles as he takes another step forwards and there's nothing human in it. "I thought I'd played my part well. You really did trust me, didn't you?"

"What are you talking about?" I flinch, unable to tear my eyes from the horror before me.

"Always thinking you're so clever. You never could solve anything on your own." The monster before me pauses, its words whispered as if speaking to itself. As if coming to an agreement, the corner of its mouth lifts in a cruel grin. "Maybe this will jog your memory." A low, sickening crack rings through the room as it raises a feathered mask and the decayed form melts away, leaving only the familiar, yet sinister, face of Dr. Collins behind. Hunching forwards his laugh fills the space.

Wiping a fake tear with his hand, his eyes soften as he speaks, his words familiar, "Once she saw potential in someone, she didn't let them give up. I have her to thank for making me part of the community here in Eldermoore. Ha! Pathetic! You said such pretty words that night, so it's too bad you wasted your breath." His words break off as he breaks off into laughter once more.

"You're an Marfóir? How could you do this?" I demand, my voice rising with disbelief and anger. "We trusted you. You taught at the Academy… and helped the students in the infirmary. The Council trusted you. Auntie Cait trusted you."

His twisted grin widens as he steps closer, his cold eyes glinting with malice. "Trust," he says, his voice low and venomous. "Trust is a tool. A weakness. And, in the end, it was your trust that brought me everything I needed." He pauses, letting the words hang in the air like poison. "You think I've been working alone? No. I've spent centuries gathering power, building what I need to finish what was started long before you even knew my name."

He steps into the flickering light, his form almost gleaming now with some unholy energy. "To rule over magic itself, to control its very essence… there are always sacrifices. People like you… You're just obstacles in the grand scheme of things."

His voice drops into a murmur, barely above a whisper, as he steps into the flickering candlelight, revealing the true extent of his decaying form once more. "I was known by another name once: Abhartach." He lets the name slither into the space between us, thick with the weight of ancient darkness. "The one who can never truly die. A legend, a nightmare. The one who walks between worlds. And now, I have everything I need to remake them."

I clench my fists, heart hammering as I try to process his words. "Where is she?" I demand, my voice shaking with desperation. "Where's my sister?"

Still in his true form, his grin deepens, eyes glinting with cruel amusement as he looks down at Shade. "Not so clever, after all." With a satisfied click of his tongue, he finally acknowledges me "Rowan? She's safely in the Veil.

Well, at least, as safe as anyone can be when they're trapped between worlds. Why fight what you are? You should be thanking me, really. I just showed her where monsters like us belong. But soon enough, you'll join her there." He takes a slow step forwards, his dark presence overwhelming. "Why struggle? Why fight it? You know the inevitable. Come with me now, and I'll make it quick."

His voice pulls me in, my brain wrapped in a fog of self-doubt that I can't seem to navigate. What if I can't save her from the Veil? What if it's the only way to be with her again? As if sensing my fear, a blue light takes form. The one becomes many as the will-o-wisps form a circle around me. I'm not dreaming, but I swear I hear their voices. Their whispered guidance leads me through the fog. That's when I know. I can't—won't—let him win.

"No." The word comes out low and fierce. "I'm not going anywhere with you."

At my words, the air shifts, and I feel more than see Aisling and Maeve stand beside me as Aiden and Declan take up our flanks. Maeve's hands rise as she calls for her magic. As she does, the shadows seem to come to a standstill, the wind they've created being pulled towards her fingertips. Aisling takes up the stance Aiden and Saoirse taught us, her dagger held in front of her as she assesses the monster for any weakness.

Taking Aiden's advice, I grab for the disk, bringing it to ear level as I prepare to throw it at the slightest movement. "We're ending this now," I say, my voice steady despite the fear clawing at my chest.

Dr. Collins's, no, *Abhartach's* smile never falters. "If you insist."

His transformation is swift as he bares his teeth, his eyes glowing in the darkness. Throwing the disk, the blade slices through the air before hitting his shoulder with a satisfying sound as it hits bone. With a growl, he gives the blade a sharp yank, letting it clatter to the floor as the metallic scent of his blood permeates the air. No longer embedded in his chest, it returns to my throwing hand.

My stomach turns as he swipes a clawed hand across the wound on his chest, bringing it to his mouth. His sharp teeth part and his tongue slides over the blood on his fingers. As he does, the wound begins to close.

With a laugh, his teeth now stained a dark umber, he hisses, "Was that supposed to hurt? Maybe I should give you some target practice."

From the corner of my eye, I watch as the shadows that have remained dormant begin to rush us. Before I focus on the new threat, I catch the subtle sway in Abhartach's step before he stumbles towards one of the tunnels, the shadows swallowing him from view. A piercing scream punctures through the air as Aisling uses her dagger on one coming towards me. We watch in horror as the shadow begins to reform.

The whizz of a blade passes by my ear as Aiden spears one from behind me. Lifting his left hand, he blocks them with his shield as Maeve pushes them towards the back wall.

"I'll buy you some time. Find him," Aiden yells over the turbulence of the wind.

Without wasting any time, the four of us dash towards the tunnel alongside Shade, the darkness swallowing us. The air is thick, the only sound our rushed breaths and the crunch of gravel beneath our boots. We can barely make out each other's forms, let alone if we're going the right way, but every instinct screams at me to go quicker to catch up to him.

At first, I notice the subtle shift in the ground beneath our feet, the dry pebbles sinking into the mud with each step. Then we hear it—footsteps. They're faint at first but rapidly grow louder the closer we get. That's when I see a faint light appear ahead of us, Abhartach's shadow cast on the wall before he disappears.

Reaching the end of the tunnel, the world suddenly opens again. The air is cool against my skin, but the adrenaline pumping through me makes me barely notice. I glance around, hoping for any sign of him, any trace of where he's gone.

Taking a moment to catch my breath, I take in the iron gate and towering architecture of Foyle Hall. From here I can see the clock tower, the setting sun illuminating the clock hands as it strikes five-fifty. *How?* Thinking back to the moment we fell down the well and felt the remnants of dark magic, I fear the entrance wasn't as abandoned as we believed. The magic had somehow entrapped us, warping time until he was ready. *Just like my dream…*

"There!" Maeve gasps through shallow breaths.

Abhartach stands just ahead, his back turned, as if he hadn't thought we'd follow him so soon. The shadows swirl around him, as though drawn to his very presence. I tense, ready to move, but before any of us can get closer, a low, eerie moan fills the space around us, followed by a sudden burst of energy. Spectral figures materialize from the shadows, no longer the souls Declan once came across. Their eyes glowing with an unnatural hunger as they surge towards us. On instinct, we form a circle, our backs touching as we prepare to fight.

Aisling reacts first, her eyes narrowing with determination. With a swift motion, she draws her dagger, before it rips through the air. The force of it slashes at the spectral figures, scattering them momentarily as they screech in protest. It's not enough. They keep coming.

We fight our way towards the ancient oak, its twisted bare branches reaching out like skeletal hands. Aisling and I wield our daggers in front of us, our steps remaining slow but deliberate as we force Abhartach to hobble backwards. Just as she'd done in the cave, Maeve calls for the wind— only now, she has full access to the elements around her. The amber and red-coloured leaves on the ground swirl into the air with each quick swipe of her arms. With a sharp pull of her magic, the wind pushes him towards the trunk of the tree with brutal force.

He stumbles, shadows still clinging to him like a second skin. His eyes narrow as he glances at the giant oak. "The tree?" he sneers, his voice dripping with venom. "You think this rotting relic can stop me?" Then, as if hearing something, his eyes flicker with a hunger I've never seen before. "I've waited for this. The veil calls me… and I know it's calling you too, Elodie. It wants me to finish what I started. No one will ever stop me again."

Breaking Maeve's hold, he materializes in front of me, his cold fingers digging into my skin as he pulls me towards him. I try to struggle, but his grip is unyielding. The darkness around me deepens, suffocating the light, and the veil stretches its tendrils to pull me in.

Suddenly, there's a sharp tug at my arm, and I look up, only to freeze in shock. Shade is there, but not as the cat sìth I know. Her body ripples and shifts, fur giving way to skin and long black hair. She transforms before my eyes into a woman, a witch, tall and fierce, with eyes burning with raw intent. The sight knocks the breath from my chest.

Without hesitation, she steps between me and the tendrils, her hands gripping my arm as she tries to pull me back. With a swift movement, she turns towards Abhartach, her face set in grim determination.

"Now, Elodie!" Shade's voice rings out, low and urgent, vibrating with a power not of this realm.

I can barely process what I'm seeing. She bellows the words again, her command turning frantic. In a desperate rush, I grab for the stake still held in the leather garter secured to my thigh, its weight grounding me just enough to focus as the first fog begins to swirl around us. I can't waste any more time.

I lunge forwards, slashing wildly with the stake, the only defence I have left. I feel the sickening sludge of his blood, his bones cracking, as I push the stake through his palm. At the same moment, Shade claws at his face, leaving a gaping hole where an eye had been. With a growl, he swipes back at us, the power from the Veil seeming to give him a burst of strength as he strikes Shade. I can do nothing as she's thrown, her body hitting the ground unnaturally. As she curls into herself, her breaths uneven, she returns to her cat form, falling unconscious.

The others shout my name, their voices frantic, but their calls grow dim. I try to fight it, my heart racing as the shadows close in around me.

"No!" I scream, but the sound is lost, consumed by the void just as I hear the clock tower ring.

Abhartach's eyes glint with triumph as the world begins to tear apart.

That's when everything I know—everything I am—slips away.

32

THE VEIL BETWEEN STARS

ELODIE

The Obsidian Veil- Time…unknown

I try to move, but it's like I'm not even there. The world around me is slipping away, and I can't hold on to anything. My thoughts scatter through the cracks in my mind, and I'm left grasping at nothing, trying to summon any shred of myself. My heart pounds, but the beat is distant, muffled, and I can't tell if it's fear or simply the emptiness swallowing me whole. I call out, but the words barely form. I reach for the threads that used to connect me to my sister, my friends, my world, but it's like they were never there.

Nothing.

Just as the weight of hopelessness threatens to consume me, a voice pierces the silence, accompanied by a burst of light, pure and radiant.

"Even in emptiness, you shall always find life. You need only have hope to guide you."

"Hello? Who's there?" My voice echoes as if the light that has begun to envelop me is endless.

A calming, ethereal chuckle dances through the air, as soft and comforting as the lullabies my Mam would sing to Rowan and me. It's like the sun's first light touching the earth after a long night. "Sorry, I apologize. She mentioned you might not recognize me." Then with a warmth that eases the weight of the darkness around me, she says, "I've missed you, my friend."

A tall figure steps from the light, her gown woven from radiant threads that shimmer and glow with an intensity that seems to draw from the sun's core. The fabric shifts and pulses as though it's alive. Behind her, feathers of a Bennu bird unfurl, each one alight with golden fire, trailing behind her in a cascade of flickering light.

My heart skips as the void I've been trapped in begins to recede, and beneath my feet, solid ground begins to form. It's like the earth has come alive, responding to her presence, grounding me in a way I haven't felt since the moment I was taken here. All at once, I hear the sounds of life: the fluttering of wings as a flock of birds pass me, the rush of water as it crashes against rock, the way the grass beneath my feet rustles in the wind.

I turn towards her, and my gaze falls on her face for the first time. Her skin glows with the same radiant warmth as the light around her, and her kohl-lined eyes shimmer with a golden hue I've only seen once before. My eyes sting, a flood of emotions threatening to overwhelm me, but I can't look away from her, can't stop myself from hoping, from wanting it to be true.

Leila steps closer, the ground beneath her feet blossoming with flowers, each step leaving a trail of life in its wake. Her voice, soft but insistent, cuts through the stillness.

"Know yourself, Elodie," she says, gently taking my hands. "And in doing so, you'll know the gods. Your power, your purpose—it's always been inside you."

I feel the weight of her words, but they don't fully make sense. "I don't understand," I say, my voice trembling. "How am I supposed to—"

Leila's gaze sharpens, yet there's a warmth in her eyes that calms me. "When you fought beside Aiden and Rowan, you felt their strength. But it wasn't just a fleeting thing, Elodie. It wasn't just something you borrowed through your bond. Their power became a part of you."

I blink, trying to make sense of her words. "So, you're saying I… absorbed it?"

She nods slowly, her expression steady. "Yes. You allowed it to merge with your own. It's not about drawing from one singular source, Elodie. That's what made you feel like you couldn't grasp the threads of magic. You were never meant to hold just one form of it. When you need it, the strength of those around you, their power is within you, waiting to be called on."

"I wish I could tell you more, but we're running out of time," Leila says softly, her voice steady but filled with a quiet urgency. "I'm here to help you defeat him, once and for all. He's taken enough from us, Elodie. It's time to make him pay."

I feel it—her strength, her belief in me. It ignites something deep inside. I'm ready.

"I'm with you," she says, voice firm. "We'll destroy him together."

Leila steps forwards, and her energy floods into me. It's fierce and blinding as her essence, her warmth, merges with mine. I feel her strength, but also her sorrow—and my own at knowing this is the end of something. Her power burns through me, a fire that refuses to be put out.

"I'll never forget you," I whisper, though I know she can't hear me now.

Leila's presence remains in my heart, guiding me, urging me forwards. With her power inside me, I open my eyes, filled with resolve, but also with the ache of her absence already starting to settle in.

Without looking back, I let Leila's light guide me.

⊹ ⟩ ⟩ ● ⟨ ⟨ ⊹

Each step forwards grows easier, and the shadows that once crept into view quickly scatter. Their movements are frantic as I extend the light towards them, their forms desperately trying to retreat into the fog that surrounds me.

275

Following where they flee, their black forms weaving between low-hanging branches, I hear the frantic voice of the one I've been looking for.

Elodie!

I stumble, a branch scratching my cheek as I catch myself. Through the fog, I can just make out the sounds of rippling water. My feet sink into the muddy earth, the soaked grass brushing against my legs as water splashes with each step I take. Her voice resonates within me, growing louder the closer I get. Ahead, Rowan floats in the murky water, the veil weaving the current that holds her suspended. Her hair cascades around her in a glowing halo of white, and though her eyes are shut, I can see the rise and fall of her chest. It's proof that I've finally found her.

Dragging her from the icy water, I lay her on the grass. "Rowan, I'm here. We need to go. Please wake up." My voice seems too loud in this void, even as I try to whisper the words.

Shaking her by the shoulders, I try to rouse her, but it's no use. I track the water, my ears searching for any hint that he's nearby. At first, there's only silence, broken only by the soft breaths from Rowan and me. Then, I hear it. The footsteps are faint at first, slow. I duck lower, using my body to get as close to the ground as possible as I use my coat to cover us. On instinct, I grab my dagger, the blade ready to aim at their throat. Without warning, a hand grabs my shoulder, their face coming into view as they kneel beside me.

"Declan? How are you here?" My eyes go round as I see his grey eyes under the cape he wears.

Throwing the hood off, he pushes the dagger away from his face. His breaths come in short pants, as though he's been running for miles, but he doesn't seem to notice. As he glances past me, his eyes rest on Rowan, a look of worry crossing his face. "There's no time. She won't last much longer in the Veil. This place isn't meant for the living." His arms cradle her neck and legs as he stands, his movements steady so as to not jostle her.

There's a cold breeze as we walk forwards and I know he's found us. I can't see him, but I feel his presence. Then, there he is, stepping into view with a twisted grin.

"Oh, how noble, but this just won't do." His body is a blur of movement that my eyes can't follow.

I slowly back away from where Declan holds Rowan in hopes of keeping them safe. Then, there's a whisper by my ear, "Help." Spinning towards the trees I watch as ravens crowd around bones. Their beaks peck at flesh and fabric, the Academy's crest hanging on by mere threads. Rónán.

Another whisper comes from the water, the deep voice pleading for me to save them. I watch as Liam begins to sink, his hand reaching out towards me as his screams cause bubbles to rise to the surface. Then, he's lost to the water's deep abyss.

I close my eyes tight, my head shaking from left to right as I physically try to block their words from my mind. Their pleading cries repeat over and over. Fingers, cold as ice, grab my face and force me to turn.

"Look at all you've done," Auntie Cait's voice growls. Her hair is splattered with blood, and her other hand pushes a red oozing mass towards me. It thumps in her hand, the beat steady, *alive*. In the centre of her chest is a cavernous pit where her heart should be. "I trusted you, but instead of saving Eldermoore, you've turned it into a grave." She screams the words in my face, drops of blood sticking to the tears that I can't contain.

I watch as she falls to the ground in a mass of broken limbs, and then more hands are pulling me. Golden eyes peek out from behind my coat, a vicious smile turning Leila into someone unrecognizable, insidious, as she crouches low.

"So many promises broken… just like you. No more sister. No more family. You're all alone."

I cover my ears, her words hitting too close to the truth.

"Why don't you just give up?" Leila's words meld with Abhartach's deep voice as her eyes shift between gold and red hues. She circles me, her form becoming a cyclone of shadows of darkness and chaos.

A scream pierces the air and a break in the shadows forms, a warning of death. *My death*. Just at the water's edge, I see her. Rowan's sliver eyes, like starlight, pierce through the fog that wraps around her as if embracing her. The Tyet is secure around her neck like a beacon of hope.

Together.

Leila's voice is soft in my mind, freeing me of the illusions he wove.

"I'm not alone," I whisper as I rise to my feet. I drag my hand across my face, cleansing me of the blood, the tears, and, more importantly the remnants of my guilt. "I know who I am. It's you who has always been alone, the one who will fail," I shout as I search for magic around me, the Veil's power amplifying my own.

I grasp at a thread that feels familiar, its warm breeze surrounding me. Then the next, this one ancient, more deadly, but I recognize it all the same. I can sense another, its blue thread piercing through the dark. In my soul, it feels almost like home. When there's nothing left, I reach for the power within me, the power Leila gave me.

"How will you defeat me when not even your parents could?" His shadows surround me once more, his red eyes glowing in front of me. "Did you know she cried for you in her last breath?" Pushing through the shadows, his sickly pale face is inches from mine his rotting flesh burning my nose as he cries, "Please, my girls. My leanaí."

At last, I release the power, its threads unravelling as I focus on him.

Maeve's wind ensnares him, a torrent that forces him to his knees and stops his breath. His eyes are no longer squinted in revelry. They widen in fear and then pure agony as I open my mouth. My piercing cry makes blood pour from his ears, the wind too strong for him to lift his arms or wipe away the blood to heal himself. Latching onto Aiden's power, I pull on the blue thread, the Veil transforming into a colourful landscape of pure energy.

My hands rise on instinct alone as I harness it. Orbs of power form in my hands like sharp daggers, the red and black shards of fear and hate cast from his shadows *from him* forge the magic into deadly weapons. His shadows lash out like an extension of him, as if they can sense my intent. Like claws, they try to pierce my skin, but they no longer hold power here.

I do.

It wasn't just hope guiding me anymore—it was love. As if called forth from the thought alone, a Bennu rises above me. A battle cry pierces the air as it dives straight towards him. His shadows shudder as the bird's flames engulf him, the vortex of wind aiding its efforts. The spectral forms of Rónán, Liam, and Auntie Cait move as one alongside its light, keeping him caged, waiting until his body becomes nothing but ash.

Only choked gasps can be heard, the lack of oxygen drawing out his pain. Without his shadows, his form flickers between that of Dr. Collins and Abhartach, reminding me of that night on the balcony of the pub. Of our conversation. Of Aiden.

"I was wrong. Loneliness is a lie, an infliction that only people with hate convince themselves of. But love is never absent unless we choose to ignore it, and choose to let the darkness take root and remake you. Unlike you, I have never been alone."

Taking a deep breath, I release the orbs, the crystallized obsidian daggers piercing his heart. His mouth opens in a silent scream as the magic he stole erupts. What remains of his soul is shredded into a million pieces, succumbing to the inevitable truth that evil, no matter how persistent, never survives. He becomes one with the Veil, becomes nothing.

The threads I pulled snap, the energy I'd taken draining me as it releases back into the Veil. My knees weaken before I fall to the ground. Declan and Rowan catch me, lowering me gently.

Kneeling next to me, Rowan pulls me into her tight embrace. "I can't believe it. He's finally gone." Her hands run over my hair, the soothing motion reassuring her that I'm okay. "I love you, sis."

With her arms wrapped around me, the other half of my soul snaps back into place, so I do the only thing left. I hold her just as tight.

Breaking the moment, Declan clears his throat. "I hate to interrupt this beautiful moment, but we really need to find a way out of here."

Before I can respond, the air shifts and the ground beneath us hums with power.

Bastet and Isis step through the fog as the Bennu bird above them lands on Bastet's shoulder.

"You have done well, child" Bastet's voice rings out. With a note of sadness, she continues, "But even in triumph, there are prices to be paid. Not everything can be returned to as it was."

The weight of their words sink in, tightening my chest. "I don't understand…"

Stepping closer, Isis places a gentle hand on both Rowan and me. "I think you both have known for a while now that Rowan's power no longer belongs to the earthly realm. Her essence has shifted, and although she is still alive, she is no longer bound to your world. She exists between both the earth and spirit realms now, and until she learns to harness this new power, returning will put both her life and others' at risk."

"You mean… she has to stay?" The words feel like they don't belong to me, as if they're too cruel to say aloud.

Eyes filled with regret, her answer rings through the space between us. "For now, yes. But fear not, child; the Tyet will protect her from harm while she is here. We will guide her and help her find her path. She is not lost to you."

Declan's voice cuts through the heavy silence. "I'll stay with her," he says, his words steady. "I'll look after her and bring her back when the time is right."

I turn to Rowan. She steps towards me, her eyes bright with unshed tears, and pulls me into a hug so tight it feels like I'm holding her for the first time once more.

"I can't leave you again," I whisper, my voice breaking.

Rowan pulls back just enough to look at me, her eyes filled with a quiet strength. "You've always known what was best for me," she says softly, her voice filled with sorrow, but also acceptance. "This is my journey now. I'll be okay. I promise."

Tears fill my eyes, but I can't hold her any longer. I have to let her go. "I don't know if I can do this," I admit, my voice trembling.

Rowan smiles through her own tears, her hands gently cupping my face. "You were right, sis…."

The goddesses raise their hands in unison, and the Veil begins to ripple, dissolving around us, the world shifting with its passing. I try to hold onto Rowan, take one last look, my heart breaking all over again.

"Everything will be alright," she whispers, the words echoing in my soul as the light from the goddesses surrounds us both.

With one final glance, I'm pulled back to Eldermoore, my heart heavy with the knowledge that I can do nothing to save her. That, maybe, I never had control over who I could save—their paths preordained. The words from my Mam's riddle that very first night come back to me. Unlike all those weeks ago, I finally have the answer: *death*. She'd been trying to warn me of this very instance—had likely known this would be Rowan's fate.

Perhaps death truly is inevitable. It is an untamable beast that is bound to leave scars that heal slowly and have the potential to break me or help make me stronger. And yet, the loss of my parents and friends— of Rowan's absence—is not what breaks me. No, it's the realization that I risk losing Rowan forever but choosing to set her free anyway.

EPILOGUE PART I

MAEVE

The spectrals stop fighting in Abhartach's absence. Like prisoners, invisible chains pulling them along, they sprint into the Veil. One by one, their forms shudder, becoming black inky shadows as the thick fog envelopes them.

I rush to where Shade lies, her body unnervingly still. I kneel beside her, my hands trembling as I gently cradle her limp form. Her fur is cold to the touch, colder than usual, and I can feel the faintest pulse beneath my fingers.

With a sharp cry, Aisling begins to run, pulling me alongside her as she heads in the direction we saw the spectrals disappear. "The fog… It's moving."

She's right.

In horror, I watch as the mist that had been surrounding Foyle Hall recedes, almost reaching the back fence line of the Academy. With the wind at my fingertips, the fog parts and mist sticks to my skin. Breaking through, I pull my dagger out, preparing for the battle ahead of us.

My breath catches as I stare at the front gate of the Academy. I hear footsteps close behind, Aisling appearing just as confused as she takes in the stone pillars. *No.* Grabbing her wrist, I charge back into the fog. As we exit once more, I see Declan speaking with Aiden despite my brother's attempts to get past him. In horror, I realize that whatever doorway he pulled Elodie through has already been sealed.

Calling out to them, I try to quickly tell them about our current predicament. "The Veil." I take a deep breath before I continue, my side beginning to ache from both the earlier fall and all the running we've done, "It's closed. We can't get through. They're alone in there."

I watch as whatever hope my brother had been clinging to fade. He stares at the Veil, trying to see through it as if searching for something. No, searching for someone. His stance is rigid as I reach for him, his jaw tensing as if refusing to say the words aloud, to admit they may be gone. That we failed.

Taking hold of his shoulder in comfort, Declan says the unexpected. "I think you know there's only one way we're getting them back." His eyes trail to the Veil before he begins to walk towards it, his outstretched hand disappearing within. "You know, I never understood why I felt like I couldn't leave here— why I needed to stay." His words pause as he takes his hand back out and lifts the edge of his cloak. "I think somehow, Leila had known it'd come to this, had known he might use the Veil."

Declan's words are strong, resolute, and I fear there's nothing I can say to stop him. In a final plea, I take his arm, pulling him away from the fog. "You saw it yourself. The spectrals turned to shadows when they followed him. The same could happen to you. We'll find another way."

"There are no other options. Perhaps this will absolve me of the failures of my past." With a sad smile, he looks at each of us as he says, "Fear not for my soul. I was never meant to stay forever, anyway."

His eyes are the last thing I see before they seamlessly blend into the shroud of silver haze.

In what seems like mere seconds, Elodie appears from a bright burst of light. As the Obsidian Veil falls, the smoke that has separated our town dissolves in front of my eyes. Her clothes have tears and scorch marks, but I see no sign of an injury. *What happened?*

Together we rush towards her. Aiden crashes into her, his arms lifting her off the ground as he grabs ahold of her like he never wants to let go of her again.

"I've got you, mo thrioblóir beag," I hear him whisper into her hair where his head rests against hers.

At his words, she seems to crumble, her shoulders shaking in a way I've only seen her do twice now.

"Elodie… where are Rowan and Declan?"

EPILOGUE PART ii

MAEVE

1 February, 1971

For weeks now, ships have been arriving in town, especially with the spectacle of the now missing Veil, though that quickly became old news when the Creevan Court's life sentences for Doyle and Brennan made the headline. Apparently, witnesses from Blackthorn arrived shortly after news of their capture surfaced with proof that they'd been involved in a series of bombings that had taken multiple lives. Now, with the Trial of Lir starting tomorrow, the Council has been in a mad rush to finish preparations. Though, with Elodie and Aisling at the helm, this year's tournament is sure to go off without a hitch.

Not to mention, it's taken Elodie's mind off missing Rowan. When we first got her back from the Veil, she wouldn't speak, as if just the memory of what happened was too much for her to bear. It's been hard, but we've been making some progress. Yet, I still see how she comes into the office every morning, looking unrested before she crosses off another date on the calendar.

Aiden seems to help, though. When he's not working a case, I often catch them on the balcony at the pub as I make my way home. It was nice to finally see her smile again, to watch her have more good days than bad.

As she walks into the office, her eyes darkened by lack of sleep, I can tell today is not one of those days.

With a small wave in greeting, she makes her way to her desk overflowing with files and books from cases she refuses to turn down. "Have we got any new cases today?"

Placing the file she begrudgingly assigned me on my desk, I grab my coat from the hook. "Don't even think about it. What you need to do is get some sleep, ya hear? I'll check out this lead I got last night and, on my way back, I'll meet you at the Stout & Sip. I hear Lennon's baking something new with the competition coming up. He's determined to win the tourists' hearts."

"Oh, alright. Message received loud and clear, but add a cuppa to my order and I'll let you go." With a wink, she turns to her desk, looking at the clutter with a sigh, before plopping down on the couch instead. "Maeve? Thank you."

"Don't go thanking me yet. Saoirse's called a mandatory session. She says the ocean air will do ya some good. Plus, she's promised me a front row seat to some prime real estate if I convince you to go." Sitting in the chair across from her, I give her my best dog-eyed expression. As the corner of her mouth lifts in a reluctant laugh, I clap my hands in success. "I'll meet you there in an hour."

It was one unsuccessful attempt after another to try and calm my witness. His fingers surely left bruises where he grabbed me. His words still ring in my ear as I remember his wife's unheard attempts to soothe him as he kept repeating how he could hear a song from the waters calling to him as he slept. When he became hysterical, I told the poor man I'd return tomorrow.

Making my way from the lighthouse, I smell the seawater on the wind, reminding me once more of the note I hurriedly hid in my pocket on that day that feels so long ago now. Patting it to assure myself it's still there and safe, I pick up my pace as I check my watch face, the time alerting me that I'm now five minutes late to meet the girls.

Just as I turn onto Fiddler's Lane, I hear a rushing of several footsteps behind me. Before I can turn around to defend myself, a brown sack is thrown over my head that smells slightly sweet and yet pungent at the same time. *Think Maeve. What is it?* Just as I realize what's happening, my consciousness starts to slip away, and I hear one of my captors speak. The deep, soothing Irish lilt of his voice causes my heart to skip a beat.

"I'm sorry, mo siréine bheag."

To be continued...

ECHOES OF ÉIRE:
FOLKTALES OF
VALOR AND
VILLAINY

Súil

Magic that allows the wielder to detect and manipulate auras. They can also see the dead.

Red—Irritation   Gold—Wisdom

Black—Trauma   Brown—Anxiety

Blue—Spiritual   Yellow—Happiness

Gray—Sadness   Indigo—Peace

Spectral

A spirit who has not yet passed over to the Otherworld.

Echo

Can be seen by you or someone else

Fetch

Unlike a twin or doppelganger, seeing your fetch foretells your death.

Typically a memory of how they died

Dark energy from a spectrals death that is left behind to help them travel to Tir na nÓg.

Not coherent

Sluagh

host of the undead that may appear as a flock of birds.

Eye of Horus

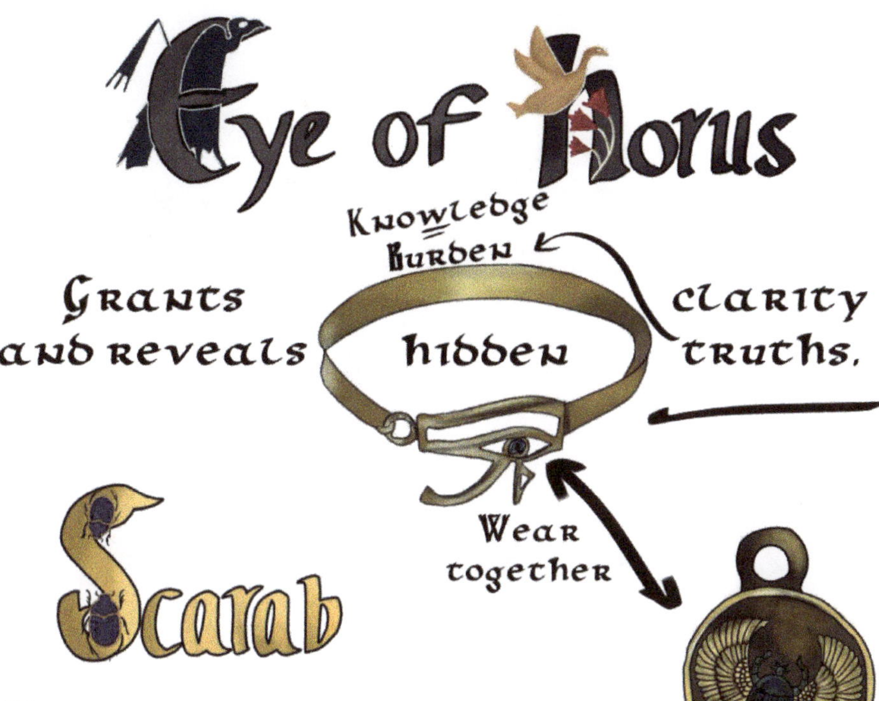

Scarab

A charm of protection that can shield against magic.

Must focus on intent

Tyet

Shield's one from dark magic, In the hand of evil— BEWARE!

The Puca

A shapeshifter who loves tricks and secrets.

Banshee

Beware, for her mournful cry heralds the death of a loved one.

Cat Sí

A spectral/witch that can only transform 9 times.

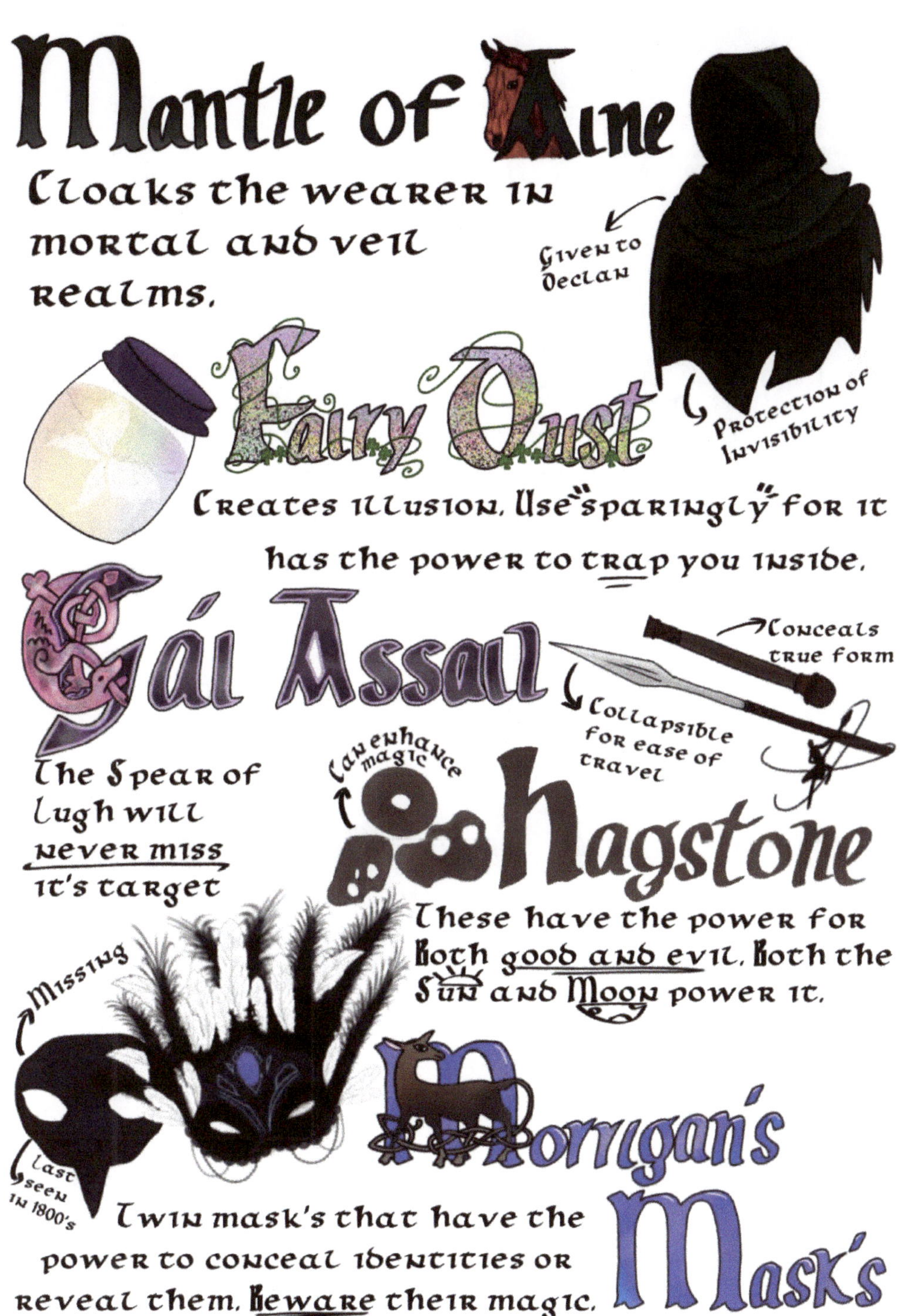

Mantle of Áine

Cloaks the wearer in mortal and veil realms.

Given to Declan

Protection of Invisibility

Fairy Dust

Creates illusion. Use "sparingly" for it has the power to trap you inside.

Gái Assail

The Spear of Lugh will never miss it's target

Conceals true form

Collapsible for ease of travel

Hagstone

Can enhance magic

These have the power for both good and evil. Both the Sun and Moon power it.

Morrigan's Masks

Missing

last seen in 1800's

Twin mask's that have the power to conceal identities or reveal them. Beware their magic.

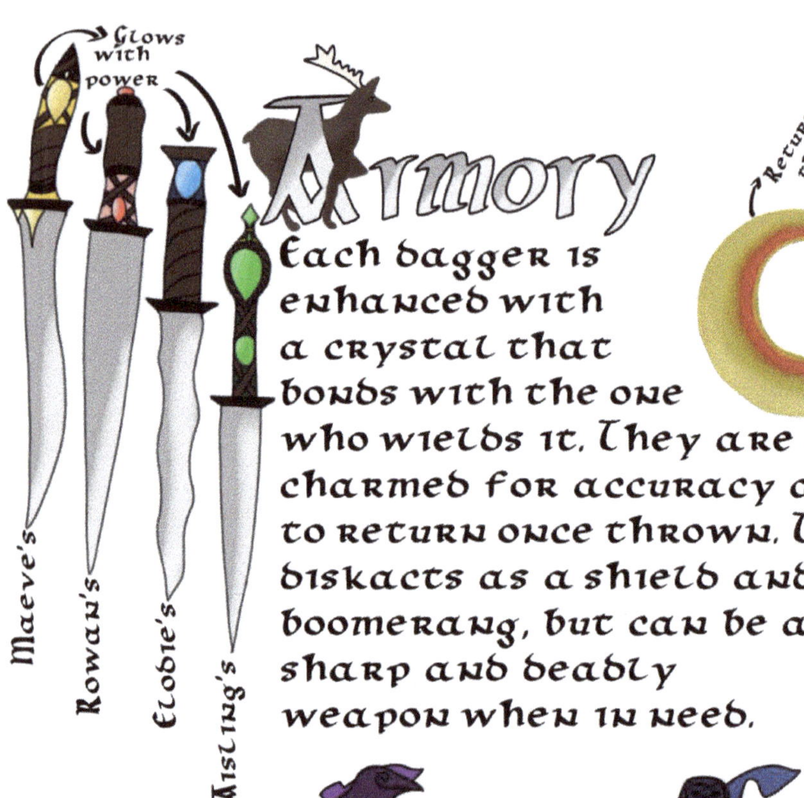

Armory

Each dagger is enhanced with a crystal that bonds with the one who wields it. They are also charmed for accuracy and to return once thrown. The disk acts as a shield and a boomerang, but can be a sharp and deadly weapon when in need.

Fianna Fáil

Legendary warriors who protect the land and it's people. The first female warrior to join and singlehandedly lead her warriors to victory when it seemed all hope was lost was none other that Saoirse Murphy. A true warrior of

★DESTINY!★

Aegis
Egyptian collar used for protection. Blessed by the goddess Bastet.
lion head
Menat
Mennu
Uses it's burning light to defeat evil.
Breathes fire!
Reincarnates
Scale of Ma'at
Used by Ma'at to weigh a soul based on Truth and Justice.

BONUS SCENE

I've spent months researching, trying anything I can think of to connect to Rowan, now that the Veil no longer exists in Eldermoore. The remnants of Rowan's last words haunt my mind. In my dreams, I see her, I try to call her back home—to tell her I need her—but I always get the same answer. *It's not time.*

That's why I force myself to work day and night. I've convinced myself it's better to focus on the problems I can solve. I should be happy now that our office has gained traction from neighboring towns and tourists who fill our small cobbled street daily, especially as word spreads of our skills as investigators and Eldermoore's latent powers. Yet, as I catch a glimpse of the empty desk across the room, Rowan's absence dims any happiness I might have felt. She should be here.

The bell above the door snaps me out of my wallowing. I quickly mask my pain by putting on a smile to greet whoever has arrived, the same way I've been practicing in the mirror every morning.

"Good morn', mo thrioblóir beag. I've got a fresh cuppa and a chocolate croissant calling your name right here—courtesy of Lennon." Aiden holds up the paper bag with a giant grin on his face, before making his way towards me. Placing a quick peck on my lips, he places the tea on the desk before opening the to-go bag.

"Thank you, a stór. If I didn't know any better, I'd say you're trying to bribe me."

"Who? Me? Never. Though I did want to run something by you." His eyebrow is raised in a hopeful stare.

"Only if it's quick, some of us do need to work around here, you know," I say as I reach for the warm chocolatey goodness.

"Ah ah ah," he says disapprovingly as he places the bag out of reach. "You only get this if you agree."

"You're not helping yourself any by getting between me and that croissant. Out with it already," I pout as I longingly stare at the bag he holds above both our heads.

Looking nervous now, he grabs my hands, and his cheeks seem to redden in embarrassment the longer I stare. In a rush, the words seem to tumble out of his mouth. "Well, I had this whole big speech planned, and I know this might be bad timing considering Rowan is still gone and it's not the same without her." His eyes widen as if he already thinks I'll say no to whatever he's going to ask, and quickly continues, "Don't get me wrong, I know I could never replace her, but I was thinking…you have magic now, I have magic, we're both investigators who get along…" Taking a knee in front of me, he takes a shaky breath before asking, "What I'm trying to say is, would you like to become partners?"

There are so many what-ifs that come to mind, but I push them aside. I've learned the importance of following my heart, and that's exactly what I do when I answer him now. "Yes. That sounds wonderful."

Seemingly lost in his thoughts, he continues as if he hasn't even heard me. "And before you say no, I spent the last few weeks coming up with a list of pros and cons that I think you would appreciate….Hold on, did you say yes?"

"Hmm. It would seem so. I can offer some listening tips—just mark my words: you'll be in for a rough time," I tease.

"Game on," Aiden smirks before wrapping me up in a hug.

With my feet dangling in the air and my arms trapped between both of our bodies, I giggle at his antics. Gently, I kick his legs as I beg him to put me down. I'd never admit it to him—it would probably go to his head—but he's given me a reason to get up every morning. By his side, I don't feel so lost.

"Well, now that that's settled, I have a little surprise for you," he says as he places me back on the ground.

"Does it involve me finally getting to eat the croissant?" I ask hopefully.

"Not yet!" He chuckles as he pulls me to follow him.

I stumble a step as I look longingly behind me at the brown paper bag we left behind.

To my surprise, instead of heading outside, we only walk a few steps before he stops at the bookcase near Aisling and Maeve's desks.

Leaning against the shelves, his grin widens as he points at a book titled *Rocket Landing for Dummies.* "Go ahead…"

I roll my eyes at the book, but follow his instructions. As I begin to pull it off the shelf, I hear a faint click before the bookcase slides open and the book returns to its original upright position.

"Turns out my great-grandfather owned this building before he decided to renovate the building next door. I happened to find the old deed of his transfer of ownership to your Aunt when I was asking Niamh to help me come up with ways to win you over. I've put in all the necessities to match the one back at my place."

Excited and overwhelmed that he would go to this extent for me, I grab his offered hand, following him into the dark entryway. I can hear the bookcase behind us slide on tracks before clicking back into place. Aiden's hand holds mine in a strong but gentle grip as we walk.

Stopping, he whispers, "Let me get the lights."

He's gone for only a moment before the lights turn on, and I'm able to take in the room around us. Much like his own hideout, there is a weapons training area that the girls and I can use alongside some newer balance boards he must have asked Saoirse's advice on. What catches my eye next is the desk to the right. A new Xerox Alto PC, just like the one Aisling had, sits there. Only this one looks to have a lot more gadgets.

Coming to stand behind me, he easily follows my gaze, and I feel him squeeze my shoulder before whispering, "For when she comes home."

Unable to control my emotions around him, my tears fall freely down my face once more. As I close my eyes, trying to compose myself, I feel the brush of his thumb against my face as he wipes them away. "You don't have to pretend around me, Elodie. I know you're hurting; your pain is my pain."

"I'm sorry, I can't seem to help it. I've tried to do what everyone's been telling me. I keep trying to live without her—*for* her—but I feel like I'm drowning. Everything reminds me of her… Sometimes I can't even pass my reflection in the mirror without seeing her," I grip his hand where it's still holding my face.

"Shh, mo thrioblóir beag, it will get better. Maybe not now, or even tomorrow, but I'll be here for you every step of the way."

As I stare up at him, his own eyes are glassy as tears fall down his face. I wipe them away as he continues, "I know Declan is out there taking good care of Rowan for you. Just like he promised, and I've never known him to break a promise he's made. I'll continue to watch every sunset with you, research every known and unknown magic out there to bring her back, and help you face your reflection until you see the woman I love staring back, and I won't stop until they're back with us—and not even then a stór. I swear it."

"I'll hold you to that, a stór," I say.

I snuggle deeper into his embrace, knowing that despite all the trouble and heartache we'll likely face in this lifetime, I can do anything—conquer anything—as long as he's right there by my side.

ACKNOWLEDGMENTS

TO EACH OTHER

Lindsey: This book took months of sleepless nights, endless cups of tea, too many inside jokes to count, and just the two of us in the world of our making. For our debut into the writing world, I wouldn't have wanted to write this story with anyone else. Thanks for cheering me on (and letting me know when I should rewrite, lol). I can't wait to continue bringing these characters to life with you!

To Shannon. The greatest twin and friend I could ever ask for! Thank you for pushing us down this path full of adventure; and for saying it was worth a try. I've had so much fun since we started! Between bouncing ideas off one another or sharing a laugh when things got way off track, I can't wait to see where we go next!

TO OUR FAMILY & FRIENDS

A special thank you to our Mom and Aunt! You both were the first to get eyes on the world of Eldermoore. We'll admit that it was a very daunting experience. We have put so much of ourselves into these characters that it was like asking you to peer into our souls to find what needed improvement. Dramatic— we know ;)

We would also like to thank our Dad. You helped us pursue our degrees in Criminal Justice and Information Science. Many of the classes we took have been the inspiration for our characters. Thank you for always cheering us on, even though you're not the biggest fan of reading in the family.

To our family and friends who've cheered us on since we first told them we were writing a book. Your support has meant the most to us—more than you'll ever know!

TO OUR WONDERFUL TEAM OF ANNA'S (We swear. It was just a coincidence!)

They say not to judge a book by its cover, but boy, did we judge!

Annalise Jensen (@annalisejensen), you exceeded every one of our expectations. We cried happy tears every time you sent us an update, and it took everything in us to keep it a secret until reveal day! You have been an absolute joy to work with, and we cannot wait to work with you again on the rest of this series.

However, our story— our words— were just as important to us to perfect. For helping us make it what it is today, we cannot thank our editor, Annalise Healey (@beeandquilledits), enough. Every time you made a suggestion, we learned how to make our writing better. With your help, we can proudly self-publish When the Raven Soars. We can't wait to work with you in the future and wish you much success in your writing and editing journey!

ARC READERS

Thank you all for taking a chance on us. As indie authors, it is always in the back of our minds that no one will connect with our world or characters. But for those who found strength in Elodie and Rowan, could laugh along with Maeve, Niamh, or Declan, and found the power of love and forgiveness in characters like Cait, Aisling, Leila, and Aiden, you make it all worth it!

TO OUR GRANDPARENTS

A big thanks to our Grandma who's always asks us questions about how our book is coming along— whether it's on our morning walks or over a cup of tea. We can't wait for you to read our book!

To our PopPop who motivates us to keep writing and is always impressed when we tell him we've written yet another chapter. The humorous part of this book can definitely be credited to your love of jokes and sarcasm.

A most heartfelt thank you to our grandparents and family members who are no longer with us. We wouldn't be the people we are today without you.

TO OUR KICKSTARTER BACKERS

Your support and enthusiasm have truly been the heartbeat of this project, and we're beyond grateful you believed in us. You helped turn our dream of creating a special edition of When the Raven Soars into reality. We can't wait for you to dive in and explore the world of Eldermoore with us! Now, let's celebrate the 71 amazing people who made it all possible:

Alicia	Victoria Wash
Florentina	Victoria P
Krystal England	Eileen
Krys Galvez	Amanda Balter
Megan Astell	Jordan Murray (@lovelyliterary)
R Tesauro	Cindy Giesbrecht
Bonnie Sue S.	Charlotte Pleym
Samantha Traunfeld	Amanda Siri Hill
Kelsey B.	Julianna
Zilla	Alexandra Corrsin
Sunny Ryan	Jessica Hoppe
Mellissa Boslow	Johanna Miller
Miss Pepita	Natalie Duleba
Mike Wall	Chumyshka
Enalia T	TiffMarieTicer
Samantha Newberry	Eleftheria Small
Barb	G.W. Bloke
U. Donnie & A. Lisa	J. Hearns
A. Eileen	Violet Mae
Tori	Nixie Jade
Mark Hal	Grandma
DonnaLee	Niki Kuhlman
Jennifer Markowski	Ash
Qavee	KJ Benson
Yueyea	Puugu
A. Barb	Michelle Glover
Samantha Curran	Rachael Barcellano
Liz Semkiu	Carol MacLennan-Gonzales
Christy Mitchiner	Morgan
Kelly Ann Parmelee Giselle	Sherry Mock

Kristen Schleif

Jennifer Matuschak

Midnightmare

Karina Krogh

Hannah Scott

Bec Taba

Viviane Descombes

Claire Smith-Simmons

Liana

Lady A Taylor

* * *

And now, we're off to write BOOK 2 …

If you would like to be a part of our Title Reveal, make sure you're following us on Instagram. We will be opening a street team interest form very soon!

about the author

Shaelyn Rose is the pen name for twin sisters who enjoy cozying up on the couch with their two pups, a hot cup of cocoa, a good book, and *Ghost Adventures* re-runs playing in the background. Their shared passion for coded messages/secret languages, crime podcasts, fantasy novels, and Irish folklore inspired them to write together. With a B.A. in Criminology and a dream of publishing a fantasy mystery, they brought the world of Eldermoore to life. When they're not writing, they run a small bookish shop where they sell handmade goods that bring other authors' characters to reality!

You can connect with us on:

https://authorshaelynrose.my.canva.site/authorshaelynrose

https://www.facebook.com/authorshaelynrose

https://www.instagram.com/authorshaelynrose

Subscribe to our newsletter:

https://author-shaelyn-rose.beehiiv.com/subscribe

www.ingramcontent.com/pod-product-compliance
Lightning Source LLC
Chambersburg PA
CBHW061117100726